PARAGONS

EDITED BY ROBIN WILSON

PARAGONS

Twelve Master

Science Fiction

Writers Ply

Their Craft

ST. MARTIN'S PRESS ❧ NEW YORK

For all the workshop faculty and staff everywhere and in particular Tess Tavormina and Mary Sheridan at Clarion East and Eileen Gunn at Clarion West.

Edited by Gordon Van Gelder
Design by Pei Loi Koay

ISBN 0-312-14023-1

CONTENTS

▼

This book is the work of fourteen people who are contributing to an odd literary tradition which, if not singular, has found its most exuberant expression among writers of contemporary American science fiction. For over half a century, some of the most skilled artisans in our field have spent significant time and energy passing on to newcomers what they know about their craft.

They have done so out of a variety of motives, few pecuniary. For some writers and editors, aiding new authors has been a way to bolster what started as a small and somewhat suspect form of literary art, to seek respectability in numbers. For others, new writers have meant more hands to meet what has been a rapidly expanding demand for science fiction, a consequence of our age of technological threat and promise. For most (those of my acquaintance), this mutual aid springs from uncomplicated affection for both the genre and its practitioners.

And then there is Fandom; perhaps only rock music and basketball have attracted so many young people seriously bent on imitating the performers they admire. As with neighborhood shooters of hoops and thumpers of air guitars, a few talented science fiction fans go from admiration to emulation and graduate to the ranks of professionals. Many have been helped along the way by one or another of the dozen first-class practitioners of their craft represented here.

▼

In his amusing and revealing history of *The Futurians* (John Day, 1977), Science Fiction and Fantasy Writers of America Grand Master Damon Knight tells of a cabal within this bohemian collective of fifteen or so SF pioneers (circa 1940) that met once a week for group readings of members' manuscripts. "This Futurian pattern of mutual help and criticism was part of a counterculture, opposed to the dominant culture of professional science fiction writers centering around John Campbell. Out of it later came the Milford Conference and the Clarion Workshop, both still viewed with alarm and suspicion by Campbell writers."

But Campbell's dominant culture also took a hand in developing new talent, although their approach—at least as Campbell expressed it to me—was Darwinian: "Either a guy's got it, and uses it, or he ain't got it, and you can't give it to him!"

A quarter of a century after the Futurians had disbanded, I was the fortunate professor who solicited Knight's help (and that of Fritz Leiber, Harlan Ellison, Judith Merril—another Futurian—and Kate Wilhelm) in an attempt to graft the "pattern of mutual help and criticism" onto the academic mainstream in what became the Clarion Writers Workshop. I also sought help from Campbell, who—although he would undoubtedly have agreed with Gore Vidal that "teaching has ruined more American novelists than drink"—was himself a splendid teacher, if principally through his remarkable correspondence. As a novice writer with a couple of sales to *Analog* under my belt, I had already benefited greatly from his letters, each filled with sapient criticism expressed in language that exactly matched his gravelly *ex cathedra* conversational tone. You knew when you spoke with Campbell that This Was the Word.

"I'll be glad to back your play on the Science Fiction Workshop," he wrote me in 1967, "despite my conviction that school courses for writers are of somewhat negative value!

"The one flaw I have found with most writers' school courses is the tendency to induce borderline . . . writers to gather the idea that story-telling is like painting by-the-numbers; you give 'em the numbers, and they start painting just like you said."

He continued, then, instructing me on rule-breaking with an account of how some prominent members of his stable of writers had done so. I pass along a sample of his pedagogy:

> The one sure way to fail is to do just what succeeded yesterday.
> Will Jenkins, the <u>real</u> Old Pro in the business once told me that for about three years he made his living from a book on How To Write Short Stories. His technique was to read the book carefully, pick out something You Should Never Do,

then write a story based on doing that, and selling it to one of the big slicks. Or on <u>not</u> doing what You Must Always Do. He also did well for some years on the old Detective Story Weekly; they used to put out a tip-sheet to their authors, explaining what they <u>must</u> have, and what they considered taboo. Like their stories <u>must</u> have action————something happening all the way through. So he sold 'em a story in which everybody in the yarn was suffering from spring fever; the desk sergeant was asleep at the desk, the detective mooches in slowly, sits down and puts his feet up on the desk, and through the story sits there waiting for a watch to run down.

A <u>real</u> author takes any statement as a challenge to prove he can do a story that proves the reverse of the obvious necessity!

Like "Do a story in which the hero's self-sacrificing nobility of character damn near causes a catastrophe, while the ill-mannered, self-centered villain wins the girl because he uses his evil skills and black-hearted ways to save the situation." (He'd get clobbered in the catastrophe too, if he didn't).

Harry Stubbs' (Hal Clement's) classic "Needle" resulted from my statement that you can't write a satisfactory detective story in science fiction.

So naturally he wrote one, and sold it to me. . . .

A. E. Van Vogt did a story————about 8000 words———— using an 800 word Basic English vocabulary; you didn't notice it until he pointed it out.

Henry Kuttner did one that started with the ending, followed by the middle, and wound up with the beginning.

Poul Anderson started one with a scene in which the toothy, reptilian bug-eyed monster shrinks in terror from the pretty blonde heroine.

Randy Garrett did an accurate-to-known-history novelette called "Despoilers of the Golden Empire," which read exactly like an early pulp science-fiction story, with improbable sounding superhero and all. Actually a true account of the conquest of Peru by an overage (55 to start!) adventurer.

You name it———and a real author can take either side
of the issue and make a story. . . .

The point of all this is not to set Campbell's iconoclasm against
Knight's mutual help and criticism (a modus operandi in nearly thirty
years of successful Clarion workshops), or either of these against the staid
academic dichotomy between teacher and pupil, but to show how science fiction has enjoyed a long tradition of professionals selflessly giving
to each other and to talented tyros, some in academic settings, some in
professional conclaves, some via amateur forums in fanzines, and some
in private communications, especially those between editor and author.

I and the twelve authors represented in this volume (and our St. Martin's Press editor, Gordon Van Gelder, who makes the 14th member of
our cabal) have all benefited from one or another of these opportunities
to learn. Each of us in turn has contributed to the mutual aid of fellow
writers via an editor's pen or within the Stakhanovite atmosphere of one
or another workshop, the longest-running of which are Clarion East at
Michigan State University and Clarion West, currently in rented space
at Seattle Central Community College and Seattle University. And so,
in this volume, we further the tradition by offering to fellow authors,
novices or not, a few of our ideas about writing science fiction.

A final conjecture: Perhaps this interesting tradition of communal
artistic enterprise results from the very nature of science, the essence of
art, and their curious union in science fiction. French scientist Claude
Bernard, who was a so-so playwright but a world-renowned Third Re-
public physiologist, put it this way:

"Art," he wrote, "is I; science is we."

Perhaps the melding of these two in our genre has hatched the idea
of the (perforce) lone artist working within a network of supportive col-
leagues and mentors which seems to be such an integral part of the
American science fiction scene.

Paragons is divided into sections on plot, character, setting, theme, point of view, and style. Each section is prefaced by a short essay for which I alone am responsible. These are minor rewrites of essays I prepared for a similar volume twenty-five years ago; I have learned little since then.

As I wrote to each contributor, "the essays are designed to provide newcomers to critical reading with a reasonably straightforward vocabulary of literary terms. I neither ask nor expect that you will agree with an essay's particulars, only that you accept it as a pad from which to launch your own ideas on the subject as they are realized in your work."

I ask the same of the reader.

▼

O what a tangled web we weave,
When first we practice to deceive!

Yes indeed, Sir Walter. And although the writer's business is truth, her primary tool is a kind of deception achieved through the (apparently) tangled web of plot.

Some writers plot consciously, building a structure to which such other elements as character, setting, and style are tailored. Others plant characters in an opening situation and watch what grows, pruning and shaping the result until it seems satisfying. Whatever the process, all plots display certain characteristics: there is a series of events in time causally related (although "time" may be variously interpreted and "cause" may be obscure); there is conflict (between people, between a person and nature or society or a machine, or between two facets of a single character); and there are some structural elements, the terms for which have been borrowed from the drama.

Exposition is the explanation of events or circumstances not given narrative or dramatic treatment in the story. Sometimes referred to as the "expository lump"—because, I suppose, it is so hard for the reader to swallow if presented clumsily—exposition is conspicuously thin in much contemporary fiction, which may work the reader a little harder, but lets the writer get on with his business without distracting interruptions.

Another structural device is *involution* (or *noument* if you prefer the French), the winding together of the threads of action and motivation which heighten conflict, add complications, or promise (falsely) an early end to things.

Climax is the point of maximum conflict, when apparently irreconcilable forces meet, the issue is in maximum doubt, and some decisive event is demanded.

Last comes the *resolution* (or *denoument*), when the issue is decided, all is clear, a kind of equilibrium has returned to the little world of the story, and wiser or sadder or happier, the reader is released from his contract with the writer.

These structural elements may be combined in a variety of ways and may enjoy greatly varying degrees of emphasis. True climax may not be perceptible to the reader until after the resolution and the new information it conveys; exposition may take place imperceptibly through the implications of events rather than through direct statement; involution may follow or precede climax; the resolution itself may be so equivocal as to leave even the careful reader unsure of the full meaning of what he has read. Writing fiction is not an exact science; there really are no plot formulas for anything worth reading.

Two more words are useful in discussions of plot: An *organic* plot is based upon direct and perceptible relationships between events, each being linked to its predecessor and successor by strong bonds of causality. In an *episodic* plot, events are knit together less by causality than by their common relationship to some central event or character or theme. The plot of Poe's "Cask of Amontillado" is highly organic, a chain of events stretched tightly from opening to resolution; *Tom Jones* is more episodic, a series of events — some causally related, some not — bound together like the spokes of a wheel by their common hub, the theme of Tom's maturation as a good *and* prudent man.

Finally, in plot time is of the essence. Some plots move along a smooth chronological line; others reverse time, or employ it as an element of conflict, or negate it as much as possible to focus the reader's attention on other matters. Then there is *tempo* (the pace of the author's presentation of events in the story, not the ticking of the clocks in the little world that *is* the story). *Normal tempo* is the conventional balance between the realistic slowness of most human happenings and the need to compress these happenings to fit the limitations of the reader's patience. *Retarded tempo* expands time, often to a pace far slower than real time, to allow the writer to examine events in great detail. (*Tristram Shandy* and Henry James' *The American* are examples.) *Accelerated tempo* is the pace of the action-adventure tale or the documentary history, the furious rush of events that leaves the hero (and the reader) breathless. Tempo is not necessarily uniform throughout a story; its variation in conformity with the author's intentions is part of his craft, something he achieves as much through stylistic devices as through his selection and arrangement of events in plot.

No apology for the accelerated tempo of this cursory treatment of an enormously complex subject; I will only add that good plotting is the first (if not the most important) skill of the writer, that an understanding of plot is essential to the critical reader, and that—for me—it is the most troublesome aspect of fiction.

THE PRICE OF ORANGES

by Nancy Kress

▼

"I'm worried about my granddaughter," Harry Kramer said, passing half of his sandwich to Manny Feldman. Manny took it eagerly. The sandwich was huge, thick slices of beef and horseradish between fresh slabs of crusty bread. Pigeons watched the park bench hopefully.

"Jackie. The granddaughter who writes books," Manny said. Harry watched to see that Manny ate. You couldn't trust Manny to eat enough; he stayed too skinny. At least in Harry's opinion. Manny, Jackie—the world, Harry sometimes thought, had all grown too skinny when he somehow hadn't been looking. Skimpy. Stretch-feeling. Harry nodded to see horseradish spurt in a satisfying stream down Manny's scraggly beard.

"Jackie. Yes," Harry said.

"So what's wrong with her? She's sick?" Manny eyed Harry's strudel, cherry with real yeast bread. Harry passed it to him. "Harry, the whole thing? I couldn't."

"Take it, take it, I don't want it. You should eat. No, she's not sick. She's miserable." When Manny, his mouth full of strudel, didn't answer, Harry put a hand on Manny's arm. *"Miserable."*

Manny swallowed hastily. "How do you know? You saw her this week?"

"No. Next Tuesday. She's bringing me a book by a friend of hers. I know from this." He drew a magazine from an inner pocket of his coat. The coat was thick tweed, almost new, with wooden buttons. On the cover of the glossy magazine a woman smiled contemptuously. A woman with hollow, starved-looking cheeks who obviously didn't get enough to eat either.

"That's not a book," Manny pointed out.

"So she writes stories, too. Listen to this. Just listen. 'I stood in my backyard, surrounded by the false bright toxin-fed green, and realized that the earth was dead. What else could it be, since we humans swarmed upon it like maggots on carrion, growing our hectic gleaming molds, leaving our slime trails across the senseless surface?' Does that sound like a happy woman?"

"Hoo boy," Manny said.

"It's all like that. 'Don't read my things, Popsy,' she says. 'You're not in the audience for my things.' Then she smiles without ever once showing her teeth." Harry flung both arms wide. "Who else should be in the audience but her own grandfather?"

Manny swallowed the last of the strudel. Pigeons fluttered angrily. "She never shows her teeth when she smiles? Never?"

"Never."

"Hoo boy," Manny said. "Did you want all of that orange?"

"No, I brought it for you, to take home. But did you finish that whole half a sandwich already?"

"I thought I'd take it home," Manny said humbly. He showed Harry the tip of the sandwich, wrapped in the thick brown butcher paper, protruding from the pocket of his old coat.

Harry nodded approvingly. "Good, good. Take the orange, too. I brought it for you."

Manny took the orange. Three teenagers carrying huge shrieking radios sauntered past. Manny started to put his hands over his ears, received a look of dangerous contempt from the teenager with green hair, and put his hands on his lap. The kid tossed an empty beer bottle onto the pavement before their feet. It shattered. Harry scowled fiercely but Manny stared straight ahead. When the cacophony had passed, Manny said, "Thank you for the orange. Fruit, it costs so much this time of year."

Harry still scowled. "Not in 1937."

"Don't start that again, Harry."

Harry said sadly, "Why won't you ever believe me? Could I afford to bring all this food if I got it at 1988 prices? Could I afford this coat? Have you seen buttons like this in 1988, on a new coat? Have you seen sandwiches wrapped in that kind of paper since we were young? Have you? Why won't you believe me?"

Manny slowly peeled his orange. The rind was pale, and the orange had seeds. "Harry. Don't start."

"But why won't you just come to my room and *see?*"

Manny sectioned the orange. "Your room. A cheap furnished room in a Social Security hotel. Why should I go? I know what will be there. What will be there is the same thing in my room. A bed, a chair, a table, a hot plate, some cans of food. Better I should meet you here in the park, get at least a little fresh air." He looked at Harry meekly, the orange clutched in one hand. "Don't misunderstand. It's not from a lack of friendship I say this. You're good to me, you're the best friend I have. You bring me things from a great deli, you talk to me, you share with me the family I don't have. It's enough, Harry. It's *more* than enough. I don't need to see where you live like I live."

Harry gave it up. There were moods, times, when it was just impossible to budge Manny. He dug in, and in he stayed. "Eat your orange."

"It's a good orange. So tell me more about Jackie."

"Jackie." Harry shook his head. Two kids on bikes tore along the path. One of them swerved towards Manny and snatched the orange from his hand. "Aw riggghhhtttt!"

Harry scowled after the child. It had been a girl. Manny just wiped the orange juice off his fingers onto the knee of his pants. "Is everything she writes so depressing?"

"Everything," Harry said. "Listen to this one." He drew out another magazine, smaller, bound in rough paper with a stylized linen drawing of a woman's private parts on the cover. On the cover! Harry held the magazine with one palm spread wide over the drawing, which made it difficult to keep the pages open while he read. " 'She looked at her mother in the only way possible: with contempt, contempt for all the betrayals and compromises that had been her mother's life, for the sad soft lines of defeat around her mother's mouth, for the bright artificial dress too young for her wasted years, for even the leather handbag, Gucci of course, filled with blood money for having sold her life to a man who had long since ceased to want it.' "

"Hoo boy," Manny said. "About a *mother* she wrote that?"

"About everybody. All the time."

"And where *is* Barbara?"

"Reno again. Another divorce." How many had that been? After two, did anybody count? Harry didn't count. He imagined Barbara's life as a large roulette wheel like the ones on TV, little silver men bouncing in and out of red and black pockets. Why didn't she get dizzy?

Manny said slowly, "I always thought there was a lot of love in her."

"A lot of that she's got," Harry said dryly.

"Not Barbara—Jackie. A lot of . . . I don't know. Sweetness. Under the way she is."

"The way she is," Harry said gloomily. "Prickly. A cactus. But you're right, Manny, I know what you mean. She just needs someone to soften her up. Love her back, maybe. Although *I* love her."

The two old men looked at each other. Manny said, "Harry. . . ."

"I know, I know. I'm only a grandfather, my love doesn't count, I'm just there. Like air. 'You're wonderful, Popsy,' she says, and still no teeth when she smiles. But you know, Manny—you are right!" Harry jumped up from the bench. "You are! What she needs is a young man to love her!"

Manny looked alarmed. "I didn't say—"

"I don't know why I didn't think of it before!"

"Harry—"

"And her stories, too! Full of ugly murders, ugly places, unhappy endings. What she needs is something to show her that writing could be about sweetness, too."

Manny was staring at him hard. Harry felt a rush of affection. That Manny should have the answer! Skinny wonderful Manny!

Manny said slowly, "Jackie said to me, 'I write about reality.' That's what she said, Harry."

"So there's no sweetness in reality? Put sweetness in her life, her writing will go sweet. She *needs* this, Manny. A really nice fellow!"

Two men in jogging suits ran past. One of their Reeboks came down on a shard of beer bottle. "Every fucking time!" he screamed, bending over to inspect his shoe. "Fucking park!"

"Well, what do you expect?" the other drawled, looking at Manny and Harry. "Although you'd think that if we could clean up Lake Erie. . . ."

"Fucking derelicts!" the other snarled. They jogged away.

"Of course," Harry said, "it might not be easy to find the sort of guy to convince Jackie."

"Harry, I think you should maybe think—"

"Not here," Harry said suddenly. "Not here. *There*. In 1937."

"*Harry*. . . ."

"Yeah," Harry said, nodding several times. Excitement filled him like light, like electricity. What an idea! "It was different then."

Manny said nothing. When he stood up, the sleeve of his coat exposed the number tattooed on his wrist. He said quietly, "It was no paradise in 1937 either, Harry."

Harry seized Manny's hand. "I'm going to do it, Manny. Find someone for her there. Bring him here."

Manny sighed. "Tomorrow at the chess club, Harry? At one o'clock? It's Tuesday."

"I'll tell you then how I'm coming with this."

"Fine, Harry. Fine. All my wishes go with you. You know that."

Harry stood up too, still holding Manny's hand. A middle-aged man staggered to the bench and slumped onto it. The smell of whiskey rose from him in waves. He eyed Manny and Harry with scorn. "Fucking fags."

"Good night, Harry."

"Manny—if you'd only come . . . money goes so much farther there. . . ."

"Tomorrow at one. At the chess club."

Harry watched his friend walk away. Manny's foot dragged a little; the knee must be bothering him again. Harry wished Manny would see a doctor. Maybe a doctor would know why Manny stayed so skinny.

Harry walked back to his hotel. In the lobby, old men slumped in upholstery thin from wear, burned from cigarettes, shiny in the seat from long sitting. Sitting and sitting, Harry thought—life measured by the seat of the pants. And now it was getting dark. No one would go out from here until the next daylight. Harry shook his head.

The elevator wasn't working again. He climbed the stairs to the third floor. Halfway there, he stopped, felt in his pocket, counted five quarters, six dimes, two nickels, and eight pennies. He returned to the lobby. "Could I have two dollar bills for this change, please? Maybe old bills?"

The clerk looked at him suspiciously. "Your rent paid up?"

"Certainly," Harry said. The woman grudgingly gave him the money.

"Thank you. You look very lovely today, Mrs. Raduski." Mrs. Raduski snorted.

In his room, Harry looked for his hat. He finally found it under his bed—how had it gotten under his bed? He dusted it off and put it on. It had cost him $3.25. He opened the closet door, parted the clothes hanging from their metal pole—like Moses parting the sea, he always thought, a Moses come again—and stepped to the back of the closet, remembering with his body rather than his mind the sharp little twist to the right just past the far gray sleeve of his good wool suit.

He stepped out into the bare corner of a warehouse. Cobwebs brushed his hat; he had stepped a little too far right. Harry crossed the empty concrete space to where the lumber stacks started, and threaded his way through them. The lumber, too, was covered with cobwebs; not much building going on. On his way out the warehouse door, Harry passed the night watchman coming on duty.

"Quiet all day, Harry?"

"As a church, Rudy," Harry said. Rudy laughed. He laughed a lot. He was also indisposed to question very much. The first time he had seen Harry coming out of the warehouse in a bemused daze, he must have assumed that Harry had been hired to work there. Peering at Rudy's round, vacant face, Harry realized that he must hold this job because he was someone's uncle, someone's cousin, someone's something. Harry had felt a small glow of approval; families should take care of their own. He had told Rudy that he had lost his key and asked him for another.

Outside it was late afternoon. Harry began walking. Eventually there were people walking past him, beside him, across the street from him. Everybody wore hats. The women wore bits of velvet or wool with dotted veils across their noses and long, graceful dresses in small prints. The men wore fedoras with suits as baggy as Harry's. When he reached the park there were children, girls in long black tights and hard shoes, boys in buttoned shirts. Everyone looked like it was Sunday morning.

Pushcarts and shops lined the sidewalks. Harry bought a pair of socks, thick gray wool, for 89 cents. When the man took his dollar, Harry held his breath: each first time made a little pip in his stomach. But no one ever looked at the dates of old bills. He bought two oranges for five cents each, and then, thinking of Manny, bought a third. At a candystore he bought *G-8 And His Battle Aces* for fifteen cents. At The Collector's Cozy in the other time they would gladly give him thirty dollars for it. Finally, he bought a cherry Coke for a nickel and headed toward the park.

"Oh, excuse me," said a young man who bumped into Harry on the sidewalk. "I'm so sorry!" Harry looked at him hard: but, no. Too young. Jackie was twenty-eight.

Some children ran past, making for the movie theater. Spencer

Tracy in *Captains Courageous*. Harry sat down on a green-painted wooden bench under a pair of magnificent Dutch elms. On the bench lay a news-magazine. Harry glanced at it to see when in September this was: the 28th. The cover pictured a young blond Nazi soldier standing at stiff salute. Harry thought again of Manny, frowned, and turned the magazine cover down.

For the next hour, people walked past. Harry studied them carefully. When it got too dark to see, he walked back to the warehouse, on the way buying an apple kuchen at a bakery with a curtain behind the counter looped back to reveal a man in his shirtsleeves eating a plate of stew at a table bathed in soft yellow lamplight. The kuchen cost thirty-two cents.

At the warehouse, Harry let himself in with his key, slipped past Rudy nodding over *Paris Nights*, and walked to his cobwebby corner. He emerged from his third-floor closet into his room. Beyond the window, sirens wailed and would not stop.

"So how's it going?" Manny asked. He dripped kuchen crumbs on the chessboard; Harry brushed them away. Manny had him down a knight.

"It's going to take time to find somebody that's right," Harry said. "I'd like to have someone by next Tuesday when I meet Jackie for dinner, but I don't know. It's not easy. There are requirements. He has to be young enough to be attractive, but old enough to understand Jackie. He has to be sweet-natured enough to do her some good, but strong enough not to panic at jumping over fifty-two years. Somebody educated. An educated man—he might be more curious than upset by my closet. Don't you think?"

"Better watch your queen," Manny said, moving his rook. "So how are you going to find him?"

"It takes time," Harry said. "I'm working on it."

Manny shook his head. "You have to get somebody here, you have to convince him he *is* here, you have to keep him from turning right around and running back in time through your shirts. . . . I don't know, Harry. I don't know. I've been thinking. This thing is not simple. What if you did something wrong? Took somebody important out of 1937?"

"I won't pick anybody important."

"What if you made a mistake and brought your own grandfather? And something happened to him here?"

"My grandfather was already dead in 1937."

"What if you brought me? I'm already here."

"You didn't live here in 1937."

"What if you brought *you?*"

"I didn't live here either."

"What if you. . . ."

"Manny," Harry said, "I'm not bringing somebody important. I'm not bringing somebody we know. I'm not bringing somebody for permanent. I'm just bringing a nice guy for Jackie to meet, go dancing, see a different kind of nature. A different view of what's possible. An innocence. I'm sure there are fellows here that would do it, but I don't know any, and I don't know how to bring any to her. From there I know. Is this so complicated? Is this so unpredictable?"

"Yes," Manny said. He had on his stubborn look again. How could somebody so skimpy look so stubborn? Harry sighed and moved his lone knight.

"I brought you some whole socks."

"Thank you. That knight, it's not going to help you much."

"Lectures. That's what there was there that there isn't here. Everybody went to lectures. No TV, movies cost money, they went to free lectures."

"I remember," Manny said. "I was a young man myself. Harry, this thing is not simple."

"Yes, it is," Harry said stubbornly.

"1937 was not simple."

"It will work, Manny."

"Check," Manny said.

That evening, Harry went back. This time it was the afternoon of September 16. On newsstands *The New York Times* announced that President Roosevelt and John L. Lewis had talked pleasantly at the White House. Cigarettes cost thirteen cents a pack. Women wore cotton stockings and clunky, high-heeled shoes. Schrafft's best chocolates were sixty cents a pound. Small boys addressed Harry as "sir."

He attended six lectures in two days. A Madame Trefania lectured on theosophy to a hall full of badly-dressed women with thin, pursed lips. A union organizer roused an audience to a pitch that made Harry leave after the first thirty minutes. A skinny, nervous missionary showed slides of religious outposts in China. An archeologist back from a Mexican dig gave a dry, impatient talk about temples to an audience of three people. A New Deal Democrat spoke passionately about aiding the poor, but afterwards addressed all the women present as "Sister." Finally, just when Harry was starting to feel discouraged, he found it.

A museum offered a series of lectures on "Science of Today—and Tomorrow." Harry heard a slim young man with a reddish beard speak with idealistic passion about travel to the moon, the planets, the stars. It seemed to Harry that compared to stars, 1989 might seem reasonably close. The young man had warm hazel eyes and a sense of humor. When he spoke about life in a space ship, he mentioned in passing that women would be freed from much domestic drudgery they now endured. Throughout the lecture, he smoked, lighting cigarettes with a masculine squinting of eyes and cupping of hands. He said that imagination was the human quality that would most help people adjust to the future. His shoes were polished.

But most of all, Harry thought, he had a *glow*. A fine golden Boy Scout glow that made Harry think of old covers for the *Saturday Evening Post*. Which here cost five cents.

After the lecture, Harry stayed in his chair in the front row, outwaiting even the girl with bright red lipstick who lingered around the lecturer, this Robert Gernshon. From time to time, Gernshon glanced over at Harry with quizzical interest. Finally the girl, red lips pouting, sashayed out of the hall.

"Hello," Harry said. "I'm Harry Kramer. I enjoyed your talk. I have something to show you that you would be very interested in."

The hazel eyes turned wary. "Oh, no, no," Harry said. "Something *scientific*. Here, look at this." He handed Gernshon a filtered Vantage Light.

"How long it is," Gernshon said. "What's this made of?"

"The filter? It's made of . . . a new filter material. Tastes milder and cuts down on the nicotine. Much better for you. Look at this." He gave Gernshon a styrofoam cup from McDonald's. "It's made of a new material, too. Very cheap. Disposable."

Gernshon fingered the cup. "Who are you?" he said quietly.

"A scientist. I'm interested in the science of tomorrow, too. Like you. I'd like to invite you to see my laboratory, which is in my home."

"In your home?"

"Yes. In a small way. Just dabbling, you know." Harry could feel himself getting rattled; the young hazel eyes stared at him so steadily. *Jackie,* he thought. Dead earths. Maggots and carrion. Contempt for mothers. What would Gernshon say? When would Gernshon say *anything?*

"Thank you," Gernshon finally said. "When would be convenient?"

"Now?" Harry said. He tried to remember what time of day it was now. All he could picture was lecture halls.

Gernshon came. It was nine-thirty in the evening of Friday, September 17. Harry walked Gernshon through the streets, trying to talk animatedly, trying to distract. He said that he himself was very interested in travel to the stars. He said it had always been his dream to stand on another planet and take in great gulps of completely unpolluted air. He said his great heroes were those biologists who made that twisty model of DNA. He said science had been his life. Gernshon walked more and more silently.

"Of course," Harry said hastily, "like most scientists, I'm mostly familiar with my own field. You know how it is."

"What is your field, Dr. Kramer?" Gernshon asked quietly.

"Electricity," Harry said, and hit him on the back of the head with a solid brass candlestick from the pocket of his coat. The candlestick had cost him three dollars at a pawn shop.

They had walked past the stores and pushcarts to a point where the locked business offices and warehouses began. There were no passers-by, no muggers, no street dealers, no Guardian Angels, no punk gangs. Only him, hitting an unarmed man with a candlestick. He was no better than the punks. But what else could he do? What else could he *do?* Nothing but hit him softly, so softly that Gernshon was struggling again almost before Harry got his hands and feet tied, well before he got on the blindfold and gag. "I'm sorry, I'm sorry," he kept saying to Gernshon. Gernshon did not look as if the apology made any difference. Harry dragged him into the warehouse.

Rudy was asleep over *Spicy Stories.* Breathing very hard, Harry pulled the young man—not more than 150 pounds, it was good Harry had looked for slim—to the far corner, through the gate, and into his closet.

"Listen," he said urgently to Gernshon after removing the gag. "Listen. I can call the Medicare Emergency Hotline. If your head feels broken. Are you feeling faint? Do you think you maybe might go into shock?"

Gernshon lay on Harry's rug, glaring at him, saying nothing.

"Listen, I know this is maybe a little startling to you. But I'm not a pervert, not a cop, not anything but a grandfather with a problem. My granddaughter. I need your help to solve it, but I won't take much of your time. You're now somewhere besides where you gave your lecture. A pretty long ways away. But you don't have to stay here long, I promise. Just two weeks, tops, and I'll send you back. I promise, on my mother's grave. And I'll make it worth your while. I promise."

"Untie me."

"Yes. Of course. Right away. Only you have to not attack me, because I'm the only one who can get you back from here." He had a sudden inspiration. "I'm like a foreign consul. You've maybe traveled abroad?"

Gernshon looked around the dingy room. "Untie me."

"I will. In two minutes. Five, tops. I just want to explain a little first."

"Where am I?"

"1989."

Gernshon said nothing. Harry explained brokenly, talking as fast as he could, saying he could move from 1989 to September, 1937 when he wanted to, but he could take Gernshon back too, no problem. He said he made the trip often, it was perfectly safe. He pointed out how much farther a small Social Security check, no pension, could go at 1937 prices. He mentioned Manny's strudel. Only lightly did he touch on the problem of Jackie, figuring there would be a better time to share domestic difficulties, and his closet he didn't mention at all. It was hard to keep his eyes averted from the closet door. He did mention how bitter people could be in 1989, how lost, how weary from expecting so much that nothing was a delight, nothing a sweet surprise. He was just working up to a tirade on innocence when Gernshon said again, in a different tone, "Untie me."

"Of course," Harry said quickly, "I don't expect you to believe me. Why should you think you're in 1989? Go, see for yourself. Look at that light, it's still early morning. Just be careful out there, is all." He untied Gernshon and stood with his eyes squeezed shut, waiting.

When nothing hit him, Harry opened his eyes. Gernshon was at the door. "Wait!" Harry cried. "You'll need more money!" He dug into his pocket and pulled out a twenty-dollar bill, carefully saved for this, and all the change he had.

Gernshon examined the coins carefully, then looked up at Harry. He said nothing. He opened the door and Harry, still trembling, sat down in his chair to wait.

Gernshon came back three hours later, pale and sweating. "My God!"

"I know just what you mean," Harry said. "A zoo out there. Have a drink."

Gernshon took the mixture Harry had ready in his toothbrush glass and gulped it down. He caught sight of the bottle, which Harry had left on the dresser: Seagram's V.O., with the cluttered, tiny-print label. He threw the glass across the room and covered his face with his hands.

"I'm sorry," Harry said apologetically. "But then it cost only $3.37 the fifth."

Gernshon didn't move.

"I'm really sorry," Harry said. He raised both hands, palms up, and dropped them helplessly. "Would you . . . would you maybe like an orange?"

Gernshon recovered faster than Harry had dared hope. Within an hour he was sitting in Harry's worn chair, asking questions about the space shuttle; within two hours taking notes; within three become again the intelligent and captivating young man of the lecture hall. Harry, answering as much as he could as patiently as he could, was impressed by the boy's resilience. It couldn't have been easy. What if he, Harry, suddenly had to skip fifty-two more years? What if he found himself in 2041? Harry shuddered.

"Do you know that a movie now costs six dollars?"

Gernshon blinked. "We were talking about the moon landing."

"Not any more, we're not. I want to ask *you* some questions, Robert. Do you think the earth is dead, with people sliming all over it like on carrion? Is this a thought that crosses your mind?"

"I . . . no."

Harry nodded. "Good, good. Do you look at your mother with contempt?"

"Of course not. Harry—"

"No, it's my turn. Do you think a woman who marries a man, and maybe the marriage doesn't work out perfect, whose does, but they raise at least one healthy child—say a daughter—that that woman's life has been a defeat and a failure?"

"No. I—"

"What would you think if you saw a drawing of a woman's private parts on the cover of a magazine?"

Gernshon blushed. He looked as if the blush annoyed him, but also as if he couldn't help it.

"Better and better," Harry said. "Now, think carefully on this next one—take your time—no hurry. Does reality seem to you to have sweetness in it as well as ugliness? Take your time."

Gernshon peered at him. Harry realized they had talked right through lunch. "But not all the time in the world, Robert."

"Yes," Gernshon said. "I think reality has more sweetness than ugliness. And more strangeness than anything else. Very much more." He looked suddenly dazed. "I'm sorry, I just—all this has happened so—"

"Put your head between your knees," Harry suggested. "There—better now? Good. There's someone I want you to meet."

Manny sat in the park, on their late-afternoon bench. When he saw them coming, his face settled into long sorrowful ridges. "Harry. Where have you been for two days? I was worried, I went to your hotel—"

"Manny," Harry said, "this is Robert."

"So I see," Manny said. He didn't hold out his hand.

"*Him*," Harry said.

"Harry. Oh, Harry."

"How do you do, sir," Gernshon said. He held out his hand. "I'm afraid I didn't get your full name. I'm Robert Gernshon."

Manny looked at him—at the outstretched hand, the baggy suit with wide tie, the deferential smile, the golden Baden-Powell glow. Manny's lips mouthed a silent word: *sir?*

"I have a lot to tell you," Harry said.

"You can tell all of us, then," Manny said. "Here comes Jackie now."

Harry looked up. Across the park a woman in jeans strode purposefully towards them. "Manny! It's only Monday!"

"I called her to come," Manny said. "You've been gone from your room two days, Harry, nobody at your hotel could say where—"

"But *Manny*," Harry said, while Gernshon looked, frowning, from one to the other and Jackie spotted them and waved.

She had lost more weight, Harry saw. Only two weeks, yet her cheeks had hollowed out and new, tiny lines touched her eyes. Skinny lines. They filled him with sadness. Jackie wore a blue tee-shirt that said LIFE IS A BITCH—THEN YOU DIE. She carried a magazine and a small can of mace disguised as hair spray.

"Popsy! You're here! Manny said—"

"Manny was wrong," Harry said. "Jackie, sweetheart, you look—it's good to see you. Jackie, I'd like you to meet somebody, darling. This is Robert. My friend. My friend Robert. Jackie Snyder."

"Hi," Jackie said. She gave Harry a hug, and then Manny one. Harry saw Gernshon gazing at her very tight jeans.

"Robert's a . . . a scientist," Harry said.

It was the wrong thing to say; Harry knew the moment he said it that it was the wrong thing. Science—all science—was, for some reason not completely clear to him, a touchy subject with Jackie. She tossed her long hair back from her eyes. "Oh, yeah? Not *chemical*, I hope?"

"I'm not actually a scientist," Gernshon said winningly. "Just a dabbler. I popularize new scientific concepts, write about them to make them intelligible."

"Like what?" Jackie said.

Gernshon opened his mouth, closed it again. A boy suddenly flashed past on a skateboard, holding a boom box. Metallica blasted in the air. Overhead, a jet droned. Gernshon smiled weakly. "It's hard to explain."

"I'm capable of understanding," Jackie said coldly. "Women *can* understand science, you know."

"Jackie, sweetheart," Harry said, "what have you got there? Is that your new book?"

"No," Jackie said, "this is the one I said I'd bring you, by my friend. It's brilliant. It's about a man whose business partner betrays him by selling out to organized crime and framing the man. In jail he meets a guy who has founded his own religion, the House of Divine Despair, and when they both get out they start a new business, Suicide Incorporated, that helps people kill themselves for a fee. The whole thing is just a brilliant denunciation of contemporary America."

Gernshon made a small sound.

"It's a comedy," Jackie added.

"It sounds . . . it sounds a little depressing," Gernshon said.

Jackie looked at him. Very distinctly, she said, "It's reality."

Harry saw Gernshon glance around the park. A man nodded on a bench, his hands slack on his knees. Newspapers and McDonald's wrappers stirred fitfully in the dirt. A trash container had been knocked over. From beside a scrawny tree enclosed shoulder-height by black wrought iron, a child watched them with old eyes.

"I brought you something else, too, Popsy," Jackie said. Harry hoped that Gernshon noticed how much gentler her voice was when she spoke to her grandfather. "A scarf. See, it's llama wool. Very warm."

Gernshon said, "My mother has a scarf like that. No, I guess hers is some kind of fur."

Jackie's face changed. "What kind?"

"I—I'm not sure."

"Not an endangered species, I hope."

"No. Not that. I'm sure not . . . that."

Jackie stared at him a moment longer. The child who had been watching strolled towards them. Harry saw Gernshon look at the boy with relief. About eleven years old, he wore a perfectly tailored suit and Italian shoes. Manny shifted to put himself between the boy and Gernshon. "Jackie, darling, it's so good to see you. . . ."

The boy brushed by Gernshon on the other side. He never looked up, and his voice stayed boyish and low, almost a whisper. "Crack. . . ."

"Step on one and you break your mother's back," Gernshon said brightly. He smiled at Harry, a special conspiratorial smile to suggest that children, at least, didn't change in fifty years. The boy's head jerked up to look at Gernshon.

"You talking about my mama?"

Jackie groaned. "No," she said to the kid. "He doesn't mean anything. Beat it."

"I don't forget," the boy said. He backed away slowly.

Gernshon said, frowning, "I'm sorry. I'm not sure exactly what all that was, but I'm sorry."

"Are you for real?" Jackie said angrily. "What the fucking hell *was* all that? Don't you realize this park is the only place Manny and my grandfather can get some fresh air?"

"I didn't—"

"That punk runner meant it when he said he won't forget!"

"I don't like your tone," Gernshon said. "Or your language."

"My language!" The corners of Jackie's mouth tightened. Manny looked at Harry and put his hands over his face. The boy, twenty feet away, suddenly let out a noise like a strangled animal, so piercing all four of them spun around. Two burly teenagers were running towards him. The child's face crumpled; he looked suddenly much younger. He sprang away, stumbled, made the noise again, and hurled himself, all animal terror, toward the street behind the park bench.

"No!" Gernshon shouted. Harry turned towards the shout but Gernshon already wasn't there. Harry saw the twelve-wheeler bearing down, heard Jackie's scream, saw Gernshon's wiry body barrel into the boy's. The truck shrieked past, its air brakes deafening.

Gernshon and the boy rose in the street on the other side.

Car horns blared. The boy bawled, "Leggo my suit! You tore my suit!" A red light flashed and a squad car pulled up. The two burly teenagers melted away, and then the boy somehow vanished as well.

"Never find him," the disgruntled cop told them over the clipboard on which he had written nothing. "Probably just as well." He went away.

"Are you hurt?" Manny said. It was the first time he had spoken. His face was ashen. Harry put a hand across his shoulders.

"No," Gernshon said. He gave Manny his sweet smile. "Just a little dirty."

"That took *guts*," Jackie said. She was staring at Gernshon with a frown between her eyebrows. "Why did you do it?"

"Pardon?"

"Why? I mean, given what that kid is, given—oh, all of it—" she gestured around the park, a helpless little wave of her strong young hands that tore at Harry's heart. "Why bother?"

Gernshon said gently, "What that kid is, is a kid."

Manny looked skeptical. Harry moved to stand in front of Manny's expression before anyone wanted to discuss it. "Listen, I've got a wonderful idea, you two seem to have so much to talk about, about . . . bothering, and . . . everything. Why don't you have dinner together, on me? My treat." He pulled another twenty dollar bill from his pocket. Behind him he could feel Manny start.

"Oh, I couldn't," Gernshon said, at the same moment that Jackie said warningly, "Popsy. . . ."

Harry put his palms on both sides of her face. "Please. Do this for me, Jackie. Without the questions, without the female protests. Just this once. For me."

Jackie was silent a long moment before she grimaced, nodded, and turned with half-humorous appeal to Gernshon.

Gernshon cleared his throat. "Well, actually, it would probably be better if all four of us came. I'm embarrassed to say that prices are higher in this city than in . . . that is, I'm not able to . . . but if we went somewhere less expensive, the Automat maybe, I'm sure all four of us could eat together."

"No, no," Harry said. "We already ate." Manny looked at him.

Jackie began, offended, "I certainly don't want—just what do you think is going on here, buddy? This is just to please my grandfather. Are you afraid I might try to jump your bones?"

Harry saw Gernshon's quick, involuntary glance at Jackie's tight jeans. He saw, too, that Gernshon fiercely regretted the glance the instant he had made it. He saw that Manny saw, and that Jackie saw, and that Gernshon saw that they saw. Manny made a small noise. Jackie's face began to turn so black that Harry was astounded when Gernshon cut her off with a dignity no one had expected.

"No, of course not," he said quietly. "But *I* would prefer all of us to have dinner together for quite another reason. My wife is very dear to me, Miss Snyder, and I wouldn't do anything that might make her feel uncomfortable. That's probably irrational, but that's the way it is."

Harry stood arrested, his mouth open. Manny started to shake with what Harry thought savagely had better not be laughter. And Jackie, after staring at Gernshon a long while, broke into the most spontaneous smile Harry had seen from her in months.

"Hey," she said softly. "That's nice. That's really, genuinely, fucking nice."

The weather turned abruptly colder. Snow threatened but didn't fall. Each afternoon Harry and Manny took a quick walk in the park and then went inside, to the chess club or a coffee shop or the bus station or the library, where there was a table deep in the stacks on which they could eat lunch without detection. Harry brought Manny a poor boy with mayo, sixty-three cents, and a pair of imported wool gloves, one dollar on pre-season sale.

"So where are they today?" Manny asked on Saturday, removing the gloves to peek at the inside of the poor boy. He sniffed appreciatively. "Horseradish. You remembered, Harry."

"The museum, I think," Harry said miserably.

"What museum?"

"How should I know? He says, 'The museum today, Harry,' and he's gone by eight o'clock in the morning, no more details than that."

Manny stopped chewing. "What museum opens at eight o'clock in the morning?"

Harry put down his sandwich, pastrami on rye, thirty-nine cents. He had lost weight the past week.

"Probably," Manny said hastily, "they just talk. You know, like young people do, just talk. . . ."

Harry eyed him balefully. "You mean like you and Leah did when you were young and left completely alone."

"You better talk to him soon, Harry. No, to her." He seemed to re-consider Jackie. "No, to *him*."

"Talk isn't going to do it," Harry said. He looked pale and deter-mined. "Gershon has to be sent back."

"Be sent?"

"He's *married*, Manny! I wanted to help Jackie, show her life can hold some sweetness, not be all struggle. What kind of sweetness is she going to find if she falls in love with a married man? You know how that goes! Jackie—" Harry groaned. How had all this happened? He had intended only the best for Jackie. Why didn't that count more? "He has to go back, Manny."

"How?" Manny said practically. "You can't hit him again, Harry. You were just lucky last time that you didn't hurt him. You don't want that on your conscience. And if you show him your, uh . . . your—"

"My closet. Manny, if you'd only come see, for a dollar you could get—"

"—then he could just come back any time he wants. So how?"

A sudden noise startled them both. Someone was coming through the stacks. "Librarians!" Manny hissed. Both of them frantically swept the sandwiches, beer (fifteen cents), and strudel into shopping bags. Manny, panicking, threw in the wool gloves. Harry swept the table free of crumbs. When the intruder rounded the nearest bookshelf, Harry was bent over *Making Paper Flowers* and Manny over *Porcelain of the Yung Cheng Dynasty*. It was Robert Gernshon.

The young man dropped into a chair. His face was ashen. In one hand he clutched a sheaf of paper, the handwriting on the last one trailing off into shaky squiggles.

After a moment of silence, Manny said diplomatically, "So where are you coming from, Robert?"

"Where's Jackie?" Harry demanded.

"Jackie?" Gernshon said. His voice was thick; Harry realized with a sudden shock that he had been crying. "I haven't seen her for a few days."

"A few *days?*" Harry said.

"No. I've been . . . I've been. . . ."

Manny sat up straighter. He looked intently at Gernshon over *Porcelain of the Yung Cheng Dynasty* and then put the book down. He moved to the chair next to Gernshon's and gently took the papers from his hand. Gernshon leaned over the table and buried his head in his arms.

"I'm so awfully sorry, I'm being such a baby. . . ." His shoulders trembled. Manny separated the papers and spread them out on the library table. Among the hand-copied notes were two slim books, one bound between black covers and the other a pamphlet. A *Memoir of Auschwitz. Countdown to Hiroshima.*

For a long moment nobody spoke. Then Harry said, to no one in particular, "I thought he was going to science museums."

Manny laid his arm, almost casually, across Gernshon's shoulders. "So now you'll know not to be at either place. More people should have only known." Harry didn't recognize the expression on his friend's face, nor the voice with which Manny said to Harry, "You're right. He has to go back."

"But Jackie. . . ."

"Can do without this 'sweetness,' " Manny said harshly. "So what's so terrible in her life anyway that she needs so much help? Is she dying? Is she poor? Is she ugly? Is anyone knocking on her door in the middle of the night? Let Jackie find her own sweetness. She'll survive."

Harry made a helpless gesture. Manny's stubborn face, carved wood under the harsh fluorescent light, did not change. "Even *him* . . . Manny, the things he knows now—"

"You should have thought of that earlier."

Gernshon looked up. "Don't, I—I'm sorry. It's just coming across it, I never thought human beings—"

"No," Manny said. "But they can. You been here, every day, at the library, reading it all?"

"Yes. That and museums. I saw you two come in earlier. I've been reading, I wanted to *know*—"

"So now you know," Manny said in that same surprisingly casual, tough voice. "You'll survive, too."

Harry said, "Does Jackie know what's going on? Why you've been doing all this . . . learning?"

"No."

"And you—what will you do with what you now know?"

Harry held his breath. What if Gernshon just refused to go back? Gernshon said slowly, "At first, I wanted to not return. At all. How can I watch it, World War II and the camps—I have *relatives* in Poland. And then later the bomb and Korea and the gulags and Vietnam and Cambodia and the terrorists and AIDS—"

"Didn't miss anything," Harry muttered.

"—and not be able to *do* anything, not be able to even hope, knowing that everything to come is already set into history—how could I watch all that without any hope that it isn't really as bad as it seems to be at the moment?"

"It all depends what you look at," Manny said, but Gernshon didn't seem to hear him.

"But neither can I stay, there's Susan and we're hoping for a baby . . . I need to think."

"No, you don't," Harry said. "You need to go *back*. This is all my mistake. I'm sorry. You need to go back, Gernshon."

"Lebanon," Gernshon said. "D.D.T. The Cultural Revolution. Nicaragua. Deforestation. Iran—"

"Penicillin," Manny said suddenly. His beard quivered. "Civil rights. Mahatma Gandhi. Polio vaccines. Washing machines." Harry stared at him, shocked. Could Manny once have worked in a hand laundry?

"Or," Manny said, more quietly, "Hitler. Auschwitz. Hoovervilles. The Dust Bowl. What you *look* at, Robert."

"I don't know," Gernshon said. "I need to think. There's so much . . . and then there's that girl."

Harry stiffened. "Jackie?"

"No, no. Someone she and I met a few days ago, at a coffee shop. She just walked in. I couldn't believe it. I looked at her and just went into shock—and maybe she did too, for all I know. The girl looked exactly like me. And she *felt* like—I don't know. It's hard to explain. She felt like *me*. I said hello but I didn't tell her my name; I didn't dare." His voice fell to a whisper. "I think she's my granddaughter."

"Hoo boy," Manny said.

Gernshon stood. He made a move to gather up his papers and booklets, stopped, left them there. Harry stood, too, so abruptly that Gernshon shot him a sudden, hard look across the library table. "Going to hit me again, Harry? Going to kill me?"

"Us?" Manny said. "Us, Robert?" His tone was gentle.

"In a way, you already have. I'm not who I was, certainly."

Manny shrugged. "So be somebody better."

"Damn it, I don't think you understand—"

"I don't think *you* do, Reuven, boychik. This is the way it *is*. That's all. Whatever you had back there, you have still. Tell me, in all that reading, did you find anything about yourself, anything personal? Are you in the history books, in the library papers?"

"The Office of Public Documents takes two weeks to do a search for birth and death certificates," Gernshon said, a little sulkily.

"So you lost nothing, because you really *know* nothing," Manny said. "Only history. History is cheap. Everybody gets some. You can have all the history you want. It's what you make of it that costs."

Gernshon didn't nod agreement. He looked a long time at Manny, and something moved behind the unhappy hazel eyes, something that made Harry finally let out a breath he didn't know he'd been holding. It suddenly seemed that Gernshon was the one that was old. And he *was*—with the fifty-two years he'd gained since last week, he was older than Harry had been in the 1937 of *Captains Courageous* and wide-brimmed fedoras and clean city parks. But that was the good time, the one that Gernshon was going back to, the one Harry himself would choose, if it weren't for Jackie and Manny . . . still, he couldn't watch as Gernshon walked out of the book stacks, parting the musty air as heavily as if it were water.

Gernshon paused. Over his shoulder he said, "I'll go back. Tonight. I will."

After he had left, Harry said, "This is my fault."

"Yes," Manny agreed.

"Will you come to my room when he goes? To . . . to help?"

"Yes, Harry."

Somehow, that only made it worse.

Gernshon agreed to a blindfold. Harry led him through the closet, the warehouse, the street. Neither of them seemed very good at this; they stumbled into each other, hesitated, tripped over nothing. In the warehouse Gernshon nearly walked into a pile of lumber, and in the sharp jerk Harry gave Gernshon's arm to deflect him, something twisted and gave way in Harry's back. He waited, bent over, behind a corner of a building while Gernshon removed his blindfold, blinked in the morning light, and walked slowly away.

Despite his back, Harry found that he couldn't return right away. Why not? He just couldn't. He waited until Gernshon had a large head start and then hobbled towards the park. A carousel turned, playing bright organ music: September 24. Two children he had never noticed before stood just beyond the carousel, watching it with hungry, hopeless eyes. Flowers grew in immaculate flower beds. A black man walked by, his eyes fixed on the sidewalk, his head bent. Two small girls jumping rope were watched by a smiling woman in a blue-and-white uniform. On the sidewalk, just beyond the carousel, someone had chalked a swastika. The black man shuffled over it. A Lincoln Zephyr V-12 drove by, $1,090. There was no way it would fit through a closet.

When Harry returned, Manny was curled up on the white chenille bedspread that Harry had bought for $3.28, fast asleep.

"What did I accomplish, Manny? What?" Harry said bitterly. The day had dawned glorious and warm, unexpected Indian summer. Trees in the park showed bare branches against a bright blue sky. Manny wore an old red sweater, Harry a flannel workshirt. Harry shifted gingerly, grimacing, on his bench. Sunday strollers dropped ice cream wrappers, cigarettes, newspapers, Diet Pepsi cans, used tissues, popcorn. Pigeons quarreled and children shrieked.

"Jackie's going to be just as hard as ever—and why not?" Harry continued. "She finally meets a nice fellow, he never calls her again. Me, I leave a young man miserable on a sidewalk. Before I leave him, I ruin his life. While I leave him, I ruin my back. *After* I leave him, I sit here guilty. There's no answer, Manny."

Manny didn't answer. He squinted down the curving path.

"I don't know, Manny. I just don't know."

Manny said suddenly, "Here comes Jackie."

Harry looked up. He squinted, blinked, tried to jump up. His back made sharp protest. He stayed where he was, and his eyes grew wide.

"Popsy!" Jackie cried. "I've been looking for you!"

She looked radiant. All the lines were gone from around her eyes, all the sharpness from her face. Her very collarbones, Harry thought dazedly, looked softer. Happiness haloed her like light. She held the hand of a slim, red-haired woman with strong features and direct hazel eyes.

"This is Ann," Jackie said. "I've been looking for you, Popsy, because . . . well, because I need to tell you something." She slid onto the bench next to Harry, on the other side from Manny, and put one arm around Harry's shoulders. The other hand kept a close grip on Ann, who smiled encouragement. Manny stared at Ann as at a ghost.

"You see, Popsy, for a while now I've been struggling with something, something really important. I know I've been snappy and difficult, but it hasn't been — everybody needs somebody to love, you've often told me that, and I know how happy you and Grammy were all those years. And I thought there would never be anything like that for me, and certain people were making everything all so hard. But now . . . well, now there's Ann. And I wanted you to know that."

Jackie's arm tightened. Her eyes pleaded. Ann watched Harry closely. He felt as if he were drowning.

"I know this must come as a shock to you," Jackie went on, "but I also know you've always wanted me to be happy. So I hope you'll come to love her the way I do."

Harry stared at the red-haired woman. He knew what was being asked of him, but he didn't believe in it, it wasn't real, in the same way weather going on in other countries wasn't really real. Hurricanes. Drought. Sunshine. When what you were looking at was a cold drizzle.

"I think that of all the people I've ever known, Ann is the most together. The most compassionate. And the most moral."

"Ummm," Harry said.

"Popsy?"

Jackie was looking right at him. The longer he was silent, the more her smile faded. It occurred to him that the smile had showed her teeth. They were very white, very even. Also very sharp.

"I . . . I . . . hello, Ann."

"Hello," Ann said.

"See, I told you he'd be great!" Jackie said to Ann. She let go of Harry and jumped up from the bench, all energy and lightness. "You're wonderful, Popsy! You, too, Manny! Oh, Ann, this is Popsy's best friend, Manny Feldman. Manny, Ann Davies."

"Happy to meet you," Ann said. She had a low, rough voice and a sweet smile. Harry felt hurricanes, drought, sunshine.

Jackie said, "I know this is probably a little unexpected—"

Unexpected. "Well—" Harry said, and could say no more.

"It's just that it was time for me to come out of the closet."

Harry made a small noise. Manny managed to say, "So you live here, Ann?"

"Oh, yes. All my life. And my family, too, since forever."

"Has Jackie . . . has Jackie met any of them yet?"

"Not yet," Jackie said. "It might be a little . . . tricky, in the case of her parents." She smiled at Ann. "But we'll manage."

"I wish," Ann said to her, "that you could have met *my* grandfather. He would have been just as great as your Popsy here. He always was."

"Was?" Harry said faintly.

"He died a year ago. But he was just a wonderful man. Compassionate *and* intelligent."

"What . . . what did he do?"

"He taught history at the university. He was also active in lots of organizations—Amnesty International, the ACLU, things like that. During World War II he worked for the Jewish rescue leagues, getting people out of Germany."

Manny nodded. Harry watched Jackie's teeth.

"We'd like you both to come to dinner soon," Ann said. She smiled. "I'm a good cook."

Manny's eyes gleamed.

Jackie said, "I know this must be hard for you—" but Harry saw that she didn't really mean it. She didn't think it was hard. For her it was so real that it was natural weather, unexpected maybe, but not strange, not out of place, not out of time. In front of the bench, sunlight striped the pavement like bars.

Suddenly Jackie said, "Oh, Popsy, did I tell you that it was your friend Robert who introduced us? Did I tell you that already?"

"Yes, sweetheart," Harry said. "You did."

"He's kind of a nerd, but actually all right."

After Jackie and Ann left, the two old men sat silent a long time. Finally Manny said diplomatically, "You want to get a snack, Harry?"

"She's happy, Manny."

"Yes. You want to get a snack, Harry?"

"She didn't even recognize him."

"No. You want to get a snack?"

"Here, have this. I got it for you this morning." Harry held out an orange, a deep-colored navel with flawless rind: seedless, huge, guaranteed juicy, nurtured for flavor, perfect.

"Enjoy," Harry said. "It cost me ninety-two cents."

ONE DAMN THING AFTER ANOTHER

by Nancy Kress

▼

"Plot" is perhaps the trickiest term in SF. "I want well-plotted stories," says the Eminent Editor (don't we all?). "What's it about?" asks True Fan, holding a new novel in his hand and meaning "What's the plot?" "But it doesn't have any plot!" wails the devoted reader of Asimov, having just finished a story by J. G. Ballard. Plot, plot, plot. It's enough to make you think we're all conspirators in an endless Machiavellian takeover.

And so we are. We all want—at least vicariously—drama, action, things to *happen*. But not just any things. Things that catch and hold our interest, which usually means things that have gotten screwed up. Nobody wants to read about things that are humming along in tranquillity. In our lives we want tranquillity; in our fiction we want an unholy mess, preferably getting unholier page by page. We want conflict. The title of this essay should actually read "One Damned Thing After Another," because events that are damned—that bedevil our characters with mental or physical pitchforks—are what make up plot.

When I wrote "The Price of Oranges" I knew all this, but it didn't help. As Robin Wilson has so sagely written in this volume's mini-essay "The Tangled Web," there are writers that can outline plot ahead of time, and there are writers who must "plant characters in an opening situation and watch what grows." I'm a literary farmer.

What I had when I began was an old man who had a tremendous nostalgia for the Depression years, who could visit them through his closet, and who was bringing things back cheaply. I could *see* this character—old, shabby, impractical, shortsighted, but still optimistic and lovable. So far, so good. But a character, alone, is not a plot. A situation, alone, is not a plot. I needed something to be bedeviling Harry.

▼ SETTING UP THE CONFLICT

I started with the "lovable" part of Harry. If he's so lovable, who does he love? The answer came easily: his granddaughter, and his best friend. Which should the conflict revolve around? I decided the granddaughter. Harry is a lovable and optimistic guy—he wants people to be happy. His granddaughter is not happy. I didn't know at this point why she wasn't happy; I just knew she wasn't. I began writing, to see what my unconscious knew about this situation that I didn't know, and I didn't stop writing until the first scene was complete.

This is, for me, the best part of writing. The characters and situation take over, and I don't know what words will flow through me until they do. When I run out of inspiration, I stop, and the conscious part of my mind—the part that "plots"—takes over. Time to assess where I, Harry, and Jackie have got to.

At the end of the first scene of "Oranges," I discovered, there were several areas of evolving conflict. One way to look at conflict is as "tension"—two forces pulling in opposite directions. Reading the scene, I found that I had Harry's desire for Jackie's happiness pulling against her misery. I had Harry's enthusiasm for his great idea pulling against Manny's attempts to restrain his friend. And I had the glamour with which Harry sees 1937 pulling against what I (and Manny) knew to be the actuality of 1937.

Now came a major decision for this story. Did I want to write a traditional plotted story, or did I want to write what, for lack of a better name, I call a "contemporary literary short story?"

The difference between them is real. The plotted story, having aroused conflict, then makes it its business to resolve that conflict. We the readers discover—because the author tells us—how each issue is resolved, what happens to each character, and how we should feel about the whole thing. In the contemporary literary short story, in contrast, the conflict is raised but not resolved. It is considered enough to raise the question; the author does not presume to have the answers. Consider, as examples, Damon Knight's classic "The Handler," or Ursula K. Le Guin's "The Day Before The Revolution," or Terry Bison's "Bears Discover Fire." The very human ambivalences set up in these stories concern, respectively, prejudice, sacrifice, and death. The questions raised are not—perhaps cannot—be resolved. They can only be endured.

I have written both kinds of stories (and, indeed, the differences between them exist as a continuum, not a dichotomy). Reading over my first scene of "Oranges," I decided it wanted to be a traditional plotted story. The tone was too playful, the characters too sentimental, and the potential plot complications too intriguing to me for this to simply set forth unresolved conflict. For this particular story, I wanted to play the whole thing through.

▼ KEEPING THE CONFLICT GOING

The second scene was logically dictated by the first: Harry would need to go back to 1937 and try to bring back a lover for Jackie. But how should that work out? Clearly, he couldn't just succeed, or the story would be over. But if he just failed (if, for instance, no one would come, or it turned out that only Harry could go through the time portal in his closet), the story would also be over. So what should happen next in the plot?

"Character is plot," said Henry James, who did pretty well with both. My translation of this is "Why are these people doing what they're doing?" Understanding the motivations of all your major characters, not just the protagonist, can suggest plot developments. Plot and character—the double helix of fiction. So, I asked myself, the man that Harry snares and forcibly brings back to 1989—what does *that* character want?

Not Jackie. Or the story would be over.

Okay, start here. He doesn't want Jackie. Why not? Because their personalities clash. Because the man has a life in his own time. Because he's married. Yes—that would fit with poor Harry's attempts: well-meaning but inept. After all, if Harry were good at time travel, he'd bring back not oranges but stock certificates, and end up rich. Harry, however, is not that sort of man ("Plot is character"). Harry, even when acting out of love, screws up ("Plot is one damned thing after another").

Again I started writing, interested in seeing what Jackie and this unknown character had to say to each other. First, of course, this unknown character had to arrive in 1989. Getting him there, having him meet Jackie, and having him develop his own individual reactions to the difference between 1937 and 1989 (more educated and far-seeing than Harry's)—all this took me through five more scenes.

The second of these scenes deserves comment. In it, nothing happens. Harry returns to 1937, looks around, studies the situation. It's a scene to demonstrate the time-travel mechanism (such as it is), establish setting and mood, and deepen character (Harry refuses to consider the saluting Nazi on the magazine cover). But shouldn't it also advance plot? Aren't *all* scenes supposed to advance plot?

Not necessarily. The Kress Swimming Pool Theory of Fiction comes into play here. This theory says that scene order is like kicking off from the side of a swimming pool. The harder the initial kick, the longer and farther you can glide. A first scene with conflict and action and rapid introduction of new information earns you the right to a slower following scene that adds backfill and focuses on comparative subtleties of tone, character, setting, or motif. Scene two of "Oranges" is all exposition.

By the end of the sixth scene, Harry has screwed things up royally. He now has more problems than he did at the start of the story. Jackie is still miserable. He's afraid she might fall in love with a married man. It has occurred to Harry, belatedly, that Gernshon has his own reactions to 1989 and that Harry is responsible for helping Gernshon resolve these. And, in an appalling development, Gernshon has actually met a woman who he thinks is his own granddaughter. What if Gernshon, like Harry, tries to meddle in *his* granddaughter's happiness? Harry now has the reverse of his initial problem. Now he has to find a way to keep Jackie and Gernshon apart.

I realized this at the same moment Harry did. Writing along, I suddenly arrived in a place where the situation dictated the next plot step: Send Gernshon back. But how? Voluntarily? Would this particular character go back? Well, yes, he probably would. But Gernshon would be changed by what he'd seen. What would he do about that in 1937? And how would Jackie be affected? And what about her unhappiness, which was Harry's original problem?

It began to seem as if I'd plotted myself into a corner.

▼ **RESOLVING THE CONFLICT**

I'd been working on this story every day for a week. Now I set it aside, to see what might occur to me. This sometimes works: An ending will come to me as I wash dishes or drive the car or fold laundry. Not this time. I was as stuck as Harry.

All right, no help from an uncooperative unconscious. For me, the second choice is to reason out the ending. There are questions I use to do this.

One such question is: How do I want the protagonist to end up changed by the events of the story? Knowing that can sometimes help the writer to work backward. This is the way events changed him—what events do I need to bring about such a change? That's the climax.

However, this reasoning didn't work for "Oranges." I knew how Harry would be changed. He would come to have a more balanced view of 1937 and 1989. He would see more clearly, partly through Manny's help, the bad side of 1937, and the good side of 1989. I even knew how I would show that ending: Through Harry's paying 1989 prices for an orange, a better orange than 1937 could produce, to give to Manny. Oranges had evolved as a motif throughout the story, and so oranges I must have in the last paragraph. The theme of the story was now clear to me: Everything has its price. Oranges, history, love.

However, knowing theme and motif and even the last line was no real help to me in resolving my plot. I still had no idea how a newly and reluctantly knowledgeable Gernshon affected 1937, or how Harry was to solve his Jackie problem, or what to do to keep my story from fizzling.

A second question to help figure out endings is: Who won and who lost? This derives from a useful metaphor about fiction, which is that every story—every single one, from *Hamlet* to *The Meatloaf that Ate Toledo*—is a war.

In a war, you have something being fought over. You have combatants who care fiercely about the outcome. You have skirmishes or battles or bloody massacres. And you have winners and losers, who are sometimes the same people. I've always been partial to the Pyrrhic victory story, in which the winner pays a stiff price for his victory. Many of my stories follow this pattern. Was it applicable here?

Harry was already paying a high price—the loss of some cherished illusions. So was Gernshon. So who else should win or lose here?

And as soon as I asked myself this question, the resolution of the plot came to me.

Jackie was the major character left. And she would have to be the winner, because I had made her so miserable up till now that she was entitled to some happiness. The tone of this story, which was playful, demanded a winner. Both Harry and Gernshon ended up with mixed gains. Therefore, Jackie needed to win. She would have to get what she wanted, not what Harry thought she should want. So—what did Jackie want?

I didn't consciously decide that the answer was a female lover. The answer just presented itself to me, out of that ever-useful unconscious. But once Ann was there, I immediately saw that she would work, for several reasons. First, Jackie's unhappiness would be logical if she'd been struggling with such a major issue as sexual orientation. Second, a gay relationship openly and lovingly engaged in was certainly a lot more 1989 than 1937, and thus fit in with what had evolved as my theme. Finally, Gernshon's granddaughter had been alluded to earlier in the story, and bringing her back would keep me from violating the usually-true dictum not to introduce important characters only at the last minute (the "deus ex machina" plot resolution).

Most of all, however, bringing Jackie and Ann together *felt* right to me. When you grow plots organically, you take deep pleasure in a new mutation of rose.

I was aware, however, that this ending did violate another usually-true plot dictum: A protagonist is supposed to solve his own difficulties, not sit passively by while life solves them for him. However, I decided (perhaps self-servingly) that Harry could be an exception to this rule. He could be an exception because I hadn't set him up as an effective actor in his own life, but rather as an inept one who can't even create a plausible scientific alibi to offer Gernshon at their first meeting. After all, Harry isn't exactly Heinlein's "competent man." In addition, "The Price of Oranges" is a gentle comedy. Resolution by outside events, leaving all the protagonist's efforts looking faintly foolish, is a staple of comedy (consider, for example, *Much Ado About Nothing*, or Avram Davidson's "Or All The Sea with Oysters"). That, I decided, was the effect I wanted for Harry.

The last two scenes almost wrote themselves. Harry returns Gernshon to 1937, in a way that prevents Gernshon's return. And then, just as Harry is in total despair ("What did I accomplish, Manny? What?"), Jackie and Ann show up to resolve all the plot problems: Jackie has found her own way to be happy. Jackie only met Ann because of Gernshon. Ann is the kind of person she is because of the kind of person her grandfather was, for which Harry's ill-planned time abduction was at least partly responsible.

The story was done—at least in first draft. But the plotting wasn't.

▼ THE REWRITE: FINE-TUNING THE CONFLICT

After I finished "The Price of Oranges" and tinkered with it a little, I took it to Sycamore Hill, a writer's workshop at which professionals critique each other's manuscripts. This is not an essay on workshopping, so I won't discuss all the participants' reactions (although Bruce Sterling's, which saw the story as an extended metaphor on writing SF, with Gernshon as Hugo Gernsback and Ann as eighties feminist revisionism of SF tropes, was pretty funny). Suffice it to say that as a result of the Sycamore Hill critiques, the plot stayed the same in its basics but changed in significant details.

For instance, in the first draft Harry and Manny had made two attempts to kidnap someone from 1937. The first, failed attempt involved chloroforming the abductee. The workshop participants felt (correctly) that two attempts only slowed the story down without adding anything new. In the rewrite, one attempt has been eliminated.

Another change: Gernshon was originally named Callahan and described as slim and blond. No, said many people—he sounds like the stereotypical Nazi. And besides, wouldn't Harry look for a nice Jewish boy for his granddaughter? Well, of course he would, I realized as soon as it was pointed out to me. And this suggested the (admittedly offstage) plot detail that Gernshon became the kind of person he was because, knowing that World War II was on the way, he felt compelled to work for Jewish rescue leagues. Which in turn contributed to the compassionate person Ann became.

Not everyone at the workshop liked the story's plot. A few people objected to the coincidence of having Gernshon just happen to meet his own granddaughter in a coffee shop. A few more felt Ann appears too conveniently at the end, a reaching into the literary hat to pull out something—anything—to end the story. My sense is that writers who do not plot organically, who carefully outline the whole story before they write, do not end up with these kinds of strains on some readers' disbelief. But I don't know for sure—I'm not an outliner. And perhaps outliners have other difficulties.

In the end, I think "The Price of Oranges" works as plot, but not flawlessly. I've written stories with tighter structure. But what "The Price of Oranges" *does* do is illustrate that plot is only one of the many aspects of fiction. The story was a Hugo nominee not for its plot, but for its char-

acters or tone or details or some other attribute apart from plot. But—
how apart, really? Without Harry's struggles to resolve his particular problem, none of the other attributes could exist at all.

"Devise incidents," was W. Somerset Maugham's succinct advice on
how to write fiction. Devising incidents means creating a plot. Not just
any incidents will do. You need motivated incidents ("Character is plot"),
damned incidents ("That poor guy!"), interesting incidents ("The war
heated up today. . . ."), logically connected incidents, significant incidents. Fortunately, you don't have to think them up all by yourself. Once
you have an initial situation, the characters will help, courtesy of your
unconscious. Interesting characters live in very fertile soil. Start planting,
and see what grows.

MONSTERS

by James Patrick Kelly

▼

When Henry looked in his dad's old mirror, he couldn't see the monster. He touched his reflection. Nothing. No shock, no secret thrill, not even a tingle. Usually his nipples tightened or the insides of his knees would get crinkly and if he were in a certain mood he'd crawl back under the covers and think very hard about women in black strapless bras. But this morning—zero. He stared at a fattish naked white man with thinning hair and yellow teeth. A face as interesting as lint. He wished for a long purple tongue or a disfiguring scar that forked down his cheek, except he didn't want any pain. Not for himself, anyway. Henry hated looking so vanilla. There was nothing terrifying about him except the bad thoughts, which he told no one, not even God. But this morning the monster was cagy. It wanted to get loose and he was tired of holding it back. Something was going to happen. He decided not to shave.

The gray Dacron shirt and shiny blue polyester pants hanging on the line over the bathtub had dripped dry overnight. His nylon underwear was dry too, but the Orlon socks were still damp so he draped them over the towel bar. Henry wore synthetics because they wouldn't shrink or wrinkle and he could wash them in the sink. Some days, after wallowing in other people's mung, he boiled his clothes. He liked his showers hot, too; he stood in the rusty old clawfooted tub for almost half and hour until his skin bloomed like a rose. The water beat all the thoughts out of his head; nothing wormy had ever happened in the tub. He opened his mouth, let it fill with hot water and spat at the wall.

He owned just five shirts: gray, white, beige, blue, and blue-striped; and three pairs of pants: blue, gray, and black. As he tried to decide what to wear to work, he had a bad thought. Not a thought exactly—he flashed an image of himself bending toward a TV minicam, hands locked behind him as he was pushed into a police car. Blue or blue-striped would show up best on the six o'clock news.

He petted the shirts. Maybe he was already crazy, but it seemed to him that if he wore blue today, it might set off the chain reaction of choices the creature was always trying to start. He pulled the white shirt from its hanger.

Henry ate only two kinds of breakfast cereal, Cheerios and Rice Chex. Over the years he had tried to simplify his life; routines were a defense against bad thoughts. That's why he always watched the Weather Channel when he ate Cheerios. He liked the satellite pictures of storms sweeping across the country because he thought that was what weather must look like to God. He didn't understand how people could think weather was boring; obviously they hadn't seen it get loose.

After breakfast he tried to slip past the shrine and out the front door, but he couldn't. The monster was stirring even though he had chosen the white shirt. He dug the key out of his pocket, opened the shrine and turned on the light. He was in the apartment's only closet, seven feet by four. Henry bolted the door behind him.

The walls were shaggy with pictures he'd ripped out of magazines but he didn't look at them. Not yet. He pressed the *play* button on the boom box and the Rolling Stones bongoed into "Sympathy for the Devil." He knelt at the oak chest which served as the altar. Inside was a plastic box. Inside the box, cradled in pink velvet, was the Beretta.

He had bought the 92SB because of its honest lines. A little bulky in the grip, the salesman had said, but only because inside was a fifteen shot double-column magazine. It was cool as a snake to the touch, thirty-five hard ounces of steel, anodized aluminum, and black plastic. He wrapped his right hand around the grip and felt the gentle bite of the serrations on the front and rear of the frame. He stood, supported his right hand with his left, extended his arms, and howled along with Jagger. "Ow!"

Schwartzenegger trembled in his sights; even cyborgs feared the thing lurking inside Henry West. "Now!" The pistol had a thrilling heft; it was more real than he was. *"Wham!"* he cried, then let his arms drop. Manson gave him a shaggy grimace of approval. Madonna shook her tits. The monster was stretching; its claw slid up his throat.

He spun then and ruined Robert Englund, *wham*, David Duke, *wham*, and Mike Tyson, *wham*, *wham*, *wham*. Metallica gave him sweaty glares. Imelda Marcos simpered. Henry let a black rain of bad thoughts drench him. He'd give in and let it loose on the Market Street bus or in the First Savings where that twisty young teller never looked at him when she cashed his paycheck. He'd blaze into Rudy's Lunch Bucket like that guy in Texas and keep slapping magazines into the Beretta until he had the mass murder record. Only not when Stefan was behind the counter. Stefan always gave him an extra pickle. Or else he'd just suck on the gun himself, take a huge bloody gulp of death. He sagged against Jim Jones, laughing so he wouldn't scream.

"Why me, God?" he said, rubbing the barrel along the stubble on his chin. "Let me pass on this, okay?" But He wasn't listening. Just because He could be everywhere, didn't mean He'd want to be. He wouldn't stoop to this place, not while Henry was celebrating slaughter.

When the music ended, he fit the pistol back into its velvet cradle. He felt split into two different Henrys, both of them moist and expended. Part of him suspected this was nothing more than a bughouse riff, like old Jagger prancing across some stage playing Lucifer. The Beretta wasn't even loaded; he'd hidden the ammo under the sink behind the paper towels. But if this were nothing but pretend, why did it give him more pleasure than a mushroom pizza and a jug of Carlo Rossi Pink Chablis and a new stroke flick? It may have started as a game, but it felt real now. Under the influence of the gun, he was solid as a brick. The rest of his life was smog.

He locked the shrine behind him and went back to the mirror, the only thing he'd kept when he closed dad's house. The creature leered at him. He stuck out his thumb and smudged his reflected eye. The hair on the back of his neck prickled. He thought then he knew what was going to happen. It wanted to touch someone else and he was going to let it.

The new bus driver was a plush moon-faced woman. She didn't even bother to look at him as he slid a dollar onto her outstretched hand, brushing fingertips quickly across the ridges of her skin. He was nobody to her, another zero. The monster's looping murderous rage was building like an electric charge as she jabbed at the coin dispenser for his change. Notice me, pay attention. She dropped the quarter into his palm and he curled his fingers suddenly, grazing her palm. The unholy spark of madness crackled between them. She yipped, jerked her hand away and stared at him. "Oops," he said. "Sorry." She gave him an uneasy laugh, like someone who has just suffered through a sick joke she didn't want to hear. She'd think it was just static—what else could it be? She couldn't know how good it felt to give away pain. He was still grinning when he swung into an empty seat and saw her watching him in the rearview mirror.

Another monster worked at Kaplan's Cleaners. Celeste Sloboda pressed and folded shirts across the room. Only she didn't count. She hadn't made the choice; she'd been born a hunchback. Besides, she wore her thick black hair down to her belt when she wasn't working, trying to cover her deformity. She would've had better luck hiding a chainsaw in her purse. What made it worse was that Celeste was tiny, barely five feet; she looked like a twelve-year-old going on forty, complete with sags and wrinkles and a hump the size of a turkey. She smiled too much and hummed to herself and yattered about her cats as if they were smarter than she was. Jerry said she was kind of cute if you pretended she wasn't lopsided but Henry didn't have that kind of imagination.

He knew that the reason Celeste kept honeying up to him was that she wanted to switch over to the cleaning side. Kaplan kept crabbing that there was no money in shirts, that he only took them so that shirt customers would bring in cleaning business. If Kaplan axed shirts, he'd have to axe Celeste too—or else move her over to Henry's side. But Henry already had a helper and, even though Jerry was a jack-around, at least he left Henry alone.

Celeste perched on a stool, steaming shirts on the form press they called the susie. The laundry had delivered just three mesh bags; usually there were between five and eight. "Guess what I had for breakfast today?" she said.

Henry, at the spotting bench, did not reply. In the six months Celeste had been at Kaplan's, he'd learned to pretend that he couldn't hear her over the rumble of the cleaning drum.

"Broccoli in Velveeta sauce. I know you think that's weird but then you think everything I do is weird. Besides, I like leftovers for breakfast. Meat loaf, potatoes, lasagna, I don't care. When I was a kid I knew this girl poured root beer on her cornflakes so I guess broccoli for breakfast isn't so bad."

Henry followed a trail of coffee splatters up the placket of a silk blouse, sponging them with wet spotter. He blotted the blouse and set it aside for a few moments.

"What if our bodies don't wake up all at once? I mean, the eyes are always last, right? Ears wake up before. I swear I can smell coffee brewing even though I'm asleep. So maybe my taste buds have insomnia or something. Say they're up at two in the morning. By six-thirty, it's lunch time. I can't remember the last time I ate bacon and eggs. What did you have for breakfast, Henry?"

He scraped the splotch on the lapel of a charcoal suit jacket with his fingernail. Some kind of wax—a candlelight dinner gone sour? The cleaning machine buzzed and the drum creaked to a stop.

Celeste cupped a hand over her mouth. "I said, what did you have for breakfast?"

"You talking to me?" He flushed the wax away with the steam gun. "Cheerios." He tossed the jacket into a basket filled with darks. "With milk." There were enough clothes in it to make a new load. "Jerry," he called. "Yo, Jerry!"

"He's pretending he can't hear you." Celeste giggled. "Probably trying to get into Maggie's pants."

That was his squawk with Jerry. When something needed doing, Jerry was either at the front counter flirting with the cashier or in the bathroom. Henry ducked around the coat hanging beside the spotting bench, grabbed an empty basket and wheeled it to the cleaning machine. As he gathered the warm clothes from the drum he breathed in harsh perchloroethylene fumes. He wheeled the basket over to the empty rail next to the presses. Perk nauseated some people, but Henry liked the smell. It filled his head like "Stairway to Heaven."

"How do you clean a syrup stain, anyway?" said Celeste.

"Huh?" He started pulling the clothes onto hangers and setting them on the rail. "You want my job, is that it?"

"Your job?" She buttoned a white spread-collar shirt onto the susie and stepped on the compressed air pedal. With a hiss, steam ballooned the shirt away from the form and jetted from the neck and sleeves. "Don't be paranoid, Henry—you're the best. Just trying for a little friendly chitchat, is all." She pulled at her hair net. "Hey, I'm a slob. Syrup's an accident I'll probably have someday."

He grunted and hung the last of the load on the rail. "Sponge it with water then use wet spotter with a couple drops of vinegar. When it's loose, you blot."

"Now was that so hard? Shit, how come getting you to say anything is like moving a refrigerator?" She wiped her forehead. Her work smock, already limp with moisture, clung to her child's body. Pressing shirts on the susie was hot, dreary work. At least on his side, every garment was different. Henry didn't blame her for being bored; he just didn't want to entertain her.

Henry was pitching darks into the machine when Kaplan elbowed the back door open. He was carrying a bag filled with takeout from Rudy's.

"Gonna rain." Louis Kaplan was a pink little man who wore a short-sleeved shirt and a paisley tie that some customer had neglected to pick up—probably on purpose. He set the bag on a shelf next to a jug of acetone. "What're you doing?" he said to Henry. Without waiting for an answer, he turned to Celeste. "What's he doing?"

"Getting ready to run a load?" she said.

"I can see that. But I'm not paying him to do the idiot work. Where's Jerry?"

"I didn't know it was my turn to watch him." She pulled a damp shirt from the blue mesh laundry bag beside her and snapped it out. Kaplan scuttled toward the front of the store.

"If that's what being boss does to you, I'm sure as hell glad it's him in charge and not me." She draped the shirt over the susie. "Well, I'm ready for a break."

While Henry finished emptying the basket into the drum, she pulled an assortment of styrofoam coffee cups and cardboard sandwich boxes from the bag and sorted through them. "Want yours now?"

"Not yet." He didn't want her near him. Touching the bus driver hadn't satisfied the thing inside him. Maybe she hadn't felt enough pain. All morning long it had been swelling like a balloon. If Celeste accidentally touched him, he wasn't sure he could keep it from striking out at her. He had never let it touch anyone at work before.

"You get time off for good behavior, Henry."

"I said, in a minute."

She shrugged and went back to her stool, unwrapped an egg bagel with cream cheese and lox. Only when she was settled back on her stool did he pick out his tea with extra milk and the English muffin. Coffee break could be the longest fifteen minutes of the day. He needed Jerry right now to shield him from Celeste. That was about all the kid was good for. What were they doing up there?

"Don't you ever get bored eating the same damn muffin over and over again?" she said.

"It's a new muffin every day."

He was dunking the tea bag when he heard someone up front shouting; the racks of clean clothes muffled the sound. "Shush!" As he strained to hear, he felt a twinge of dread. He hadn't worn the blue but still, something was happening. The noise got closer; he recognized Jerry's whine.

"What do you want me to say? No, *really*, tell me what I'm supposed to say. I mean, I'm sorry and all and it won't happen again."

Kaplan was the first through the door; his pink face had flushed a meaty red.

"Why won't you *listen* to me?" Jerry tagged behind like a bad dog on a short leash. "Nobody saw, really. How could they? We were way, way back, behind the 'W' rack."

Kaplan hesitated, trapped by his own machines. If he wanted to keep walking away from Jerry, he'd have to leave the store. He glanced blindly around before deciding his only escape was to dive into a cup of Rudy's coffee.

"*Please*, Louis."

Jerry tried to come around to face him but Kaplan veered away. He clutched the styrofoam cup close to him and fixed on it as if it were telling him secrets.

"Nobody could've seen us back there," said Jerry. "Go see for yourself. Besides there *weren't* any customers. Maggie was listening for the door chime. Mr. Kaplan, please say something."

The creature squirmed in delight at Kaplan's distress, watching as he worried at the drink tab on the lid. "You had your hand in her pants."

Celeste used both hands to smother a giggle and Jerry realized he had an audience. Since Kaplan's back was turned, he let a grin slink across his face.

"No, no," he said. You don't understand. Yes, we were kissing. That's what you saw and I'm sorry but it's not what you think."

Kaplan tore the plastic lid off and hot coffee slopped onto his hand and down his trousers. "Shit!" When he tried to dance out of the way, he bumped into Jerry and half the cup splatted onto his shoes. Celeste laughed out loud.

"Okay, okay, so I was playing with the elastic a little." Jerry's smirk curdled what little sincerity he had left. "But that was as far as we were going. I mean, this is a public place. We're not stupid or anything."

"You're right, Jerry. You're not stupid." Kaplan put the dripping coffee cup back on the shelf as if it were a weight he was glad to set down. "I'm the stupid." He finally turned to confront Jerry. "You've worked here for two whole months and done nothing but screw up. I guess that makes me dumb as a box of rocks. But I've learned my lesson, kid. Get your stuff and go. You're finished."

"You're firing me?" Jerry seemed to shrink six inches. "What is this, a joke?"

"I'll give you a week's severance. The check will be ready by closing. You can come back then."

"Oh come on, Mr. Kaplan. Give me a break."

His voice was hard as the sidewalk. "Take your lunch, you can even take your coffee, if you want. But go."

"*Henry.*" Jerry spun toward him in desperation. "You can't let this happen. He'll make you do both our jobs, Henry. Tell him you need help."

Henry was certain that if he opened his mouth the monster would leap out and strangle them all. Jerry plucked a vest from the basket and shook it at Henry. "Who do you think is going to clean this? Miss Dumpty Humpty?"

"He already does most of your work," said Celeste. "Asshole."

"Celeste," said Kaplan. "Enough."

"*No.*" Jerry threw the vest to the floor. "I'm not going anywhere unless you ask Henry. He runs this place but you're all afraid of him. I'm the only one he ever talks to."

A sound like the squealing of brakes filled Henry's head. He knew it wasn't real but held his breath, waiting for the crash.

"Celeste," said Kaplan, "I think you should call the police. Tell them we're having a little problem here."

"See, Henry?" Jerry was full of scorn. "They don't even trust you with the phone."

"Get the hell out of my store!" Kaplan stepped toward Jerry.

Celeste edged off her stool. Henry tried to think of a way to stop her.

He knew Jerry and Kaplan were very close to fighting; she was going to keep them from hurting each other. When he closed his eyes, Henry saw broken teeth and dark blood beading on the floor tiles. His fists clenched. This was so much better than the shrine. He had never been so close to real violence before.

"Aww, fuck all of you." Jerry snatched his coat. "I never liked working here anyway. The pay sucks and you're nothing but a bunch of loonies and losers." He retreated toward the back door. "Just make sure my check is ready." He stalked out, not even bothering to slam the door behind him.

Kaplan slumped against the spotting bench. "I'm sorry you had to listen to that." Henry guessed he meant both of them, even though he was speaking to Celeste. "I should've taken care of him after work, but I . . . Listen, we're going to have to pull together for a couple of days." He looked about as together as dust. "I'll get an ad in the paper right away. I—I should stay up front today, keep an eye on Maggie. What I think we need to do is keep pushing the cleaning out on schedule, which means you'll have to help Henry. If there's time left, we'll worry about the shirts. No money in goddamn shirts, anyway." He considered for a moment, then gathered himself. "That little weasel." He pushed away from the bench and clapped his hands. "So, then, can we handle this?"

Henry had been flashing Kaplan firing Jerry after work, when there'd be no witnesses. Jerry coldcocked the brittle old man, then straddled him and grasped the pink head between his hands. When he pounded it against the floor, it exploded like a light bulb. The monster was frustrated that nothing had happened. "It stinks," Henry said.

"I'm sorry, Henry. Just give me a couple of days."

"Don't worry, Louis," said Celeste. "We'll handle it."

Kaplan shot her a grateful look and hurried off to keep Maggie from ransacking the till. Henry bent to snare the vest Jerry had thrown. He dropped it in the hamper.

"Look at you." Celeste chuckled. "He's gone and you're still picking up after him."

"It's your fault." He snapped at her. "You laughed, you got him fired."

"That's bullshit, Henry, and you know it. Jerry blew this job off long ago. If you ask me, he got what he deserved. I'm sorry if that bothers you.

I'm sorry if you hate my guts. But other people don't make you do bad things. You do them yourself."

Even though she was wrong, he didn't reply; she'd only chew his ear some more. He folded his untouched muffin and rammed it into the cup still half full of lukewarm tea. Of course other people could make you do wrong. Henry was proof of that. And he didn't really hate her. Yes, the grotesque hump repelled him and she had the personality of Brillo but he was also a little sorry for her.

It was the monster who hated her.

"So what do you want me to do?" she said.

Henry figured that the reason it was always dark in church was because God didn't like bright places. His God tended to lurk in the shadows and not say much, like a stranger at a wedding. When He spoke in His midnight whisper, it always took Henry by surprise. God certainly wasn't a rattletongue like Celeste or a smartmouth like Jerry. Henry believed that He preferred the dark because, like Henry, He was shy.

Even though Our Lady of Mercy was only two blocks from Kaplan's, Henry's midday routine was to bring his lunch to St. Sebastian's because the light there was so bad that it was hard for anyone to see him eating. Also, Sebastian was the martyr that some Roman emperor had shot full of arrows; his painting was in the side chapel. Henry liked to sit in the third pew from the back with his regular tuna sandwich, pickle, and chocolate milk. The priests usually left him alone because he never made a mess, but sometimes parishioners would crab at him.

The rain had come earlier than predicted, chasing at least a dozen other people into the church, so he had to be cagy about eating. And the clouds had dulled his favorite stained glass; the reds had gone to mud, the blues almost black. Each of the fourteen narrow windows of St. Sebastian's depicted one of the Stations of the Cross. Henry liked to pray to the sixth: Veronica wiping the face of Jesus. Once, years ago, he had wondered whether the impression of His face that Jesus had left on Veronica's handkerchief could be removed with wet spotter, or maybe a hydrogen peroxide soak. It was as close as he had ever come to having a bad thought in a church.

After he finished the pickle, he slid forward onto the kneeler to say a Hail Mary. The monster snuffed the prayer by ramming a fist up Henry's windpipe. He rocked back onto the pew, choking. People turned to stare; Henry put a hand to his mouth and pretended to cough into it. It took a moment before he could breathe again. He sat very still, closed his eyes and tried not to panic. *Our Father,* he thought, *Who art in . . .* His head snapped back as veins of fire pulsed across his lids; it felt as if someone were squashing his eyes into his skull. He couldn't speak, couldn't even think to Him. Henry had never needed God's help more. Why couldn't he ask for it? Nothing else had changed: Up at the altar, votive candles still flickered like angels and the tabernacle glittered with the gold of heaven. But Henry could not pray. He covered his face with his hands.

"Hey, you. *Bum.*"

Henry turned and blinked at a pale twitchy man in a rain-spattered blue jacket stitched with the name Phil.

"This is a church, scumbag." Phil's voice swelled with outrage, snapping through the gloom like a sermon. "Not some flop where you can sleep off a drunk. You understand? And look at all this garbage. Go on, get out of here!"

Henry crumbled the sandwich box and the wax paper into a ball. The last place he wanted something to happen was in God's house. He sensed the creature plugging into the man's anger, feeding off it into a frenzy. If Phil tried to hurt him, it would hurt him back. *Oh God.* He had to get away before it was too late. As he gathered in the milk carton, Phil decided he wasn't hurrying fast enough.

"Now, bum! Or I'm calling the cops." He grabbed at Henry to haul him out of the pew.

He tried to twist away but Phil's hand closed on his shoulder. Henry moaned with dread and pleasure as he yielded to the madness. The spark surged down his arm; muscles spasmed in an explosion of awful strength. He snapped his attacker back as easily as a wet shirt. Phil hit the wall of the church with a sharp *crack.* He sagged to the floor, face slack, eyes like eggs.

Someone screamed. The shock of monstrous pleasure had left Henry momentarily limp; now he shuddered and flung himself out of the pew past the body. The touch had never been this good before, this vicious. He sprinted through the baptistry out the side door into the rain. He ran five blocks before he realized no one was paying attention to him. Everyone was hunkered down against the weather.

He slowed to a walk. His cheeks were hot; he was in no hurry to get out of the rain. The monster was spent and he was back in control. He hadn't felt this relaxed in weeks. What harm had been done, really? Phil would wake up with a headache and a story he'd exaggerate down at the corner bar for years. So Henry would have lunch at Our Lady of Mercy for a while. Or find an even darker church.

"Hail Mary, full of grace," he said to a parking meter. "The Lord is with thee." He fished a dime from his pocket, cranked it into the slot and the violation flag clicked down. "Deliver us from evil." He laughed. "Amen."

By the time he got back to Kaplan's he had convinced himself that for today, at least, he'd left the nightmare behind.

▼

It rained that afternoon on everyone but Henry; he was still shining hours after lunch. Even Celeste's yattering failed to rile him, perhaps because she talked mostly about dry-cleaning instead of her cats and rice pudding and the world's tallest woman. And she worked much harder than Jerry; he was secretly impressed. She may have been a rattletongue, but when Celeste started something, it got done.

He was pressing pants and she was hanging whites. "How long ago did you start in cleaning anyway?" She said. "Ten years, twenty?"

"Before your time."

"Really?" She brightened. "How old do you think I am?"

He didn't understand why she was still honeying up to him, now that she had what she wanted. Henry pulled a pair of gray pinstripes off the rail and ignored her.

"Don't be such a gentleman. The answer is thirty-six, same age as you. Or at least that's how old Jerry said you were. Unless he was making it up."

"No."

"So how come you never opened a store of your own?"

He stepped on the compressor pedal; steam billowed through the pants. His own shop? That's what his dad used to say. But the thought had never appealed to Henry; he had enough to worry about.

"After all," said Celeste, "you know the business."

"Twenty-five pounder is the smallest rig they make." He nodded at the dry-cleaning machine. "Cost Kaplan thirty grand." He took his foot off the steam pedal and the pants deflated. "You've got to be smart to play for those stakes."

"So? You're smart. All you need is a rich uncle. Or else hit the lottery. I play my birthday and Madonna's every week. 7/28/56 and 8/16/58. Tell you what: When I win, I'll stake you. Only you have to name the store after me. Sloboda's Cleaners."

Brown gabardines were next on the rail. He said nothing.

"Because it's nice work," she said, "dry-cleaning. I mean, it's fun because there's progress. You can see what you've done at the end of the day, not like bagging groceries or stitching shoes. You start with something ugly and it ends up pretty. How many jobs are there where you try to make the world a more beautiful place?"

Henry had no idea; he cared zero for the world. He liked the iron tang of steam hissing from the presses, the furriness of wet wool, the backbeat of the spinning drum, the way silk clung like caterpillars to his rough skin, the perfect chemical luster of nylon, the attic smell of shirt cardboards, leather jackets as heavy as raw steak, the airiness of rayon, the delicate crinkling of plastic bags fresh off the roll, and especially the intoxicating palette of chemicals at the spotting table. He liked sweating through his tank top in the numbing heat of July and basking in the cozy humidity of the back room at Christmas. What mattered to Henry was that the job filled his senses and kept away the bad thoughts. Mostly.

"Yeah," she was saying, "I like it here just fine even though it's not exactly what I want to do for the rest of my life." She waved her finger at him. "Don't you dare tell Kaplan I said that. I'm trusting you."

A pair of tan suit pants.

"No, what I really want to be someday is a travel agent. That way I'll get to go all over so I can tell people where the best times are. You know, like a librarian has to read all those books? Because I'd love to see the pyramids and China and San Francisco and the Disneys—all the Disneys. I read where they have one in France now. And learn to ski. And I'm going to try all those warm places where you just lay around on the beach in your bikini and waiters bring you drinks with cherries in them."

The idea of Celeste in a bikini made him laugh. She'd need to buy a third piece to cover her hump.

"Yeah, what's so funny?" She was suddenly brittle, as if a cruel word might shatter her. "You don't think I could do it?"

He had never seen her fold up like this; maybe she had never told him anything that mattered before. He sensed that if he said what he really thought, she might never speak to him again. A couple hours ago he would've killed for this chance. Now he let it pass. "Don't you have to go to school for that?" He waved vaguely toward downtown.

"Probably. I don't know. Never mind." She picked an armful off the rail of hanging clothes and carried them over to the big press. "It's just something I've been thinking about."

She didn't speak, sing, or hum for fifteen minutes. She just hurled clothes around like curses: yanked them onto the press, jerked down the cover, threw them onto hangers when they were done. Kaplan wheeled in a basket filled with dirty clothes from up front and parked it by the spotting bench. He beamed when he saw the long line of finished orders ready for bagging.

"I should've gotten you two together weeks ago." He rubbed his hands. "This is great; I really mean it. Look, it's been a tough day. Go ahead and finish up the shirts and you can knock off a half hour early."

Olive twills.

"Thanks, Louis," said Celeste. She watched him go with a lemon expression on her face. "Half an hour early? Shit, we should go home now. We've already done a hell of a lot more than he had any right to expect." Then she chuckled; Celeste wasn't built to pout. "Well, if you'll bag up the cleaning, I'll move over to shirts."

"Sure."

"You're an odd one, you know that, Henry? At first I thought that you didn't like me. Then Jerry said you didn't like anyone. But we talked today and you survived. My guess is that you're just shy."

He hung the last pair of pants.

"Mind if I ask you a question?"

He sighed.

"What are you doing after work?"

It had been three years since Henry had last ridden in a car—not since he first started having bad thoughts. Now he remembered why. The bus might be crowded and slow but it was safe as the living room couch. Cars were vicious. The streets seethed with tense, drunk, angry, worried, impatient drivers. They were lost, late, stuck in traffic, and their windshields kept fogging up. There was no place to park, some scut had just cut them off, so they screamed back at their radios. He could see them jittering behind the steering wheels of their weapons, feel the darkness inside him feasting on their anger.

He should have known better than to disrupt the routines. The monster was back.

"It's because they think I'm their mother," said Celeste, who drove as if she were alone on the road. "For a cat, leaving a dead mouse in the middle of the kitchen floor is the best way to say 'I love you.' They can't understand why I'm not grateful. Probably think I'm crazy."

Her junker '82 Escort would have lost a collision with a lunchbox. He grasped the shoulder belt with his left arm; his right hand crushed the armrest on the door. Something was happening.

"My mom used to say that there are two kinds of people in the world, cat people and dog people. But come to find out there're all kinds of people. Bird people, fish people, snake people, plant people, even petless people. Bet that's you. You don't strike me as the pet type."

He shook his head.

"See? So what does that mean? That you're not human?"

Riding a tuna wagon down the mean streets was bad enough, but what really spooked him was Celeste's driving. She was barely tall enough to see over the dashboard. He had never realized how big her hump was until he had watched her wiggle it into the tiny car. It forced her forward so that she seemed to be looking through the steering wheel at the road. Except she wasn't. She kept trying to make eye contact with him while she babbled about cats.

"Of course, Slippers leaves most of the little prizes, these days. Figaro isn't quite the mouser he used to be since the operation. They cut a tumor off his chest. Cost me two hundred dollars. So what about your dad? You didn't say whether he's covered by insurance or not."

"We're okay." Henry should never have told her that he always visited his dad on the way home from work. And then he should've realized what would happen when she'd asked what hospital he was in. And then he should've lied about the forty minute bus ride that got him there fifteen minutes before visiting hours ended. He and his dad did not have that much to say to one another anyway.

"Pick a lane, Grandma!" She swerved around a LeBaron with Alabama plates. "That's good, because a hospital bill can kill you faster than any peckerhead doctor. Believe me, it'd be cheaper for him to stay in the presidential suite at the Sheraton. Probably more fun. How is he taking it anyway? My mother died of lung cancer, which isn't surprising seeing as how she smoked like Pittsburgh. She was an okay mom, better than I deserved. But I'll tell you, she was a bitch at the end. It was really hard."

"He's drugged," said Henry. "Doesn't talk much."

She signalled for a left turn and the Escort rattled up the ramp onto the interstate. "See," she said. "Almost there. Dad will have a nice surprise." As the speedometer skulked toward seventy, Henry braced against the floorboards hard enough to leave footprints. "I think the worst of it was when she decided she had to find God before she died. She hadn't been within spitting distance of a church for forty years and the next thing I know she's a born-again Baptist. Three weeks later I buried her. Only I have to put up with this douchebag in a collar who throws dirt on her and talks about how she's eating bonbons with Jesus in the Kingdom of God. And charging me fifty bucks for the privilege. You're not a believer, are you Henry?"

Henry hesitated, fighting a bad thought. If he touched her now, she'd faint. He could whip the wheel over and they'd jump the median into the oncoming traffic. "I go to church every day," he said.

"Oh." She turned pale, as if he'd said his hobby was drowning kittens. "Me and my big mouth." She signalled for Exit 7. "Sorry. I guess I fucked up." At the bottom of the ramp, Memorial loomed like a giant's headstone. She pulled up to the main entrance. "See you tomorrow then. Sorry."

"Yeah." Henry bolted from the car before the monster ripped her hump off and stuffed it down her throat.

▼

"You look like a bum." Roger West had been cranked into a semi-upright position and propped in his hospital bed with pillows. "You come in here again, you shave." Cancer had chewed on him until there was only the wrinkled brown pit of a man left. "Why're you here?" His eyes were bright with pain.

"I came to visit, Dad. I always come."

"Not before the pill, you don't. Time is it?"

Henry glanced at his watch. "Four-eleven."

"Jesus God, nineteen years until four-thirty. Go find the nurse, tell her I can't wait. Service stinks in this lousy hospital you stuck me in, kid. I keep begging them for the pill, but they don't bring me nothing." His fingers curled and scrabbled at the sheet. "Why am I here? I hate this."

"You're sick, Dad. The doctor brought you here to take care of you."

"That's right." He licked his lips. "Okay."

"The reason I'm early today is I didn't take the bus. I got a ride over."

His dad closed his eyes. He sounded like he was breathing through a straw; the arms that used to hold Henry were limp as wet cardboard. He sat beside the bed and gazed out the window. At least his dad had the view. The middle bed was empty. The privacy curtain was drawn around Mr. DeCredico's bed near the door.

"What she say?" His dad didn't open his eyes.

"Who?"

"The nurse. My son's coming, don't you understand? I need my pill."

The room got very small then so Henry went to the hall. He leaned against the doorway and listened to the fluorescents hum. Down the hall someone was watching "Jeopardy." The PA system chimed. He scuffed the carpet. It was gun-barrel gray. The wallpaper was beige and shiny and easy to wash. Henry rubbed a hand through the stubble along his jaw. It wasn't a bad thought to want to kill dad. He could do it with a pillow; he wouldn't even need the Beretta. Dad would be grateful for the favor. It'd be payback for everything he had done for Henry, bringing him up all by himself. But this was the only murder the monster didn't lust for and Henry didn't have the spunk to do it by himself. He went back in.

"You're early," his dad said. "You didn't get fired did you?"

"No dad, I told you, I got a ride with someone."

"A ride? With someone?"

The monster hated Celeste and, for the moment, so did Henry. She had done this to them by disrupting the routine. He should've taken the bus and his dad would've scarfed the pill and none of this mung would've happened.

"Time is it?"

"Almost four-thirty."

His dad's laugh sounded like a cough. There was a plant with long shiny leaves like swords that he had bought for his dad by the window. Snake plant, the florist had said. Nothing could kill it. Henry could see the interstate, the bridges, and the river glittering like the road to heaven. His dad had a room with a view on the twelfth floor. All the fabric snobs in the worsted wool suits he cleaned would kill for the chance to sit behind a desk with a view like this.

"Know why I can't get a pill? I can't pay. If I still had a credit card, I could charge all the pills I need." He swallowed painfully. "I know what they're trying to do. They're hoping I'll get sick of the lousy service and leave. I should. Just go home."

"You're sick, Dad."

"Don't tell me that. You don't know what sick is. You get a runny nose, you take a day off. But I'm empty. Nothing inside me. At least the pills fill me up." His mouth hung open as he gasped for breath. "But they're not giving me mine because you sold the house. That's why I can't go home, isn't it? I get sick and you let them take everything. I built that house. Where's my furniture, Henry?"

"Take it easy, dad. It's safe in the warehouse."

"You think I can live in some damn warehouse?"

"Don't swear. When you get out, we'll rent an apartment."

"I'm not getting out. You're just like the nurses. Here I'm dying and you want to wait until four-thirty. I don't know why I had you, you useless bum. We would've been better off buying a dog."

"Why Mr. West, good afternoon." The nurse carried a tray with a clear plastic cup of apple juice and a tiny paper cup with the pill. "You're early today." Her acrylic uniform dress was whiter than anything Henry had ever cleaned. There was so much pain in the room, it was hard not to touch her. He flashed on the monster hurling her through the window. There'd be stains on her uniform that would never come out.

"He wants his pill," he said.

"Of course he does, it's four-thirty."

"Don't mind him." Roger West lifted his head off the pillow. "He's having a rough day." He opened his mouth for the pill as if he were taking the sacrament.

Henry was dancing with the boom box. No more routines; it was finally happening. Guns 'N' Roses was cranked to the bughouse level. He cradled the noise to his chest, balanced it across his shoulders like an electronic hump, swung it in a straight-arm loop over his head. Someone was out to get Axl Rose but he wasn't going to take it. Neither was Henry, not as long as Slash was allowed to perform brain surgery with a guitar. Henry's underwear was not as white as a nurse's uniform. He had pulled one sock halfway off. The bathtub was filling up.

He whirled into the bedroom, set the boom box on the nightstand and hurled himself at the unmade bed. He bounced up and sprang again. Again, three, five times, as if the mattress were the plane of sanity that he might crash through, if only he tried hard enough. The song ended, the next one was about drugs. Henry didn't need drugs; he was high on death. He punched the eject button, flung the tape across the room and carried the boom box to the shrine. The door was wide open.

He slapped the Talking Heads into the player and snatched the Beretta off the altar. *Wham!* No more Louis Farrakhan. *Wham!* Die, Robert De Niro. But pretending wasn't enough anymore. He wanted to flash like he had when Phil had put a hand on him. He wanted to feel the gun kick when he pulled the trigger. While David Byrne was quavering about psycho killers, Henry decided to show the Beretta the rest of their nasty little apartment. The boom box came along for the ride. They turned off the water in the bathtub and changed channels on the TV and straightened the picture of Henry and Dad at the lake. They were on their way to the kitchen to look behind the paper towels under the sink when the phone rang. *Qu'est-ce que c'est?*

As soon as he turned off the music, he knew it was the hospital calling to tell him dad had died. Henry had let him down, hadn't given him what he wanted. It rang five times, six. A hand he wasn't quite in control of trembled over the phone but did not pick up. *Ring.* He was crying. *Ring.*

"Hello," he said.

"Henry? This is Celeste."

Hail Mary, he thought, full of grace. "Yeah?"

"Hey look, I'm sorry for what I said this afternoon. You know, about religion and all. It's my problem, okay? It has nothing to do with you."

He dabbed at a tear running down his cheek. "Uh-huh."

"Anyway, I've been driving around ever since then, thinking about what a jerk I was and I just looked at my watch and saw that it was six-thirty and realized I was hungry and I'm just around the block from Angelina's and I was wondering . . . I was wondering if you liked pizza? Because I was thinking I'd spring for a large with pepperoni or mushroom or extra cheese or whatever you want and bring it over and we could split it and then maybe I could convince you to forgive me for being such an idiot. I mean, it's okay if you're busy but . . ."

"Mushroom," said the monster.

Her squeal of delight made the speaker buzz. "Mushroom? All right! How about something to drink? Beer? Wine?"

"Carlo Rossi Pink Chablis."

"No problem. This is great, Henry. I knew you'd understand. This shouldn't take long; what if we say I'll be there around seven-fifteen. I mean if that's too soon, I can come later."

"Seven-fifteen," it said. "You know where I live?"

"Sure, 117 Queensberry, apartment 22. Jerry told me. See you then."

The monster hung up the phone and glanced around. The apartment needed some straightening up. Things needed to be put in their places. It stuck the gun in its belt and went out to the kitchen to check behind the paper towels.

The bed was made, the breakfast dishes were washed and put away, the living room floor was vacuumed, the door to the shrine was locked and the Beretta was loaded and stashed under a cushion of the couch. The sound of Henry's mewling for it to stop came as if from a great distance, as it opened the door for its guest.

"Pouring out there." The rain had flattened Celeste's hair but hadn't washed away her smile. "It's a good night to stay home."

"Thanks for coming." It took the pizza box from her. "Come in." The top was soaked but the bottom was still hot.

"Ta-da!" She pulled a squat jug of wine from a paper bag. "Took me three stores to find it."

It hung her slicker over the bathtub and saw that she'd changed her clothes. She'd been wearing a red pocket tee and acid-washed jeans under her work smock. Now she had on a ramie skirt that hung just above the knee and a fake batik polyester blouse—a smart choice of fabrics. You could get blood stains out of ramie, as long as they were fresh.

It had already decided not to rush. Now that it was in charge, there was no need to lunge; it could enjoy the moment. Besides, even monsters liked mushroom pizza and it hadn't eaten since lunch.

They sat at the kitchen table and tucked away all but a slice and drank sweet wine out of coffee cups while she babbled about crusts and exotic toppings and Roseanne and the high cost of mufflers and kitty litter. She asked what kind of movies it liked and it told her comedies but that its VCR was broken. She confessed to staying up too many late nights with horror flicks. Her favorite was the *Nightmare on Elm Street* series.

"Too violent for me." The monster couldn't help but notice that she was watching it like a movie. Her eyes never left its face. She was lit with an expression of fascinated suspense that got brighter and brighter with each cup of wine.

"The problem is," she was saying, "they're running out of ideas. You can watch just so many decapitations before you stop taking them seriously. Half the horror flicks these days play for laughs. The other half are about as scary as Count Chocula."

It offered the jug for a refill. She laughed and waved it away. "I've still got plenty left. You trying to get rid of it or what?"

"Maybe we should move to the couch?" It was excited now. "More comfortable there."

She stumbled coming out of her chair and it caught her, exercising so much restraint it thought it might burst." 'Scuse me," she said, her voice suddenly husky, "Hell of a lot drunker up here than I thought." She steadied herself with an arm around its waist and let it lead her down the hall. Her body was firm under her clothes; it could feel her heart pumping. "Where'd you say we were going?"

It steered her through the door. "You remember the living room?"

"Ah, yes. We were introduced earlier. Miss Lamp." She bowed. "Mr. TV. Mr. Table." She giggled and twisted around in a deft way that took it by surprise. She pressed closer and closer, arching up on tiptoes, stretching until their lips touched. Her tongue nipped against his teeth and she was kissing Henry, not the monster. When he realized he was back in control, he began to tremble.

"I know." She moaned softly and pushed him toward the couch. "Me too," she said. "But sit down first."

He slid as far away from the gun as he could and gaped as she unbuttoned her blouse.

"You probably think I do this all the time." She was wearing more underwear than he had expected. Her bra was white lace, sheer enough that he could see her nipples. Above it was a wide elastic harness made of ace bandages stitched together. He remembered the three piece bathing suit but he didn't laugh. Her skin frightened him. "Well, you're wrong," she said. "I don't get many requests and the ones that do ask are always perverts." She released three metal clips and the harness unwrapped itself and fell to the floor.

The hump on her back unfolded with a sound like hands rubbing together. Celeste grunted and twisted her head back and forth as if she had a crick. "No, it's all right," she said. "They just get a little stiff after being cooped up all day." She shook herself and two pointed masses of flesh dropped low behind her back and then slowly rose up past her shoulder.

She smiled shyly at him and beat her wings; he could feel air on his face. They were double-jointed; he could see outlines of bones that reminded him of posters of starving children.

"Oh my God," he said.

The skin stretched between the needle digits was the same color as her face, flushed an embarrassed red. He could see a filagree of arteries. She had a span of about four feet.

"Can you fly?"

She shook her head. "I'm afraid they're pretty useless." She giggled. "Except maybe as fans."

"I don't . . . this is . . . my God, Celeste." He shivered. "Can I touch them?"

"Mister, you can touch anything you want."

It was as if he was swimming across the room toward her. The wine burned in his belly like a pool of fire. She turned her back to him and held her wings still. They were covered with downy black hair and were hot as her lips. "Hey you, I'm standing here in my underwear and you're still dressed." She faced him. "Time to catch up." Her fingers tickled his chest as she took off his white shirt. She laughed drunkenly as she fumbled at his belt.

His legs went out beneath him and he sank to his knees. "Thank you, God." Now he knew he could beat the monster. "You've sent me an angel."

She grabbed a fistful of his hair and hauled him up.

"Listen, Henry." He had never seen her angry before. "I walked in here on my own two feet because you're the only man who never stared at me. Nobody pushed me in here, especially not God. There is no fucking God! Or if there is, he's got to be the most heartless asshole in the universe." Her wings were flapped like pennants. "You look at me. Go ahead. I'm a freak, a monster. I didn't ask to be one and I had to learn to live with these damn things. And nobody helped — my mother gave me this dumb name — I still haven't got any goddamn help. So if you want to thank somebody, you can thank Celeste Sloboda for staying sane despite the way most everyone stares." She was crying. "So that's the way it is, okay? I've pissed you off, you pissed me off and now we can go home and hate each other."

"Celeste." She could think whatever she wanted. He knew God's work when he saw it. She was full of a kind of pain the monster couldn't use. Only he could. He knew that as long as he believed in this miracle, nobody, nothing could stop him from being himself. "Let go of my hair?"

She released him and immediately stroked the back of his head. "I didn't mean to hurt you." Her gaze softened. "I'm sorry. I didn't want it like this."

He could feel the monster slipping away. "I want you," he said. Her face kept getting bigger until it was the only thing Henry could see. They kissed forever and amen. Henry wasn't sure how he got naked. As he led her to the bedroom he couldn't remember if any woman had ever seen him naked before.

She paused by the bathroom, traced the line of his chin, and smiled. "Henry," she said, "Do you think you might shave?"

▼

Much later, he eased out from under the covers so as not to wake her. He realized where the monster had gone when it left him. He pulled on his jeans, padded into the living room and felt under the cushion. It was in the Beretta. He stared at the gun without comprehension. Even though it was still as hard and black and cold as ever, it didn't seem real to him anymore. His first thought was to lose it in the dumpster behind his apartment, but he was barefoot and it had set him back five hundred and thirty-eight dollars. Tomorrow after work he could pawn it and buy some nice woman thing for Celeste.

He stripped the magazine, picked the shells out, and wrapped everything in a green garbage bag. Or maybe he should keep the gun for protection—God knows there were monsters loose in the city. He hid it under the sink and snuck back to bed with his angel.

MAKING MONSTERS
by James Patrick Kelly

▼

This essay isn't turning out quite the way I expected. I was going to begin with one of my favorite anecdotes about making art but, when I checked into it, I found out the story I'd heard was a myth. Well, almost.

It's about the film classic *Casablanca*. According to legend, the actors weren't told the ending—mostly because the writers couldn't come up with one until almost two months after shooting started. Ingrid Bergman, Humphrey Bogart, and Paul Henreid had to enact their wrenching love triangle so that it made emotional sense whether Ilsa stayed with Rick in Casablanca or flew off into the fog with Victor Laslow. In other words, the actors faced the same uncertainties as do we who muddle through real life. I've always found the idea immensely appealing. As yet, nobody has handed *me* those last few pages of the *Jim Kelly Story*—those which reveal whether I am destined for a tragic fall or happy ever-after. I'm just making me up as I go along.

Unfortunately, there never was an Ilsa-stays-with-Rick option for *Casablanca*. Although Bergman claims in her autobiography that such an ending was discussed several times, the reality was that no censor in 1942 would pass a movie in which a woman deserted her war hero husband for her lover. Yes, the writers were still casting about for an ending late in the production, but their problem was not *whether* to send Ilsa off with Laslow, but just *how* to get her onto that plane. Does Rick persuade her to leave? Order her? Trick her? Slug her and then load her on? Why does he want her to go, anyway? And how could she ever agree?

To me, these questions point up the difficulty of discussing plot without sliding into character analysis. This is the wave/particle duality of fiction. In a story, things happen for reasons. It makes sense to say that *what someone does* falls for the most part in the domain of plot and *why she does it* is largely a matter of character, but I can't always make a hard distinction, nor do I see the profit in it.

Some writers are assiduous planners; I am not one of them. In fact, the outline is probably the rustiest tool in my kit. Of course, different projects require different strategies. I wouldn't launch into a novel without making notes, timelines, and character sketches; complex, episodic stories sprawling over someone's entire lifetime might require a diagram. But in general, my approach to plotting is to procrastinate. I don't necessarily want to work out everything that's going to happen ahead of time. Whenever possible, I prefer to wait until I can collaborate with my characters. I ruefully acknowledge that this isn't the most efficient way to write, but it's what works for me.

Procrastination serves two purposes. First, by keeping myself in the dark as long as possible, I'm better able to maintain my own interest in the story. The reader can sense when a writer is bored, so I try never to be. And without doubt, the most exhilarating moment in the creation of any story is when what I see on the screen surprises *me*. Second, I think that developing plot/character using the *Casablanca* model adds verisimilitude. Characters who navigate precisely through a storyline to some well known destination all too often turn out to be plot robots who never come alive on the page. Even if they do, I worry what they are missing along the way. I prefer to send my people out to discover the story. If, on the road to denouement, they chance across a cave which leads to a secret empire, I let them climb down for a look.

"Monsters" began with Henry. I wanted to write about a character on the day before he became a mass murderer. The conceit is that he feels possessed by some interior "monster," so that the infliction of pain on others gives him intense, almost sexual pleasure. The plot arises from his struggle to contain the monster within. To help him suppress his craving for violence, I gave him a strong religious impulse. However, as I considered what might happen to Henry, I doubted God would save him. I believed he would lose the struggle with his monster in a splatterpunk explosion.

Note that I decided to tell about the day before he became a killer. This was an important structural decision, since it dictated that "Monsters" have an organic plot which observed the unities of time and, to some extent, of place. This story could have been about how Henry got to be the way he was, in which case I could have ranged through his childhood, his sad careers at school and work and his non-existent love life, picking and choosing key moments to dramatize. This would have been a longer, more episodic story, possibly more complex but less immediate and therefore less scary.

All by himself, Henry doesn't necessarily suggest a plot. A plot arises out of conflict; the protagonist needs a strong antagonist. I wanted to put someone in Henry's way; a final obstacle to overcome before he began his killing spree. Celeste is a character I conceived of over twenty years ago. She is an oxymoron: at once a caterpillar and a butterfly, the ugly angel. Because she has what the world perceives as a deformity, it has brutalized her. Yet, she still clings to an unlikely dream of love. I made several pages of notes on Celeste when I first thought of her, but for some reason she never seemed to throw off any plot lines. I relegated her to the idea drawer with the dozens of other half-baked characters, openings, suggestive titles and snippets of dialogue I had scrawled on scrap paper over the years. (The contents of the idea drawer have since migrated to a file in my computer.) Just as I was trying to figure out what to do with Henry, Celeste popped out of the drawer and volunteered to help.

The plot flows from their interactions. In her desperate attempt to get his attention, Celeste unwittingly puts Henry under the stress that will release his monster. She thinks she's in a romantic comedy; he's in a horror story. My first thought was that he would kill her, only to discover, too late, that she was the angel whom his God had sent to save him. Although I did not have a firm notion of everything that was going to occur in "Monsters," the plot did have a destination image which, when fully developed, was my intended climax: Celeste must be undressed so that her miraculous wings could unfold.

Most adults I know spend the greater part of their day on the job, yet surprisingly few genre stories take place in the workplace. Whenever possible I like to show what my characters do for a living. So Kaplan's Cleaners becomes the setting of much of what Robin Wilson calls the involution of the plot, the purpose of which is to push Henry past his breaking point. The scene in St. Sebastian's, set outside Kaplan's, serves as a kind of gauge on which the reader can read Henry's rising tension. It is also a blunt foreshadowing of the violent climax I anticipated at the time I wrote it.

Foreshadowing is perhaps the most useful tool in my plot kit. It is a way to create expectations and to prepare the reader for what may come.

To foreshadow is to parallel some climatic event at a strategic moment early on in the story. Foreshadowing can be as subtle as a passing, perhaps enigmatic reference; it can be as blatant as a pattern of repetition or a particularly striking image. All the monster's appearances foreshadow its final possession of Henry. When Henry imagines Celeste in a three piece bikini, it foreshadows the scene in which she reveals her wings. While overindulgence in foreshadowing can become affectation, the careful writer can use it to make even the most improbable twist believable. Foreshadowing can also be used like a magician's handkerchief to distract the reader from the author's true intentions, to create a seeming inevitability where none exists. More on misdirection in a moment.

I remember getting stuck as I approached the end of Henry's work day. This is the price one pays for plotting on the fly. Outliners have it easy; they always knows what comes next. I regard getting stuck as nature's way of telling me that what I am about to do is wrong; the problem crops up in almost every project.

The plot point I needed was for something very bad to happen to revive Henry's monster. But what? An obnoxious seatmate on the commute home? A fight at the bus stop? A burst pipe in the apartment? All these seemed either too tame or generic. The real problem was that I didn't know enough about Henry at that time to write a scene powerful enough to free his monster. Such a scene would have to be deeply personal. My early plot/character decision not to delve into Henry's psychopathology was now catching up with me. It was time to answer the question Damon Knight had taught me to ask twenty years ago at the Clarion Writers Workshop: What mattered most to my character?

I had long since decided that Henry's parents would be conveniently dead; it almost always pays to economize on characters. However, if the reader was to understand my tortured loner, I needed to stage some of his history. A clumsy way to accomplish this would have been to have him gaze at a picture of himself and his dad, say standing on the dock at the lake, then cut to flashback. In fact, just such a picture was hanging in the story at the time. Or else that obnoxious seatmate on the bus might say or do something that jogged his memory . . . nah! Eventually I got it. Henry's dad wasn't dead; he was dying.

This insight remade the plot of "Monsters" in a way I could never have imagined before I started writing. The hospital scene was perfect for scraping Henry's emotions raw—and I was able to implicate Celeste in the disaster too. But I found the old man's rebuke so scarifying that my sympathies turned. It became clear that the emergence of the monster coincided with the onset of Roger West's long illness and his unfair, pain-wracked censure of Henry, who was trying as hard as he could. Pardon my hubris, but the god Henry was praying to was *me*; what kind of universe was I running here? By the time I finished the hospital scene, I no longer wanted Henry's monster to win, even though that had been the climax toward which I had been working for the previous 7,420 words.

Which brings us back to the craft of misdirection and the uses of the surprise. Did I now owe it to the reader to *un*foreshadow the murder ending? I believe I did not. After all, I hadn't changed the actual destination image of my plot: the unfolding of Celeste's wings. I'd simply changed its meaning. In no way had I made it impossible for Henry to beat the monster. Indeed, there are glimmerings of humanity in him. Certainly, he loves his father. He also refuses to crush Celeste emotionally when he has the chance. Building on that fragile foundation, Celeste might be able to save him. It would probably take a miracle, but then I was already committed to the miracle of Celeste's wings. If I wasted her, literally and figuratively, "Monsters" would have ended as one more splatter-fest with an ironic twist. The potential for redemption had always been there, I had just never considered it.

There are reasons why science fiction and fantasy writers try so hard to inject suprise into their plots—particularly into their endings. We're writing popular literature here; surprise may be the most special of our effects. And it's part of our heritage. After all, we're the folks who gave Western Civilization *Amazing* and *Astounding*. Surprises sustain and even enhance the reader's interest in a developing plot. Remember that when most critics use "predictable," it is as a pejorative. Nobody wants to hear, "I guessed how it all came out on page two," whereas a well-wrought twist ending can prolong the life of the story in the imagination. For some time after that last page is turned, the reader will still be thinking about what happened.

Surprise forms part of the philosophical underpinnings of the genre as well. If science fiction is about things that could happen but haven't yet, and fantasy is about impossible things, then astonishment is our natural condition. We deal in the shock of the new—and the strange. Moreover, the genre has a proud history of subverting cultural assumptions and challenging the common wisdom. What if we didn't have to die? What if we're not the crown of creation? What if reality is a lie?

Up until the moment that Celeste undresses, "Monsters" can be read as a mainstream story; its many commonplaces invite the reader to map the real world onto it. For example, it's entirely possible that Henry has multiple personalities and his monster is one of them. If this is a "realistic" story, the reader's dread must soar when Celeste arrives at Henry's apartment, because in the real world Celeste would seem to be doomed. It would take a miracle to save her, and the common wisdom is that, in reality, there are no miracles, more's the pity. Actually, two miracles occur in the seduction scene and only one is fantastic. When Celeste kisses the monster, a disoriented Henry reappears; when Henry sees her wings, he finds the strength to banish the monster.

Which was more important?

I mentioned earlier that I attended Clarion. In the years since, I've become a workshop enthusiast; I've been to Milford, Philford, Sycamore Hill, and am currently a member of the monthly Cambridge (Massachusetts) Science Fiction Workshop. While workshops are not for everyone, I find that listening to a group of very creative readers analyze and interpret my work is always instructive. In particular, what workshops do best is scrutinize plot and character. "Monsters" was the first manuscript I put through the Cambridge Workshop. Their comments helped me fix a number of problems, most related to the midcourse plot/character correction. The remains of the splatter ending were distorting the salvation ending. Henry was at times too bloody-minded and psychotic; he did not appear to be a good candidate for redemption. In part because I had intended to kill her off, I had drawn Celeste as an annoying and superficial chatterbox; she did not seem to have enough self-insight to deliver her tirade against the deity. These flaws in characterization undermined the climax of the plot. I made what I thought were the appropriate revisions and sent the story to *Isaac Asimov's Science Fiction Magazine.*

Gardner Dozois and Sheila Williams have published sixteen of my stories, including much of my best work thus far. When they make suggestions, I always pay attention. They wanted to buy "Monsters" but worried that the last few pages were too rushed. After all, Henry goes from crazed blood lust to peaceful postcoital sanity in a very short span. They wondered whether I'd lurched toward the happy ending too abruptly. My recollection is that they wanted me to provide more foundation for Henry's profound change—perhaps by means of some pillow talk right before the denouement.

As Robin Wilson points out, the ending of a work of fiction consists of climax and denouement. The climax, as the turning point of the plot and the moment of highest reader interest, gets the most attention, as well it should. However, the denouement, the sorting out and sending off, all too often is treated as an afterthought. A grievous mistake, in my opinion, because it's here the writer gets to make one last statement about the meaning of the story. It is also the perfect place to impart what politicians these days call spin.

A story I wrote once upon a time as a student at Clarion involved a woman scientist who, against her better judgment, participates in an unspeakable experiment. In the process she nearly wrecks her marriage. After much techno-mayhem, she alone is left of the research team; the experiment has succeeded but at a horrific cost. At the denouement, she retreats in a daze to her office, where she finds a dozen roses from her estranged husband—a peace offering. In the version I workshopped, she decides impulsively to take the bouquet, go to him and leave everything else behind. It was the bland conclusion to a There-Are-Some-Things-We-Are-Not-Meant-To-Know story. In her critique Kate Wilhelm taught me the importance of the denouement. After reading my manuscript, Kate suggested a change: What if my heroine tossed all but a single flower out, stuck that one into a bud vase and sat down to write up the experiment? All it took was two sentences and one red rose to transform the piece into a chilling and powerful Scientist-Loses-Her-Soul story.

After mulling over Sheila and Gardner's criticism of "Monsters," what I decided was that rather than pad the climax, I'd put a new spin on the denouement. Here's the last paragraph of the version they read:

Much later, he eased out from under the covers so as not to wake her. He realized where the monster had gone when it left him. He pulled on his jeans, padded into the living room and felt under the cushion. It was in the Beretta. He stared at the gun without comprehension. Even though it was still as hard and black and cold as ever, it didn't seem real to him anymore. He stripped the magazine, picked the shells out one by one, and hid them under the sink. He stuffed the gun in the trash under the pizza box and went back to bed with his angel.

Compare this to the revised denouement, as published in *Asimov's*.

There are several ways to interpret the penultimate sentence, but at least one valid reading is that the monster is not permanently defeated. As Henry vacillates and then decides not to get rid of the Beretta, the monster may once again be insinuating itself into his psyche. Henry has not yet been completely redeemed; however, he does seem to have mastered his madness—for the time being. This is not necessarily a happy ending, although it *is* hopeful. Like so much of what I write, "Monsters" didn't turn out quite the way I expected.

Which comes as no surprise.

▼

What is character but the determination of incident?
What is incident but the illustration of character?

Henry James' felicitous formulation underscores the futility of considering aspects of fiction separately. All—plot, character, point of view, setting, theme, and a dozen others—are interrelated and mutually dependent in the gestalt of the story; no two more so than plot and character. To paraphrase James: Every story has its unique characters; every character has its own story.

Functioning characters are not stock items, carefully labeled and stored on shelves in the writer's mind until she needs them. Instead, they are meticulously constructed within the framework of their stories, imagined in a depth and detail that usually surpasses the demands of the drama they act out. They are, of course, modeled after life; a writer has no other source for her knowledge of behavior and motivation.

Characters are presented in accord with two judgments the writer must make: the *quantity* of information about the character the reader must have and the *function* of the character in the story. The quantitative decision is particularly important in short fiction, where every word must count, and the writer—who is as interested in her creations as any fond parent—must struggle against prolixity. The functional decision helps to determine the quantitative one by distinguishing between central and marginal characters. But even here, the writer who plots by the "plant some characters in a situation and see what grows" method is likely to see some unimportant little sprout suddenly develop great leaves and strong tentacles threatening to strangle the rest of the tale.

Again from the drama, we borrow some useful terms for the functions of characters. There are, of course, the *protagonist* and *antagonist* (or hero and villain), who must be understood to be not just good guys and bad guys but the two parties to the central dramatic conflict of the story. They may be people or animals or natural forces or social movements or odd bits of machinery or even opposing views within one person, just so long as they are, in some way or another, personified. George R. Stewart managed to make a *Fire* and a *Storm* the central characters in the two novels with those titles, and perhaps "central character" is a better term than "hero" or "villain," avoiding the value judgments those words imply.

Other character functions are the *foil*, whose character contrasts with that of the central character, thus illuminating it; the *confidant*, to whom the central character may speak with some honesty, revealing himself to the reader or delivering necessary expository information in the process; the *narrator*, who tells the story (and more on this in the section on point of view); and a host of non-specific spear carriers who leave important messages on the telephone answering machine, pour drinks behind the bar, arrest the villain, or act as nameless persons from Porlock who are important simply through their presence.

The writer characterizes through two basic methods, the *explicit* and the *dramatic*. The choice between the two seems to follow a kind of faddish cycle, with James' reaction to the explicit techniques of the nineteenth century novel expressed in his exhortation to "Dramatize! Dramatize!" now appearing in writers workshops as "Show, don't tell!" But the pendulum swings, and if the explicit method is not yet in vogue, it is holding its own. The writer who chooses the explicit method of characterization has limited her choice of point of view (she requires omniscience or a third-person narrator), but she has two powerful tools: the *essay method*, concentrated expository character portraits, and the *method of progressive analysis*, a running commentary on the actions and motivations of the character.

The dramatic (or implicit) method of characterization requires that the character be revealed through the opinions of other characters, through his interactions with his environment, and through his acted-out attitudes toward others. Specifically, the implicit method demands careful attention to the character's appearance, speech, mannerisms, possessions, and reactions to others. It is one thing to characterize George as a mean man, another to describe him swiping empties from a homeless person's shopping cart, yet another to describe the scene and tell the reader why George did it and what was going through his mind at the time, obviously a combination of the explicit and dramatic methods.

One last revelation: Writers construct characters partly from their observations of others, partly from their understanding of certain general principles of human behavior, but mostly from their analyses of themselves. Good writers develop introspection into a high art, become professional schizoids, experiment dangerously in the laboratories of their own souls, and sometimes drink too much.

SISTERS
by Greg Bear

▼

"But you're the only one, Letitia." Reena Cathcart lay a light, slender hand on her shoulder with a look of utmost sincerity. "You know none of the others can. I mean . . ." She stopped, the slightest hint of awareness of her faux pas dawning. "You're simply the only one who can play the old—the older—woman."

Letitia Blakely looked down at the hall floor, eyes and face hot, then circled her gaze up to the ceiling, trying to keep the fresh tears from spilling over. Reena tossed her long black hair, perfect hazel eyes imploring. A few stragglers sauntered down the clean and carpeted hall of the new school wing to their classes. "We're late for first period," Letitia said. "Why the old woman? Why didn't you come to me when there was some other part to play?"

Reena was too smart not to know what she was doing. Smart, but not terribly sensitive. "You're the type."

"You mean frowsy?"

Reena didn't react. She was intent on a yes answer, the perfect solution to her problems.

"Or just dumpy?"

"You shouldn't be ashamed of how you look."

"I look frowsy and *dumpy*! I'm perfect for the old woman in your lysing play, and you're the only one with the guts to ask me."

"We'd like to give you a chance. You're such a loner, and we want you to feel like you're part—"

"Bullmusk!" The moisture spilled over and Reena backed away. "Leave me alone. Just leave me alone."

"No need to swear." Petulant, offended.

Letitia raised her hand as if to strike. Reena swung her hair again defiantly and turned to walk away. Letitia leaned against the tile wall and wiped her eyes, trying to avoid damage to her carefully applied makeup. The damage was already done, however. She could feel the tear tracks of her mother's mascara and the smudged eyeshadow. With a sigh, she walked off to the bathroom, not caring how late she was. She wanted to go home.

Coming into class fifteen minutes after the bell, Letitia was surprised to find the students in self-ordered discussion, with no sign of Mr. Brant. Several of Reena's drama group gave her frosty looks as she took her seat.

"TB," Edna Corman said beneath her breath from across the aisle.

"RC you," Letitia replied, head cocked to one side and tone matching Edna's precisely. She poked John Lockwood in the shoulder. Lockwood didn't care much for socializing; he seldom noticed the exchanges going on around him. "Where's Mr. Brant?"

"Georgia Fischer blitzed and he took her to the counselors. He told us to plug in and pursue."

"Oh." Georgia Fischer had transferred two months ago from a superwhiz class in Oakland. She was brighter than most but she blitzed about once every two weeks. "I may be fat and ugly," Letitia said for Lockwood's ears only, "but I never blitz."

"Nor I," Lockwood said. He was PPC, like Georgia, but not a superwhiz. Letitia liked him, but not enough to feel threatened by him. "Better pursue."

Letitia leaned back in her seat and closed her eyes to concentrate. Her mod activated and projections danced in front of her, then steadied. She had been cramming patient psych for a week and was approaching threshold. The little computer graphics nursie in whites and pillcap began discussing insanouts of terminal patient care, which all seemed very TB to Letitia; who died of disease now, anyway? She made her decision and cut to the same CG nursie discussing the shock of RoR-replacement and recovery. What she really wanted to study was colony medicine, but how could she ever make it Out There?

Some PPCs had been designed by their parents to qualify physically and mentally for space careers. Some had been equipped with bichemistries, one of which became active in Earth's gravity, the other in space. How could an NG compete with that?

Of the seven hundred adolescents in her high school training programs, Letitia Blakely was one of ten NGs—possessors of natural, unaltered genomes. Everyone else was the proud bearer of juggled genes, PPCs or Pre-Planned Children, all lovely and stable with just the proper amount of adipose tissue and just the proper infusion of parental characteristics and chosen features to be beautiful and different; tall, healthy, hair manageable, skin unblemished, well-adjusted (except for the occasional blitzer) with warm and sunny personalities. The old derogatory slang for PPCs was RC-Recombined.

Letitia Blakely, slightly overweight, skin pasty, hair frizzy, bulbous-nosed and weak-chinned, one breast larger than the other and already showing a droop pronounced enough to grip a stylus—with painful menstrual periods and an absolute indisposition to athletics—was the Sport. That's what they were called. NG sports. TBs-throwbacks. Neanderthals.

All the beautiful PPCs risked a great deal if they showed animosity toward the NGs. Her parents had the right to sue the system if she was harassed to the detriment of her schooling. This wasn't a private school where all parents paid astronomical tuitions; this was an old-fashioned public school, with public school programs and regulations. Teachers tended to nuke out on raggers. And, she admitted to herself with a painful loop of recrimination, she wasn't making it any easier for them.

Sure, she could join in, play the old woman—how much realism she would contribute to their little drama, with her genuine TB phys! She could be jolly and self-deprecating like Helen Roberti, who wasn't all that bad-looking anyway—she could pass if she straightened her hair. Or she could be quiet and camouflaged like Bernie Thibhault.

The CG nursie exited from RoR care. Letitia had hardly absorbed a thing. Realtime mod education was a bore, but she hadn't yet qualified for experience training. She had only one course of career study now—no alternatives—and two aesthetic programs, individual orchestra on Friday afternoon and LitVid publishing on alternating weekends.

For pre-med, she was a washout, but she wouldn't admit it. She was NG. Her brain took longer to mature; it wasn't as finely wired.

She thought she was incredibly slow. She doubted whether she would ever be successful as a doctor; she was squeamish, and nobody, not even her fellow NGs, would want to be treated by a doctor who grew pale at the sight of blood.

Letitia silently told nursie to start over again, and nursie obliged.

Reena Cathcart, meanwhile, had dropped into her mod with a

vengeance. Her blissed expression told it all. The realtime ed slid into her so smooth, so quick, it was pure joy.

No zits on her brain.

Mr. Brant returned ten minutes later with a pale and bleary-eyed Georgia Fischer. She sat two seats behind Letitia and over one aisle. She plugged in her mod dutifully and Brant went to his console to bring up the multimedia and coordinate the whole class. Edna Corman whispered something to her.

"Not a bad blitz, all in all," Georgia commented softly.

"How are you doing, Letitia?" the autocounselor asked. The CG face projected in front of her with some slight wirehash, which Letitia paid no attention to. CG ACs were the jams and she didn't appreciate them even in pristine perfection.

"Poorly," she said.

"Really? Care to elaborate?"

"I want to talk to Dr. Rutger."

"Don't trust your friendly AC?"

"I'd like some clear space. I want to talk to Dr. Rutger."

"Dr. Rutger is busy, dear. Unlike your friendly AC, humans can only be in one place at a time. I'd like to help if I may."

"Then I want program sixteen."

"Done, Letitia." The projection wavered and the face changed to a real-person simulation of Marian Tempesino, the only CG AC Letitia felt comfortable with.

Tempesino had no wirehash, which indicated she was a seldom-used program, and that was just fine with Letitia. "Sixteen here. Letitia? You're looking cut. More adjustment jams?"

"I wanted to talk with Dr. Rutger but he's busy. So I'll talk to you. And I want it on my record. I want out of school. I want my parents to pull me and put me in a special NG school."

Tempesino's face didn't wear any particular expression, which was one of the reasons Letitia liked Program 16 AC. "Why?"

"Because I'm a freak. My parents made me a freak and I'd like to know why I shouldn't be with all the other freaks."

"You're a natural, not a freak."

"To look like any of the others—even to look like Reena Cathcart—I'd have to spend the rest of my life in bioplasty. I can't take it anymore.

They asked me to play an old lady in one of their dramas. The only part I'm fit for. An old lady."

"They tried to include you in."

"That *hurt!*" Letitia said, tears in her eyes.

Tempesino's image wavered a bit as the emotion registered and a higher authority AC kicked in behind 16.

"I just want out. I want to be alone."

"Where would you like to go, Letitia?"

Letitia thought about it for a moment. "I'd like to go back to when being ugly was normal."

"Fine, then. Let's simulate. Sixty years should do it. Ready?"

She nodded and wiped away more mascara with the back of her hand.

"Then let's go."

It was like a dream, somewhat fuzzier than plugging in a mod. CG images compiled from thousands of miles of old films and tapes and descriptive records made her feel as if she were flying back in time, back to a place she would have loved to call home. Faces came to her—faces with ugly variations, growing old prematurely, wearing glasses, even beautiful faces which could have passed today—and the faces pulled away to become attached to bodies. Bodies out of shape, in good condition, overweight, sick and healthy, red-faced with high blood pressure: the whole variable and disaster-prone population of humanity, sixty years past. This was where Letitia felt she belonged.

"They're beautiful," she said.

"They didn't think so. They jumped at the chance to be sure their children were beautiful, smart, and healthy. It was a time of transition, Letitia. Just like now."

"Everybody looks alike now."

"I don't think that's fair," the AC said. "There's a considerable variety in the way people look today."

"Not my age."

"Especially your age. Look." The AC showed her dozens of faces. Few looked alike, but all were handsome or lovely. Some made Letitia ache just looking at them; faces she could never be friends with, never love, because there was always someone more beautiful and desirable than an NG.

"My parents should have lived back then. Why did they make me a freak?"

"You're developmentally normal genotype. You're not a freak."

"Sure. I'm a DNG. Dingy. That's what they call me."

"Don't you invite the abuse sometimes?"

"No!" This was getting her nowhere.

"Letitia, we all have to adjust. Not even today's world is fair. Are you sure you're doing all you can to adjust?"

Letitia squirmed in her seat and said she wanted to leave. "Just a moment," the AC said. "We're not done yet." She knew that tone of voice. The ACs were allowed to get a little tough at times. They could make unruly students do grounds duty or detain them after hours to work on assignments usually given to computers. Letitia sighed and settled back. She hated being lectured.

"Young woman, you're carrying a giant chip on your shoulder."

"That's all the more computing capacity for me."

"Quiet, and listen. We're all allowed to criticize policy, whoever makes it. Dignity of office and respect for superiors has not survived very well into Century Twenty-one. People have to earn respect. That goes for students, too. The average student here has four major talents, each of them fitting into a public planning policy which guarantees them a job incorporating two or more of those talents. They aren't forced to accept the jobs, and if their will falters, they may not keep those jobs. But the public has tried to guarantee every one of us a quality employment opportunity. That goes for you, as well. You're DNG, but you show as much intelligence and at least as many developable talents as the PPCs. You are young, and your maturation schedule is a natural one—but you are not inferior or impaired, Letitia. That's more than can be said for the offspring of some parents even more resistive than your own. You at least were given prenatal care and nutrition adjustment, and your parents let the biotechs correct your allergies."

"So?"

"So for you, it's all a matter of will. If your will falters, you won't be given any more consideration than a PPC. You'll have to choose secondary or tertiary employment, or even . . ." The AC paused. "Public support. Do you want that?"

"My grades are up. I'm doing fine."

"You are choosing career training not matching your developable talents."

"I like medicine."

"You're squeamish."

Letitia shrugged.

"And you're hard to get along with."

"Just tell them to lay off. I'll be civil . . . but I don't want them treating me like a freak. Edna Corman called me . . ." She paused. That could get Edna Corman into a lot of trouble. Among the students, TB was a casual epithet; to school authorities, applied to an NG, it might be grounds for a blot on Corman's record. "Nothing. Not important."

The AC switched to lower authority and Tempesino's face took a different counseling track. "Fine. Adjustment on both sides is necessary. Thank you for coming in, Letitia."

"Yeah. I still want to talk with Rutger."

"Request has been noted. Please return to your class in progress."

"Pay attention to your brother when he's talking," Jane said. Roald was making a nuisance of himself by chattering about the preflight training he was getting in primary. Letitia made a polite comment or two, then lapsed back into contemplation of the food before her. She didn't eat. Jane regarded her from the corner of her eye and passed a bowl of sugared berries. "What's eating you?"

"I'm doing the eating," Letitia said archly.

"Ha," Roald said. "Full load from this angle." He grinned at her, his two front teeth missing. He looked hideous, she thought. Any other family would have given him temporaries; not hers.

"A little more respect from both of you," said Donald. Her father took the bowl from Roald and scooped a modest portion into his cup, then set it beside Letitia. "Big fifteen and big eight." That was his homily; behave big whether eight or fifteen.

"Autocounselor today?" Jane asked. She knew Letitia much too well.

"AC," Letitia affirmed.

"Did you go in?"

"Yes."

"And?"

"I'm not tuned."

"Which means?" Donald ask.

"It means she hisses and crackles," Roald said, mouth full of berries, juice dripping down his chin. He cupped his hand underneath and sucked it up noisily. Jane reached out and finished the job with a napkin. "She complains," Roald finished.

"About what?"

Letitia shook her head and didn't answer.

The dessert was almost finished when Letitia slapped both palms on the table. "Why did you do it?"

"Why did we do what?" her father asked, startled.

"Why are Roald and I normal? Why didn't you design us?"

Jane and Donald glanced at each other quickly and turned to Letitia. Roald regarded her with wide eyes, a bit shocked himself.

"Surely you know why by now," Jane said, looking down at the table, either nonplussed or getting angry. Now that she had laid out her course, Letitia couldn't help but forge ahead.

"I don't. Not really. It's not because you're religious."

"Something like that," Donald said.

"No," Jane said, shaking her head firmly.

"Then why?"

"Your mother and I —"

"I am *not* just their mother," Jane said.

"Jane and I believe there is a certain plan in nature, a plan we shouldn't interfere with. If we had gone along with most of the others and tried to have PPCs — participated in the boy-girl lotteries and signed up for the prebirth opportunity counseling — why, we would have been interfering."

"Did you go to a hospital when we were born?"

"Yes," Jane said, still avoiding their faces.

"That's not natural," Letitia said. "Why not let nature decide whether we'd be born alive or not?"

"We have never claimed to be consistent," Donald said.

"Donald," Jane said ominously.

"There are limits," Donald expanded, smiling placation. "We believe those limits begin when people try to interfere with the sex cells. You've had all that in school. You know about the protests when the first PPCs were born. Your grandmother was one of the protesters. Your mother and I are both NGs; of course, our generation has a much higher percentage of NGs."

"Now we're freaks," Letitia said.

"If by that you mean there aren't many teenage NGs, I suppose that's right," Donald said, touching his wife's arm. "But it could also mean you're special. Chosen."

"No," Letitia said. "Not chosen. You played dice with both of us. We could have been DDs. Duds. Not just dingies, but retards or spaz."

An uncomfortable quiet settled over the table. "Not likely," Donald said, his voice barely above a whisper. "Your mother and I both have good genotypes. Your grandmother insisted your mother marry a good genotype. There are no developmentally disabled people in our families."

Letitia had been hemmed in. There was no way she could see out of it, so she pushed back her chair and excused herself from the table.

As she made her way up to her room, she heard arguing below. Roald raced up the stairs behind her and gave her a dirty look. "Why'd you have to bring all that up?" he asked. "It's bad enough at school, we don't have to have it here."

She thought about the history the AC had shown her. Back then, a family with their income wouldn't have been able to live in a four-bedroom house. Back then, there had been half as many people in the United States and Canada as there were now. There had been more unemployment, much more economic uncertainty, and far fewer automated jobs. The percentage of people doing physical labor for a living — simple construction, crop maintenance and harvesting, digging ditches and hard work like that — had been ten times greater then than it was now. Most of the people doing such labor today belonged to religious sects or one of the Wendell Berry farming communes.

Back then, Roald and Letitia would have been considered gifted children with a bright future.

She thought about the pictures and the feeling of the past, and wondered if Reena hadn't been right.

She would be a perfect old woman.

Her mother came into her room while Letitia was putting up her hair. She stood in the door frame. It was obvious she had been crying. Letitia watched her reflection in the mirror of her grandmother's dressing table, willed to her four years before. "Yes?" she asked softly, ageless bobby pin in her mouth.

"It was more my idea than your father's," Jane said, stepping closer, hands folded before her. "I mean, I am your mother. We've never really talked about this."

"No," Letitia said.

"So why now?"

"Maybe I'm growing up."

"Yes." Jane looked at the soft and flickering pictures hung on the walls, pastel scenes of improbable forests. "When I was pregnant with you, I was very afraid. I worried we'd made the wrong decision, going against what everybody else seemed to think and what everybody was advising or being advised. But I carried you and felt you move . . . and I knew you were ours, and ours alone, and that we were responsible for you body and soul. I was your mother, not the doctors."

Letitia looked up with mixed anger and frustration . . . and love.

"And now I see you. I think back to what I might have felt, if I were your age again, in your position. I might be mad, too. Roald hasn't had time to feel different yet; he's too young. I just came up here to tell you; I know that what I did was right, not for us, not for them" — she indicated the broad world beyond the walls of the house — "but right for you. It will work out. It really will." She put her hands on Letitia's shoulders. "They aren't having an easy time either. You know that." She stopped for a moment, then from behind her back revealed a book with a soft brown cover. "I brought this to show you again. You remember Great-grandma? Her grandmother came all the way from Ireland, along with her grandpa." Jane gave her the album. Reluctantly, Letitia opened it up. There were real photographs inside, on paper, ancient black and white and faded color. Her great-grandmother did not much resemble Grandmother, who had been big-boned, heavy-set. Great-grandmother looked as if she had been skinny all her life. "You keep this," Jane said. "Think about it for a while."

The morning came with planned rain. Letitia took the half-empty metro to school, looking at the terraced and gardened and occasionally neglected landscapes of the extended suburbs through raindrop-smeared glass. She walked onto the school grounds and went to one of the older buildings in the school, where there was a little-used old-fashioned lavatory. This sometimes served as her sanctuary. She stood in a white stall and breathed deeply for a few minutes, then went to a sink and washed her hands as if conducting some ritual. Slowly, reluctantly, she looked at herself in the cracked mirror. A janitorial worker went about its duties, leaving behind the fresh, steamy smell of clean fixtures.

The early part of the day was a numb time. Letitia began to fear her own distance from feeling, from the people around her. She might at any minute step into the old lavatory and simply fade from the present, find herself sixty years back. . . .

And what would she really think of that?

In her third period class she received a note requesting that she appear in Rutger's counseling office as soon as was convenient. That was shorthand for immediately; she gathered up her mods and caught Reena's unreadable glance as she walked past.

Rutger was a handsome man of forty-three (the years were registered on his desk life clock, an affectation of some of the older PPCs) with a broad smile and a garish taste in clothes. He was head of the counseling department and generally well-liked in the school. He shook her hand as she entered the counseling office and offered her a chair. "Now. You wanted to talk to me?"

"I guess," Letitia said.

"Problems?" He spoke in a pleasant baritone; he was probably a fairly good singer. That had been a popular trait in the early days of PPCs.

"The ACs say it's my attitude."

"And what about it?"

"I . . . am ugly. I am the ugliest girl . . . the only girl in this school who is ugly."

Rutger nodded. "I don't think you're ugly, but which is worse, being unique or being ugly?" Letitia lifted the corner of one lip in snide acknowledgment of the funny.

"Everybody's *unique* now," she said.

"That's what we teach. Do you believe it?"

"No," she said. "Everybody's the same. I'm . . ." She shook her head. She resented Rutger prying up the pavement over her emotions. "I'm TB. I wouldn't mind being a PPC, but I'm not."

"I think it's a minor problem," Rutger said quickly. He hadn't even sat down; obviously he was not going to give her much time.

"It doesn't feel minor," she said, anger poking through the cracks he had made.

"Oh, no. Being young often means that minor problems feel major. You feel envy and don't like yourself, at least not the way you look. Well, looks can be helped by diet, or at the very least by time. If I'm any judge, you'll look fine when you're older. And I am something of a judge. As for the way the others feel about you . . . I was a freak once."

Letitia looked up at him.

"Certainly. Bona fide. Much more of a freak than you. There are ten NGs like yourself in this school now. When I was your age, I was the only PPC in my school. There was still suspicion and even riots. Some PPCs were killed in one school when parents stormed the grounds."

Letitia stared.

"The other kids hated me. I wasn't bad-looking, but they knew. They had parents who told them PPCs were Frankenstein monsters. Do you remember the Rifkin Society? They're still around, but they're extreme fringies now. Just as well. They thought I'd been grown in a test tube somewhere and hatched out of an incubator. You've never experienced real hatred, I suspect. I did."

"You were nice-looking," Letitia said. "You knew somebody would like you eventually, maybe even love you. But what about me? Because of what I am, the way I look, who will ever want me? And will a PPC ever want to *be* with a Dingy?"

She knew these were hard questions and Rutger made no pretense of answering them. "Say it all works out for the worst," he said. "You end up a spinster and no one ever loves you. You spend the rest of your days alone. Is that what you're worried about?"

Her eyes widened. She had never quite thought those things through. Now she really hurt.

"Everybody out there is choosing beauty for their kids. They're choosing slender, athletic bodies and fine minds. You have a fine mind, but you don't have an athletic body. Or so you seem to be convinced; I have no record of you ever trying out for athletics. So when you're out in the adult world, sure, you'll look different. But why can't that be an advantage? You may be surprised how hard we PPCs try to be different. And how hard it is, since tastes vary so little in our parents. You have that built in."

Letitia listened, but the layers of paving were closing again. "Icing on the cake," she said.

Rutger regarded her with his shrewd blue eyes and shrugged. "Come back in a month and talk to me," he said. "Until then, I think auto-counselors will do fine."

Little was said at dinner and less after. She went upstairs and to bed at an early hour, feeling logy and hoping for escape.

Her father did his usual bedcheck an hour after she had put on her pajamas and lain down. "Rolled tight?" he asked.

"Mmph," she replied.

"Sleep tighter," he said. Rituals. Her life had been shaped by parents who were comfortable with nightly rituals and formulas.

Almost immediately after falling sleep, or so it seemed, she came abruptly awake. She sat up in bed and realized where she was, and who, and began to cry. She had had the strangest and most beautiful dream, the finest ever without a dream mod. She could not remember details now, try as she might, but waking was almost more than she could bear.

In the first period class, Georgia Fischer blitzed yet again and had to go to the infirmary. Letitia watched the others and saw a general stony cover-up of feelings. Edna Corman excused herself in second period and came back with puffy red eyes and pink cheeks. The tension built through the rest of the day until Letitia wondered how anyone could concentrate. She did her own studying without conviction; she was still wrapped in the dream, trying to decide what it meant.

In eighth period, she once again sat behind John Lockwood. It was as if she had completed a cycle beginning in the morning and ending with her last class. She looked at her watch anxiously. Once again, they had Mr. Brant supervising. He seemed distracted, as if he, too, had had a dream, but it hadn't been as pleasant as hers.

Brant had them cut mods mid-period and begin a discussion on what had been learned. These were the so-called integrative moments when the media learning was fixed by social interaction; Letitia found these periods a trial at the best of times. The others discussed their economics, Reena Cathcart as usual standing out in a class full of dominant personalities.

John Lockwood listened intently, a small smile on his face as he presented a profile to Letitia. He seemed about to turn around and talk to her. She placed her hand on the corner of her console and lifted her finger to attract his attention.

He glanced at her hand, turned away, and with a shudder looked at it again, staring this time, eyes widening. His mouth began to work as if her hand was the most horrible thing he had ever seen. His chin quivered, then his shoulder, and before Letitia could react he stood up and moaned. His legs folded and he fell to the console, arms hanging, then slid to the floor. On the floor, John Lockwood—who had never done such a thing in his life—twisted and groaned and shivered, locked in a violent blitz.

Brant pressed the class emergency button and came around his desk. Before he could reach Lockwood, the boy became still, eyes open, one hand letting go its tight grip on the leg of his seat. Letitia could not move, watching his empty eyes; he appeared so horribly *limp*.

Brant grabbed the boy by the shoulders, swearing steadily, and dragged him outside the classroom. Letitia followed them into the hall, wanting to help. Edna Corman and Reena Cathcart stood beside her, faces blank. Other students followed, staying well away from Brant and the boy.

Brant lowered John Lockwood to the concrete and began pounding his chest and administering mouth-to-mouth. He pulled a syringe from his coat pocket and uncapped it, shooting its full contents into the boy's skin just below the sternum. Letitia focused on the syringe, startled. Right in his pocket; not in the first-aid kit.

The full class stood in the hallway, silent, in shock. The medical arrived, Rutger following; it scooped John Lockwood onto its gurney and swung around, lights flashing. "Have you administered KVN?" the robot asked Brant.

"Yes. Five cc's. Direct to heart."

Room after room came out to watch, all the PPCs fixing their eyes on the burdened medical as it rolled down the hall. Edna Corman cried. Reena glanced at Letitia and turned away as if ashamed.

"That's five," Rutger said, voice tired beyond grimness. Brant looked at him, then at the class, and told them they were dismissed. Letitia hung back. Brant screwed up his face in grief and anger. "Go! Get out of here!"

She ran. The last thing she heard Rutger say was, "More this week than last."

▼

Letitia sat in the empty white lavatory, wiping her eyes, ashamed at her sniveling. She wanted to react like a grownup—she saw herself being

calm, cool, offering help to whoever needed it in the classroom—but the
tears and the shaking would not stop.

Mr. Brant had seemed angry, as if the entire classroom were at fault.
Not only was Mr. Brant adult, he was PPC.

So did she expect adults, especially adult PPCs, to behave better?
Wasn't that what it was all about?

She stared at herself in the cracked mirror. "I should go home, or go
to the library and study," she said. Dignity and decorum.

Two girls walked into the lavatory, and her private moment passed.

Letitia did not go to the library. Instead, she went to the old concrete
and steel auditorium, entering through the open stage entrance, standing in darkness in the wings. Three female students sat talking in the
front row, below the stage level and about ten meters away from Letitia.
Letitia recognized Reena but not the other two; they did not share classes
with her.

"Did you know him?" the first girl asked.

"No, not very well," Reena said. "He was in my class."

"No ducks!" the third snorted.

"Trish, keep it *interior*, please. Reena's had it rough."

"He hadn't blitzed. He wasn't a superwhiz. Nobody expected it."

"When was his incept?"

"I don't know," Reena said. "We're all about the same age, within a
couple of months. We're all the same model year, same supplements, if
it's something in the genotype, in the supplements . . ."

"I heard somebody say there had been five so far. I haven't heard anything," the third said.

"I haven't either," said the second.

"Not in our school," Reena said. "Except for the superwhizes. And
none of them have died before."

Letitia stepped back in the darkness, hand on mouth. Had Lockwood
actually died?

She thought for a mad moment of stepping out of the wings, going
into the seats and telling the three she was sorry. The impulse faded fast.
That would have been intruding.

They weren't any older than she was, and they didn't sound much
more mature. They sounded scared.

▼

In the morning, at the station room for pre-med secondary, Brant confirmed that John Lockwood had died the day before. "He had a heart attack," Brant said. Letitia sensed that was not the complete truth. A short eulogy was read, and special hours for psych counseling were arranged for those students who felt they might need it.

The word "blitzing" was not mentioned by Brant, nor by any of the PPCs throughout that day. Letitia tried to research the subject but found precious few materials in the libraries accessed by her mod. She presumed she didn't know where to look; it was hard to believe that *nobody* knew what was happening.

The dream came again, even stronger, the next night, and Letitia awoke out of it cold and shivering with excitement. She saw herself standing before a crowd, no single face visible, for she was in light and they were in darkness. She had felt, in the dream, an almost unbearable happiness, grief mixed with joy, unlike anything she had ever experienced before. She *loved* and did not know what she loved—not the crowd, precisely, not a man, not a family member, not even herself.

She sat up in her bed, hugging her knees, wondering if anybody else was awake. It seemed possible she had never been awake until now; every nerve was alive. Quietly, not wanting anybody to intrude on this moment, she slipped out of bed and walked down the hall to her mother's sewing room. There, in a full-length cheval mirror, she looked at herself as if with new eyes.

"Who are you?" she whispered. She lifted her cotton nightshirt and stared at her legs. Short calves, lumpy knees, thighs not bad—not fat, at any rate. Her arms looked soft, not muscular, but not particularly plump, a rosy vanilla color with strawberry blotches on her elbows where she leaned on them while reading in bed. She had Irish ancestors on her mother's side; that showed in her skin color, recessed cheekbones, broad face. On her father's side, Mexican and German; not much evidence in her of the Mexican. Her brother looked more swarthy. "We're mongrels," she said. "I look like a mongrel compared to PPC purebreds." But PPCs were not purebred; they were *designed*.

She lifted her nightshirt higher still, pulling it over her head finally and standing naked. Shivering from the cold and from the memory of her dream, she forced herself to focus on all of her characteristics. Whenever she had seen herself naked in mirrors before, she had blurred her eyes at one feature, looked away from another, special-effecting her body into a more acceptable fantasy. Now she was in a mood to know herself for what she was.

Broad hips, strong abdomen—plump, but strong. From her pre-med, she knew that meant she would probably have little trouble bearing children. "Brood mare," she said, but there was no critical sharpness in the words. To have children, she would have to attract men, and right now there seemed little chance of that. She did not have the "Attraction Peaks" so often discussed on the TV, or seen faddishly headlined on the LitVid mods; the culturally prescribed geometric curves allocated to so few naturally, and now available to so many by design. *Does Your Child Have the Best Design for Success?*

Such a shocking triviality. She felt a righteous anger grow—another emotion she was not familiar with—and sucked it back into the excitement, not wanting to lose her mood. "I might never look at myself like this again," she whispered.

Her breasts were moderate in size, the left larger than the right and more drooping. She could indeed hold a stylus under her left breast, something a PPC female would not have to worry about for decades, if ever. Rib cage not really distinct; muscles not distinct; rounded, soft, gentle-looking, face curious, friendly, wide-eyed, skin blemished but not so badly it wouldn't recover on its own; feet long and toenails thick, heavily cuticled. She had never suffered from ingrown toenails.

Her family line showed little evidence of tendency to cancer—correctable now, but still distressing—or heart disease or any of the other diseases of melting pot cultures, of mobile populations and changing habits. She saw a strong body in the mirror, one that would serve her well.

And she also saw that with a little makeup, she could easily play an older woman. Some shadow under the eyes, lines to highlight what would in thirty or forty years be jowls, laugh lines. . . .

But she did not look old *now*.

Letitia walked back to her room, treading carefully on the carpet. In the room, she asked the lights to turn on, lay down on the bed, pulled the photo album Jane had given her from the top of her nightstand and gingerly turned the delicate black paper pages. She stared at her great-grandmother's face, and then at the picture of her grandmother as a little girl.

Individual orchestra was taught by three instructors in one of the older drama classrooms behind the auditorium. It was a popular aesthetic;

the school's music boxes were better than most home units, and the instructors were very popular. All were PPCs.

After a half hour of group, each student could retire to box keyboard, order up spheres of countersound to avoid cacophony, and practice.

Today, she practiced for less than half an hour. Then, tongue between her lips, she stared into empty space over the keyboard. "Countersound off, please," she ordered, and stood up from the black bench. Mr. Teague, the senior instructor, asked if she was done for the day.

"I have to run an errand," she said.

"Practice your polyrhythms," he advised.

She left the classroom and walked around to the auditorium's stage entrance. She knew Reena's drama group would be meeting there.

The auditorium was dark, the stage lighted by a few catwalk spots. The drama group sat in a circle of chairs in one illuminated corner of the stage, reading lines aloud from old paper scripts. Hands folded, she walked toward the group. Rick Fayette, a quiet senior with short back hair, spotted her first but said nothing, glancing at Reena. Reena stopped reading her lines, turned, and stared at Letitia. Edna Corman saw her last and shook her head, as if this was the last straw.

"Hello," Letitia said.

"What are you doing here?" There was more wonder than disdain in Reena's voice.

"I thought you might still . . ." She shook her head. "Probably not. But I thought you might still be able to use me."

"*Really*," Edna Corman said.

Reena put her script down and stood. "Why did you change your mind?"

"I thought I wouldn't mind being an old lady," Reena said. "It's just not that big a deal. I brought a picture of my great-grandmother." She took a plastic wallet from her pocket and opened it to a copy she had made from the photo in the album. "You could make me up like this. Like my great-grandmother."

Reena took the wallet. "You look like her," she said.

"Yeah. Kind of."

"Look at this," Reena said, holding the picture out to the others. They gathered around and passed the wallet from hand to hand, staring in wonder. Even Edna Corman glanced at it briefly. "She actually *looks* like her great-grandmother."

Rick Fayette whistled with wonder. "You," he said, "will make a really great old lady."

Rutger called her into his office abruptly a week later. She sat quietly before his desk. "You've joined the drama class after all," he said. She nodded.

"Any reason why?"

There was no simple way to express it. "Because of what you told me," she said.

"No friction?"

"It's going okay."

"Good. They gave you another role?"

"No. I'm the old lady. They'll use makeup on me."

"You don't object to that?"

"I don't think so."

Rutger seemed to want to find something wrong, but he couldn't. With a faintly suspicious smile, he thanked her for her time. "Come back and see me whenever you want," he said. "Tell me how it goes."

The group met each Friday, an hour later than her individual orchestra. Letitia made arrangements for home keyboard hookup and practice. After a reading and a half hour of questions, she obtained the permission of the drama group advisor, a spinsterish non-PPC seldom seen in the hallways, Miss Darcy. Miss Darcy dressed very TB and addressed all of her students as either "Mister" or "Miss," but she knew drama and stagecraft. She was the oldest of the six NG teachers in the school.

Reena stayed with Letitia during the audition and made a strong case for her late admittance, saying that the casting of Rick Fayette as an older woman was not going well. Fayette was equally eager to be rid of the part; he had another nonconflicting role, and the thought of playing two characters in the production worried him.

Fayette confessed his appreciation at their second Friday meeting. He introduced her to slender, elfishly handsome, large-eyed Frank Leroux. Leroux was much too shy to go on stage, Fayette said, but he would be doing their makeup. "He's pretty amazing."

Letitia stood nervously while Leroux examined her. "You've really got a *face*," he said softly. "May I touch you, to see where your bone contours are?"

Letitia giggled and abruptly sobered, embarrassed. "Okay," she said. "You're going to draw lines and make shadows?"

"Much more than that," Leroux said.

"He'll take a video of your face in motion," Fayette said. "Then he'll digitize it and sculpt a laserfoam mold—much better than sitting for a life mask. He made a life mask of *me* last year to turn me into the Hunchback of Notre Dame. No fun at all."

"This way is much better," Leroux agreed, touching her skin delicately, poking under her cheeks and chin, pulling back her hair to feel her temples. "I can make two or three sculptures showing what your face and neck are like when they're in different positions. Then I can adjust the appliance molds for flex and give."

"When he's done with you, you won't know yourself," Fayette said.

"Reena says you have a picture of your great-grandmother. May I see it?" Leroux asked. She gave him the wallet and he looked at the picture with squint-eyed intensity. "What a wonderful face," he said. "I never met my great-grandmother. My own grandmother looks about as old as my mother. They might be sisters."

"When he's done with you," Fayette said, his enthusiasm becoming a bit tiresome, "you and your *great-grandmother* will look like sisters!"

When she went home that evening, taking a late pay metro from the school, she wondered just exactly what she was doing. Throughout her high school years, she had cut herself off from most of her fellow students; the closest she had come to friendship had been occasional banter while sitting at the mods with John Lockwood, waiting for instructors to arrive. Now she actually liked Fayette, and strange Leroux, whose hands were thin and pale and strong and cool. Leroux was a PPC, but obviously his parents had different tastes; was he a superwhiz? Nobody had said so; perhaps it was a matter of honor among PPCs that they pretended not to care about their classifications.

Reena was friendly and supportive, but still distant.

As Letitia walked up the stairs, across the porch and through the door of their home, setting her keyboard down by the closet, she saw the edge of a news broadcast in the living room. Nobody was watching; she surmised everybody was in the kitchen.

From this angle, the announcer appeared translucent and blue, ghostly. As Letitia walked around to the premium angle, the announcer solidified, a virtual goddess of Oriental-negroid features with high cheek-

bones, straight golden hair and copper-bronze skin. Letitia didn't care
what she looked like; what she was saying had attracted her attention.

"—revelations made today that as many as one-fourth of all PPCs in-
ceived between sixteen and seventeen years ago may be possessors of a defective chromosome sequence known as T56-WA 5659. Originally part
of an intelligence enhancement macrobox used in ramping creativity and
mathematical ability, T56-WA 5659 was refined and made a standard
option in almost all pre-planned children. The effects of this defective
sequence are not yet known, but at least twenty children in our city have
already died. They all suffered from initial symptoms similar to grand mal
epilepsy. Nationwide casualties are as yet unknown. The Rifkin Society
is charging government regulatory agencies with a wholesale cover-up."

Letitia squatted on her knees before the image, chin in hand,
stunned.

"The Parental Pre-Natal Design Administration has advised parents
of PPC children with this incept to immediately contact your medicals
and design specialists for advice and treatment. Younger children may
be eligible to receive wholebody retroviral therapy. For more detailed
information, please refer to our LitVid on-line at this moment, and
call—"

Letitia turned and saw her mother watching with a kind of grim satisfaction. When she noticed her daughter's shocked expression, she suddenly appeared sad. "How unfortunate," she said. "I wonder how far it
will go."

Letitia did not eat much dinner. Nor did she sleep more than a couple of hours that night. The weekend seemed to stretch on forever.

Leroux compared the laserfoam sculptures to her face, turning her
chin this way and that with gentle hands before the green room mirror.
As Leroux worked to test the various molds on Letitia, humming softly
to himself, the rest of the drama group rehearsed a scene that did not require her presence. When they were done, Reena walked into the green
room and stood behind them, watching. Letitia smiled stiffly through the
hastily applied sheets and mounds of skinlike plastic.

"You're going to look great," Reena said.

"I'm going to look *old*," Letitia said, trying for a joke.

"I hope you aren't worried about that," Reena said. "Nobody cares, really. They all like you. Even Edna."

"I'm not worried," Letitia said.

Leroux pulled off the pieces and laid them carefully in a box. "Just about got it," he said. "I'm so good I could make *Reena* look old if she'd let me."

The implication, rather than the meaning, was embarrassingly obvious. Reena blushed and stared angrily at Leroux. Leroux caught her stare, looked between them, and said, "Well, I could." Reena could not argue without sinking them all deeper. Letitia blinked, then decided to let them off this particular hook. "She wouldn't look like a grandmother, though. I'll be a much better old lady."

"Of course," Leroux said, picking up his box and the sculptures. He walked to the door, a mad headsman. "Like your great-grandmother."

For a long silent moment, Reena and Letitia faced each other alone in the green room. The old incandescent makeup lights glared around the cracked mirror, casting a pearly glow on the white walls behind them. "You're a good actress," Reena said. "It really doesn't matter what you look like."

"Thank you."

"Sometimes I wish I looked like somebody in my family," Reena said.

Without thinking, Letitia said, "But you're beautiful." And she meant it. Reena *was* beautiful; with her Levantine darkness and long black hair, small sharp chin, large hazel-colored almond eyes and thin, ever-so-slightly bowed nose, she was simply lovely, with the kind of face and bearing and intelligence that two or three generations before would have moved her into entertainment, or pushed her into the social circles of the rich and famous. Behind the physical beauty was a sparkle of reserved wit, and something gentle. PPCs were healthier, felt better, and their minds, on the average, were more subtle, more balanced. Letitia did not feel inferior, however; not this time.

Something magic touched them. The previous awkwardness, and her deft destruction of that awkwardness, had moved them into a period of charmed conversation. Neither could offend the other; without words, that was a given.

"My parents are beautiful, too. I'm second generation," Reena said.

"Why would you *want* to look any different?"

"I don't, I suppose. I'm happy with the way I look. But I don't look much like my mother or my father. Oh, complexion, color, hair, eyes, that sort of thing. . . . Still, my mother wasn't happy with her own face. She didn't get along well with my grandmother. . . . She blamed her for not matching her face with her personality." Reena smiled. "It's all rather silly."

"Some people are never happy," Letitia observed.

Reena stepped forward and leaned over to face Letitia's mirror image. "How do you feel, looking like your grandmother?"

Letitia bit her lip. "Until you asked me to join, I don't think I ever knew." She told about her mother giving her the album, and looking at herself in the mirror—though she did not describe being naked—and comparing herself with the old pictures.

"I think that's called an epiphany," Reena said. "It must have been nice. I'm glad I asked you, then, even if I was stupid."

"Did you . . ." Letitia paused. The period of charm was fading, regrettably; she did not know whether this question would be taken as she meant it. "Did you ask me to give me a chance to stop being so silly and stand-offish?"

"No," Reena said steadily. "I asked because we needed an old lady."

They laughed suddenly, and the charmed moment was gone, replaced by something steadier and longer-lasting: friendship. Letitia took Reena's hand and pressed it. "Thank you," she said.

"You're welcome." Then, with hardly a pause, Reena said, "At least you don't have to worry."

Letitia stared up at her, mouth open slightly, eyes searching.

"Got to go home now," Reena said. She squeezed Letitia's shoulder with more than gentle strength, revealing a physical anger or jealousy that ran counter to all they had said and done. She turned and walked through the green room door, leaving Letitia alone to pick off a few scraps of latex and adhesive.

The disaster grew. Letitia listened to the news in her room late that night, whispers in her ear, projected ghosts of newscasters and doctors and scientists dancing before her eyes, telling her things she did not really understand, could only feel.

A monster walked through her generation, but it would not touch her.

Going to school on Monday, she saw students grouping in hallways before the bell, somber, talking in low voices, glancing at her as she passed. In her second period class, she learned from overheard conversation that Leroux had died during the weekend. Her throat seemed to close, and she held back a strangled cough.

"He was superwhiz," a tall, athletic girl told her neighbor. "They don't die, usually, they just blitz. But he died."

Letitia retreated to the old lavatory at the beginning of lunch break, found it empty, but did not stare into the mirror. She knew what she looked like and accepted it.

What she found difficult to accept was a new feeling inside her. The young Letitia was gone. She could not live on a battlefield and remain a child. She thought about slender, elfin Leroux, carrying her heads under his arms, touching her face with gentle, professional admiration. Strong, cool fingers. Her eyes filled but the tears would not fall, and she went to lunch empty, fearful, confused.

She did not apply for counseling, however. This was something she had to face on her own.

Nothing much happened the next few days. The rehearsals went smoothly in the evenings as the date of the play approached. She learned her lines easily enough. Her role had a sadness that matched her mood. On Wednesday evening, after rehearsal, she joined Reena and Fayette at a supermarket sandwich stand near the school. Letitia did not tell her parents she would be late; she felt the need to not be responsible to anybody but her immediate peers. Jane would be upset, she knew, but not for long; this was a *necessity*.

Neither Reena nor Fayette mentioned the troubles directly. They were fairylike in their gaiety. They kidded Letitia about having to do without makeup now, and it seemed funny, despite their hidden grief. They ate sandwiches and drank fruit sodas and talked about what they would be when they grew up.

"Things didn't used to be so easy," Fayette said. "Kids didn't have so many options. Schools weren't very efficient at training for the real world; they were academic."

"Learning was slower," Letitia said.

"So were the kids," Reena said, tossing off an irresponsible grin.

"I resent that," Letitia said. Then, together, they all said, "*I don't deny it, I just resent it!*" Their laughter caught the attention of an older couple sitting in a corner. Even if the man and woman were not angry, Letitia wanted them to be, and she bowed her head down, giggling into her straw, snucking bubbles up her nose and choking. Reena made a disapproving face and Fayette covered his mouth, snorting with laughter.

"You could paste rubber all over your face," Fayette suggested.

"I'd look like Frankenstein's monster, not an old woman," Letitia said.

"So what's the difference?" Reena said.

"Really, you guys," Letitia said. "You're acting your age."

"Don't have to act," Fayette said. "Just *be.*"

"I wish we could act our age," Reena said.

Not once did they mention Leroux, but it was as if he sat beside them the whole time, sharing their levity.

It was the closest thing to a wake they could have.

"Have you gone to see your designer, your medical?" Letitia asked Reena behind the stage curtains. The lights were off. Student stagehands moved muslin walls on dollies. Fresh paint smells filled the air.

"No," Reena said. "I'm not worried. I have a different incept."

"Really?"

She nodded briskly. "It's okay. If there was any problem, I wouldn't be here. Don't worry." And nothing more was said.

The night of dress rehearsal came. Letitia put on her own makeup, drawing pencil lines and applying color and shadow; she had practiced and found herself reasonably adept at aging. With her great-grandmother's photograph before her, she mimicked the jowls she would have in her later years, drew laugh lines around her lips, and completed the effect with a smelly old gray wig dug out of a prop box.

The actors gathered for a prerehearsal inspection by Miss Darcy. They seemed quite adult now, dressed in their period costumes, tall and handsome. Letitia didn't mind standing out. Being an old woman gave her special status.

"This time, just relax, do it smooth," said Miss Darcy. "Everybody expects you to flub your lines, so you'll probably do them all perfectly.

We'll have an audience, but they're here to forgive our mistakes, not laugh at them. This one," Miss Darcy said, pausing, "is for Mr. Leroux."

They all nodded solemnly.

"Tomorrow, when we put on the first show, that's going to be for you."

They took their places in the wings. Letitia stood behind Reena, who would be first on stage. Reena shot her a quick smile, nervous.

"How's your stomach?" she whispered.

"Where's the sick bag?" Letitia asked, pretending to gag herself with a finger.

"TB," Reena accused lightly.

"RC," Letitia replied. They shook hands firmly.

The curtain went up. The auditorium was half filled with parents and friends and relatives. Letitia's parents were out there. The darkness beyond the stagelights seemed so profound it should have been filled with stars and nebulae. Would her small voice reach that far?

The recorded music before the first act came to its quiet end. Reena made a move to go on stage, then stopped. Letitia nudged her. "Come on."

Reena pivoted to look at her, face cocked to one side, and Letitia saw a large tear dripping from her left eye. Fascinated, she watched the tear fall in slow motion down Reena's cheek and spot the satin of her gown.

Reena's lips twitched. "I'm sorry," she whispered. "I can't do it now. Tell. Tell."

Horrified, Letitia reached out, tried to stop her from falling, to lift her, push her back into place, but Reena was too heavy and she could not stop her descent, only slow it. Reena's feet kicked out like a horse's, bruising Letitia's legs, all in apparent silence, and her eyes fluttered bright and empty and wet, showing the whites. Then Reena's legs stopped kicking.

Letitia bent over her, hands raised, afraid to touch her, afraid not to, unaware she was shrieking.

Fayette and Edna Corman stood behind her, equally helpless.

Reena lay like a twisted doll, face upturned to the flies, eyes moving slowly to Letitia, vibrating, becoming still.

"Not you!" Letitia screamed, and barely heard the commotion in the audience. "Please, God, not her!"

Fayette backed away and Miss Darcy came into the light, grabbing Letitia's shoulders. She shook free.

"Not her," Letitia sobbed. The medicals arrived and surrounded Reena, blocking her from the eyes of all around. Miss Darcy firmly, almost brutally, pushed her students from the stage and herded them into the green room. Her face was stiff as a mask, eyes stark in the paleness.

"We have to *do* something!" Letitia said, holding up her hands, beseeching.

"Get control of yourself," Miss Darcy said sharply. "Everything's being done that can be done."

Fayette said, "What about the play?"

Everyone stared at him.

"Sorry," he said, lip quivering. "I'm an idiot."

Jane, Donald, and Roald came to the green room and Letitia hugged her mother fiercely, eyes shut tight, burying her face in Jane's shoulder. They escorted her outside, where a few students and parents still milled about in the early evening. "We should go home," Jane said.

"We have to stay here and find out if she's all right." Letitia pushed away from Jane's arms and looked at the people. "They're so frightened. I know they are. She's frightened, too. I saw her. She told me—" Her voice hitched. "She told me—"

"We'll stay for a little while," her father said. He walked off to talk to another man. The man shook his head, they parted. Roald stood away from them, hands stuffed into his pockets, dismayed, young, uncomfortable.

"All right," Donald said a few minutes later. "We're not going to learn anything tonight. Let's go home."

This time, Letitia did not protest. Home, she locked herself in her bedroom. She did not need to know. She had seen it happen; anything else was self-delusion.

Her father came to the door an hour later, rapped gently. Letitia came up from a troubled doze and got off the bed to let him in.

"We're very sorry," he said.

"Thanks," she murmured, returning to the bed. He sat beside her. She might have been eight or nine again; she looked around the room, at toys and books, knickknacks.

"Your teacher, Miss Darcy, called. She said to tell you, Reena Cathcart died. She was dead by the time they got her to the hospital. Your mother and I have been watching the vids. A lot of children are sick now. A lot have died." He touched her head, patted the crown gently. "I think you know now why we wanted a natural child. There were risks."

"That's not fair," she said. "You didn't have us . . ." She hiccuped, "the way you did, because you thought there would be risks. You talk as if there's something *wrong* with them."

"Isn't there?" Donald asked, eyes suddenly flinty. "They're defective."

"They're my *friends!*" Letitia shouted.

"Please," Donald said, flinching.

She got to her knees on the bed, tears coming again. "There's nothing wrong with them! They're people! They're just sick, that's all."

"You're not making sense," Donald said.

"I talked to her," Letitia said. "She must have known. You can't just say there's something wrong with them. That isn't enough."

"Their parents should have known," Donald said, voice rising. "Letitia . . ."

"Leave me alone," she demanded. He stood up hastily, confused, and walked out, closing the door. She lay back on the bed, wondering what Reena had wanted her to say, and to whom.

"I'll do it," she whispered.

In the morning, breakfast was eaten in silence. Roald picked at his cereal, glancing at the others with wide, concerned eyes. Letitia ate little, pushed away from the table, said, "I'm going to her funeral."

"We don't know her parents—" Jane said.

"I'm going."

Letitia went to only one funeral: Reena's. With a puzzled expression, she watched Reena's parents from across the grave, wondering about them, comparing them to Jane and Donald. She did not cry. She came home and wrote down the things she had thought.

That school year was the worst. One hundred and twelve students from the school died. Another two hundred became very ill.

John Fayette died.

The drama class continued, but no plays were presented. The school was quiet. Many students had been withdrawn from classes; Letitia watched the hysteria mount, listened to rumors that it was a plague, not a PPC error.

It was not a plague.

Across the nation, two million children became ill. One million died.

Letitia read, without really absorbing the truth all at once, that it was the worst disaster in the history of the United States. Riots destroyed PPC centers. Women carrying PPC babies demanded abortions. The Rifkin Society became a political force of considerable influence.

Each day, after school, listening to the news, everything about her existence seemed trivial. Her family was healthy. They were growing up normally.

Edna Corman approached her in school toward the end of one day, two weeks before graduation. "Can we talk?" she asked. "Some place quiet."

"Sure," Letitia said. They had not become close friends, but she found Edna Corman tolerable. Letitia took her into the old bathroom and they stood surrounded by the echoing white tiles.

"You know, everybody, I mean the older people, they stare at me," Edna said. "Like I'm going to fall over any minute. It's really bad. I don't think I'm going to get sick, but . . . it's like people are afraid to touch me."

"Yeah," Letitia said.

"Why is that?" Edna said, voice trembling.

"I don't know," Letitia said.

Edna stood before her, hands limp. "Was it our fault?" she asked.

"No. You know that."

"Please tell me."

"Tell you what?"

"What we can do to make it right."

Letitia looked at her for a moment, and then extended her arms, took her by the shoulders, drew her closer, and hugged her. "Remember," she said.

Five days before graduation, Letitia asked Rutger if she could give a speech at the ceremonies. Rutger sat behind his desk, folded his hands, and said, "Why?"

"Because there are things nobody's saying," Letitia told him. "They should be said. If nobody else will say them, then . . ." She swallowed hard. "Maybe I can."

He regarded her dubiously. "You really think there's something important that you can say?"

She faced him down. Nodded.

"Write the speech," he said. "Show it to me."

She pulled a piece of paper out of her pocket. He read it carefully, shook his head — she thought at first in denial — and then handed it back to her.

▼

Waiting in the wings to go on stage, Letitia Blakely listened to the low murmur of the young crowd in the auditorium. She avoided the spot near the curtain.

Rutger acted as master of ceremonies. The proceedings were somber. She began to feel she was making a terrible mistake. She was too young to say these things; it would sound horribly awkward, even childish.

Rutger made his opening remarks, then introduced her and motioned for her to come on stage. Letitia deliberately walked to the spot near the curtain, paused, closed her eyes and took a deep breath, as if to infuse herself with whatever remained there of Reena. She walked past Miss Darcy, who seemed to glare at her.

Her throat closed tight. She rubbed her neck, blinked at the bright lights on the catwalk overhead, tried to see the faces beyond the glare, smudges in great darkness. She glanced out of the corner of her eye and saw Miss Darcy nodding, *Go ahead.*

"This has been a bad time for all of us," Letitia began, voice high and scratchy. She cleared her throat. "I've lost a lot a friends and so have you. Maybe you've lost sons and daughters. I think, looking at me, you can tell I'm not designed. I don't have to wonder whether I'll get sick and die. But I . . ." She cleared her throat again. It was not getting easier. "I thought someone like me could tell you something important.

"People have made mistakes, bad mistakes. But you are not the mistakes. I mean . . . they weren't mistaken to make you. I can only dream about doing some of the things you'll do. Some of you are made to live in space for a long time, and I can't do that. Some of you will think things I can't, and go places I won't . . . travel to see the stars. We're different in a lot of ways, but I just thought it was important to tell you . . ." She wasn't following the prepared speech. She couldn't. "I don't care what the others say. We love you. You are very important. Please don't forget that. And don't forget what it costs us all."

The silence was complete. She felt like slinking away. Instead, she straightened, thanked them, hearing not a word, not a restless whisper, then bowed her head from the catwalk glare and the interstellar darkness beyond.

Miss Darcy, stiff and formal, stretched out her arm as Letitia passed by. They shook hands firmly, and Letitia saw, for the first time, that Miss Darcy looked upon her as an equal.

Letitia stood backstage while the ceremonies continued, examining the old wood floor, the curtains, counterweights, and flies, the catwalk.

It seemed very long ago, she had dreamed what she felt now, this unspecified love, not for family, not for herself. Love for something she could not have known back then; love for children not her own, yet hers none the less. Brothers.

Sisters.

Family.

CHARACTERS GREAT AND
SMALL IN SF: "SISTERS"

by Greg Bear

▼

In "Sisters," the viewpoint character, Letitia Blakely, is familiar
enough—an adolescent girl, struggling with painful problems. In outline,
"Sisters" reads much like a contemporary story of growing up—with a few
words and some set dressing changed to indicate the near future. Yet my
intent in this story—as in many of my stories—is to deal with characters
within larger characters, to explore how individuals react to change within
a larger setting.

If anything has become more and more clear in the past five hundred years, it is that men and women are not the measure of all things,
but the *measurers*. A richer, more powerful literature must take into account the nature of larger entities than human individuals.

There's nothing that stops science fiction—often dismissed as merely
a literature of ideas—from also being a literature of character, so long as
readers understand a larger definition of character. Character is not limited to the nature and actions of a single individual, or even a group of
individuals. Character may also describe a nation, a culture, a species, a
world—or a universe.

For me, the story of character is not limited to the Jamesian small
group of individuals in an unchanging social setting, with all change aris-
ing from individually willed action. Yet since James this has been touted
as the datum of literature—and not without reason.

Human readers (the only kind I've encountered) enjoy reading about
people not greatly unlike themselves. We enjoy watching the lives of others we can relate to. For relaxation, or a historical refresher, we also enjoy
reading about the mores and social patterns of the past, in Dickens and
Austen and Joyce, or Tolstoy and Hemingway and Dostoevsky. But what
involves us most of all is fiction that directly or indirectly models our present situation and stimulates thought about the choices we have and the

decisions we make. We enjoy discovering patterns and relationships between strangers and ourselves, and between different societies in different times.

In a sense, science fiction takes its cues from historical fiction, but with no specific arrow of time. The future as well as the past is open. (Alternate times and realities may qualify as well!)

Since there are few if any societies where change from outside—forced by history, the weather, or other natural phenomena—does not have a major impact on individual lives, to focus on change coming about solely through the willed actions of the individual is a very artificial limitation. It produces attractive and moving works, but these works are no more than an aspect, perhaps just a genre. At their worst, they give a false sense of comfort. Even at their best, they do not define the range of literature.

Most of my stories draw the lives of characters *within* larger characters, exploring how individuals react to change within a larger setting. Science fiction stories at their most ambitious model changes in nations, in cultures, even in species and worlds.

Writing science fiction puts added burdens on me as a storyteller. I have to do more than just closely observe: I have to extrapolate. This takes me into dangerous territory, since to extrapolate, I must try to understand the laws and forces that direct the greater characters. I see sociology, psychology, technology, and history as interrelated subsets of biology. This is far from the static and isolating world view common in many religions and much philosophy; it is also far from the gooey and shapeless "holistic" approach of New Age thinking, where anything goes, and the universe caters to our personal whims.

Just as a sharp observer of individual character strives not to be guided by sentiment and personal animus, an observer of larger characters must adopt a similar objectivity. In my stories, individuals are often shaped by environments that may be only marginally familiar, if at all, to the average reader. Bringing the environment to life is important, and inevitably takes some of the center spotlight away from so-called "pure" exploration of character and motive. But it returns the focus with additional rewards by giving insight into how characters shape and are shaped.

No character great or small lives in splendid isolation. Everything an individual does reflects back, and the mirror is not just society, but nature. Discovering how a larger nature works in a story is as thrilling (and dangerous) to my characters as internal discovery.

Letitia's world has changed in significant ways, and offers her challenges no modern young woman has to face. Facing those challenges reveals her inner self as no contemporary setting can.

Moving between the internal world, the social world, and the external world breaks down the barriers between. Inside becomes outside. There is no mirror, after all.

Letitia Blakely sees herself as ugly and handicapped because her parents have chosen to give her their own natural genotypes, rather than go with a trend and engage in biological engineering. A medical mistake of immense proportions is about to decimate her "enhanced" classmates, and she will escape through no personal action, but by the *inaction* of her parents. The heart of the story is not individual action, but a deeper blossoming—an epiphany.

Letitia's story unfolds within a larger story: the story of Reena and those like her, but also the story of a society about to be badly burned in its exploration of what is possible. (Note that I'm not at all concerned with "what is permissible.")

Letitia's heroism comes from refusing to place blame on the victims, or even to see deep differences between victims and survivors. She is not "smug," she is not limited by horrid prejudices from old half-baked faiths and philosophies. In her deepest self she finds a resonance with those who she once thought more fortunate than her, and soon realizes are not, and she sees beyond small differences to find great similarities.

By the story's end, she understands that reaching out for something new is not necessarily evil, however much failure may hurt and even kill.

Some may see a real weakness in the story. Blame is not placed squarely on any group. The doctors and scientists who screw up are not brought on stage. There is no awful conspiracy promoted by an evil government or group. The tragedy is not pinned to the shoulders of any scapegoat, who is then belled and sent off into the wilderness to be satisfactorily devoured by wolves. This is not a story about the horrors of eugenics, or the revenge of society on "mad" doctors.

It's about coming of age, for an individual—the small character—and for a society, the larger character. Both are adolescents. The tragedy is only heightened when Letitia realizes her friends were *not* monstrous mistakes—they were pioneers.

RACHEL IN LOVE
by Pat Murphy

▼

It is a Sunday morning in summer and a small brown chimpanzee named Rachel sits on the living room floor of a remote ranch house on the edge of the Painted Desert. She is watching a Tarzan movie on television. Her hairy arms are wrapped around her knees and she rocks back and forth with suppressed excitement. She knows that her father would say that she's too old for such childish amusements — but since Aaron is still sleeping, he can't chastise her.

On the television, Tarzan has been trapped in a bamboo cage by a band of wicked pygmies. Rachel is afraid that he won't escape in time to save Jane from the ivory smugglers who hold her captive. The movie cuts to Jane, who is tied up in the back of a jeep, and Rachel whimpers softly to herself. She knows better than to howl: She peeked into her father's bedroom earlier, and he was still in bed. Aaron doesn't like her to howl when he is sleeping.

When the movie breaks for a commercial, Rachel goes to her father's room. She is ready for breakfast and she wants him to get up. She tiptoes to the bed to see if he is awake.

His eyes are open and he is staring at nothing. His face is pale and his lips are a purplish color. Dr. Aaron Jacobs, the man Rachel calls father, is not asleep. He is dead, having died in the night of a heart attack.

When Rachel shakes him, his head rocks back and forth in time with her shaking, but his eyes do not blink and he does not breathe. She places his hand on her head, nudging him so that he will waken and stroke her. He does not move. When she leans toward him, his hand falls to dangle limply over the edge of the bed.

In the breeze from the open bedroom window, the fine wisps of gray hair that he had carefully combed over his bald spot each morning shift and flutter, exposing the naked scalp. In the other room, elephants trumpet as they stampede across the jungle to rescue Tarzan. Rachel whimpers softly, but her father does not move.

Rachel backs away from her father's body. In the living room, Tarzan is swinging across the jungle on vines, going to save Jane. Rachel ignores the television. She prowls through the house as if searching for comfort—stepping into her own small bedroom, wandering through her father's laboratory. From the cages that line the walls, white rats stare at her with hot red eyes. A rabbit hops across its cage, making a series of slow dull thumps, like a feather pillow tumbling down a flight of stairs.

She thinks that perhaps she made a mistake. Perhaps her father is just sleeping. She returns to the bedroom, but nothing has changed. Her father lies open-eyed on the bed. For a long time, she huddles beside his body, clinging to his hand.

He is the only person she has ever known. He is her father, her teacher, her friend. She cannot leave him alone.

The afternoon sun blazes through the window, and still Aaron does not move. The room grows dark, but Rachel does not turn on the lights. She is waiting for Aaron to wake up. When the moon rises, its silver light shines through the window to cast a bright rectangle on the far wall.

Outside, somewhere in the barren land surrounding the ranch house, a coyote lifts its head to the rising moon and wails, a thin sound that is as lonely as a train whistling through an abandoned station. Rachel joins in with a desolate howl of loneliness and grief. Aaron lies still and Rachel knows that he is dead.

When Rachel was younger, she had a favorite bedtime story. *Where did I come from?* she would ask Aaron, using the abbreviated gestures of ASL, American Sign Language. *Tell me again.*

"You're too old for bedtime stories," Aaron would say.

Please, she would sign. *Tell me the story.*

In the end, he always relented and told her. "Once upon a time, there was a little girl named Rachel," he would say. "She was a pretty girl, with long golden hair like a princess in a fairy tale. She lived with her father and her mother and they were all very happy."

Rachel would snuggle contentedly beneath her blankets. The story, like any good fairy tale, had elements of tragedy. In the story, Rachel's father worked at a university, studying the workings of the brain and charting the electric fields that the nervous impulses of an active brain produced. But the other researchers at the university didn't understand Rachel's father; they distrusted his research and cut off his funding. (During this portion of the story, Aaron's voice took on a bitter edge.) So he left the university and took his wife and daughter to the desert, where he could work in peace.

He continued his research and determined that each individual brain produced its own unique pattern of fields, as characteristic as a fingerprint. (Rachel found this part of the story quite dull, but Aaron insisted on including it.) The shape of this Electric Mind, as he called it, was determined by habitual patterns of thoughts and emotions. Record the Electric Mind, he postulated, and you could capture an individual's personality.

Then one sunny day, the doctor's wife and beautiful daughter went for a drive. A truck barreling down a winding cliffside road lost its brakes and met the car head-on, killing both the girl and her mother. (Rachel clung to Aaron's hand during this part of the story, frightened by the sudden evil twist of fortune.)

But though Rachel's body had died, all was not lost. In his desert lab, the doctor had recorded the electrical patterns produced by his daughter's brain. The doctor had been experimenting with the use of external magnetic fields to impose the patterns from one animal onto the brain of another. From an animal supply house, he obtained a young chimpanzee. He used a mixture of norepinephrin-based transmitter substances to boost the speed of neural processing in the chimp's brain, and then he imposed the pattern of his daughter's mind on the brain of this young chimp, combining the two after his own fashion, saving his daughter in his own way. In the chimp's brain was all that remained of Rachel Jacobs.

The doctor named the chimp Rachel and raised her as his own daughter. Because the limitations of the chimpanzee larynx made speech very difficult, he instructed her in ASL. He taught her to read and to write. They were good friends, the best of companions.

By this point in the story, Rachel was usually asleep. But it didn't matter—she knew the ending. The doctor, whose name was Aaron Jacobs, and the chimp named Rachel lived happily ever after.

Rachel likes fairy tales and she likes happy endings. She has the mind of a teenage girl, but the innocent heart of a young chimp.

▼

Sometimes, when Rachel looks at her gnarled brown fingers, they seem alien, wrong, out of place. She remembers having small, pale, delicate hands. Memories lie upon memories, layers upon layers, like the sedimentary rocks of the desert buttes.

Rachel remembers a blond woman who smelled sweetly of perfume. On a Halloween long ago, this woman (who was, in these memories, Rachel's mother) painted Rachel's fingernails bright red because Rachel was dressed as a gypsy and gypsies liked red. Rachel remembers the woman's hands: white hands with faintly blue veins hidden just beneath the skin, neatly clipped nails painted rose pink.

But Rachel also remembers another mother and another time. Her mother was dark and hairy and smelled sweetly of overripe fruit. She and Rachel lived in a wire cage in a room filled with chimps and she hugged Rachel to her hairy breast whenever any people came into the room. Rachel's mother groomed Rachel constantly, picking delicately through her fur in search of lice that she never found.

Memories upon memories: jumbled and confused, like random pictures clipped from magazines, a bright collage that makes no sense. Rachel remembers cages: cold wire mesh beneath her feet, the smell of fear around her. A man in a white lab coat took her from the arms of her hairy mother and pricked her with needles. She could hear her mother howling, but she could not escape from the man.

Rachel remembers a junior high school dance where she wore a new dress: She stood in a dark corner of the gym for hours, pretending to admire the crepe paper decorations because she felt too shy to search among the crowd for her friends.

She remembers when she was a young chimp: She huddled with five other adolescent chimps in the stuffy freight compartment of a train, frightened by the alien smells and sounds.

She remembers gym class: gray lockers and ugly gym suits that revealed her skinny legs. The teacher made everyone play softball, even Rachel who was unathletic and painfully shy. Rachel at bat, standing at the plate, was terrified to be the center of attention. "Easy out," said the catcher, a hard-edged girl who ran with the wrong crowd and always smelled of cigarette smoke. When Rachel swung at the ball and missed, the outfielders filled the air with malicious laughter.

Rachel's memories are as delicate and elusive as the dusty moths that
dance among the rabbit brush and sage. Memories of her girlhood never
linger; they land for an instant, then take flight, leaving Rachel feeling
abandoned and alone.

Rachel leaves Aaron's body where it is, but closes his eyes and pulls
the sheet up over his head. She does not know what else to do. Each day
she waters the garden and picks some greens for the rabbits. Each day,
she cares for the rats, bringing them food and refilling their water bot-
tles. The weather is cool, and Aaron's body does not smell too bad,
though by the end of the week, a wide line of ants runs from the bed to
the open window.

At the end of the first week, on a moonlit evening, Rachel decides
to let the animals go free. She releases the rabbits one by one, climbing
on a stepladder to reach down into the cage and lift each placid bunny
out. She carries each one to the back door, holding it for a moment and
stroking the soft warm fur. Then she sets the animal down and nudges it
in the direction of the green grass that grows around the perimeter of the
fenced garden.

The rats are more difficult to deal with. She manages to wrestle the
large rat cage off the shelf, but it is heavier than she thought it would be.
Though she slows its fall, it lands on the floor with a crash and the rats
scurry to and fro within. She shoves the cage across the linoleum floor,
sliding it down the hall, over the doorsill, and onto the back patio. When
she opens the cage door, rats burst out like popcorn from a popper, white
in the moonlight and dashing in all directions.

Once, while Aaron was taking a nap, Rachel walked along the dirt
track that led to the main highway. She hadn't planned on going far.
She just wanted to see what the highway looked like, maybe hide near
the mailbox and watch a car drive past. She was curious about the outside world and her fleeting fragmentary memories did not satisfy that
curiosity.

She was halfway to the mailbox when Aaron came roaring up in his
old jeep. "Get in the car," he shouted at her. "Right now!" Rachel had

never seen him so angry. She cowered in the jeep's passenger seat, covered with dust from the road, unhappy that Aaron was so upset. He didn't speak until they got back to the ranch house, and then he spoke in a low voice, filled with bitterness and suppressed rage.

"You don't want to go out there," he said. "You wouldn't like it out there. The world is filled with petty, narrow-minded, stupid people. They wouldn't understand you. And anyone they don't understand, they want to hurt. They hate anyone who's different. If they know that you're different, they punish you, hurt you. They'd lock you up and never let you go."

He looked straight ahead, staring through the dirty windshield. "It's not like the shows on TV, Rachel," he said in a softer tone. "It's not like the stories in books."

He looked at her then and she gestured frantically. *I'm sorry. I'm sorry.* "I can't protect you out there," he said. "I can't keep you safe."

Rachel took his hand in both of hers. He relented then, stroking her head. "Never do that again," he said. "Never."

Aaron's fear was contagious. Rachel never again walked along the dirt track and sometimes she had dreams about bad people who wanted to lock her in a cage.

Two weeks after Aaron's death, a black-and-white police car drives slowly up to the house. When the policemen knock on the door, Rachel hides behind the couch in the living room. They knock again, try the knob, then open the door, which she had left unlocked.

Suddenly frightened, Rachel bolts from behind the couch, bounding toward the back door. Behind her, she hears one man yell, "My God! It's a gorilla!"

By the time he pulls his gun, Rachel has run out the back door and away into the hills. From the hills she watches as an ambulance drives up and two men in white take Aaron's body away. Even after the ambulance and the police car drive away, Rachel is afraid to go back to the house. Only after sunset does she return.

Just before dawn the next morning, she wakens to the sound of a truck jouncing down the dirt road. She peers out the window to see a pale green pickup. Sloppily stenciled in white on the door are the words:

PRIMATE RESEARCH CENTER. Rachel hesitates as the truck pulls up in front of the house. By the time she decides to flee, two men are getting out of the truck. One of them carries a rifle.

She runs out the back door and heads for the hills, but she is only halfway to hiding when she hears a sound like a sharp intake of breath and feels a painful jolt in her shoulder. Suddenly, her legs give way and she is tumbling backward down the sandy slope, dust coating her red-brown fur, her howl becoming a whimper, then fading to nothing at all. She falls into the blackness of sleep.

The sun is up. Rachel lies in a cage in the back of the pickup truck. She is partially conscious and she feels a tingling in her hands and feet. Nausea grips her stomach and bowels. Her body aches.

Rachel can blink, but otherwise she can't move. From where she lies, she can see only the wire mesh of the cage and the side of the truck. When she tries to turn her head, the burning in her skin intensifies. She lies still, wanting to cry out, but unable to make a sound. She can only blink slowly, trying to close out the pain. But the burning and nausea stay.

The truck jounces down a dirt road, then stops. It rocks as the men get out. The doors slam. Rachel hears the tailgate open.

A woman's voice: "Is that the animal the county sheriff wanted us to pick up?" A woman peers into the cage. She wears a white lab coat and her brown hair is tied back in a single braid. Around her eyes, Rachel can see small wrinkles, etched by years of living in the desert. The woman doesn't look evil. Rachel hopes that the woman will save her from the men in the truck.

"Yeah. It should be knocked out for a least another half hour. Where do you want it?"

"Bring it into the lab where we had the rhesus monkeys. I'll keep it there until I have an empty cage in the breeding area."

Rachel's cage scrapes across the bed of the pickup. She feels each bump and jar as a new pain. The man swings the cage onto a cart and the woman pushes the cart down a concrete corridor. Rachel watches the walls pass just a few inches from her nose.

The lab contains rows of cages in which small animals move sleepily. In a sudden stark light of the overhead fluorescent bulbs, the eyes of white rats gleam red.

With the help of one of the men from the truck, the woman man-handles Rachel onto a lab table. The metal surface is cold and hard, painful against Rachel's skin. Rachel's body is not under her control; her limbs will not respond. She is still frozen by the tranquilizer, able to watch, but that is all. She cannot protest or plead for mercy.

Rachel watches with growing terror as the woman pulls on rubber gloves and fills a hypodermic needle with a clear solution. "Mark down that I'm giving her the standard test for tuberculosis; this eyelid should be checked before she's moved in with the others. I'll add thiabendazole to her feed for the next few days to clean out any intestinal worms. And I suppose we might as well deflea her as well," the woman says. The man grunts in response.

Expertly, the woman closes one of Rachel's eyes. With her open eye, Rachel watches the hypodermic needle approach. She feels a sharp pain in her eyelid. In her mind, she is howling, but the only sound she can manage is a breathy sigh.

The woman sets the hypodermic aside and begins methodically spraying Rachel's fur with a cold, foul-smelling liquid. A drop strikes Rachel's eye and burns. Rachel blinks, but she cannot lift a hand to rub her eye. The woman treats Rachel with casual indifference, chatting with the man as she spreads Rachel's legs and sprays her genitals. "Looks healthy enough. Good breeding stock."

Rachel moans, but neither person notices. At last, they finish their torture, put her in a cage, and leave the room. She closes her eyes, and the darkness returns.

Rachel dreams. She is back at home in the ranch house. It is night and she is alone. Outside, coyotes yip and howl. The coyote is the voice of the desert, wailing as the wind wails when it stretches itself thin to squeeze through a crack between two boulders. The people native to this land tell tales of Coyote, a god who was a trickster, unreliable, change-able, mercurial.

Rachel is restless, anxious, unnerved by the howling of the coyotes. She is looking for Aaron. In the dream, she knows he is not dead, and she searches the house for him, wandering from his cluttered bedroom to her small room to the linoleum-tiled lab.

She is in the lab when she hears something tapping: a small dry scratching, like a windblown branch against the window, though no tree grows near the house and the night is still. Cautiously, she lifts the curtain to look out.

She looks into her own reflection: a pale oval face, long blond hair. The hand that holds the curtain aside is smooth and white with carefully clipped fingernails. But something is wrong. Superimposed on the reflection is another face peering through the glass: a pair of dark brown eyes, a chimp face with red-brown hair and jug-handle ears. She sees her own reflection and she sees the outsider; the two images merge and blur. She is afraid, but she can't drop the curtain and shut the ape face out.

She is a chimp looking in through the cold, bright windowpane; she is a girl looking out; she is a girl looking in; she is an ape looking out. She is afraid and the coyotes are howling all around.

Rachel opens her eyes and blinks until the world comes into focus. The pain and tingling have retreated, but she still feels a little sick. Her left eye aches. When she rubs it, she feels a raised lump on the eyelid where the woman pricked her. She lies on the floor of a wire mesh cage. The room is hot and and the air is thick with the smell of animals.

In the cage beside her is another chimp, an older animal with scruffy dark brown fur. He sits with his arms wrapped around his knees, rocking back and forth, back and forth. His head is down. As he rocks, he murmurs to himself, a meaningless cooing that goes on and on. On his scalp, Rachel can see a gleam of metal: a permanently implanted electrode protrudes from a shaven patch. Rachel makes a soft questioning sound, but the other chimp will not look up.

Rachel's own cage is just a few feet square. In one corner is a bowl of monkey pellets. A water bottle hangs on the side of the cage. Rachel ignores the food, but drinks thirstily.

Sunlight streams through the windows, sliced into small sections by the wire mesh that covers the glass. She tests her cage door, rattling it gently at first, then harder. It is securely latched. The gaps in the mesh are too small to admit her hand. She can't reach out to work the latch.

The other chimp continues to rock back and forth. When Rachel rattles the mesh of her cage and howls, he lifts his head wearily and looks at her. His red-rimmed eyes are unfocused; she can't be sure he sees her.

Hello, she gestures tentatively. *What's wrong?*

He blinks at her in the dim light. *Hurt,* he signs in ASL. He reaches up to touch the electrode, fingering skin that is already raw from repeated rubbing.

Who hurt you? she asks. He stares at her blankly and she repeats the question. *Who hurt you?*

Men, he signs.

As if on cue, there is the click of a latch and the door to the lab opens. A bearded man in a white coat steps in, followed by a clean-shaven man in a suit. The bearded man seems to be showing the other man around the lab. ". . . Only preliminary testing, so far," the bearded man is saying. "We've been hampered by a shortage of chimps trained in ASL." The two men stop in front of the old chimp's cage. "This old fellow is from the Oregon center. Funding for the language program was cut back and some of the animals were dispersed to other programs." The old chimp huddles at the back of the cage, eyeing the bearded man with suspicion.

Hungry? the bearded man signs to the old chimp. He holds up an orange where the old chimp can see it.

Give orange, the old chimp gestures. He holds out his hand, but comes no nearer to the wire mesh than he must to reach the orange. With the fruit in hand, he retreats to the back of his cage.

The bearded man continues. "This project will provide us with the first solid data on neural activity during use of sign language. But we really need greater access to chimps with advanced language skills. People are so damn protective of their animals."

"Is this one of yours?" the clean-shaven man asks, pointing to Rachel. She cowers in the back of the cage, as far from the wire mesh as she can get.

"No, not mine. She was someone's household pet, apparently. The county sheriff had us pick her up." The bearded man peers into her cage. Rachel does not move; she is terrified that he will somehow guess that she knows ASL. She stares at his hands and thinks about those hands putting an electrode through her skull. "I think she'll be put in breeding stock," the man says as he turns away.

Rachel watches them go, wondering at the cruelty of these people. Aaron was right: They want to punish her, they want to put an electrode in her head.

After the men are gone, she tries to draw the old chimp into conversation but he will not reply. He ignores her as he eats his orange. Then he returns to his former posture, hiding his head and rocking himself back and forth.

Rachel, hungry despite herself, samples one of the food pellets. It has a strange medicinal taste, and she puts it back in the bowl. She needs to pee, but there is no toilet and she cannot escape the cage. At last, unable to hold it, she pees in one corner of the cage. The urine flows through the wire mesh to soak the litter below, and the smell of warm piss fills her cage. Humiliated, frightened, her head aching, her skin itchy from the flea spray, Rachel watches as the sunlight creeps across the room.

The day wears on. Rachel samples her food again, but rejects it, preferring hunger to the strange taste. A black man comes and cleans the cages of the rabbits and rats. Rachel cowers in her cage and watches him warily, afraid that he will hurt her too.

When night comes, she is not tired. Outside, coyotes howl. Moonlight filters in through the high windows. She draws her legs up toward her body, then rests with her arms wrapped around her knees. Her father is dead, and she is a captive in a strange place. For a time, she whimpers softly, hoping to awaken from this nightmare and find herself at home in bed. When she hears the click of a key in the door to the room, she hugs herself more tightly.

A man in green coveralls pushes a cart filled with cleaning supplies into the room. He takes a broom from the cart, and begins sweeping the concrete floor. Over the rows of cages, she can see the top of his head bobbing in time with his sweeping. He works slowly and methodically, bending down to sweep carefully under each row of cages, making a neat pile of dust, dung, and food scraps in the center of the aisle.

The janitor's name is Jake. He is a middle-aged deaf man who has been employed by the Primate Research Center for the last seven years. He works the night shift. The personnel director at the Primate Research Center likes Jake because he fills the federal quota for handicapped employees, and because he has not asked for a raise in five years. There have been some complaints about Jake—his work is often sloppy—but never enough to merit firing the man.

Jake is an unambitious, somewhat slow-witted man. He likes the Primate Research Center because he works alone, which allows him to drink on the job. He is an easygoing man, and he likes the animals. Sometimes, he brings treats for them. Once, a lab assistant caught him feeding an apple to a pregnant rhesus monkey. The monkey was part of an experiment on the effect of dietary restrictions on fetal brain development, and the lab assistant warned Jake that he would be fired if he was ever caught interfering with the animals again. Jake still feeds the animals, but he is more careful about when he does it, and he has never been caught again.

As Rachel watches, the old chimp gestures to Jake. *Give banana*, the chimp signs. *Please banana.* Jake stops sweeping for a minute and reaches down to the bottom shelf of his cleaning cart. He returns with a banana and offers it to the old chimp. The chimp accepts the banana and leans against the mesh while Jake scratches his fur.

When Jake turns back to his sweeping, he catches sight of Rachel and sees that she is watching him. Emboldened by his kindness to the old chimp, Rachel timidly gestures to him. *Help me.*

Jake hesitates, then peers at her more closely. Both his eyes are shot with a fine lacework of red. His nose displays the broken blood vessels of someone who has been friends with the bottle for too many years. He needs a shave. But when he leans close, Rachel catches the scent of whiskey and tobacco. The smells remind her of Aaron and give her courage.

Please help me, Rachel signs. *I don't belong here.*

For the last hour, Jake has been drinking steadily. His view of the world is somewhat fuzzy. He stares at her blearily.

Rachel's fear that he will hurt her is replaced by the fear that he will leave her locked up and alone. Desperately she signs again. *Please, please, please. Help me. I don't belong here. Please help me go home.*

He watches her, considering the situation. Rachel does not move. She is afraid that any movement will make him leave. With a majestic speed dictated by his inebriation, Jake leans his broom on the row of cages behind him and steps toward Rachel's cage again. *You talk?* he signs.

I talk, she signs.

Where did you come from?

From my father's house, she signs. *Two men came and shot me and put me here. I don't know why. I don't know why they locked me in jail.*

Jake looks around, willing to be sympathetic, but puzzled by her talk of jail. *This isn't jail. This is a place where scientists raise monkeys.*

Rachel is indignant. *I am not a monkey. I am a girl.*

Jake studies her hairy body and her jug-handle ears. *You look like a monkey.*

Rachel shakes her head. *No. I am a girl.*

Rachel runs her hands back over her head, a very human gesture of annoyance and unhappiness. She signs sadly, *I don't belong here. Please let me out.*

Jake shifts his weight from foot to foot, wondering what to do. *I can't let you out. I'll get in big trouble.*

Just for a little while? Please?

Jake glances at his cart of supplies. He has to finish off this room and two corridors of offices before he can relax for the night.

Don't go, Rachel signs, guessing his thoughts.

I have work to do.

She looks at the cart, then suggests eagerly, *Let me out and I'll help you work.*

Jake frowns. *If I let you out, you will run away.*

No, I won't run. I will help. Please let me out.

You promise to go back?

Rachel nods.

Warily he unlatches the cage. Rachel bounds out, grabs a whisk broom from the cart, and begins industriously sweeping bits of food and droppings from beneath the row of cages. *Come on,* she signs to Jake from the end of the aisle. *I will help.*

When Jake pushes the cart from the room filled with cages, Rachel follows him closely. The rubber wheels of the cleaning cart rumble softly on the linoleum floor. They pass through a metal door into a corridor where the floor is carpeted and the air smells of chalk dust and paper.

Offices let off the corridor, each one a small room furnished with a desk, bookshelves, and a blackboard. Jake shows Rachel how to empty the wastebaskets into a garbage bag. While he cleans the blackboards, she wanders from office to office, trailing the trash-filled garbage bag.

At first, Jake keeps a close eye on Rachel. But after cleaning each blackboard, he pauses to sip whiskey from a paper cup. At the end of the corridor, he stops to refill the cup from the whiskey bottle that he keeps wedged between the Saniflush and the window cleaner. By the time he is halfway through the second cup, he is treating her like an old friend, telling her to hurry up so that they can eat dinner.

Rachel works quickly, but she stops sometimes to gaze out the office windows. Outside, moonlight shines on a sandy plain, dotted here and there with scrubby clumps of rabbit brush.

At the end of the corridor is a larger room in which there are several desks and typewriters. In one of the wastebaskets, buried beneath memos and candybar wrappers, she finds a magazine. The title is *Love Confessions* and the cover has a picture of a man and woman kissing. Rachel studies the cover, then takes the magazine, tucking it on the bottom shelf of the cart.

Jake pours himself another cup of whiskey and pushes the cart to another hallway. Jake is working slower now. As he works he makes humming noises, tuneless sounds that he feels only as pleasant vibrations. The last few blackboards are sloppily done, and Rachel, finished with the wastebaskets, cleans the places that Jake missed.

They eat dinner in the janitor's storeroom, a stuffy windowless room furnished with an ancient grease-stained couch, a battered black-and-white television, and shelves of cleaning supplies. From a shelf, Jake takes the paper bag that holds his lunch: a baloney sandwich, a bag of barbecued potato chips, and a box of vanilla wafers. From behind the gallon jugs of liquid cleanser, he takes a magazine. He lights a cigarette, pours himself another cup of whiskey, and settles down on the couch. After a moment's hesitation, he offers Rachel a drink, pouring a shot of whiskey into a chipped ceramic cup.

Aaron never let Rachel drink whiskey, and she samples it carefully. At first the smell makes her sneeze, but she is fascinated by the way that the drink warms her throat, and she sips some more.

As they drink, Rachel tells Jake about the men who shot her and the woman who pricked her with a needle. He nods. *The people here are crazy*, he signs.

I know, she says, thinking of the old chimp with the electrode in his head. *You won't tell them I can talk, will you?*

Jake nods. *I won't tell them anything.*

They treat me like I'm not real, Rachel signs sadly. Then she hugs her knees, frightened at the thought of being held captive by crazy people. She considers planning her escape: She is out of the cage and she is sure she could outrun Jake. As she wonders about it, she finishes her cup of whiskey. The alcohol takes the edge off her fear. She sits close beside Jake on the couch, and the smell of his cigarette smoke reminds her of

Aaron. For the first time since Aaron's death she feels warm and happy.

She shares Jake's cookies and potato chips and looks at the *Love Confessions* magazine that she took from the trash. The first story that she reads is about a woman named Alice. The headline reads: "I became a go-go dancer to pay off my husband's gambling debts, and now he wants me to sell my body."

Rachel sympathizes with Alice's loneliness and suffering. Alice, like Rachel, is alone and misunderstood. As Rachel slowly reads, she sips her second cup of whiskey. The story reminds her of a fairy tale: The nice man who rescues Alice from her terrible husband replaces the handsome prince who rescued the princess. Rachel glances at Jake and wonders if he will rescue her from the wicked people who locked her in the cage.

She has finished the second cup of whiskey and eaten half Jake's cookies when Jake says that she must go back to her cage. She goes reluctantly, taking the magazine with her. He promises that he will come back for her the next night, and with that she must be content. She puts the magazine in one corner of the cage and curls up to sleep.

She wakes early in the afternoon. A man in a white coat is wheeling a low cart into the lab.

Rachel's head aches with hangover and she feels sick. As she crouches in one corner of her cage, the man stops the cart beside her and locks the wheels. "Hold on there," he mutters to her, then slides her cage onto the cart.

The man wheels her through long corridors, where the walls are cement blocks, painted institutional green. Rachel huddles unhappily in the cage, wondering where she is going and whether Jake will ever be able to find her.

At the end of a long corridor, the man opens a thick metal door. A wave of warm air comes from the doorway. It stinks of chimpanzees, excrement, and rotting food. On either side of the corridor are metal bars and wire mesh. Behind the mesh, Rachel can see dark hairy shadows. In one cage, five adolescent chimps swing and play. In another, two females huddle together, grooming each other. The man slows as he passes a cage in which a big male is banging on the wire with his fist, making the mesh rattle and ring.

"Now, Johnson," says the man. "Cool it. Be nice. I'm bringing you a new little girlfriend."

With a series of hooks, the man links Rachel's cage with the cage next to Johnson's and opens the doors. "Go on, girl," he says. "See the nice fruit." In the new cage is a bowl of sliced apples with an attendant swarm of fruit flies.

At first, Rachel will not move into the new cage. She crouches in the cage on the cart, hoping that the man will decide to take her back to the lab. She watches him get a hose and attach it to a water faucet. But she does not understand his intention until he turns the stream of water on her. A cold blast strikes her on the back and she howls, fleeing into the new cage to avoid the cold water. Then the man closes the doors, unhooks the cage, and hurries away.

The floor is bare cement. Her cage is at one end of the corridor and two of its walls are cement block. A doorway in one of the cement block walls leads to an outside run. The other two walls are wire mesh: one facing the corridor; the other, Johnson's cage.

Johnson, quiet now that the man has left, is sniffing around the door in the wire mesh wall that joins their cages. Rachel watches him anxiously. Her memories of other chimps are distant, softened by time. She remembers her mother; she vaguely remembers playing with other chimps her age. But she does not know how to react to Johnson when he stares at her with great intensity and makes a loud huffing sound. She gestures to him in ASL, but he only stares harder and huffs again. Beyond Johnson, she can see other cages and other chimps, so many that the wire mesh blurs her vision and she cannot see the other end of the corridor.

To escape Johnson's scrutiny, she ducks through the door into the outside run, a wire mesh cage on a white concrete foundation. Outside there is barren ground and rabbit brush. All the other runs are deserted until Johnson appears in the run beside hers. His attention disturbs her and she goes back inside.

She retreats to the side of the cage farthest from Johnson. A crudely built wooden platform provides her with a place to sit. Wrapping her arms around her knees, she tries to relax and ignore Johnson. She dozes off for a while, but wakes to a commotion across the corridor.

In the cage across the way a female chimp is in heat. Rachel recognizes the smell from her own times in heat. Two keepers are opening the door that separates the female's cage from the adjoining cage, where a male stands, watching with great interest. Johnson is shaking the wire mesh and howling as he watches.

"Mike here is a virgin, but Susie knows what she's doing," one keeper was saying to the other. "So it should go smoothly. But keep the hose ready."

"Yeah?"

"Yeah. Sometimes they fight. We only use the hose to break it up if it gets real bad. Generally, they do okay."

Mike stalks into Susie's cage. The keepers lower the cage door, trapping both chimps in the same enclosure. Susie seems unalarmed. She continues eating a slice of orange while Mike sniffs at her genitals with every indication of great interest. She bends over to let Mike finger her pink bottom, the sign of estrus.

Rachel finds herself standing at the wire mesh, making low moaning noises. She can see Mike's erection, hear his grunting cries. He squats on the floor of Susie's cage, gesturing to the female. Rachel's feelings are mixed: She is fascinated, fearful, confused. She keeps thinking of the description of sex in the *Love Confessions* story: When Alice feels Danny's lips on hers, she is swept away by the passion of the moment. He takes her in his arms and her skin tingles as if she were consumed by an inner fire.

Susie bends down and Mike penetrates her with a loud grunt, thrusting violently with his hips. Susie cries out shrilly and suddenly leaps up, knocking Mike away. Rachel watches, overcome with fascination. Mike, his penis now limp, follows Susie slowly to the corner of the cage, where he begins grooming her carefully. Rachel finds that the wire mesh has cut her hands where she gripped it too tightly.

It is night, and the door at the end of the corridor creaks open. Rachel is immediately alert, peering through the wire mesh and trying to see down to the end of the corridor. She bangs on the mesh. As Jake comes closer, she waves a greeting.

When Jake reaches for the lever that will raise the door to Rachel's cage, Johnson charges toward him, howling and waving his arms above his head. He hammers on the mesh with his fists, howling and grimacing at Jake. Rachel ignores Johnson and hurries after Jake.

Again Rachel helps Jake clean. In the laboratory, she greets the old chimp, but the animal is more interested in the banana that Jake has brought than in conversation. The chimp will not reply to her questions, and after several tries, she gives up.

While Jake vacuums the carpeted corridors, Rachel empties the trash, finding a magazine called *Modern Romance* in the same waste-basket that had provided *Love Confessions*.

Later, in the janitor's lounge, Jake smokes a cigarette, sips whiskey, and flips through one of his own magazines. Rachel reads love stories in *Modern Romance*.

Every once in a while, she looks over Jake's shoulder at grainy pictures of naked women with their legs spread wide apart. Jake looks for a long time at a picture of a blond woman with big breasts, red fingernails, and purple-painted eyelids. The woman lies on her back and smiles as she strokes the pinkness between her legs. The picture on the next page shows her caressing her own breasts, pinching the dark nipples. The final picture shows her looking back over her shoulder. She is in the position that Susie took when she was ready to be mounted.

Rachel looks over Jake's shoulder at the magazine, but she does not ask questions. Jake's smell began to change as soon as he opened the magazine; the scent of nervous sweat mingles with the aromas of tobacco and whiskey. Rachel suspects that questions would not be welcome just now.

At Jake's insistence, she goes back to her cage before dawn.

Over the next week, she listens to the conversations of the men who come and go, bringing food and hosing out the cages. From the conversations, she learns that the Primate Research Center is primarily a breeding facility that supplies researchers with domestically bred apes and monkeys of several species. It also maintains its own research staff. In indifferent tones, the men talk of horrible things. The adolescent chimps at the end of the corridor are being fed a diet high in cholesterol to determine cholesterol's effects on the circulatory system. A group of pregnant females is being injected with male hormones to determine how that will affect the offspring. A group of infants is being fed a low-protein diet to determine adverse effects on their brain development.

The men look through her as if she were not real, as if she were a part of the wall, as if she were no one at all. She cannot speak to them; she cannot trust them.

Each night, Jake lets her out of her cage and she helps him clean. He brings treats: barbecued potato chips, fresh fruit, chocolate bars, and cookies. He treats her fondly, as one would treat a precocious child. And he talks to her.

At night, when she is with Jake, Rachel can almost forget the terror of the cage, the anxiety of watching Johnson pace to and fro, the sense of unreality that accompanies the simplest act. She would be content to stay with Jake forever, eating snack food and reading confessions magazines. He seems to like her company. But each morning, Jake insists that she must go back to the cage and the terror. By the end of the first week, she has begun plotting her escape.

Whenever Jake falls asleep over his whiskey, something that happens three nights out of five, Rachel prowls the center alone, surreptitiously gathering things that she will need to survive in the desert: a plastic jug filled with water, a bag of food pellets, a large beach towel that will serve as a blanket on the cool desert nights, a discarded shopping bag in which she can carry the other things. Her best find is a road map on which the Primate Research Center is marked in red. She knows the address of Aaron's ranch and finds it on the map. She studies the roads and plots a route home. Cross-country, assuming that she does not get lost, she will have to travel about fifty miles to reach the ranch. She hides these things behind one of the shelves in the janitor's storeroom.

Her plans to run away and go home are disrupted by the idea that she is in love with Jake, a notion that comes to her slowly, fed by the stories in the confessions magazines. When Jake absentmindedly strokes her, she is filled with a strange excitement. She longs for his company and misses him on the weekends when he is away. She is happy only when she is with him, following him through the halls of the center, sniffing the aroma of tobacco and whiskey that is his own perfume. She steals a cigarette from his pack and hides it in her cage, where she can savor the smell of it at her leisure.

She loves him, but she does not know how to make him love her back. Rachel knows little about love: She remembers a high-school crush where she mooned after a boy with a locker near hers, but that came to nothing. She reads the confessions magazines and Ann Landers's column in the newspaper that Jake brings with him each night. From these sources, she learns about romance. One night, after Jake falls asleep, she types a badly punctuated, ungrammatical letter to Ann. In the letter, she explains her situation and asks for advice on how to make Jake love her. She slips the letter into a sack labeled "Outgoing Mail," and for the next week she reads Ann's column with increased interest. But her letter never appears.

Rachel searches for answers in the magazine pictures that seem to fascinate Jake. She studies the naked women, especially the big-breasted woman with the purple smudges around her eyes.

One night, she finds a plastic case of eyeshadow in a secretary's desk. She steals it and takes it back to her cage. The next evening, as soon as the center is quiet, she upturns her metal food dish and regards her reflection in the shiny bottom. Squatting, she balances the eye shadow case on one knee and examines its contents: a tiny makeup brush and three shades of eye shadow—Indian Blue, Forest Green, and Wildly Violet. Rachel chooses the shade labeled Wildly Violet.

Using one finger to hold her right eye closed, she dabs her eyelid carefully with the makeup brush, leaving a gaudy orchid-colored smudge on her brown skin. She studies the smudge critically, then adds to it, smearing the color beyond the corner of her eyelid until it disappears in her brown fur. The color gives her eye a carnival brightness, a lunatic gaiety. Working with great care, she matches the effect on the other side, then smiles at her reflection, blinking coquettishly.

In the other cage, Johnson bares his teeth and shakes the mesh. She ignores him.

When Jake comes to let her out, he frowns at her eyes. *Did you hurt yourself?* he asks.

No, she says. Then, after a pause, *Don't you like it?*

Jake squats beside her and stares at her eyes. Rachel puts a hand on his knee and her heart pounds at her own boldness. *You are a very strange monkey,* he signs.

Rachel is afraid to move. Her hand on his knee closes into a fist; her face folds in on itself, puckering around the eyes.

Then, straightening up, he signs, *I liked your eyes better before.*

He likes her eyes. She nods without taking her eyes from his face.

Later, she washes her face in the women's restroom, leaving dark smudges the color of bruises on a series of paper towels.

▼

Rachel is dreaming. She is walking through the Painted Desert with her hairy brown mother, following a red rock canyon that Rachel somehow knows will lead her to the Primate Research Center. Her mother is lagging behind: She does not want to go to the center; she is afraid. In the shadow of a rock outcrop, Rachel stops to explain to her mother that they must go to the center because Jake is at the center.

Rachel's mother does not understand sign language. She watches Rachel with mournful eyes, then scrambles up the canyon wall, leaving Rachel behind. Rachel climbs after her mother, pulling herself over the edge in time to see the other chimp loping away across the windblown red cinder rock and sand.

Rachel bounds after her mother, and as she runs she howls like an abandoned infant chimp, wailing her distress. The figure of her mother wavers in the distance, shimmering in the heat that rises from the sand. The figure changes. Running away across the red sands is a pale blond woman wearing a purple sweatsuit and jogging shoes, the sweet-smelling mother that Rachel remembers. The woman looks back and smiles at Rachel. "Don't howl like an ape, daughter," she calls. "Say Mama."

Rachel runs silently, dream running that takes her nowhere. The sand burns her feet and the sun beats down on her head. The blond woman vanishes in the distance, and Rachel is alone. She collapses on the sand, whimpering because she is alone and afraid.

She feels the gentle touch of fingers grooming her fur, and for a moment, still half-asleep, she believes that her hairy mother has returned to her. She opens her eyes and looks into a pair of dark brown eyes, separated from her by wire mesh. Johnson. He has reached through a gap in the fence to groom her. As he sorts through her fur, he makes soft cooing sounds, gentle comforting noises.

Still half-asleep, she gazes at him and wonders why she was so fearful. He does not seem so bad. He grooms her for a time, and then sits nearby, watching her through the mesh. She brings a slice of apple from her dish of food and offers it to him. With her free hand, she makes the sign for apple. When he takes it, she signs again: *apple*. He is not a particularly quick student, but she has time and many slices of apple.

▼

All Rachel's preparations are done, but she cannot bring herself to leave the center. Leaving the center means leaving Jake, leaving potato chips and whiskey, leaving security. To Rachel, the thought of love is always accompanied by the warm taste of whiskey and potato chips.

Some nights, after Jake is asleep, she goes to the big glass doors that lead to the outside. She opens the doors and stands on the steps, looking down into the desert. Sometimes a jackrabbit sits on its haunches in the rectangles of light that shine through the glass doors. Sometimes she sees kangaroo rats, hopping through the moonlight like rubber balls bouncing on hard pavement. Once, a coyote trots by, casting a contemptuous glance in her direction.

The desert is a lonely place. Empty. Cold. She thinks of Jake snoring softly in the janitor's lounge. And always she closes the door and returns to him.

Rachel leads a double life: janitor's assistant by night, prisoner and teacher by day. She spends her afternoons drowsing in the sun and teaching Johnson new signs.

On a warm afternoon, Rachel sits in the outside run, basking in the sunlight. Johnson is inside, and the other chimps are quiet. She can almost imagine she is back at her father's ranch, sitting in her own yard. She naps and dreams of Jake.

She dreams that she is sitting in his lap on the battered old couch. Her hand is on his chest: a smooth pale hand with red-painted fingernails. When she looks at the dark screen of the television set, she can see her reflection. She is a thin teenager with blond hair and blue eyes. She is naked.

Jake is looking at her and smiling. He runs a hand down her back and she closes her eyes in ecstasy.

But something changes when she closes her eyes. Jake is grooming her as her mother used to groom her, sorting through her hair in search of fleas. She opens her eyes and sees Johnson, his diligent fingers searching through her fur, his intent brown eyes watching her. The reflection on the television screen shows two chimps, tangled in each other's arms.

Rachel wakes to find that she is in heat for the first time since she came to the center. The skin surrounding her genitals is swollen and pink.

For the rest of the day, she is restless, pacing to and fro in her cage.

On his side of the wire mesh wall, Johnson is equally restless, following her when she goes outside, sniffing long and hard at the edge of the barrier that separates him from her.

That night, Rachel goes eagerly to help Jake clean. She follows him closely, never letting him get far from her. When he is sweeping, she trots after him with the dustpan and he almost trips over her twice. She keeps waiting for him to notice her condition, but he seems oblivious.

As she works, she sips from a cup of whiskey. Excited, she drinks more than usual, finishing two full cups. The liquor leaves her a little disoriented, and she sways as she follows Jake to the janitor's lounge. She curls up close beside him on the couch. He relaxes with his arms resting on the back of the couch, his legs stretching out before him. She moves so that she is pressed against him.

He stretches, yawns, and rubs the back of his neck as if trying to rub away stiffness. Rachel reaches around behind him and begins to rub his neck gently, reveling in the feel of his skin. The thoughts that hop and skip through her mind are confusing. Sometimes it seems that the hair that tickles her hands is Johnson's; sometimes, she knows it is Jake's. And sometimes it doesn't seem to matter. Are they really so different? They are not so different.

She rubs his neck, not knowing what to do next. In the confessions magazines, this is where the man crushes the woman in his arms. Rachel climbs into Jake's lap and hugs him, waiting for him to crush her in his arms. He blinks at her sleepily. Half-asleep, he strokes her, and his moving hand brushes near her genitals. She presses herself against him, making a soft sound in her throat. She rubs her hip against his crotch, aware now of a slight change in his smell, in the tempo of his breathing. He blinks at her again, a little more awake now. She bares her teeth in a smile and tilts her head back to lick his neck. She can feel his hands on her shoulders, pushing her away, and she knows what he wants. She slides from his lap and turns, presenting him with her pink genitals, ready to be mounted, ready to have him penetrate her. She moans in anticipation, a low inviting sound.

He does not come to her. She looks over her shoulder and he is still sitting on the couch, watching her through half-closed eyes. He reaches over and picks up a magazine filled with pictures of naked women. His other hand drops to his crotch and he is lost in his own world.

Rachel howls like an infant who has lost its mother, but he does not look up. He is staring at the picture of the blond woman.

Rachel runs down dark corridors to her cage, the only home she has. When she reaches the corridor, she is breathing hard and making small lonely whimpering noises. In the dimly lit corridor, she hesitates for a moment, staring into Johnson's cage. The male chimp is asleep. She remembers the touch of his hands when he groomed her.

From the corridor, she lifts the gate that leads into Johnson's cage and enters. He wakes at the sound of the door and sniffs the air. When he sees Rachel, he stalks toward her, sniffing eagerly. She lets him finger her genitals, sniff deeply of her scent. His penis is erect and he grunts in excitement. She turns and presents herself to him and he mounts her, thrusting deep inside. As he penetrates, she thinks, for a moment, of Jake and of the thin blond teenage girl named Rachel, but then the moment passes. Almost against her will she cries out, a shrill exclamation of welcoming and loss.

After he withdraws his penis, Johnson grooms her gently, sniffing her genitals and softly stroking her fur. She is sleepy and content, but she knows that they cannot delay.

Johnson is reluctant to leave his cage, but Rachel takes him by the hand and leads him to the janitor's lounge. His presence gives her courage. She listens at the door and hears Jake's soft breathing. Leaving Johnson in the hall, she slips into the room. Jake is lying on the couch, the magazine draped over his legs. Rachel takes the equipment that she has gathered and stands for a moment, staring at the sleeping man. His baseball cap hangs on the arm of a broken chair, and she takes that to remember him by.

Rachel leads Johnson through the empty halls. A kangaroo rat, collecting seeds in the dried grass near the glass doors, looks up curiously as Rachel leads Johnson down the steps. Rachel carries the shopping bag slung over her shoulder. Somewhere in the distance, a coyote howls, a long yapping wail. His cry is joined by others, a chorus in the moonlight.

Rachel takes Johnson by the hand and leads him into the desert.

A cocktail waitress, driving from her job in Flagstaff to her home in Winslow, sees two apes dart across the road, hurrying away from the bright beams of her headlights. After wrestling with her conscience (she does not want to be accused of drinking on the job), she notifies the county sheriff.

A local newspaper reporter, an eager young man fresh out of journalism school, picks up the story from the police report and interviews the waitress. Flattered by his enthusiasm for her story and delighted to find a receptive ear, she tells him details that she failed to mention to the police: One of the apes was wearing a baseball cap and carrying what appeared to be a shopping bag.

The reporter writes up a quick humorous story for the morning edition, and begins researching a feature article to be run later in the week. He knows that the newspaper, eager for news in a slow season, will play a human-interest story up big—kind of a *Lassie, Come Home* with chimps.

Just before dawn, a light rain begins to fall, the first rain of spring. Rachel searches for shelter and finds a small cave formed by three tumbled boulders. It will keep off the rain and hide them from casual observers. She shares her food and water with Johnson. He has followed her closely all night, seemingly intimidated by the darkness and the howling of distant coyotes. She feels protective toward him. At the same time, having him with her gives her courage. He knows only a few gestures in ASL, but he does not need to speak. His presence is comfort enough.

Johnson curls up in the back of the cave and falls asleep quickly. Rachel sits in the opening and watches dawn light wash the stars from the sky. The rain rattles against the sand, a comforting sound. She thinks about Jake. The baseball cap on her head still smells of his cigarettes, but she does not miss him. Not really. She fingers the cap and wonders why she thought she loved Jake.

The rain lets up. The clouds rise like fairy castles in the distance and the rising sun tints them pink and gold and gives them flaming red banners. Rachel remembers when she was younger and Aaron read her the story of Pinocchio, the little puppet who wanted to be a real boy. At the end of his adventures, Pinocchio, who has been brave and kind, gets his wish. He becomes a real boy.

Rachel had cried at the end of the story and when Aaron asked why, she had rubbed her eyes on the backs of her hairy hands. *I want to be a real girl,* she signed to him. *A real girl.*

"You are a real girl," Aaron had told her, but somehow she had never believed him.

The sun rises higher and illuminates the broken rock turrets of the desert. There is a magic in this barren land of unassuming grandeur. Some cultures send their young people to the desert to seek visions and guidance, searching for true thinking spawned by the openness of the place, the loneliness, the beauty of emptiness.

Rachel drowses in the warm sun and dreams a vision that has the clarity of truth. In the dream, her father comes to her. "Rachel," he says to her, "it doesn't matter what anyone thinks of you. You're my daughter."

I want to be a real girl, she signs.

"You are real," her father says. "And you don't need some two-bit drunken janitor to prove it to you." She knows she is dreaming, but she also knows that her father speaks the truth. She is warm and happy and she doesn't need Jake at all. The sunlight warms her and a lizard watches her from a rock, scurrying for cover when she moves. She picks up a bit of loose rock that lies on the floor of the cave. Idly, she scratches on the dark red sandstone. A lopsided heart shape. Within it, she awkwardly prints: Rachel and Johnson. Between them, a plus sign. She goes over the letters again and again, leaving scores of fine lines on the smooth rock surface. Then, late in the morning, soothed by the warmth of the day, she sleeps.

Shortly after dark, an elderly rancher in a pickup truck spots two apes in a remote corner of his ranch. They run away and lose him in the rocks, but not until he has a good look at them. He calls the police, the newspaper, and the Primate Research Center.

The reporter arrives first thing the next morning, interviews the rancher, and follows the men from the Primate Research Center as they search for evidence of the chimps. They find monkey shit near the cave, confirming that the runaways were indeed nearby. The reporter squirms on his belly into the cave and finds the names scratched on the cave wall. He peers at them. He might have dismissed them as the idle scratching of kids, except that one of the names matched the name of one of the missing chimps. "Hey," he calls to his photographer, "Take a look at this."

The next morning's newspaper displays Rachel's crudely scratched letters. In a brief interview, the rancher had mentioned that one of the chimps was carrying a bag. "Looked like supplies," he had said. "They looked like they were in for the long haul."

On the third day, Rachel's water runs out. She heads toward a small town, marked on the map. They reach it in the early morning—thirst forces them to travel by day. Beside an isolated ranch house, she finds a faucet. She is filling her bottle when Johnson grunts in alarm.

A dark-haired woman watches from the porch of the house. She does not move toward the apes, and Rachel continues filling the bottle. "It's all right, Rachel," the woman, who has been following the story in the papers, calls out. "Drink all you want."

Startled, but still suspicious, Rachel caps the bottle and, keeping her eyes on the woman, drinks from the faucet. The woman steps back into the house. Rachel signals to Johnson, telling him to hurry and drink. She turns off the faucet when he is done.

They are turning to go when the woman emerges from the house carrying a plate of tortillas and a bowl of apples. She sets them on the edge of the porch and says, "These are for you."

The woman watches through the window as Rachel packs the food in her bag. Rachel puts away the last apple and gestures her thanks to the woman. When the woman fails to respond to the sign language, Rachel picks up a stick and writes in the sand of the yard. "THANK YOU," Rachel scratches, then waves good-bye and sets out across the desert. She is puzzled, but happy.

The next morning's newspaper includes an interview with the dark-haired woman. She describes how Rachel turned on the faucet and turned it off when she was through, how the chimp packed the apples neatly in her bag and wrote in the dirt with a stick.

The reporter also interviews the director of the Primate Research Center. "These are animals," the director explains angrily. "But people want to treat them like they're small hairy people." He describes the Center as "primarily a breeding center with some facilities for medical research." The reporter asks some pointed questions about their acquisition of Rachel.

But the biggest story is an investigative piece. The reporter reveals that he has tracked down Aaron Jacobs's lawyer and learned that Jacobs left a will. In this will Jacobs bequeathed all his possessions—including his house and surrounding land—to "Rachel, the chimp I acknowledge as my daughter."

The reporter makes friends with one of the young women in the typing pool at the research center, and she tells him the office scuttlebutt: People suspect that the chimps may have been released by a deaf and drunken janitor, who was subsequently fired for negligence. The reporter, accompanied by a friend who can communicate in sign language, finds Jake in his apartment in downtown Flagstaff.

Jake, who has been drinking steadily since he was fired, feels betrayed by Rachel, by the Primate Research Center, by the world. He complains at length about Rachel: They had been friends, and then she took his baseball cap and ran away. He just didn't understand why she had run away like that.

"You mean she could talk?" the reporter asks through his interpreter.

Of course she can talk, Jake signs impatiently. *She is a smart monkey.*

The headline reads: "Intelligent chimp inherits fortune!" Of course, Aaron's bequest isn't really a fortune and she isn't just a chimp, but close enough. Animal rights activists rise up in Rachel's defense. The case is discussed on the national news. Ann Landers reports receiving a letter from a chimp named Rachel; she had thought it was a hoax perpetrated by the boys at Yale. The American Civil Liberties Union assigns a lawyer to the case.

By day, Rachel and Johnson sleep in whatever hiding places they can find: a cave; a shelter built for range cattle; the shell of an abandoned car, rusted from long years in a desert gully. Sometimes Rachel dreams of jungle darkness, and the coyotes in the distance become a part of her dreams, their howling becomes the cries of fellow apes.

The desert and the journey have changed her. She is wiser, having passed through the white-hot love of adolescence and emerged on the other side. She dreams, one day, of the ranch house. In the dream, she has long blond hair and pale white skin. Her eyes are red from crying and she wanders the house restlessly, searching for something that she has lost. When she hears coyotes howling, she looks through a window at the darkness outside. The face that looks in at her has jug-handle ears and shaggy hair. When she sees the face, she cries out in recognition and opens the window to let herself in.

By night, Rachel and Johnson travel. The rocks and sands are cool beneath Rachel's feet as she walks toward her ranch. On television, scientists and politicians discuss the ramifications of her case, describe the technology uncovered by investigation of Aaron Jacobs's files. Their debates do not affect her steady progress toward her ranch or the stars that sprinkle the sky above her.

It is night when Rachel and Johnson approach the ranch house. Rachel sniffs the wind and smells automobile exhaust and strange humans. From the hills, she can see a white van marked with the name of a local television station. She hesitates and considers returning to the safety of the desert. Then she takes Johnson by the hand and starts down the hill. Rachel is going home.

IMAGINARY FRIENDS
by Pat Murphy

▼

I've talked to writers who sit down before they begin writing and compile a complete biography for their main characters. Such writers know where their characters went to school, what their characters like to eat for lunch, when they lost their virginity, and all the other significant details of their lives. That seems like a very sensible, straightforward way to approach a story.

Of course, that's not the way I work.

When I start thinking about a story, I know a few facts about the main characters: age, sex, social status, general attitude toward life, and maybe likes and dislikes. And I have many questions that are, in the beginning, largely unanswered. What motivates this character? What does she want? What does she need? What does she fear?

By working on a story, I learn—or I suppose, to be more accurate, I invent—the details of the character's life. As I shape the story, I consider the character—and I figure out the answers to all my initial questions.

For me, getting to know my characters is a bit like getting to know anyone else. It takes time; it takes patience; it takes a little thought and care. By writing a story, I ask my characters questions—and I learn the answers. As I write, I put my characters in situations of stress and trouble and I see how they react. I think about why they react the way they do—and how that reaction affects the story.

Of course, the advantage to being a writer is that I can influence how my characters react. I can't just push a character around and make her do this or that—if I did that, I'd end up with a character I couldn't believe in. But by thinking about what a particular character wants or needs, I can give her a reason to behave in the way that I would like her to, one that moves the story in the direction that I want it to move.

All of this may sound terribly analytical. It's not. Writing a story and creating a character is, for me, an organic process of give and take. As a story takes form, it shapes my view of the character. At the same time, my view of the character helps shape the story.

▼

Take "Rachel in Love," for instance. This story began when I interviewed a woman who wrote stories for true confessions magazines. To prepare for the interview, I read a number of the magazines: *Modern Romance*, *True Confessions*, and the like. Many of the stories followed a simple formula. A young woman meets a charming man who gambles, drinks, sleeps around, or engages in some other unacceptable behavior. Though he is clearly the wrong man for her, the young woman falls in love with him—and suffers as a result. A staunch friend supports her through her suffering. Then, in the end, when the man she loves treats her very badly, she realizes that she doesn't really love him after all. She loves her loyal friend.

I had, some time before, learned in a neurophysiology class that nerve impulses—like the ones zipping around in your brain as you read these words—are electrical in nature. In a physics class, I had learned of the interaction of electricity and magnetism: An electric current generates a magnetic field and a magnetic field can generate an electric current. In a fit of wild speculation, I thought about how you might record the magnetic fields generated by the working brain and then impose that pattern on another brain, transferring habitual patterns of thought and personality.

The true confessions formula and the unlikely scientific speculation came together in "Rachel in Love." The true confessions formula contains all the plot elements in the story. The scientific speculation has just enough basis in fact to get the story rolling. I couldn't have started writing the story without both of those. But the plot elements and the scientific speculation weren't enough to make the story. The real story of Rachel emerged from what I learned about Rachel's character.

Rachel has the mind of a teenage girl and the heart of a chimp—I knew that early on. That's the emotional center of the story. Rachel has all the longings and pains of adolescence, compounded by her unusual situation. Like every adolescent, she is trying to figure out who she is and where in the world she belongs. She's struggling to learn about the mysteries of sex and love; she's growing up and coming of age. That's not an easy task for anyone, but Rachel's situation makes it particularly difficult for her.

I knew from the beginning that Rachel would fall in love with someone inappropriate—I was, after all, following the true confessions formula. But who exactly would that someone be? And where would all this happen? Where did this story take place?

I struggled for a long time to figure that out. For me, the struggle to figure out particulars often takes the form of writing bits and pieces of rough drafts. I put Rachel in a variety of situations, trying to find the one that generated the best story. In one draft, Rachel was a student on a college campus, in love with a graduate student. In another, she was a chimp in a language lab, well-treated by the researchers who worked with her.

As I wrote these drafts, I learned more about Rachel and realized that this story could not take place in circumstances that were comfortable for her. An important part of the story was Rachel's struggle to find her identity in a world where people failed to recognize her for who she was. Rachel not only wants to understand the world—she wants the world to understand her. She wants to be a real girl.

Understanding that about Rachel—an understanding that I came to by writing drafts that went nowhere—made me aware that I had to change the circumstances of the story. Rachel wasn't a free agent on a college campus, recognized as an intelligent chimp. Rachel wasn't in a comfortable language lab, respected by those around her. Instead, she was a helpless prisoner in a research facility, misunderstood by the people who worked there. She is in a situation where she has reason to be afraid, where she is always threatened and dehumanized.

Once I knew the circumstances of the story, I could figure out more about Rachel. For me, the elements of the story are continuously influencing each other, a constant process of give and take. Here's one example of how this works. Rachel can speak in American Sign Language; she can write in English. Once she is in the Primate Research Center, she could simply tell the researchers her history. Why doesn't she?

Rachel doesn't tell them who she is because she is afraid—and her fears are justified. When she was a young chimp, eager to explore the world, her father warned her that people hated anyone who was different—if they found her, they would hurt her. And in the Primate Research Center, she sees that her father was right. The chimp in the next cage has had an electrode placed in his brain to monitor neural activity during sign language. Rachel is understandably afraid to tell the researchers who she is.

I didn't know about the incident in Rachel's childhood and I didn't know about Aaron's bitter rejection of the outside world until I started wondering about why Rachel didn't speak to the researchers. When I knew she couldn't tell her story, I had to figure out why—and the answers came.

In the hostile environment of the Primate Research Center, I searched for the person with whom Rachel would fall in love. She could not fall in love with any of the researchers—they were her captors and part of the threatening environment. The man she loved had to be someone who was not part of the scientific team. And for Rachel to fall in love, she needed to meet this person at a time when she could get to know him, learn to trust him. That was when Jake, the night janitor, came along.

Jake is no threat. Though he works for the Primate Research Center, he is not a part of it. He works when no one else is around. He does what he needs to do to get by, but no more than that. His deafness, which allows him to converse with Rachel, also makes him an asset to the Center—he fulfills their quota of handicapped employees. He ignores the researchers' rules, bringing treats for the animals. He can talk with Rachel—but he'd never think of reporting his conversations to anyone else at the Center.

Johnson, the third member of the love triangle, was inevitable. Since Jake was the wrong man (the wrong species, for one thing), Johnson had to be the right one—though of course that wasn't obvious to Rachel.

Once I had figured out the circumstances, I could explore the characters further. I realized that Rachel herself read true confessions magazines. Of course she did. She is trying to figure out how the world works, where she fits into it, and she picks up information wherever she can. Her notions about love and sex come from what she reads: true confessions magazines and Ann Landers—and also from the circumstances around her. When she watches two chimps mating in a nearby cage, when she peeks over Jake's shoulder at his cheesecake magazines, she is fascinated and confused, struggling to reconcile the things she observes with the romantic stories she has read.

At this point in my writing, the characters can also interact in ways that tell me—and the reader—more about them. When Rachel applies

Wildly Violet eyeshadow, she wants to make herself beautiful for Jake. When Jake says casually that he liked her eyes better before, she misinterprets his words as any teenager in love might. She hears only that he likes her eyes. The reader, who can see the situation from the outside, knows that Rachel's hopes are misplaced, but Rachel does not.

As I continued working on the story, aspects of Rachel's character emerged both from the needs of the story I wanted to tell—and from my memories of adolescence and its traumas. Rachel wants to run away from the Primate Research Center—but she can't bring herself to run away. She does not want to be alone and afraid. She loves Jake and will not leave the momentary comfort of her relationship with him.

All of this tells you something about how I shape a character as I shape a story—but I suppose it doesn't tell you much about where the initial character comes from. All of my characters, even the most reprehensible, include bits of the person I know best: myself. Some of Rachel's memories are my own. I remember standing in a corner at a junior high school dance; I remember gym class and the hard-edged girls who smelled of cigarette smoke. I remember discussing with friends the peculiarities of sex, as it had been described to us by older kids, and trying to make sense of it all. I remember being confused because the way that people treated me didn't match my own image of myself.

Of course, some of Rachel's memories are events that I imagined, modified versions of my own experience. I've never been a chimp in a freight compartment of a train—but I've felt lost and alone and confused. I've never fallen in love with a drunken janitor—but I had my share of unrequited adolescent crushes.

Though my own experience serves as the primary source for material, I also learn about people by observing others. Like most writers, I eavesdrop on buses and watch people on the street, listen closely to friends and observe how they behave. I try to be aware of the traits that I notice when I first meet someone: The way they dress? The way they smile? The things they say? These are the things that I can use in my writing to communicate who a character is.

I feel quite close to all my characters—even characters whose viewpoint may not reflect my own. To write about them, I have to discover—in them and in myself—points of commonality. Very few people regard themselves as evil. Instead, people justify their actions to themselves. Though I may see someone's actions as evil, to write about that person, I need to figure out how he or she is justifying those actions.

Recently I realized that the best stories (that is, the stories I like best) have characters that are neither clearly good nor clearly bad. I think that's true in "Rachel in Love." There are no evil characters in the story. The woman who sprays Rachel for fleas is not evil. She does not intend to torture Rachel; that's just incidental. The men who fetch her from her father's ranch are not evil. Rather, they are simply oblivious to her situation.

When my friend Karen Fowler is writing, her kids say that she's "playing with her imaginary friends." I like that description. Writing stories—and creating (or discovering) the characters that inhabit them—is very much like playing games with people who don't really exist. It's fun, an element that beginning writers sometimes seem to forget. I find it fascinating—since I think that people (even imaginary people) are about the most interesting thing around. And it's a cooperative venture—I modify the game to suit my imaginary friends and sometimes modify the friends to suit the game. Since my imaginary friends are my own creation, I suppose that I'm cooperating with myself in a schizophrenic sort of way. Somehow, through this oddly bumbling process, a story emerges. And I have a good time along the way.

A Local Habitation and a Name

▼

. . . as imagination bodies forth
The forms of things unknown, the poet's pen
Turns them to shapes, and gives to airy nothing
A local habitation and a name.

Lumping poets with lovers and lunatics as beings "of imagination all compact," Shakespeare's Theseus defines the process by which writers furnish their fictive worlds. *Setting* in the short story is the sum of all factors—tangible and intangible—which form a background for and interact with characters and their doings.

The setting of a short story performs three functions. Like theatrical scenery, it attempts to give a palpable and pictorial locus for the action. Unlike the flats and sets behind the proscenium, it can constitute an environmental force which influences character and affects plot. And, with far greater freedom and effect than anything short of the Grand Guignol, it is productive of that elusive quality called *atmosphere*.

Mood, ambiance, atmosphere, all are terms descriptive of the larger affective context within which a story takes place and which is carefully designed to lend emotional force to characters and their actions. Setting is always productive of atmosphere, but unless it is carefully constructed it may generate the wrong atmosphere, one that fails to reinforce (or effectively contrast with) emotional qualities established by plot and character. Some settings are clichés: the dark and stormy nights and gloomy castles of the gothic novel, the sagebrush and big sky of the western, the intimate midwestern or southern or New England town, the ghetto, the inky, awesome blackness of interstellar space.

Some settings push the reader's psychological buttons too hard and too frequently. Snakes and spiders and heights and rats and nostalgia and sealed caves and food and money and even erotic paraphernalia of one kind or another—if presented clumsily—can produce so strong a reaction, so powerful an atmosphere, as to drown out everything else in the story. Here, as in every other aspect of artistic composition, the writer is above all selective, choosing just those elements of setting that will pro-

vide the precise emotional loading he wishes to give the incidents he relates.

Not everything a writer does is fully conscious or deliberate; setting
is. Faced on one hand by the necessity of making every word count, and
on the other by the desire to make her work as sensuous and emotionally gratifying as possible, the writer trolls in her own memories for sense
impressions (since they are at the heart of setting) which have been, for
her, very strong and meaningful. She uses all five senses, although—for
most writers—the visual predominates. She tests her memories against
what she understands of others' reactions to similar stimuli, aware at all
times that she runs the risk of becoming a closet writer, truly effective to
no one but herself. And she continues, consciously, to increase her stock
of impressions, observing what goes on around her, looking for events and
characters and elements of setting which are powerful and hold some
promise of universality. Writers are seldom bored in waiting rooms.

Above all, the writer remembers that setting is a means to an end,
not an end in itself, no matter how carried away he is with sun-washed
Acapulco, the streets of Soho or SoHo, or breasts in lace.

Setting—describing "the forms of things unknown"—is particularly
important in science fiction. Indeed, one might argue that it is distin-
guishable from other fictions only in setting. After all, people will fall in
love or hate each other or grow frustrated or achieve success in very
much the same manner in 2073 or on the moon or in some parallel world
as they do today, here. If they do not, they are not people (as we understand the term), and if they are alien, we will personify them and try to
understand them in our own terms.

Unlike the writer of more traditional forms of fiction, the science fiction writer cannot entirely depend upon his own learning or store of sense
impressions; he must extrapolate from them, decide upon some incre-
ment of change, and carefully relate his wonders to our familiar world,
or he will lose us. To do this deftly, unobtrusively, convincingly, requires
great skill, but it is a significant part of the fascination of science fiction.

GLACIER

by Kim Stanley Robinson

▼

"This is Stella," Mrs. Goldberg said. She opened the cardboard box and a gray cat leaped out and streaked under the corner table.

"That's where we'll put her blanket," Alex's mother said.

Alex got down on hands and knees to look. Stella was a skinny old cat; her fur was an odd mix of silver, black, and pinkish tan. Yellow eyes. Part tortoise-shell, Mom had said. The color of the fur over her eyes made it appear her brow was permanently furrowed. Her ears were laid flat.

"Remember she's kind of scared of boys," Mrs. Goldberg said.

"I know." Alex sat back on his heels. Stella hissed. "I was just looking." He knew the cat's whole story. She had been a stray that began visiting the Goldbergs' balcony to eat their dog's food, then—as far as anyone could tell—to hang out with the dog. Remus, a stiff-legged ancient thing, seemed happy to have the company, and after a while the two animals were inseparable. The cat had learned how to behave by watching Remus, and so it would go for a walk, come when you called it, shake hands and so on. Then Remus died, and now the Goldbergs had to move. Mom had offered to take Stella in, and though Father sighed heavily when she told him about it, he hadn't refused.

Mrs. Goldberg sat on the worn carpet beside Alex, and leaned forward so she could see under the table. Her face was puffy. "It's okay, Stell-bell," she said. "It's okay."

The cat stared at Mrs. Goldberg with an expression that said *You've got to be kidding.* Alex grinned to see such skepticism.

Mrs. Goldberg reached under the table; the cat squeaked in protest as it was pulled out, then lay in Mrs. Goldberg's lap quivering like a rabbit. The two women talked about other things. Then Mrs. Goldberg put Stella in Alex's mother's lap. There were scars on its ears and head. It breathed fast. Finally it calmed under Mom's hands. "Maybe we should feed her something," Mom said. She knew how distressed animals could get in this situation: They themselves had left behind their dog Pongo, when they moved from Toronto to Boston. Alex and she had been the ones to take Pongo to the Wallaces; the dog had howled as they left, and walking away Mom had cried. Now she told Alex to get some chicken out of the fridge and put it in a bowl for Stella. He put the bowl on the couch next to the cat, who sniffed at it disdainfully and refused to look at it. Only after much calming would it nibble at the meat, nose drawn high over one sharp eyetooth. Mom talked to Mrs. Goldberg, who watched Stella eat. When the cat was done it hopped off Mom's lap and walked up and down the couch. But it wouldn't let Alex near; it crouched as he approached, and with a desperate look dashed back under the table. "Oh Stella!" Mrs. Goldberg laughed. "It'll take her a while to get used to you," she said to Alex, and sniffed. Alex shrugged.

▼

Outside the wind ripped at the treetops sticking above the buildings. Alex walked up Chester Street to Brighton Avenue and turned left, hurrying to counteract the cold. Soon he reached the river and could walk the path on top of the embankment. Down in its trough the river's edges were crusted with ice, but midstream was still free, the silty gray water riffled by white. He passed the construction site for the dam and came to the moraine, a long mound of dirt, rocks, lumber, and junk. He climbed it with big steps, and stood looking at the glacier.

The glacier was immense, like a range of white hills rolling in from the west and north. The Charles poured from the bottom of it and roiled through a cut in the terminal moraine; the glacier's snout loomed so large that the river looked small, like a gutter after a storm. Bright white iceberg chunks had toppled off the face of the snout, leaving fresh blue scars and clogging the river below.

Alex walked the edge of the moraine until he was above the glacier's side. To his left was the razed zone, torn streets and fresh dirt and cellars open to the sky; beyond it Allston and Brighton, still bustling with city life. Under him, the sharp-edged mound of dirt and debris. To his right, the wilderness of ice and rock. Looking straight ahead it was hard to believe that the two halves of the view came from the same world. Neat. He descended the moraine's steep loose inside slope carefully, following a path of his own.

The meeting of glacier and moraine was a curious juncture. In some places the moraine had been undercut and had spilled across the ice in wide fans; you couldn't be sure if the dirt was solid or if it concealed crevasses. In other places melting had created a gap, so that a thick cake of ice stood over empty air, and dripped into gray pools below. Once Alex had seen a car in one of these low wet caves, stripped of its paint and squashed flat.

In still other places, however, the ice sloped down and overlay the moraine's gravel in a perfect ramp, as if fitted by carpenters. Alex walked the trough between dirt and ice until he reached one of these areas, then took a big step onto the curved white surface. He felt the usual quiver of excitement: He was on the glacier.

It was steep on the rounded side slope, but the ice was embedded with thousands of chunks of gravel. Each pebble, heated by the sun, had sunk into a little pocket of its own, and was then frozen into position in the night; this process had been repeated until most chunks were about three-quarters buried. Thus the glacier had a peculiarly pocked, rocky surface, which gripped the torn soles of Alex's shoes. A non-slip surface. No slope on the glacier was too steep for him. Crunch, crunch, crunch: Tiny arabesques of ice collapsed under his feet with every step. He could change the glacier, he was part of its action. Part of it.

Where the side slope leveled out the first big crevasses appeared. These deep blue fissures were dangerous, and Alex stepped between two of them and up a narrow ramp very carefully. He picked up a fist-sized rock, tossed it in the bigger crack. *Clunk clunk . . . splash.* He shivered and walked on, ritual satisfied. He knew from these throws that at the bottom of the glacier there were pockets of air, pools of water, streams running down to form the Charles . . . a deadly subglacial world. No one who fell into it would ever escape. It made the surface ice glow with a magical danger, an internal light.

Up on the glacier proper he could walk more easily. Crunch crunch crunch, over an undulating broken debris-covered plain. Ice for miles on miles. Looking back toward the city he saw the Hancock and Prudential towers to the right, the lower MIT towers to the left, poking up at low scudding clouds. The wind was strong here and he pulled his jacket hood's drawstring tighter. Muffled hoot of wind, a million tricklings. There were little creeks running in channels cut into the ice: It was almost like an ordinary landscape, streams running in ravines over a broad rocky meadow. And yet everything was different. The streams ran into crevasses or potholes and instantly disappeared, for instance. It was wonderfully strange to look down such a rounded hole: The ice was very blue and you could see the air bubbles in it, air from some year long ago.

Broken seracs exposed fresh ice to the sun. Scores of big erratic boulders dotted the glacier, some the size of houses. He made his way from one to the next, using them as cover. There were gangs of boys from Cambridge who occasionally came up here, and they were dangerous. It was important to see them before he was seen.

A mile or more onto the glacier, ice had flowed around one big boulder, leaving a curving wall some ten feet high—another example of the glacier's whimsy, one of hundreds of odd surface formations. Alex had wedged some stray boards into the gap between rock and ice, making a seat that was tucked out of the west wind. Flat rocks made a fine floor, and in the corner he had even made a little fireplace. Every fire he lit sank the hearth of flat stones a bit deeper into the otherwise impervious ice.

This time he didn't have enough kindling, though, so he sat on his bench, hands deep in pockets, and looked back at the city. He could see for miles. Wind whistled over the boulder. Scattered shafts of sunlight broke against ice. Mostly shadowed, the jumbled expanse was faintly pink. This was because of an algae that lived on nothing but ice and dust. Pink; the blue of the seracs; gray ice; patches of white, marking snow or sunlight. In the distance dark clouds scraped the top of the blue Hancock building, making it look like a distant serac. Alex leaned back against his plank wall, whistling one of the songs of the Pirate King.

Everyone agreed the cat was crazy. Her veneer of civilization was thin, and at any loud noise—the phone's ring, the door slamming—she would jump as if shot, then stop in mid-flight as she recalled that this particular noise entailed no danger; then lick down her fur, pretending she had never jumped in the first place. A flayed sensibility.

She was also very wary about proximity to people; this despite the fact that she had learned to love being petted. So she would often get in moods where she would approach one of them and give an exploratory, half-purring mew; then, if you responded to the invitation and crouched to pet her, she would sidle just out of arm's reach, repeating the invitation but retreating with each shift you made, until she either let you get within petting distance—just—or decided it wasn't worth the risk, and scampered away. Father laughed at this intense ambivalence. "Stella, you're too stupid to live, aren't you," he said in a teasing voice.

"Charles," Mom said.

"It's the best example of approach avoidance behavior I've ever seen," Father said. Intrigued by the challenge, he would sit on the floor, back against the couch and legs stretched ahead of him, and put Stella on his thighs. She would either endure his stroking until it ended, when she could jump away without impediment—or relax, and purr. She had a rasping loud purr, it reminded Alex of a chainsaw heard across the glacier. "Bug brain," Father would say to her. "Button head."

After a few weeks, as August turned to September and the leaves began to wither and fall, Stella started to lap sit voluntarily—but always in Mom's lap. "She likes the warmth," Mom said.

"It's cold on the floor," Father agreed, and played with the cat's scarred ears. "But why do you always sit on Helen's lap, huhn, Stell? I'm the one who started you on that." Eventually the cat would step onto his lap as well, and stretch out as if it was something she had always done. Father laughed at her.

Stella never rested on Alex's lap voluntarily, but would sometimes stay if he put her there and stroked her slowly for a long time. On the other hand she was just as likely to look back at him, go cross-eyed with horror and leap desperately away, leaving claw marks in his thighs. "She's so weird," he complained to Mom after one of these abrupt departures.

"It's true," Mom said with her low laugh. "But you have to remember that Stella was probably an abused kitty."

"How can you abuse a stray?"

"I'm sure there are ways. And maybe she was abused at home, and ran away."

"Who would do that?"

"Some people would."

Alex recalled the gangs on the glacier, and knew it was true. He tried to imagine what it would be like to be at their mercy, all the time. After that he thought he understood her permanent frown of deep concentration and distrust, as she sat staring at him. "It's just me, Stell-bells."

Thus when the cat followed him up onto the roof, and seemed to enjoy hanging out there with him, he was pleased. Their apartment was on the top floor, and they could take the pantry stairs and use the roof as a porch. It was a flat expanse of graveled tar paper, a terrible imitation of the glacier's non-slip surface, but it was nice on dry days to go up there and look around, toss pebbles onto other roofs, see if the glacier was visible, and so on. Once Stella pounced at a piece of string trailing from his pants, and next time he brought up a length of Father's yarn. He was astonished and delighted when Stella responded by attacking the wind-blown yarn enthusiastically, biting it, clawing it, wrestling it from her back when Alex twirled it around her, and generally behaving in a very kittenish way. Perhaps she had never played as a kitten, Alex thought, so that it was all coming out now that she felt safe. But the play always ended abruptly; she would come to herself in mid-bite or bat, straighten up, and look around with a forbidding expression, as if to say *What is this yarn doing draped over me?*—then lick her fur and pretend the preceding minutes hadn't happened. It made Alex laugh.

▼

Although the glacier had overrun many towns to the west and north, Watertown and Newton most recently, there was surprisingly little evidence of that in the moraines, or in the ice. It was almost all natural: rock and dirt and wood. Perhaps the wood had come from houses, perhaps some of the gravel had once been concrete, but you couldn't tell that now. Just dirt and rock and splinters, with an occasional chunk of plastic or metal thrown in. Apparently the overrun towns had been plowed under on the spot, or moved. Mostly it looked like the glacier had just left the White Mountains.

Father and Gary Jung had once talked about the latest plan from MIT. The enormous dam they were building downstream, between All-ston and Cambridge, was to hold the glacier back. They were going to heat the concrete of the inner surface of the dam, and melt the ice as it advanced. It would become a kind of frozen reservoir. The meltwater would pour through a set of turbines before becoming the Charles, and the electricity generated by these turbines would help to heat the dam. Very neat.

The ice of the glacier, when you got right down to look at it, was clear for an inch or less, cracked and bubble-filled; then it turned a milky white. You could see the transition. Where the ice had been sheared vertically, however—on the side of a serac, or down in a crevasse—the clear part extended in many inches. You could see air bubbles deep inside, as if it were badly made glass. And this ice was distinctly blue. Alex didn't understand why there should be that difference, between the white ice lying flat and the blue ice cut vertically. But there it was.

Up in New Hampshire they had tried slowing the glacier—or at least stopping the abrupt "Alaskan slides"—by setting steel rods vertically in concrete, and laying the concrete in the glacier's path. Later they had hacked out one of these installations, and found the rods bent in perfect ninety degree angles, pressed into the scored concrete.

The ice would flow right over the dam.

One day Alex was walking by Father's study when Father called out. "Alexander! Take a look at this."

Alex entered the dark book-lined room. Its window overlooked the weed-filled space between buildings, and green light slanted onto Father's desk. "Here, stand beside me and look in my coffee cup. You can see the reflection of the Morgelis' window flowers on the coffee."

"Oh yeah! Neat."

"It gave me a shock! I looked down and there were these white and pink flowers in my cup, bobbing against a wall in a breeze, all of it tinted sepia as if it were an old-fashioned photo. It took me a while to see where it was coming from, what was being reflected." He laughed. "Through a looking glass."

Alex's father had light brown eyes, and fair wispy hair brushed back from a receding hairline. Mom called him handsome, and Alex agreed: tall, thin, graceful, delicate, distinguished. His father was a great man. Now he smiled in a way Alex didn't understand, looking into his coffee cup.

Mom had friends at the street market on Memorial Drive, and she had arranged work for Alex there. Three afternoons a week he walked over the Charles to the riverside street and helped the fishmongers gut fish, the vegetable sellers strip and clean the vegetables. He also helped set up stalls and take them down, and he swept and hosed the street afterwards. He was popular because of his energy and his willingness to get his hands wet in raw weather. The sleeves of his down jacket were permanently dis-

colored from the frequent soakings—the dark blue almost a brown—a
fact that distressed his mom. But he could handle the cold better than
the adults; his hands would get a splotchy bluish white and he would put
them to the red cheeks of the women and they would jump and say My
God, Alex, how can you stand it?

This afternoon was blustery and dark but without rain, and it was en-
livened by an attempted theft in the pasta stands, and by the appearance
of a very mangy, very fast stray dog. This dog pounced on the pile of fish-
heads and entrails and disappeared with his mouth stuffed, trailing slick
white-and-red guts. Everyone who saw it laughed. There weren't many
stray dogs left these days, it was a pleasure to see one.

An hour past sunset he was done cleaning up and on his way home,
hands in his pockets, stomach full, a five dollar bill clutched in one
hand. He showed his pass to the National Guardsman and walked out
onto Weeks Bridge. In the middle he stopped and leaned over the rail-
ing, into the wind. Below the water churned, milky with glacial silt. The
sky still held a lot of light. Low curving bands of black cloud swept in
from the northwest, like great ribs of slate. Above these bands the white
sky was leached away by dusk. Raw wind whistled over his hood. Light
water rushing below, dark clouds rushing above . . . he breathed the
wind deep into him, felt himself expand until he filled everything he
could see.

That night his parents' friends were gathering at their apartment for
their bi-weekly party. Some of them would read stories and poems and
essays and broadsides they had written, and then they would argue about
them; and after that they would drink and eat whatever they had brought,
and argue some more. Alex enjoyed it. But tonight when he got home
Mom was rushing between computer and kitchen and muttering curses
as she hit command keys or the hot water faucet, and the moment she
saw him she said, "Oh Alex I'm glad you're here, could you please run
down to the laundry and do just one load for me? The Talbots are staying over tonight and there aren't any clean sheets and I don't have anything to wear tomorrow either—thanks, you're a dear." And he was back
out the door with a full laundry bag hung over his shoulder and the box
of soap in the other hand, stomping grumpily past a little man in a black
coat, reading a newspaper on the stoop of 19 Chester.

Down to Brighton, take a right, downstairs into the brightly lit basement laundromat. He threw laundry and soap and quarters into their places, turned the machine on and sat on top of it. Glumly he watched the other people in there, sitting on the washers and dryers. The vibrations put a lot of them to sleep. Others stared dully at the wall. Back in his apartment the guests would be arriving, taking off their overcoats, slapping arms over chests and talking as fast as they could. David and Sara and John from next door, Ira and Gary and Ilene from across the street, the Talbots, Kathryn Grimm, and Michael Wu from Father's university, Ron from the hospital. They would settle down in the living room, on couches and chairs and floor, and talk and talk. Alex liked Kathryn especially, she could talk twice as fast as anyone else, and she called everyone darling and laughed and chattered so fast that everyone was caught up in the rhythm of it. Or David with his jokes, or Jay Talbot and his friendly questions. Or Gary Jung, the way he would sit in his corner like a bear, drinking beer and challenging everything that everyone read. "Why abstraction, why this distortion from the real? How does it help us, how does it speak to us? We should forget the abstract!" Father and Ira called him a vulgar Marxist, but he didn't mind. "You might as well be Plekhanov, Gary!" "Thank you very much!" he would say with a sharp grin, rubbing his unshaven jowls. And someone else would read. Mary Talbot once read a fairy tale about the Thing under the glacier; Alex had *loved* it. Once they even got Michael Wu to bring his violin along, and he hmm'd and hawed and pulled at the skin of his neck and refused and said he wasn't good enough, and then shaking like a leaf he played a melody that stilled them all. And Stella! She hated these parties, she spent them crouched deep in her refuge, ready for any kind of atrocity.

And here he was sitting on a washer in the laundromat.

When the laundry was dry he bundled it into the bag, then hurried around the corner and down Chester Street. Inside the glass door of Number 21 he glanced back out, and noticed that the man who had been reading the paper on the stoop next door was still sitting there. Odd. It was cold to be sitting outdoors.

Upstairs the readings had ended and the group was scattered through the apartment, most of them in the kitchen, as Mom had lit the stovetop burners and turned the gas up high. The blue flames roared airily under their chatter, making the kitchen bright and warm. "Wonderful the way white gas burns so clean." "And then they found the poor thing's head and intestines in the alley—it had been butchered right on the spot."

"Alex, you're back! Thanks for doing that. Here, get something to eat."

Everyone greeted him and went back to their conversations. "Gary you are so *conservative*," Kathryn cried, hands held out over the stove. "It's not conservative at all," Gary replied. "It's a radical goal and I guess it's so radical that I have to keep reminding you it exists. Art should be used to *change* things."

"Isn't that a distortion from the real?"

Alex wandered down the narrow hall to his parents' room, which overlooked Chester Street. Father was there, saying to Ilene, "It's one of the only streets left with trees. It really seems residential, and here we are three blocks from Comm Ave. Hi, Alex."

"Hi, Alex. It's like a little bit of Brookline made it over to Allston."

"Exactly."

Alex stood in the bay window and looked down, licking the last of the carrot cake off his fingers. The man was still down there.

"Let's close off these rooms and save the heat. Alex, you coming?"

He sat on the floor in the living room. Father and Gary and David were starting a game of hearts, and they invited him to be the fourth. He nodded happily. Looking under the corner table he saw yellow eyes, blinking back at him; Stella, a frown of the deepest disapproval on her flat face. Alex laughed. "I knew you'd be there! It's okay, Stella. It's okay."

They left in a group, as usual, stamping their boots and diving deep into coats and scarves and gloves and exclaiming at the cold of the stairwell. Gary gave Mom a brief hug. "Only warm spot left in Boston," he said, and opened the glass door. The rest followed him out, and Alex joined them. The man in the black coat was just turning right onto Brighton Avenue, toward the university and downtown.

Sometimes clouds took on just the mottled gray of the glacier, low dark points stippling a lighter gray surface as cold showers draped down. At these times he felt he stood between two planes of some larger structure, two halves: icy tongue, icy roof of mouth. . . .

He stood under such a sky, throwing stones. His target was an erratic some forty yards away. He hit the boulder with most of his throws. A rock that big was an easy target. A bottle was better. He had brought one with him, and he set it up behind the erratic, on a waist-high rock. He walked back to a point where the bottle was hidden by the erratic. Using flat rocks he sent spinners out in a trajectory that brought them curving in from the side, so that it was possible to hit the concealed target. This was very important for the rock fights that he occasionally got involved in; usually he was outnumbered, and to hold his own he relied on his curves and his accuracy in general, and on a large number of ammunition caches hidden here and there. In one area crowded with boulders and crevasses he could sometimes create the impression of two throwers.

Absorbed in the exercise of bringing curves around the right side of the boulder—the hard side for him—he relaxed his vigilance, and when he heard a shout he jumped around to look. A rock whizzed by his left ear.

He dropped to the ice and crawled behind a boulder. Ambushed! He ran back into his knot of boulders and dashed a layer of snow away from one of his big caches, then with hands and pockets full looked carefully over a knobby chunk of cement, in the direction the stone had come from.

No movement. He recalled the stone whizzing by, the brief sight of it and the *zip* it made in passing. That had been close! If that had hit him! He shivered to think of it, it made his stomach shrink.

A bit of almost frozen rain pattered down. Not a shadow anywhere. On overcast days like this one it seemed things were lit from below, by the white bulk of the glacier. Like plastic over a weak neon light. Brittle huge blob of plastic, shifting and groaning and once in a while cracking like a gunshot, or grumbling like distant thunder. Alive. And Alex was its ally, its representative among men. He shifted from rock to rock, saw movement and froze. Two boys in green down jackets, laughing as they ran off the ice and over the lateral moraine, into what was left of Watertown. Just a potshot, then. Alex cursed them, relaxed.

He went back to throwing at the hidden bottle. Occasionally he recalled the stone flying by his head, and threw a little harder. Elegant curves of flight as the flat rocks bit the air and cut down and in. Finally one rock spun out into space and turned down sharply. Perfect slider. Its disappearance behind the erratic was followed by a tinkling crash. "Yeah!" Alex exclaimed, and ran to look. Icy glass on glassy ice.

Then, as he was leaving the glacier, boys jumped over the moraine

shouting "Canadian!" and "There he is!" and "Get him!" This was more
a chase than a serious ambush, but there were a lot of them and after emptying hands and pockets Alex was off running. He flew over the crunchy
irregular surface, splashing meltwater, jumping narrow crevasses and
surface rills. Then a wide crevasse blocked his way, and to start his jump
he leaped onto a big flat rock; the rock gave under his foot and lurched
down the ice into the crevasse.

Alex turned in and fell, bringing shoe-tips, knees, elbows and hands
onto the rough surface. This arrested his fall, though it hurt. The crevasse
was just under his feet. He scrambled up, ran panting along the crevasse
until it narrowed, leaped over it. Then up the moraine and down into
the narrow abandoned streets of west Allston.

Striding home, still breathing hard, he looked at his hands and saw
that the last two fingernails on his right hand had been ripped away from
the flesh; both were still there, but blood seeped from under them. He
hissed and sucked on them, which hurt. The blood tasted like blood.

If he had fallen into the crevasse, following the loose rock down . . .
if that stone had hit him in the face . . . he could feel his heart, thump-
ing against his sternum. Alive.

Turning onto Chester Street he saw the man in the black coat, leaning against the florid maple across the street from their building. Watching them still! Though the man didn't appear to notice Alex, he did heft
a bag and start walking in the other direction. Quickly Alex picked a rock
out of the gutter and threw it at the man as hard as he could, spraying
drops of blood onto the sidewalk. The rock flew over the man's head like
a bullet, just missing him. The man ducked and scurried around the corner onto Comm Ave.

Father was upset about something. "They did the same thing to
Gary and Michael and Kathryn, and their classes are even smaller than
mine! I don't know what they're going to do. I don't know what *we're*
going to do."

"We might be able to attract larger classes next semester," Mom said.
She was upset too. Alex stood in the hall, slowly hanging up his jacket.

"But what about now? And what about later?" Father's voice was
strained, almost cracking.

"We're making enough for now, that's the important thing. As for later—well, at least we know now rather than five years down the road."

Father was silent at the implications of this. "First Vancouver, then Toronto, now here—"

"Don't worry about all of it at once, Charles."

"How can I help it!" Father strode into his study and closed the door, not noticing Alex around the corner. Alex sucked his fingers. Stella poked her head cautiously out of his bedroom.

"Hi Stell-bell," he said quietly. From the living room came the plastic clatter of Mom's typing. He walked down the long hallway, past the silent study to the living room. She was hitting the keys hard, staring at the screen, mouth tight.

"What happened?" Alex said.

She looked up. "Hi, Alex. Well—your father got bad news from the university."

"Did he not get tenure again?"

"No, no, it's not a question of that."

"But now he doesn't even have the chance?"

She glanced at him sharply, then back at the screen, where her work was blinking. "I suppose that's right. The department has shifted all the new faculty over to extension, so they're hired by the semester, and paid by the class. It means you need a lot of students. . . ."

"Will we move again?"

"I don't know," she said curtly, exasperated with him for bringing it up. She punched the command key. "But we'll really have to save money, now. Everything you make at the market is important."

Alex nodded. He didn't mention the little man in the black coat, feeling obscurely afraid. Mentioning the man would somehow make him significant—Mom and Father would get angry, or frightened—something like that. By not telling them he could protect them from it, handle it on his own, so they could concentrate on other problems. Besides the two matters couldn't be connected, could they? Being watched; losing jobs. Perhaps they could. In which case there was nothing his parents could do about it anyway. Better to save them that anger, that fear.

He would make sure his throws hit the man next time.

▼

Storms rolled in and the red and yellow leaves were ripped off the trees. Alex kicked through piles of them stacked on the sidewalks. He never saw the little man. He put up flyers for his father, who became even more distracted and remote. He brought home vegetables from work, tucked under his down jacket, and Mom cooked them without asking if he had bought them. She did the wash in the kitchen sink and dried it on lines in the back space between buildings, standing knee deep in leaves and weeds. Sometimes it took three days for clothes to dry back there; often they froze on the line.

While hanging clothes or taking them down she would let Stella join her. The cat regarded each shifting leaf with dire suspicion, then after a few exploratory leaps and bats would do battle with all of them, rolling about in a frenzy.

One time Mom was carrying a basket of dry laundry up the pantry stairs when a stray dog rounded the corner and made a dash for Stella, who was still outside. Mom ran back down shouting, and the dog fled; but Stella had disappeared. Mom called Alex down from his studies in a distraught voice, and they searched the back of the building and all the adjacent backyards for nearly an hour, but the cat was nowhere to be found. Mom was really upset. It was only after they had quit and returned upstairs that they heard her, miaowing far above them. She had climbed the big oak tree. "Oh *smart* Stella," Mom cried, a wild note in her voice. They called her name out the kitchen window, and the desperate miaows redoubled.

Up on the roof they could just see her, perched high in the almost bare branches of the big tree. "I'll get her," Alex said. "Cats can't climb down." He started climbing. It was difficult: The branches were close-knit, and they swayed in the wind. And as he got closer the cat climbed higher. "No, Stella, don't do that! Come here!" Stella stared at him, clamped to her branch of the moment, cross-eyed with fear. Below them Mom said over and over, "Stella, it's okay — it's okay, Stella." Stella didn't believe her.

Finally Alex reached her, near the tree's top. Now here was a problem: He needed his hands to climb down, but it seemed likely he would also need them to hold the terrified cat. "Come here, Stella." He put a hand on her flank; she flinched. Her side pulsed with her rapid breathing. She hissed faintly. He had to maneuver up a step, onto a very questionable branch; his face was inches from her. She stared at him without a trace of recognition. He pried her off her branch, lifted her. If she cared to claw him now she could really tear him up. Instead she clung to his shoulder and chest, all her claws dug through his clothes, quivering under his left arm and hand.

Laboriously he descended, using only the one hand. Stella began miaowing fiercely, and struggling a bit. Finally he met Mom, who had climbed the tree quite a ways. Stella was getting more upset. "Hand her to me." Alex detached her from his chest paw by paw, balanced, held the cat down with both hands. Again it was a tricky moment; if Stella went berserk they would all be in trouble. But she fell onto Mom's chest and collapsed, a catatonic ball of fur.

Back in the apartment she dashed for her blanket under the table. Mom enticed her out with food, but she was very jumpy and she wouldn't allow Alex anywhere near her; she ran away if he even entered the room. "Back to square one, I see," Mom commented.

"It's not fair! I'm the one that saved her!"

"She'll get over it." Mom laughed, clearly relieved. "Maybe it'll take some time, but she will. Ha! This is clear proof that cats are smart enough to be crazy. Irrational, neurotic—just like a person." They laughed, and Stella glared at them balefully. "Yes you are, aren't you! You'll come around again."

Often when Alex got home in the early evenings his father was striding back and forth in the kitchen talking loudly, angrily, fearfully, while Mom tried to reassure him. "They're doing the same thing to us they did to Rick Stone! But why!" When Alex closed the front door the conversation would stop. Once when he walked tentatively down the quiet hallway to the kitchen he found them standing there, arms around each other, Father's head in Mom's short hair.

Father raised his head, disengaged, went to his study. On his way he said, "Alex, I need your help."

"Sure."

Alex stood in the study and watched without understanding as his father took books from his shelves and put them in the big laundry bag. He threw the first few in like dirty clothes, then sighed and thumped in the rest in a businesslike fashion, not looking at them.

"There's a used book store in Cambridge, on Mass Ave. Antonio's."

"Sure, I know the one." They had been there together a few times.

"I want you to take these over there and sell them to Tony for me," Father said, looking at the empty shelves. "Will you do that for me?"

"Sure." Alex picked up the bag, shocked that it had come to this. Father's books! He couldn't meet his father's eye. "I'll do that right now," he said uncertainly, and hefted the bag over one shoulder. In the hallway Mom approached and put a hand on his shoulder—her silent thanks—then went into the study.

Alex hiked east toward the university, crossed the Charles River on the great iron bridge. The wind howled in the superstructure. On the Cambridge side, after showing his pass, he put the heavy bag on the ground and inspected its contents. Ever since the infamous incident of the spilled hot chocolate, Father's books had been off-limits to him; now a good twenty of them were there in the bag to be touched, opened, riffled through. Many in this bunch were in foreign languages, especially Greek and Russian, with their alien alphabets. Could people really read such marks? Well, Father did. It must be possible.

When he had inspected all the books he chose two in English—*The Odyssey* and *The Colossus of Maroussi*—and put those in his down jacket pockets. He could take them to the glacier and read them, then sell them later to Antonio's—perhaps in the next bag of books. There were many more bagfuls in Father's study.

A little snow stuck to the glacier now, filling the pocks and making bright patches on the north side of every boulder, every serac. Some of the narrower crevasses were filled with it—bright white lines on the jumbled gray. When the whole surface was white the crevasses would be invisible, and the glacier too dangerous to walk on. Now the only danger was leaving obvious footprints for trackers. Walking up the rubble lines would solve that. These lines of rubble fascinated Alex. It looked just as if bulldozers had clanked up here and shoved the majority of the stones and junk into straight lines down the big central tongue of the glacier. But in fact they were natural features. Father had attempted to explain on one of the walks they had taken up here. "The ice is moving, and it moves faster in the middle than on the outer edges, just like a stream. So rocks on the surface tend to slide over time, down into lines in the middle."

"Why are there two lines, then?"

Father shrugged, looking into the blue-green depths of a crevasse. "We really shouldn't be up here, you know that?"

Now Alex stopped to inspect a tire caught in the rubble line. Truck tire, tread worn right to the steel belting. It would burn, but with too much smoke. There were several interesting objects in this neat row of rock and sand: plastic jugs, a doll, a lampbase, a telephone.

His shelter was undisturbed. He pulled the two books from his pockets and set them on the bench, propping them with rock bookends.

He circled the boulder, had a look around. The sky today was a low smooth pearl gray sheet, ruffled by a set of delicate waves pasted to it. The indirect light brought out all the colors: the pink of the remarkable snow algae, the blue of the seracs, the various shades of rock, the occasional bright spot of junk, the many white patches of snow. A million dots of color under the pewter sheet of cloud.

Three creaks, a crack, a long shuddering rumble. Sleepy, muscular, the great beast had moved. Alex walked across its back to his bench, sat. On the far lateral moraine some gravel slid down. Puffs of brown dust in the air.

He read his books. *The Odyssey* was strange but interesting. Father had told him some of the story before. *The Colossus of Maroussi* was long-winded but funny—it reminded Alex of his uncle, who could turn the smallest incident into an hour's comic monologue. What he could have made of Stella's flight up the tree! Alex laughed to think of it. But his uncle was in jail.

He sat on his bench and read, stopped occasionally to look around. When the hand holding the book got cold, he changed hands and put the cold one in a pocket of his down jacket. When both hands were blue he hid the books in rocks under his bench and went home.

There were more bags of books to be sold at Antonio's and other shops in Cambridge. Each time Alex rotated out a few that looked interesting, and replaced them with the ones on the glacier. He daydreamed of saving all the books and earning the money some other way—then presenting his father with the lost library, at some future undefined but appropriate moment.

Eventually Stella forgave him for rescuing her. She came to enjoy chasing a piece of yarn up and down their long narrow hallway, skidding around the corner by the study. It reminded them of a game they had played with Pongo, who would chase anything, and they laughed at her, especially when she jerked to a halt and licked her fur fastidiously, as if she had never been carousing. "You can't fool us, Stell! We *remember!*"

Mom sold most of her music collection, except for her favorites. Once Alex went out to the glacier with the *Concerto de Aranjuez* coursing through him—Mom had had it on in the apartment while she worked. He hummed the big theme of the second movement as he crunched over the ice: Clearly it was the theme of the glacier, the glacier's song. How had a blind composer managed to capture the windy sweep of it, the spaciousness? Perhaps such things could be heard as well as seen. The wind said it, whistling over the ice. It was a terrifically dark day, windy, snowing in gusts. He could walk right up the middle of the great tongue, between the rubble lines; no one else would be up there today. Da-da-da . . . da da da da da da, da-da-da. . . . Hands in pockets, chin on chest, he trudged into the wind humming, feeling like the whole world was right there around him. It was too cold to stay in his shelter for more than a minute.

He read his books. The Odyssey was strange but interesting. Father had told him some of the story before. The *Colossus of Maroussi* was very

Father went off on trips, exploring possibilities. One morning Alex woke to the sound of *The Pirates of Penzance*. This was one of their favorites, Mom played it all the time while working and on Saturday mornings, so that they knew all the lyrics by heart and often sang along. Alex especially loved the Pirate King, and could mimic all his intonations.

He dressed and walked down to the kitchen. Mom stood by the stove with her back to him, singing along. It was a sunny morning and their big kitchen windows faced east; the light poured in on the sink and the dishes and the white stove and the linoleum and the plants in the window and Stella, sitting contentedly on the window sill listening.

His mom was tall and broad-shouldered. Every year she cut her hair shorter; now it was just a cap of tight brown curls, with a somewhat longer patch down the nape of her neck. That would go soon, Alex thought, and then her hair would be as short as it could be. She was lost in the song, one slim hand on the white stove top, looking out the window. She had a low, rich, thrilling voice, like a real singer's only prettier. She was singing along with the song that Mabel sings after she finds out that Frederick won't be able to leave the pirates until 1940.

When it was over Alex entered the kitchen, went to the pantry. "That's a short one," he said.

"Yes, they had to make it short," Mom said. "There's nothing funny about that one."

One night while Father was gone on one of his trips, Mom had to go over to Ilene and Ira and Gary's apartment: Gary had been arrested, and Ilene and Ira needed help. Alex and Stella were left alone.

Stella wandered the silent apartment miaowing. "I *know*, Stella," Alex said in exasperation. "They're *gone*. They'll be back tomorrow." The cat paid no attention to him.

He went into Father's study. Tonight he'd be able to read something in relative warmth. It would only be necessary to be *very careful*.

The bookshelves were empty. Alex stood before them, mouth open. He had no idea they had sold that many of them. There were a couple left on Father's desk, but he didn't want to move them. They appeared to be dictionaries anyway. "It's all Greek to me."

He went back to the living room and got out the yarn bag, tried to interest Stella in a game. She wouldn't play. She wouldn't sit on his lap. She wouldn't stop miaowing. "Stella, shut up!" She scampered away and kept crying. Vexed, he got out the jar of catnip and spread some on the linoleum in the kitchen. Stella came running to sniff at it, then roll in it. Afterwards she played with the yarn wildly, until it caught around her tail and she froze, staring at him in a drugged paranoia. Then she dashed to her refuge and refused to come out. Finally Alex put on *The Pirates of Penzance* and listened to it for a while. After that he was sleepy.

They got a good lawyer for Gary, Mom said. Everyone was hopeful. Then a couple of weeks later Father got a new job; he called them from work to tell them about it.

"Where is it?" Alex asked Mom when she was off the phone.

"In Kansas."

"So we will be moving."

"Yes," Mom said. "Another move."

"Will there be glaciers there too?"

"I think so. In the hills. Not as big as ours here, maybe. But there are glaciers everywhere."

▼

He walked onto the ice one last time. There was a thin crust of snow on the tops of everything. A fantastically jumbled field of snow. It was a clear day, the sky a very pale blue, the white expanse of the glacier painfully bright. A few cirrus clouds made sickles high in the west. The snow was melting a bit and there were water droplets all over, with little sparks of colored light in each drip. The sounds of water melting were everywhere, drips, gurgles, splashes. The intensity of light was stunning, like a blow to the brain, right through the eyes. It pulsed.

The crevasse in front of his shelter had widened, and the boards of his bench had fallen. The wall of ice turning around the boulder was splintered, and shards of bright ice lay over the planks.

The glacier was moving. The glacier was alive. No heated dam would stop it. He felt its presence, huge and supple under him, seeping into him like the cold through his wet shoes, filling him up. He blinked, nearly blinded by the light breaking everywhere on it, a surgical glare that made every snow-capped rock stand out like the color red on a slide transparency. The white light. In the distance the ice cracked hollowly, moving somewhere. Everything moved: the ice, the wind, the clouds, the sun, the planet. All of it rolling around.

▼

As they packed up their possessions Alex could hear them in the next room. "We can't," Father said. "You know we can't. They won't let us."

When they were done the apartment looked odd. Bare walls, bare wood floors. It looked smaller. Alex walked the length of it: his parents' room overlooking Chester Street; his room; his father's study; the living room; the kitchen with its fine morning light. The pantry. Stella wandered the place miaowing. Her blanket was still in its corner, but without the table it looked moth-eaten, fur-coated, ineffectual. Alex picked her up and went through the pantry, up the back stairs to the roof.

Snow had drifted into the corners. Alex walked in circles, looking at the city. Stella sat on her paws by the stairwell shed, watching him, her fur ruffled by the wind.

Around the shed snow had melted, then froze again. Little puddles of ice ran in flat curves across the the pebbled tar paper. Alex crouched to inspect them, tapping one speculatively with a fingernail. He stood up and looked west, but buildings and bare treetops obscured the view.

Stella fought to stay out of the box, and once in it she cried miserably.

Father was already in Kansas, starting the new job. Alex and Mom and Stella had been staying in the living room of Michael Wu's place while Mom finished her work; now she was done, it was moving day, they were off to the train. But first they had to take Stella to the Talbots'.

Alex carried the box and followed Mom as they walked across the Commons and down Comm Ave. He could feel the cat shifting over her blanket, scrabbling at the cardboard against his chest. Mom walked fast, a bit ahead of him. At Kenmore they turned south.

When they got to the Talbots', Mom took the box. She looked at him. "Why don't you stay down here," she said.

"Okay."

She rang the bell and went in with the buzzer, holding the box under one arm.

Alex sat on the steps of the walk-up. There were little ones in the corner: flat fingers of ice, spilling away from the cracks.

Mom came out the door. Her face was pale, she was biting her lip. They took off walking at a fast pace. Suddenly Mom said, "Oh, Alex, she was *so scared*," and sat down on another stoop and put her head on her knees.

Alex sat beside her, his shoulder touching hers. Don't say anything, don't put arm around shoulders or anything. He had learned this from Father. Just sit there, be there. Alex sat there like the glacier, shifting a little. Alive. The white light.

After a while she stood. "Let's go," she said.

They walked up Comm Ave. toward the train station. "She'll be all right with the Talbots," Alex said. "She already likes Jay."

"I know." Mom sniffed, tossed her head in the wind. "She's getting to be a pretty adaptable cat." They walked on in silence. She put an arm over his shoulders. "I wonder how Pongo is doing." She took a deep breath. Overhead clouds tumbled like chunks of broken ice.

THE PSYCHIC LANDSCAPE
by Kim Stanley Robinson

▼

Love of place is one of the most powerful human emotions, and in this time, when people are increasingly mobile and all social spaces are tending to look more and more the same, our love of place has not attenuated but rather sharpened, become a hunger for something missing. This hunger can be appeased, to some extent, in stories.

There is an idea that setting in fiction is merely the backdrop for the all-important plot. Reverse that: Imagine that plots are merely the stage business allowing us to visit places in our minds.

Then move to a more balanced view. A plot in a place: Fiction can appeal both to our addiction to stories and to our love of place, all at once. That is a powerful combination.

At its minimal value, setting contributes to what Roland Barthes called "the effect of the real." Barthes was referring to those parts of a story that do not advance the plot, deepen characters, or serve any symbolic purpose; these details seem almost to be gratuitous inclusions, deserving to be trimmed; but their usefulness then comes from that very quality, the implication being that "because the story really happened this way, these facts have to be included."

If a story's setting goes below that minimum value, is missing or very sketchy, the story then exists in a kind of no-place, or at best on a ticky-tacky stage set, as in daytime soap operas or cheap sci-fi movies; and a part of the reading mind is muttering, Well, this didn't really happen, that's why it's all so fake-looking; and the clever plot and snappy dialogue go to waste.

This is true even if the entire story takes place indoors.

Lack of setting is particularly dangerous in science fiction, where the setting is often unvisited as yet, or displaced into the future—imaginary in some way or another. One of the games we play in our genre is making these imaginary spaces seem real. Setting therefore becomes a major part of almost every SF story. In quite a few of them, setting becomes the equivalent of one of the story's characters, sometimes even the protagonist: The characters' interactions with the place form the plot. Naturally, in these stories the setting can hardly be overemphasized.

So there is a continuum, from setting-as-reality-effect to setting-as-heart-of-story. But in all cases it is important, and the writer must take it into consideration, and devote some of the text to it.

This becomes part of the text's exposition, and there lies a problem. The current Anglo-American SF scene is death on exposition. Many advise doing exposition only in snippets, tucked here and there so that at no point does the reader notice it, but merely collects data bits along the way, and constructs the background from that. The clear implication is that setting and other kinds of exposition aren't important enough to interrupt the all-important plot: The proper study of man is man, don't mention that gun on the mantle unless you're going to use it later on, show don't tell, and at all costs avoid the "expository lump" or "infodump" (there is no positive workshop term for this phenomenon).

Why slight exposition in this way? Science itself is a fairly expository process, after all, and if you are one of those who try to put some science in your science fiction, you will find exposition quite helpful. Really, the demand to serve up something so important only in snippets is a contradiction, it doesn't make sense. H. Bruce Franklin has even argued that this convention condemning exposition is a kind of ideological self-censorship, tending to prevent writers from having to say anything new or dangerous, and leaving only stage business. In any case it is a curtailment of options, it cramps your style.

I say exposition is fine. In fact expository lumps are often the place where the story is *most* interesting rather than least, the place where the writer's obsessions take over. And you have to trust your obsessions. A perfectly streamlined short story with all its elements balanced is a fine thing, if it works—but the only real rule is, make it interesting. If it's interesting then you can go on for pages in any mode you please; that's one of the glories of fiction, it can absorb all other kinds of writing.

Of course going on for pages about something and remaining interesting is difficult, but this is true in every mode of writing, so you might as well not avoid exposition just because it is hard; it is all hard. Purely descriptive writing is very difficult indeed. But it is always necessarily presented from a point of view—all landscapes are psychic landscapes—and so it's fairly easy for a fiction writer to do descriptions from a character's point of view. This is the start of one method for helping lengthy exposition of setting to stay interesting: Make it do two things at once, landscape expressing character and vice versa.

Some other suggestions:

When describing space, remember time; time of day, the weather, the season, the light, the moment in history: All these combine to fix a place in mind. In Conrad's "Typhoon" we learn about the sea, not for all time but during a storm; in *A Suitable Boy* by Vikram Seth we learn about India, not all of it always, but in certain northern states in 1951.

Weather in particular can serve as an objective correlative for the emotion desired, a symbol of the situation. The ever-present fog in Dickens' *Bleak House* is a famous example of this, physicalizing the vague ominous quality of the novel's legal and moral worlds. My feeling is you can work these effects pretty heavily before they look ham-handed.

It helps to have visited a place when writing about it. This is one of the ways writing fiction becomes a discipline for increasing your involvement in the world. Everywhere you go you must pay attention, because it may well be that you will later want to use that place in fiction. Then you will write what you remember. Writing about place is a kind of impressionism.

This leads to another method: the search for the "heraldic moment," as Lawrence Durrell called it, which is a particularly powerful image that evokes the whole experience. Some writers are superb at finding heraldic moments, giving the impression of a fully-rendered setting with great economy. A sentence early in *The Left Hand of Darkness:* "Rainclouds over dark towers, rain falling in deep streets, a dark storm-beaten city of stone, through which one vein of gold winds slowly."

Note the metaphor above. Metaphors can link the unknown to the known, and so help the reader to visualize the unknown. They can link the concrete and the abstract; they can link two familiar things never linked before; they are one of the great joys of literature, especially when they are both surprising and apt, i.e. "true." They are a great help in establishing setting.

Another method, in contrast to the "heraldic moment," is to pile a lot of detail together in a heap. Pynchon does this often in *Gravity's Rainbow;* a paragraph begins,

"The storm has blown away, the breeze is mild today and the sky lies overhead in a perfect interference-pattern, mackerel gray and blue. Someplace military machines are rooting and clanking. Men and women are hollering near and far in Russian. Otto and Slothrop dodge them down alleys flanked by the remains of half-timbered houses, stepped out story by story, about to meet overheard after centuries of imperceptible toppling. Men in black-billed caps sit on stoops, watching hands for cigarettes. In a little square market stalls are set up, wood frames and old, stained canvas shimmering when the breeze passes through. Russian soldiers lean against posts or benches, talking to girls in dirndls and white knee-socks. . . ."

—and the paragraph continues in this manner for most of another page, until that seaside town is palpable. This is perhaps easier to do in a novel than in a short story, but it is surprising how quickly a sequence of details begins to feel like a lot; it might take only half a page or less, if it is a dense list of sensory impressions. This can be worth it even in short fiction, for after that, the reader is there; and has had the enjoyment of a wonderful half-page.

If you can include an observation so detailed and unique to the situation that it had to have been observed on site, this will always help to evoke a place. Sometimes these details can even be made up by a clever deduction, but usually it is a matter of paying attention while you are there.

If you can't visit a place but want to write about it anyway, extensive reading helps, and pictures, and films; always looking to find the heraldic moment, the unique detail, always trying to integrate all the data into your own vision of the place. You can also work by analogy to places you have visited; for Mars, for instance, you could visit deserts, high mountains, Meteor Crater, etc.

As a way to decide what to include, remember that in fiction the emotion evoked by the place is what's most important about it. In the case of "Glacier," I moved to Boston in the fall of 1974, after living all my life in southern California. I was cold. I wore my down jacket and hiking boots everywhere. I was stunned to see snow in a city, and in general felt somewhat overwhelmed. I lived in the apartment described in the story, with the roommates likewise described. Making the viewpoint character a young boy felt right. Stella came from a different part of my life, but fit in. A lot of our stories process our lives in that way; this is a good thing all around.

As for the glacier, I suppose in some ways it is a symbol threatening to overrun the story, like a glacier plowing over a city. The chill of that psychic landscape. Also I spent time on Swiss glaciers in the year I wrote the story (1986), and I wanted to talk about them. But it was so much more interesting to do it in Boston, through the eyes of that boy! Why this is I cannot say.

So much of fiction is a matter of such unconscious choices. These books on the craft of writing can give the impression that their categories are the inside story, and that writers in the act of composition think about them consciously. For me it's more a matter of one sentence after another, struggling to find what to say. Afterward it's possible to analyze the story and see these various components, if you care to, and so it's good to know them, as preparation and as an aid to thought during revision. But the reader experiences the story in a way similar to the writing of it, as a flow of information and emotion, a willing suspension of disbelief, a plunge into something like dream. So it's important to remember that there are no rules, there are only suggestions. I say: Pay attention. Trust your obsessions. Make it interesting.

BEAST OF THE HEARTLAND
by Lucius Shepard

▼

Mears has a dream the night after he fought the Alligator Man. The dream begins with words: "In the beginning was a dark little god with glowing red eyes. . . ." And then, there it stands, hovering in the blackness of Mears' hotel room, a twisted mandrake root of a god, evil and African, with ember eyes and limbs like twists of leaf tobacco. Even after it vanishes, waking Mears, he can feel those eyes burning inside his head, merged into a single red pain that seems as if it will go on throbbing forever. He wonders if he should tell Leon about the pain—maybe he could give Mears something to ease it—but he figures this might be a bad idea. Leon might cut and run, not wanting to be held responsible should Mears keel over, and there Mears would be: without a trainer, without anyone to coach him for the eye exams, without an accomplice in his blindness. It's not a priority, he decides.

To distract himself, he lies back and thinks about the fight. He'd been doing pretty well until the ninth. Staying right on the Cuban's chest, mauling him in the corners, working the body. The Cuban didn't like it to the body. He was a honey-colored kid a couple of shades lighter than Mears and he punched like a kid, punches that stung but that didn't take your heart like the punches of a man. Fast, though. Jesus, he was fast! As the fight passed into the middle rounds, as Mears tired, the Cuban began to slip away, to circle out of the haze of ring light and vanish into the darkness at the corners of Mears's eyes, so that Mears saw the punches coming only at the last second, the wet-looking red blobs of the gloves looping in over his guard. Then, in the ninth, a left he never saw drove him into the turnbuckle, a flurry of shots under the ribs popped his mouthpiece halfway out and another left to the temple made him clinch, pinning the Cuban's gloves against his sides.

In the clinch, that's when he caught sight of the Alligator Man. The

Cuban pulled back his head, trying to wrench his right glove free, and
the blurred oval of his face sharpened, resolved into features: blazing yellow eyes and pebbly skin, and slit nostrils at the end of a long snout. Although used to such visions, hallucinations, whatever this was, Mears
reacted in terror. He jolted the Alligator Man with an uppercut, he spun
him, landed a clubbing right high on the head, another right, and as if
those punches were magic, as if their force and number were removing
a curse, breaking a spell, the Alligator Man's face melted away, becoming a blurred brown oval once again. Mears's terror also grew blurred,
his attack less furious, and the Cuban came back at him, throwing shots
from every angle. Mears tried to slide off along the ropes but his legs were
gone, so he ducked his head and put his gloves up to block the shots. But
they got through, anyway.

Somebody's arms went around him, hemming him in against the
ropes, and he smelled flowery cologne and heard a smooth baritone saying, "Take it easy, man! It's over." Mears wanted to tell the ref he could
have stood up through ten, the Cuban couldn't punch for shit. But he
was too weak to say anything and he just rested his head on the ref's shoulder, strings of drool hanging off his mouthpiece, cooling on his chin. And
for the first time in a long while, he heard the crowd screaming for the
Cuban, the women's voices bright and crazy, piercing up from the male
roar. Then Leon was there, Leon's astringent smell of Avitene and Vaseline and Gelfoam, and somebody shoved Mears down onto a stool and
Leon pressed the ice-cold bar of the Enswell against the lump over his
eye, and the Cuban elbowed his way through the commission officials
and nobodies in the corner and said, "Man, you one tough motherfucker. You almos' kill me with them right hands." And Mears had the
urge to tell him, "You think I'm tough, wait'll you see what's coming,"
but instead, moved by the sudden, heady love that possesses you after you
have pounded on a man for nine rounds and he has not fallen, Mears
told him that one day soon he would be champion of the world.

Mears wonders if the bestial faces that materialize in the midst of his
fights are related to the pain in his head. In his heart he believes they are
something else. It could be that he has been granted the magical power
to see beneath the surface of things. Or they may be something his mind
has created to compensate for his blindness, a kind of spiritual adrena-
line that inspires him to fiercer effort, often to victory. Since his retinas
became detached, he has slipped from the status of fringe contender to

trial horse for young fighters on the way up, and his style has changed from one of grace to that of a brawler, of someone who must keep in constant physical contact with his opponent. Nevertheless, he has won twelve of seventeen fights with his handicap, and he owes much of his success to this symptom or gift or delusion.

He knows most people would consider him a fool for continuing to fight, and he accepts this. But he does not consider himself a greater fool than most people; his is only a more dramatic kind of foolishness than the foolishness of loving a bad woman or stealing a car or speculating on gold futures or smoking cigarettes or taking steroids or eating wrong or involving yourself with the trillion other things that lead to damage and death.

As he lies in that darkened room, in the pall of his own darkness, he imagines attending a benefit held to raise his medical expenses after his secret has been disclosed. All the legends are there. Ali, Frazier, and Foreman are there, men who walk with the pride of a nation. Duran is there, Duran of the demonic fury, who TKO'd him in 1979, back when Mears was a welterweight. The Hit Man is there, Thomas Hearns, sinister and rangy, with a cobra-like jab that had once cut him so badly the flesh hung down into his eyes. Sugar Ray Leonard is there, talking about his own detached retina and how he could have gone the same way as Mears. And Hagler, who knocked Mears out in his only title shot, Hagler the tigerish southpaw, he is there, too. Mears ascends to the podium to offer thanks, and a reporter catches his arm and asks him, "What the hell went wrong, Bobby? What happened to you?" He thinks of all the things he could say in response. Bad managers, crooked promoters. Alimony, I forgot to duck. The classic answers. But there is one answer they've never heard, one that he's nourished for almost two years.

"I traveled into the heartland," he tells the reporter, "and when I got done fighting the animals there, I came out blind."

The reporter looks puzzled, but Ali and Foreman, Frazier and Hagler, Duran and Hearns, they nod sagely, they understand. They realize Mears' answer is partly a pride thing, partly intuitive, a summation of punches absorbed, hands lifted in victory, months of painful healing, hours of punishment in the gym. But mainly it is the recasting into a vow of a decision made years before. They would not argue that their sport is brutally stupid, run by uncaring bastards to whom it is a business of dollars and blood, and that tragedies occur, that fighters are swindled and

outright robbed. Yet there is something about it they have needed, something they have chosen, and so in the end, unlike the asbestos worker who
bitterly decries the management that has lied to him and led him down
a fatal path, the fighter feels no core bitterness, not even at himself for
being a fool, for making such a choice in the folly of youth, because he
has forsworn the illusion of wisdom.

Mears is not without regrets. Sometimes, indeed, he regrets almost
everything. He regrets his blindness, his taste in women, his rotten luck
at having been a middleweight during the age of Marvin Hagler. But he
has never regretted boxing. He loves what he does, loves the gym rats,
the old dozers with their half-remembered tales of Beau Jack and Henry
Armstrong, the crafty trainers, the quiet cut men with their satchels full
of swabs and chemicals. He loves how he has been in the ring, honor-
able and determined and brave. And now, nodding off in a cheap hotel
room, he feels love from the legends of the game returned in applause
that has the sound of rushing water, a pure stream of affirmation that bears
him away into the company of heroes and a restless sleep.

Three mornings later, as Mears waits for Leon in the gym, he listens
happily to the slapping of jump ropes, the grunt and thud of someone
working the heavy bag, the jabber and pop of speed bags, fighters shouting encouragement, the sandpapery whisk of shoes on canvas, the meaty
thump of fourteen-ounce sparring gloves. Pale winter light chutes
through the high windows like a Bethlehem star to Mears' eyes. The smell
is a harsh perfume of antiseptic, resin, and sweat. Now and then somebody passes by, says, "Yo, Bobby, what's happenin'?" or "Look good the
other night, man!" and he will hold out his hand to be slapped without
glancing up, pretending that his diffidence is an expression of cool, not
a pose designed to disguise his impaired vision. His body still aches from
the Cuban's fast hands, but in a few weeks, a few days if necessary, he'll
be ready to fight again.

He hears Leon rasping at someone, smells his cigar, then spots a dark
interruption in the light. Not having to see Leon, he thinks, is one of the
few virtues of being legally blind. He is unsightly, a chocolate-colored
blob of a man with jowls and yellow teeth and a belly that hangs over his
belt. The waist of Mears' boxing trunks would not fit over one of Leon's
thighs. He is especially unsightly when he lies, which is often — weakness

comes into his face, his popped eyes dart, the pink tip of the tongue slimes the gristly upper lip. He looks much better as a blur in an onion-colored shirt and dark trousers.

"Got a fight for us, my man." Leon drops onto a folding chair beside him, and the chair yields a metallic creak. "Mexican name Nazario. We gon' kick his fuckin' ass!"

This is the same thing Leon said about the Cuban, the same thing he said about every opponent. But this time he may actually be sincere. "Guy's made for us," he continues. "Comes straight ahead. Good hook, but a nothin' right. No fancy bullshit." He claps Bobby on the leg. "We need a W bad, man. We whup this guy in style, I can get us a main event on ESPN next month in Wichita."

Mears is dubious. "Fighting who?"

"Vederotta," says Leon, hurrying past the name to say the Nazario fight is in two weeks. "We can be ready by then, can't we, sure, we be ready, we gon' kill that motherfucker."

"That guy calls himself the Heat? Guy everybody's been duckin'?"

"Wasn't for everybody duckin' him, I couldn't get us the fight. He's tough, I ain't gon' tell you no lie. He busts people up. But check it out, man. Our end's twenty grand. Like that, Bobby? Tuh-wenty thousand dollars."

"You shittin' me?"

"They fuckin' desperate. They can't get nobody to fight the son of a bitch. They need a tune-up for a title shot." Leon sucks on his cigar, trying to puff it alight. "It's your ass out there, man. I'll do what you tell me. But we get past Nazario, we show good against Vederotta—I mean give him a few strong rounds, don't just fold in one—guy swears he'll book us three more fights on ESPN cards. Maybe not the main event, but TV bouts. That'd make our year, man. Your end could work out to forty, forty-five."

"You get that in writin' 'bout the three more fights?"

"Pretty sure. Man's so damn desperate for somebody with a decent chin, he'll throw in a weekend with his wife."

"I don't want his damn wife, I want it in writin' 'bout the fights."

"You ain't seen his wife! That bitch got a wiggle take the kinks outta a couch spring." Delighted by his wit, Leon laughs; the laugh turns into a wet, racking cough.

"I'm gon' need you on this one," says Mears after the coughing has subsided. "None of this bullshit 'bout you runnin' round all over after dope and pussy while I'm bustin' my balls in the gym, and then showin' up when the bell rings. I'm gon' need you really working. You hear that, Leon?"

Leon's breath comes hard. "I hear you."

"Square business, man. You gotta write me a book on that Vederotta dude."

"I'll do my thing," says Leon, wheezing. "You just take care of old Señor Nazario."

The deal concluded, Mears feels exposed, as if a vast, luminous eye—God's, perhaps—is shining on him, revealing all his frailties. He sits up straight, holds his head very still, rubs his palms along the tops of his thighs, certain that everyone is watching. Leon's breathing is hoarse and labored, like last breaths. The light is beginning to tighten up around that sound, to congeal into something cold and gray, like a piece of dirty ice in which they are all embedded.

Mears thinks of Vederotta, the things he's heard. The one-round knockouts, the vicious beatings. He knows he's just booked himself a world of hurt. As if in resonance with that thought, his vision ripples and there is a twinge inside his head, a little flash of red. He grips the seat of the chair, prepares for worse. But worse does not come, and after a minute or so, he begins to relax, thinking about the money, slipping back into the peace of morning in the gym, with the starred light shining from on high and the enthusiastic shouts of the young fighters and the slap of leather making a rhythm like a river slapping against a bank and the fat man who is not his friend beginning to breathe easier now beside him.

When Mears phones his ex-wife, Amandla, the next night, he sits on the edge of the bed and closes his eyes so he can see her clearly. She's wearing her blue robe, slim-hipped and light-skinned, almost like a Latin girl, but her features are fine and eloquently African and her hair is kept short in the way of a girl from Brazzaville or Conakry. He remembers how good she looks in big-hoop gold earrings. He remembers so much sweetness, so much consolation and love. She simply had not been able to bear his pain, coming home with butterfly patches over his stitched eyes, pissing blood at midnight, having to heave himself up from a chair like an old man. It was a weakness in her, he thinks, yet he knows it was an equiv-

alent weakness in him, that fighting is his crack, his heroin—he would
not give it up for her.

She picks up on the fourth ring, and he says, "How you been, baby?"

She hesitates a moment before saying, "Aw, Bobby, what you want?"
But she says it softly, plaintively, so he'll know that though it's not a good
thing to call, she's glad to hear his voice, anyway.

"Nothin', baby," he says. "I don't want nothin'. I just called to tell
you I'll be sendin' money soon. Few weeks, maybe."

"You don't have to. I'm makin' it all right."

"Don't tell me you can't use a little extra. You got responsibilities."

A faded laugh. "I hear that."

There is silence for a few beats, then Mears says, "How's your mama
holdin' up?"

"Not so good. Half the time I don't think she knows who I am. She
goes to wanderin' off sometimes, and I got to—" She breaks off, lets air
hiss out between her teeth. "I'm sorry, Bobby. This ain't your trouble."

That stings him, but he does not respond directly to it. "Well, maybe
I send you a little somethin', you can ease back from it."

"I don't want to short you."

"You ain't gon' be shortin' me, baby." He tells her about Nazario,
the $20,000, but not about Vederotta.

"Twenty thousand!" she says. "They givin' you twenty thousand for
fightin' a man you say's easy? That don't make any sense."

"Ain't like I'm just off the farm. I still got a name."

"Yeah, but you—"

"Don't worry about it," he says angrily, knowing that she's about to
remind him he's on the downside. "I got it under control."

Another silence. He imagines that he can hear her irritation in the
static on the line.

"But I do worry," she says. "God help me, I still worry about you after
all this time."

"Ain't been that long. Three years."

She does not seem to have heard. "I still think about you under them
lights gettin' pounded on. And now you offerin' me money you gon' earn
for gettin' pounded on some more."

"Look here—" he begins.

"Blood money. That's what it is. It's blood money."

"Stop it," he says. "You stop that shit. It ain't no more blood money than any other wage. Money gets paid out, somebody always gettin' fucked over at the end of it. That's just what money is. But this here money, it ain't comin' 'cause of nothin' like that, not even 'cause some damn judge said I got to give it. It's coming from me to you 'cause you need it and I got it."

He steers the conversation away from the topic of fighting, gets her talking about some of their old friends, even manages to get her laughing when he tells her how the cops caught Sidney Bodden and some woman doing the creature in Sidney's car in the parking lot of the A&P. The way she laughs, she tips her head and tucks her chin down onto her shoulder and never opens her mouth, just makes these pleased, musical noises like a shy little girl, and when she lifts her head, she looks so innocent and pretty he wants to kiss her, grazes the receiver with his lips, wishes it would open and let him pour through to her end of the line. The power behind the wish hits his heart like a mainlined drug, and he knows she still loves him, he still loves her, this is all wrong, this long-distance shit, and he can't stop himself from saying, "Baby, I want to see you again."

"No," she says.

It is such a terminal, door-slamming no, he can't come back with anything. His face is hot and numb, his arms and chest heavy as concrete, he feels the same bewildered, mule-stupid helplessness as he did when she told him she was leaving. He wonders if she's seeing somebody, but he promises himself he won't ask.

"I just can't, Bobby," she says.

"It's all right, baby," he says, his voice reduced to whisper. "It's all right. I got to be goin'."

"I'm sorry, I really am sorry. But I just can't."

"I'll be sending you something' real soon. You take care now."

"Bobby?"

He hangs up, an effort, and sits there turning to stone. Brooding thoughts glide through his head like slow black sails. After a while he lifts his arms as if in an embrace. He feels Amandla begin to take on shape and solidity within the circle of his arms. He puts his left hand between her shoulder blades and smooths the other along her flanks, following the arch of her back, the tight rounds of her ass, the columned thighs, and he presses his face against her belly, smelling her warmth, letting all the trouble and ache of the fight with the Cuban go out of him. All the weight of loss and sadness. His chest seems to fill with something clear and buoyant. Peace, he thinks, we are at peace.

But then some sly, peripheral sense alerts him to the fact that he is a fool to rely on this sentimental illusion, and he drops his arms, feels her fading away like steam. He sits straight, hands on knees, and turns his head to the side, his expression rigid and contemptuous as it might be during a stare-down at the center of a boxing ring. Since the onset of his blindness, he has never been able to escape the fear that people are spying on him, but lately he has begun to worry that they are not.

For once Leon has not lied. The fight with Nazario is a simple contest of wills and left hooks, and though the two men's hooks are comparable, Mears' will is by far the stronger. Only in the fourth round does he feel his control slipping, and then the face of a hooded serpent materializes where Nazario's face should be, and he pounds the serpent image with right leads until it vanishes. Early in the fifth round, he bulls Nazario into a corner and following a sequence of twelve unanswered punches, the ref steps in and stops it.

Two hours after the fight, Mears is sitting in the dimly lit bar on the bottom floor of his hotel, having a draft beer and a shot of Gentleman Jack, listening to Mariah Carey on the jukebox. The mirror is a black, rippling distance flocked by points of actinic light, a mysterious lake full of stars and no sign of his reflection. The hooker beside him is wearing a dark something sewn all over with spangles that move over breasts and hips and thighs like the scattering of moonlight on choppy water. The bartender, when he's visible at all, is a cryptic shadow. Mears is banged up some, a small but nasty cut at his hairline from a head butt and a knot on his left cheekbone, which the hooker is making much of, touching it, saying, "That's terrible-lookin', honey. Just terrible. You inna accident or somepin'?" Mears tells her to mind her own damn business, and she says, "Who you think you is, you ain't my business? You better quit yo' dissin' 'cause I ain't takin' that kinda shit from nobody!"

He buys her another drink to mollify her and goes back to his interior concerns. Although the pain from the fight is minimal, his eyes are acting up and there is a feeling of dread imminence inside his head, an apprehension of a slight wrongness that can bloom into a fiery red presence. He is trying, by maintaining a certain poise, to resist it.

The hooker leans against him. Her breasts are big and sloppy soft and her perfume smells cheap like flowered Listerine, but her waist is slender and firm, and despite her apparent toughness, he senses that she is very young, new to the life. This barely hardened innocence makes him think of Amandla.

"Don't you wan' go upstairs, baby?" she says as her hand traces loops and circles along the inside of his thigh.

"We be there soon enough," he says gruffly. "We got all night."

"Whoo!" She pulls back from him. "I never seen a young man act so stern! 'Mind me of my daddy!" From her stagy tone, he realizes she is playing to the other patrons of the place, whom he cannot see, invisible as gods on their bar stools. Then she is rubbing against him again, saying, "You gon' treat me like my daddy, honey? You gon' be hard on me?"

"Listen up," he says quietly, putting a hand on her arm. "Don't you be playin' these games. I'm payin' you good, so you just sit still and we'll have a couple drinks and talk a little bit. When the time comes, we'll go upstairs. Can you deal with that?"

He feels resentment in the tension of her arm. "OK, baby," she says with casual falsity. "What you wan' talk about?"

Mariah Carey is having a vision of love, her sinewy falsetto going high into a gospel frequency, and Mears asks the hooker if she likes the song. She shrugs. "It's all right."

"You know the words?"

"Uh-huh."

"Sing it with me?"

"Say what?"

He starts to sing, and after a couple of seconds the hooker joins in. Her voice is slight and sugary but blends well with Mears' tenor. As they sing, her enthusiasm grows and Mears feels a frail connection forming between them. When the record ends, she giggles, embarrassed, and says, "That was def, baby. You sing real good. You a musician?"

"Naw, just church stuff, you know."

"Bobby Mears!" A man's voice brays out behind him, a hand falls heavily onto his shoulder. "Goddamn, it is you! My fren', he saying, 'Ain't that Bobby Mears over there?' and I said, 'Shit, what he be doin' in here?' "

The man is huge, dark as a coal sack against the lesser darkness, and Mears has no clue to his identity.

"Yes, sir! Bobby 'the Magician' Mears! I'm your biggest fan, no shit! I seen you fight a dozen times. And I ain't talkin' TV. I mean in person. Man, this is great! Can I get you a drink? Lemme buy you one. Hey, buddy! Give us another round over here, OK?"

" 'Nother draft, 'nother shot of the Gentleman," says the bartender in a singsong delivery as he pours. He picks up the hooker's glass and says with less flair, "Vodka and coke."

"Sister," the man says to the hooker, "I don't know what Bobby's been tellin' you, but you settin' next to one of the greatest fighters ever lived."

The hooker says, "You a fighter, baby?" and Mears, who has been seething at this interruption, starts to say it's time to leave, but the man talks through him.

"The boy was slick! I'm tellin' you. Slickest thing you ever seen with that jab of his. Like to kill Marvin Hagler. That old baldhead was one lucky nigger that night. Ain't it the truth, man?"

"Bullshit," Mears says.

"Man's jus' bein' modest."

"I ain't bein' modest. Hagler was hurtin' me from round one, and all I's doin' was tryin' to survive." Mears digs a roll of bills from his pocket, peels a twenty from the top—the twenties are always on top; then the tens, then the fives. "Anybody saw that fight and thinks Hagler was lucky don't know jack shit. Hagler was the best, and it don't make me feel no better 'bout not bein' the best, you comin' round and bullshittin' me."

"Be cool, Bobby! All right, man? Be cool."

The hooker caresses Mears' shoulders, his neck, and he feels the knots of muscle, like hard tumors. It would take a thousand left hooks to work out that tension, a thousand solid impacts to drain off the poisons of fear lodged there, and he experiences a powerful welling up of despair that seems connected to no memory or incident, no stimulus whatsoever, a kind of bottom emotion, one you would never notice unless the light and the temperature and the noise level, all the conditions, were just right. But it's there all the time, the tarry stuff that floors your soul. He tells the man he's sorry for having lashed out at him. He's tired, he says, got shit on his mind.

"Hey," says the man, "hey, it's not a problem, OK?"

There follows a prickly silence that ends when Aaron Neville comes on the jukebox. Mears goes away with the tune, with the singer's liquid shifts and drops, like the voice of a saxophone, and is annoyed once again when the man says, "Who you fightin' next, Bobby? You got some-thin' lined up?"

"Vederotta," Mears says.

"The Heat, man? You fightin' the Heat? No shit! Hey, you better watch your ass with that white boy! I seen him fight Reggie Williams cou-ple months back. Hit that man so hard, two his teeth come away stuck in the mouthpiece."

Mears slides the twenty across the bar and says "Keep it" to the bar-tender.

"That's right," says the man with apparent relish. "That white boy ain't normal, you ax me. He jus' be livin' to fuck you up, know what I mean? He got somethin' wrong in his head."

"Thanks for the drink," Mears says, standing.

"Any time, Bobby, any time," the man says as Mears lets the hooker lead him toward the stairs. "You take my advice, man. Watch yourself with that Vederotta. That boy he gon' come hard, and you ain't no way slick as you used to be."

▼

Cold blue neon winks on and off in the window of Mears' room, a vague nebular shine that might be radiating from a polar beacon or a ghostly police car, and as the hooker undresses, he lies on the bed in his shorts and watches the light. It's the only thing he sees, just that chilly blue in a black field, spreading across the surface of the glass like some undersea thing, shrinking and expanding like the contractions of an icy blue heart. He has always been afraid before a fight, yet now he's afraid in a different way. Or maybe it's not the fear that's different, maybe it's his resistance to it that has changed. Maybe he's weaker, wearier. He is so accustomed to suppressing fear, however, that when he tries to exam-ine it, it slithers away into the cracks of his soul and hides there, lurking, eyes aglow, waiting for its time. Vederotta. The man's name even sounds strong, like a foreign sin, an age-old curse.

"Ain't you wan' the lights on, honey?" asks the hooker. "I wan' you be able see what you doin'."

"I see you just fine," he says. "You come on lie down."

A siren curls into the distance; two car horns start to blow in an im-patient rhythm like brass animals angry at each other; smells of barbe-cue and gasoline drift in to overwhelm the odor of industrial cleaner.

Training, he thinks. Once he starts to train, he'll handle the fear. He'll pave it over with tons of sit-ups, miles of running, countless combinations, and by fight night there'll be just enough left to motivate him.

The hooker settles onto the bed, lies on her side, leaning over him, her breasts spilling onto his chest and arm. He lifts one in his palm, squeezing its heft, and she makes a soft, pleased noise.

"Why you didn't tell me you famous?" she asks.

"I ain't famous."

"Yeah, but you was."

"What difference it make? Bein' famous ain't about nothin'."

She rolls her shoulders, making her breasts roll against him, and her hot, sweet scent seems to thicken. "Jus' nice to know is all." She runs a hand along his chest, his corded belly. "Ain't you somepin'," she says, and then, "How old're you, baby?"

"Thirty-two."

He expects her to say, "Thirty-two! Damn, baby. I thought you was twentyfive, you lookin' good." But all she does is give a little *mmm* sound as if she's filing the fact away and goes on caressing him. By this he knows that the connection they were starting to make in the bar has held and she's going to be herself with him, which is what he wants, not some play-acting bitch who will let him turn her into Amandla, because he is sick and tired of having that happen.

She helps him off with his shorts and brings him all the way hard with her hand, then touches his cock to her breasts, lets it butt and slide against her cheek, takes it in her mouth for just seconds, like into warm syrup, her tongue swirling, getting his hips to bridge up from the mattress, wise and playful in her moves, and finally she comes astride him and says, "I believe I'm ready for some of this, baby," her voice blurred, and she reaches for him, puts him where she needs it, and then her whole dark, sweet weight swings down slick and hot around him, and his neck arches, his mouth strains open and his head pushes back into the pillow, feeling as if he's dipped the back of his brain into a dark green pool, this ancient place with mossy-stone temples beneath the water and strange carvings and spirits gliding in and out the columns. When that moment passes, he finds she's riding him slow and deep and easy, not talking hooker trash, but fucking him like a young girl, her breath shaky and musical, hands braced on the pillow by his head, and he slides his hands around to cup her ass, to her back, pressing down so that her breasts graze and nudge his chest, and it's all going so right he forgets to think how good it is and gives himself over to the arc of his feelings and the steady, sinuous beat of her heart-filled body.

Afterward there is something shy and delicate between them, something he knows won't survive for long, maybe not even until morning, and maybe it's all false, maybe they have only played a deeper game, but if so, it's deep enough that the truth doesn't matter, and they are for now in that small room somewhere dark and green, the edge of that pool he dipped into for a second, a wood, sacred, with the calls of those strange metal beasts sounding in the distance from the desolate town. A shadow is circling beneath the surface of the pool, it's old, wrinkled, hard with evil, like a pale crocodile that's never been up into the light, but it's not an animal, not even a thought, it's just a name: Vederotta. He holds her tight, keeps two fingers pushed between her legs touching the heated damp of her, feeling her pulse there, still rapid and trilling, and he wants to know a little more about her, anything, just one thing, and when he whispers the only question he can think to ask, she wriggles around, holding his two fingers in place, turns her face to his chest and says her name is Arlene.

Training is like religion to Mears, the litanies of sparring, the penances of one-arm push-ups, the long retreats of his morning runs, the monastic breakfasts at four A.M., the vigils in the steam room during which he visualizes with the intensity of prayer what will happen in the ring, and as with a religion, he feels it simplifying him, paring him down, reducing his focus to a single consuming pursuit. On this occasion, however, he allows himself to be distracted and twice sleeps with Arlene. At first she tries to act flighty and brittle as she did in the bar, but when they go upstairs, that mask falls away and it is good for them again. The next night she displays no pretense whatsoever. They fuck wildly like lovers who have been long separated, and just before dawn they wind up lying on their sides, still joined, hips still moving sporadically. Mears' head is jangled and full of anxious incoherencies. He's worried about how he will suffer for this later in the gym and concerned by what is happening with Arlene. It seems he is being given a last sweetness, a young girl not yet hardened beyond repair, a girl who has some honest affection for him, who perhaps sees him as a means of salvation. This makes him think he is being prepared for something bad by God or whomever. Although he's been prepared for the worst for quite a while, now he wonders if the Vederotta fight will somehow prove to be worse than the worst, and frightened by this, he tells Arlene he can't see her again until after the fight. Being with her, he says, saps his strength and he needs all his strength for Vederotta. If she is the kind of woman who has hurt him in the past, he knows she will react badly, she will accuse him of trying to dump her, she will rave and screech and demand his attentions. And she does become angry, but when he explains that he is risking serious injury by losing his focus, her defensiveness—that's what has provoked her anger—subsides, and she pulls him atop her, draws up her knees and takes him deep, gluing him to her sticky thighs, and as the sky turns the color of tin and delivery traffic grumbles in the streets, and a great clanking and screech of metal comes from the docks, and garbage trucks groan and whine as they tip Dumpsters into their maws like iron gods draining their goblets, she and Mears rock and thrust and grind, tightening their hold on each other as the city seems to tighten around them, winching up its loose ends, notch by notch, in order to withstand the fierce pressures of the waking world.

That afternoon at the gym, Leon takes Mears into the locker room and sits him on a bench. He paces back and forth, emitting an exhaust of cigar smoke, and tells Mears that the boxing commission will be no problem, the physical exam—like most commission physicals—is going to be a joke, no eye charts, nothing, just blood pressure and heart and basic shit like that. He paces some more, then says he's finished watching films of Vederotta's last four fights.

"Ain't but one way to fight him," he says. "Smother his punches, grab him, hold him, frustrate the son of a bitch. Then when he get wild and come bullin' in, we start to throw uppercuts. Uppercuts all night long. That's our only shot. Understand?"

"I hear you."

"Man's strong." Leon sighs as he takes a seat on the bench opposite Mears. "Heavyweight strong. He gon' come at us from the bell and try to hurt us. He use his head, his elbows, whatever he gots. We can't let him back us up. We back up on this motherfucker, we goin' to sleep."

There is more. Mears can feel it, and he waits patiently, picking at the wrappings on his hands while he listens to the slap and babble from the gym.

" 'Member that kid Tony Ayala?" Leon asks. "Junior middleweight 'bout ten years ago. Mean fuckin' kid, wound up rapin' some school-teacher in Jersey. Big puncher. This Vederotta 'mind me of him. He knock Jeff Toney down and then he kick him. He hold up Reggie Williams 'gainst the ropes when the man out on his feet so he kin hit him five, six times more." Leon pauses. "Maybe he's too strong. Maybe we should pull out of this deal. What you think?"

Mears realizes that Leon is mainly afraid Vederotta will knock him into retirement, that his cut of the $20,000 will not compensate for a per-manent loss of income. But the fact that Leon has asked what he thinks, that's new, that's a real surprise. He suspects that deep within that gross bulk, the pilot light of Leon's moral self, long extinguished, has been relit and he is experiencing a flicker of concern for Mears' well-being. Rec-ognizing this, Mears is, for reasons he cannot fathom, less afraid.

"Ain't you listenin', man? I axed what you think."

"Got to have that money," Mears says.

Leon sucks on his cigar, spits. "I don't know 'bout this," he says, real doubt in his voice, real worry. "I just don't know."

Mears thinks about Leon, all the years, the lies, the petty betrayals and pragmatic loyalty, the confusion that Leon must be experiencing to be troubled by emotion at this stage of the relationship. He tries to pic-ture who Leon is and conjures the image of something bloated and mot-tled washed up on a beach—something that would have been content to float and dream in the deep blue-green light, chewing on kelp, but would now have to heave itself erect and lumber unsightly through the bright, terrible days without solace or satisfaction. He puts a hand on the man's soft, sweaty back, feels the sick throb of his heart. "I know you don't," he says. "But it's all right."

The first time he meets Vederotta, it's the morning of the fight, at the weigh-in. Just as he's stepping off the scale, he is startled to spot him standing a few feet away, a pale, vaguely human shape cut in the middle by a wide band of black, the trunks. And a face. That's the startling thing, the thing that causes Mears to shift quickly away. It's the sort of face that appears when a fight is going badly, when he needs more fear in order to keep going, but it's never happened so early, before the fight even be-gins. And this one is different from the rest. Not a comic-book image slapped on to a human mold, it seems fitted just below the surface of the skin, below the false human face, rippling like something seen through a thin film of water. It's coal black, with sculpted cheeks and a flattened bump of a nose and a slit mouth and hooded eyes, an inner mask of black lusterless metal. From its eyes and mouth leaks a crumbling red glow so radiant it blurs the definition of the features. Mears recognizes it for the face of his secret pain, and he can only stare at it. Then Vederotta smiles, the slit opening wider to show the furnace glow within, and says in a dull, stuporous voice, a voice like ashes, "You don't look so hot, man. Try and stay alive till tonight, will ya?" His handlers laugh and Leon curses them, but Mears, suddenly spiked with terror, can find no words, no solidity within himself on which to base a casual response. He lashes out at that evil, glowing face with a right hand, which Vederotta slips, and then everyone—handlers, officials, the press—is surging back and forth, pulling the two fighters apart, and as Leon hustles Mears away, saying, "Fuck's wrong with you, man? You crazy?" he hears Vederotta shouting at him, more bellowing than shouting, no words, nothing intelligible, just the raving of the black beast.

▼

Half an hour before the fight is scheduled to start, Mears is lying on a training table in the dressing room, alone, his wrapped hands folded on his belly. From the arena come intermittent announcements over the PA, the crowd booing one of the preliminary bouts, and some men are talking loudly outside his door. Mears scarcely registers any of this. He's trying to purge himself of fear but is not having much success. He believes his peculiar visual trick has revealed one of God's great killers, and that tonight the red seed of pain in his head will bloom and he will die, and nothing—no determined avowal, no life-affirming hope—will diminish that belief. He could back out of the fight, he could fake an injury of some sort, and he considers this possibility, but something—and it's not just pride—is pulling him onward. No matter whether or not that face he saw is real, there's something inhuman about Vederotta. Something evil and implacable. And stupid. Some slowness natural to sharks and demons. Maybe he's not a fate, a supernatural creature; maybe he's only malformed, twisted in spirit. Whatever, Mears senses his wrongness the way he would a change in the weather, not merely because of the mask but from a wealth of subtle yet undeniable clues. All these months of imagining beasts in the ring and now he's finally come up against a real one. Maybe the only real one there is. The one he always knew was waiting. Could be, he thinks, it's just his time. It's his time and he has to confront it. Then it strikes him that there may be another reason. It's as if he's been in training, sparring with the lesser beasts, Alligator Man, the Fang, Snakeman and the rest, in order to prepare for this bout. And what if there's some purpose to his sacrifice? What if he's supposed to do something out there tonight aside from dying?

Lying there, he realizes he's already positioned for the coffin, posed for eternity, and that recognition makes him roll up to his feet and begin his shadowboxing, working up a sweat. His sweat stinks of anxiety, but the effort tempers the morbidity of his thoughts.

A tremendous billow of applause issues from the arena, and not long thereafter, Leon pops in the door and says, "Quick knockout, man. We on in five." Then it goes very fast. The shuffling, bobbing walk along the aisle through the Wichita crowd, hearing shouted curses, focusing on that vast, dim tent of white light that hangs down over the ring. Climbing through the ropes, stepping into the resin box, getting his gloves checked a final time. It's all happening too quickly. He's being torn away from important details. Strands of tactics, sustaining memories, are being burned off him. He does not feel prepared. His belly knots and he wants to puke. He needs to see where he is, exactly where, not just this stretch of blue canvas that ripples like shallow water and the warped circles of lights suspended in blackness like an oddly geometric grouping of suns seen from outer space. The heat of those lights, along with the violent, murmurous heat of the crowd, it's sapping — it should be as bright as day in the ring, like noon on a tropic beach, and not this murky twilight reeking of Vaseline and concession food and fear. He keeps working, shaking his shoulders, testing the canvas with gliding footwork, jabbing and hooking. Yet all the while he's hoping the ring will collapse or Vederotta will sprain something, a power failure, anything to spare him. But when the announcer brays his weight, his record and name over the mike, he grows calm as if by reflex and submits to fate and listens to the boos and desultory clapping that follow.

"His opponent," the announcer continues, "in the black trunks with a red stripe, weighs in tonight at a lean and mean one hundred fifty-nine and one half pounds. He's undefeated and is currently ranked number one by both the WBC and WBA, with twenty-four wins, twenty-three by knockout! Let's have a great big prairie welcome for Wichita's favorite son, Toneee! The Heat! Ve-de-rot-taaaaa! Vederotta!"

Vederotta dances forward into the roar that celebrates him, arms lifted above his head, his back to Mears; then he turns, and as Leon and the cut man escort Mears to the center of the ring for the instructions, Mears sees that menacing face again. Those glowing eyes.

"When I say 'break'," the ref is saying, "I want you to break clean. Case of a knockdown, go to a neutral corner and stay there till I tell ya to come out. Any questions?"

One of Vederotta's handlers puts in his mouthpiece, a piece of opaque plastic that mutes the fiery glow, makes it look liquid and obscene; gassy red light steams from beneath the black metal hulls that shade his eyes.

"OK," says the ref. "Let's get it on."

Vederotta holds out his gloves and says something through his mouthpiece. Mears won't touch gloves with him, frightened of what this acquiescence might imply. Instead, he shoves him hard, and once again the handlers have to intervene. Screams from the crowd lacerate the air, and the ref admonishes him, saying, "Gimme a clean fight, Bobby, or I'll disqualify ya." But Mears is listening to Vederotta shouting fierce, garbled noises such as a lion might make with its mouth full of meat.

Leon hustles him back to the corner, puts in his mouthpiece and slips out through the ropes, saying, "Uppercuts, man! Keep throwin' them uppercuts!" Then he's alone, that strangely attenuated moment between the instructions and the bell, longer than usual tonight because the TV cameraman standing on the ring apron is having problems. Mears rolls his head, working out the kinks, shaking his arms to get them loose, and pictures himself as he must look from the cheap seats, a tiny dark figure buried inside a white pyramid. The image of Amandla comes into his head. She, too, is tiny. A doll in a blue robe, like a Madonna, she has that kind of power, a sweet, gentle idea, nothing more. And there's Arlene, whom he has never seen, of whom he knows next to nothing, African and voluptuous and mysterious like those big-breasted ebony statues they sell in the import stores. And Leon hunkered down at the corner of the ring, sweaty already, breath thick and quavery, peering with his pop eyes. Mears feels steadier and less afraid, triangulated by them: the only three people who have any force in his life. When he glances across the ring and finds that black death's head glaring at him, he is struck by something—he can see Vederotta. Since his eyes went bad, he's been unable to see his opponent until the man closes on him, and for that reason he circles tentatively at the beginning of each round, waiting for a figure to materialize from the murk, backing, letting his opponent come to him. Vederotta must know this, must have seen that tendency on film, and Mears thinks it may be possible to trick him, to start out circling and then surprise him with a quick attack. He turns, wanting to consult Leon, not sure this would be wise, but the bell sounds, clear and shocking, sending him forward as inexorably as a toy set in motion by a spark.

Less than ten seconds into the fight, goaded in equal measure by fear and hope, Mears feints a sidestep, plants his back foot and lunges forward behind a right that catches Vederotta solidly above the left eye, driving him into the ropes. Mears follows with a jab and two more rights before Vederotta backs him up with a wild flurry, and he sees that Vederotta has been cut. The cut is on the top of the eyelid, not big but in a bad place, difficult to treat. It shows as a fuming red slit in that black mask, like molten lava cracking open the side of a scorched hill. Vederotta rubs at the eye, holds up his glove to check for blood, then hurls himself at Mears, taking another right on the way in but managing to land two stunning shots under the ribs that nearly cave him in. From then on it's all downhill for Mears. Nobody, not Hagler or Hearns or Duran, has ever hit him with such terrible punches. His face is numb from Vederotta's battering jab and he thinks one of his back teeth may have been cracked. But the body shots are the worst. Their impact is the sort you receive in a car crash when the steering wheel or the dash slams into you. They sound like football tackles, they dredge up harsh groans as they sink deep into his sides, and he thinks he can feel Vederotta's fingers, his talons, groping inside the gloves, probing for his organs. With less than a minute to go in the round, a right hand to the heart drops him onto one knee. It takes him until the count of five to regain his breath, and he's up at seven, wobbly, dazed by the ache spreading across his chest. As Vederotta comes in, Mears wraps his arms about his waist and they go lurching about the ring, faces inches apart, Vederotta's arm barred under his throat, trying to push him off. Vederotta spews words in a goblin language, wet, gnashing sounds. He sprays fiery brimstone breath into Mears' face, acid spittle, the crack on his eyelid leaking a thin track of red phosphorus down a black cheek. When the ref finally manages to separate them, he tells

Mears he's going to deduct a point if he keeps holding. Mears nods, grateful for the extra few seconds rest, more grateful when he hears the bell.

Leon squirts water into Mears' mouth, tells him to rinse and spit. "You cut him," he says excitedly. "You cut the motherfucker!"

"I know," Mears says. "I can see him."

Leon, busy with the Enswell, refrains from comment, restrained by the presence of the cut man. "Left eye," he says, ignoring what Mears has told him. "Throw that right. Rights and uppercuts. All night long. That's a bad cut, huh, Eddie?"

"Could be a winner," the cut man says, "we keep chippin' on it."

Leon smears Vaseline on Mears' face. "How you holdin' up?"

"He's hurtin' me. Everything he throws, he's hurtin' me."

Leon tells him to go ahead and grab, let the ref deduct the fucking points, just hang in there and work the right. The crowd is buzzing, rumorous, and from this, Mears suspects that he may really have Vederotta in some trouble, but he's still afraid, more afraid than ever now that he has felt Vederotta's power. And as the second round begins, he realizes he's the one in trouble. The cut has turned Vederotta cautious. Instead of brawling, he circles Mears, keeping his distance, popping his jab, throwing an occasional combination, wearing down his opponent inch by inch, a pale, indefinite monster, his face sheathed in black metal, eyes burning like red suns at midnight. Each time Mears gets inside to throw his shots or grab, the price is high—hooks to the liver and heart, rights to the side of the neck, the hinge of the jaw. His face is lumping up. Near the end of the round, a ferocious straight right to the temple blinds him utterly in the left eye for several seconds. When the bell rings, he sinks onto the stool, legs trembling, heartbeat ragged. Exotic eye trash floats in front of him. His head's full of hot poison, aching and unclear. But oddly enough, that little special pain of his has dissipated, chased away by the same straight right that caused his temporary blackout.

The doctor pokes his head into the desperate bustle of the corner and asks him where he is, how he's doing. Mears says "Wichita" and "OK." When the ref asks him if he wants to continue, he's surprised to hear himself say "Yeah," because he's been doing little other than wondering if it would be all right to quit. Must be some good reason, he thinks, or else you're one dumb son of a bitch. That makes him laugh.

"Fuck you doin' laughin'?" Leon says. "We ain't havin' that much fun out there. Work on that cut! You ain't done diddly to that cut!"

Mears just shakes his head, too drained to respond.

The first minute of the third round is one of the most agonizing times of Mears' life. Vederotta continues his cautious approach, but he's throwing heavier shots now, head-hunting, and Mears can do nothing other than walk forward and absorb them. He is rocked a dozen times, sent reeling. An uppercut jams the mouthpiece edge-on into his gums and his mouth fills with blood. A hook to the ear leaves him rubber-legged. Two rights send spears of white light into his left eye and the tissue around the eye swells, reducing his vision to a slit. A low blow smashes the edge of his cup, drives it sideways against his testicles, causing a pain that brings bile into his throat. But Vederotta does not follow up. After each assault he steps back to admire his work. It's clear he's prolonging things, trying to inflict maximum damage before the finish. Mears peers between his gloves at the beast stalking him and wonders when that other little red-eyed beast inside his head will start to twitch and burn. He's surprised it hasn't already, he's taken so many shots.

When the ref steps in after a series of jabs, Mears thinks he's stopping the fight, but it's only a matter of tape unraveling from his left glove. The ref leads him into the corner to let Leon retape it. He's so unsteady, he has to grip the ropes for balance, and glancing over his shoulder, he sees Vederotta spit his mouthpiece into his glove, which he holds up like a huge red paw. He expects Vederotta to say something, but all Vederotta does is let out a maniacal shout. Then he reinserts the mouthpiece into that glowing red maw and stares at Mears, shaking his black and crimson head the way a bear does before it charges, telling him—Mears realizes—that this is it, there's not going to be a fourth round. But Mears is too wasted to be further intimidated, his fear has bottomed out, and as Leon fumbles with the tape, giving him a little more rest, his pride is called forth, and he senses again just how stupid Vederotta is, bone stupid, dog stupid, maybe just stupid and overconfident enough to fall into the simplest of traps. No matter what happens to him, Mears thinks, maybe he can do something to make Vederotta remember this night.

The ref waves them together, and Mears sucks it up, banishes his pain into a place where he can forget about it for a while and shuffles forward, presenting a picture of reluctance and tentativeness. When Vederotta connects with a jab, then a right that Mears halfway picks off with his glove, Mears pretends to be sorely afflicted and staggers back against the ropes. Vederotta's in no hurry. He ambles toward him, dipping his left shoulder, so sure of himself he's not even trying to disguise his punches, he's going to come with the left hook under, he's going to hurt Mears some more before he whacks him out. Mears peeks between his gloves, elbows tight to his sides, knowing he's got this one moment, waiting, the crowd's roar like a jet engine around him, the vicious, smirking beast planting himself, his shoulder dipping lower yet, his head dropping down and forward as he cocks the left, and it's then, right at that precise instant, when Vederotta is completely exposed, that Mears explodes from his defensive posture and throws the uppercut, aiming not at the chin or the nose, but at that red slit on the black eyelid. He lands the shot clean, feels the impact, and above the crowd noise he hears Vederotta shriek like a woman, sees him stumble into the corner, his head lowered, glove held to the damaged eye. Mears follows, spins him about and throws another shot that knocks Vederotta's glove aside, rips at the eye. The slit, it's torn open now, has become an inch-long gash, and that steaming, luminous red shit is flowing into the eye, over the dull black cheek and jaw, dripping onto his belly and trunks. Mears pops a jab, a right, then another jab, not hard punches—they don't have to be hard, just accurate—splitting Vederotta's guard, each landing on the gash, slicing the eyelid almost its entire length. Then the ref's arms wrap around him from behind and haul him back, throwing him into ring center, where he stands, confused by this sudden cessation of violence, by this solitude imposed on him after all that brutal intimacy, as the doctor is called in to look at Vederotta's eye. He feels light and unreal, as if he's been shunted into a place where gravity is weaker and thought has no emotional value. The crowd has gone quiet and he hears the voice of Vederotta's manager above the babbling in the corner. Then a second voice shouting the manager down, saying, "I can see the bone, Mick! I can see the goddamn bone!" And then—this is the most confusing thing of all—the ref is lifting his arm and the announcer is declaring, without enthusiasm, to a response of mostly silence and some scattered boos, that "the referee stops the contest at a minute fifty-six seconds of the third round. Your winner by TKO: Bobby! The Magician! Mears!"

Mears' pain has returned, the TV people want to drag him off for an interview, Leon is there hugging him, saying, "We kicked his ass, man! We fuckin' kicked his ass!" and there are others, the promoter, the nobodies, trying to congratulate him, but he pushes them aside, shoulders his way to Vederotta's corner. He has to see him, because this is not how things were supposed to play. Vederotta is sitting on his stool, someone smearing his cut with Avitene. His face is still visible, still that of the beast. Those glowing red eyes stare up at Mears, connect with the eye of pain in his head, and he wants there to be a transfer of knowledge, to learn that one day soon that pain will open wide and he will fall the way a fighter falls after one punch too many, disjointed, graceless, gone from the body. But no such transfer occurs, and he begins to suspect that something is not wrong, or rather that what's wrong is not what he suspected.

There's one thing he thinks he knows, however, looking at Vederotta, and while the handlers stand respectfully by, acknowledging his place in this ritual, Mears says, "I was lucky, man. You a hell of a fighter. But that eye's never gon' be the same. Every fight they gon' be whacking at it, splittin' it open. You ain't gon' be fuckin' over nobody no more. You might as well hang 'em up now."

As he walks away, as the TV people surround him, saying, "Here's the winner, Bobby Mears" — and he wonders what exactly it is he's won — it's at that instant he hears a sound behind him, a gush of raw noise in which frustration and rage are commingled, both dirge and challenge, denial and lament, the final roar of the beast.

▼

Two weeks after the fight he's sitting in the hotel bar with Arlene, staring into that infinite dark mirror, feeling lost, undefined, sickly, like there's a cloud between him and the light that shines him into being, because he's not sure when he's going to fight again, maybe never, he's so busted up from Vederotta. His eyes especially seem worse, prone to dazzling white spots and blackouts, though the pain deep in his head has subsided, and he thinks that the pain may have had something to do only with his eyes, and now that they're fading, it's fading, too, and what will he do if that's the case? Leon has been working with this new lightweight, a real prospect, and he hasn't been returning Mears' calls, and when the bartender switches on the TV and a rapper's voice begins blurting out his simple, aggressive rhymes, Mears gets angry, thoughts like gnats swarming around that old reeking nightmare shape in his head, that thing that may never have existed, and he pictures a talking skull on the TV shelf, with a stuffed raven and a coiled snake beside it. He drops a twenty on the counter and tells Arlene he wants to take a walk, a disruption of their usual routine of a few drinks, then upstairs. It bewilders her, but she says, "OK, baby," and off they go into the streets, where the Christmas lights are gleaming against the black velour illusion of night like green and red galaxies, as if he's just stepped into an incredible distance hung here and there with plastic angels filled with radiance. And people, lots of people brushing past, dark and shiny as beetles, scuttling along in this holy immensity, chattering their bright gibberish, all hustling toward mysterious crossroads where they stop and freeze into silhouettes against the streams of light, and Mears, who is walking very fast because walking is dragging something out of him, some old weight of emotion, is dismayed by their stopping, it goes contrary to the flow he wants to become part of, and he bursts through a group of shadows assembled like pilgrims by a burning river, and steps out, out and down — he's forgotten the curb — and staggers forward into the traffic, into squealing brakes and shouts, where he waits for a collision he envisions as swift and ultimately stunning, luscious in its finality, like the fatal punch Vederotta should have thrown. Yet it never comes. Then Arlene, who has clattered up, unsteady in her high heels, hauls him back onto the sidewalk, saying, "You tryin' to kill yo'self, fool?" And Mears, truly lost now, truly bereft of understanding, either of what he has done or why he's done it, stands mute and tries to find her face, wishes he could put a face on her, not a mask, just a face that would be her, but she's nowhere to be found, she's only perfume, a sense of presence. He knows she's looking at him, though.

"You sick, Bobby?" she asks. "Ain't you gon' tell me what's wrong?"

How can he tell her that what's wrong is he's afraid he's not dying, that he'll live and go blind? How can that make sense? And what does it say about how great a fool he's been? He's clear on nothing apart from that, the size of his folly.

"C'mon," Arlene says with exasperation, taking his arm. "I'm gon' cook you some dinner. Then you can tell me what's been bitin' yo' ass."

He lets her steer him along. He's too dazed to make decisions. Too worried. It's funny, he thinks, or maybe funny's not the word, maybe it's sad that what's beginning to worry him is exactly the opposite of what was troubling him a few seconds before. What if she proves to be someone who'll stand by him no matter how bad things get, what if the pain in his head hasn't gone away, it's just dormant, and instead of viewing death as a solution, one he feared but came to rely on, he now comes to view it as something miserable and dread? The darkness ahead will be tricky to negotiate, and the simple trials of what he's already starting to characterize as his old life seem, despite blood and attrition, unattainably desirable. But no good thing can arise from such futile longing, he realizes. Loving Amandla has taught him that.

Between two department stores, two great, diffuse masses of white light, there's an alley, a doorway, a dark interval of some sort, and as they pass, Mears draws Arlene into it and pulls her tightly to him, needing a moment to get his bearings. The blackness of street and sky is so uniform, it looks as if you could walk a black curve up among the blinking red and green lights, and as Arlene's breasts flatten against him, he feels like he is going high, like it feels when the man in the tuxedo tells you that you've won and the pain is washed away by perfect exhilaration and sweet relief. Then, as if jolted forward by the sound of a bell, he steps out into the crowds, becoming part of them, just another fool with short money and bad health and God knows what kind of woman trouble, who in another time might have been champion of the world.

GOD IS IN THE DETAILS

by Lucius Shepard

▼

The most important decisions you must make in creating an evocative setting, particularly in a short story, are the choice of the details that you will show the reader in order to make him think that you have described something, or more precisely, that he has seen what you have wanted him to see . . . when actually you have forced him to see something in his own mind, either a memory or an imaginary object or scene. Nothing can be fully described; if it could be, the result would be ridiculously long. As it bears on this, I suggest you examine the description of a sunset in the opening pages of *The Raw and the Cooked*, a book by the anthropologist Claude Lévi-Strauss. The description goes on for page after page, and includes some amazing detail; but at the end of it you still have no precise idea of how the sunset looked, and have had to plow through a daunting mass of verbiage. The overall effect is one of boredom. Browning's description in "Sordello" of a sunset resembling "a torch blown back upon the bearer's hand" is far more evocative, for with that simple image, he persuades us to dredge up a sunset from our memory and transpose it to his poem. And this of course is what good descriptive writing does—it evokes rather than describes.

In a short story, where space is at a premium, you should strive to make your descriptions serve double and triple duty; in other words, they should not merely evoke, they should inform matters of plot and character. Here's a passage from a novelette set in Latin America, "The Jaguar Hunter," that achieves this:

> . . . across from it was the appliance store, a one-story building of
> yellow stucco with corrugated metal doors that were lowered at
> night. Its facade was decorated by a mural that supposedly rep-

resented the merchandise within: sparkling refrigerators and tele-
visions and washing machines, all given the impression of enor-
mity by the tiny men and women painted below them, their hands
upflung in awe.

This not only acts as description, it comments indirectly on the fi-
nancial dominance the store's owner wields over the town, on the nature
of local consumerism, and—even more indirectly—on the attitude of the
point-of-view character toward the owner, whom he does not respect or
like. The specificity of the mural—and its commonality in our experience; we've all seen similar—takes the reader's attention away from the
shape of the building, from other elements of the environment, by the
cleverness of its relationship to other elements of the story and the power
of its resonance with those materials; it is in effect a sleight-of-hand that
makes him believe he knows where he is, even if he's never been in Latin
America.

Here's a passage from "Beast of the Heartland" that serves a different sort of multiple purpose:

Cold blue neon light winks on and off in the window of Mears'
room, a vague nebular shine that might be radiating from a
polar beacon or a ghostly police car, and as the hooker un-
dresses, he lies on the bed in his shorts and watches the light.
It's the only thing he sees, just that chilly blue in a black field,
spreading across the surface of the glass like some undersea
thing, shrinking and expanding like the contractions of an icy
blue heart. He has always been afraid before a fight, yet now
he's afraid in a different way. Or maybe it's not the fear that's
different, maybe it's his resistance to it that has changed. Maybe
he's weaker, wearier. He is so accustomed to suppressing fear,
however, that when he tries to examine it, it slithers away into
the cracks of his soul and hides there, lurking, eyes aglow, wait-
ing for its time.

Most of us have been in a hotel room with this sort of external light
source, so this detail fixes the location; but due to Mears' extreme focus
on the light, it also reinforces our sense of his impaired vision, and its cold
nature amplifies his sense of foreboding. Moments later he hears "two

car horns start to blow in an impatient rhythm like brass animals angry at each other," and this image, too, serves to reinforce the reader's impression of Mears' mood.

The classic use of descriptive writing is to establish a specific milieu or place. For an example of this kind of writing at its best, I would suggest you take a look at the opening of Yukio Mishima's novel *Spring Snow*. Here in the space of two pages, Mishima presents us with a crystallized portrait of an entire culture, that of postwar Japan, by means of a description of a photograph of some soldiers standing about a cenotaph. But in the long run of a novel and in the brief rush of a story, it is eventually the small touches that succeed in persuading the reader that he has been transported to a place of the author's imagining, and that support moment-to-moment changes in atmosphere that the author wishes to create. For instance, in a story on which I'm currently working, a man and a woman are talking. As they talk the man hears the woman's dog walking about in the kitchen, its claws clicking on the linoleum, and then a bit later he hears it lapping water from the toilet bowl. The dog is mentioned a few times, no more than a couple of phrases on each occasion, but the sounds the dog makes—tight, clicking, and echoey (in the bathroom)—add to the air of tension that is building between the man and woman. The man begins to be annoyed by the dog, and in the process, begins to realize that he doesn't like the woman very much. This is achieved without dwelling on the dog, just simple, non-metaphorical relations of sound and action, interspersed with the man's brief interiorizations, all of which give texture and added weight to a long conversational passage.

Here are a couple of excerpts from a scene in the novella, "The Ends of the Earth". Two men who don't like each other are involved in a contest over a woman, a contest that involves a strange game, and during the course of this conversation in his opponent's beach hut, the narrator begins to think that more may be at stake than he has previously realized, though he's not sure what exactly the stakes are:

The light was bad, a brownish gloom, and Konwicki was sitting cross-legged against the rear wall; beside him was something bumpy covered by a white cloth, and noticing that a corner of orange wood protruded from the cloth, I realized that he had been fooling around with the game.

"What can I do fc   ?" he said in a dry tone. "Sell you some drugs?"

I sat down close to him, off to the side, so I could watch the door; the dried palm fronds crunched beneath my weight. "How you been?"

He made a noise of amusement. "I've been fine, Ray. And you?"

I gestured at the covered board. "Playing with yourself?"

A bit later, as they are discussing the nature of the game, the light in the hut becomes so dim that Konwicki's features become indistinct. The narrator's apprehension increases—this is not stated explicitly, but is stated by the setting:

The thatched roof crackled like a small fire in a gust of wind, and behind Konwicki, mapping the darkness of the wall, were tiny points of lights, uncaulked places between the boards through which the day was showing; they lent the wall the illusion of depth, of being a vast sky mapped with stars, all arranged in a dwindling perspective so as to draw one's eyes toward a greater darkness beyond them. . . .

And then, as a sense of peril begins to overwhelm the narrator, we have this passage, which foreshadows the true nature of the game, that being a sort of interface between realities:

The doorway framed a stretch of pale brown sand and sun-spat-tered water and curving palm trunks, and the brilliance of the scene was such a contrast to the gloom within, I imagined that these things comprised a single presence that was peering in at us like an eye at a keyhole, and that Konwicki and I were microscopic creatures dwelling inside the mechanism of a lock that separated dark and light.

As can be seen from the proceeding excerpts, it is somewhat mis-leading to approach the topic of "Setting" or "Sense of Place" as being separate from certain other aspects of prose writing, because to my mind setting is always a function of character development and often relates to narrative process. I would guess that ninety-nine percent of all failures in achieving a sense of place stem from the author not recognizing setting's innate relationship to character, from an attempt to describe a place, whether it be an imagined world or a real one, as being distinct or somehow removed from the passage of his point-of-view character through that environment. The result of such failures are descriptive passages that read like excerpts from encyclopedias and lack the emotional valence that would attach had the author succeeded in showing us the landscape through the eyes of his main protagonist.

All effective descriptive writing is fueled by character and is in essence a form of interiorization. What is seen and described is purportedly not seen and described by the author, but rather through the eyes of the point-of-view character; thus everything that character sees must mirror what he or she is feeling. If your character is angry or upset, what he sees of, say, a room will be different than what he sees when feeling calm. In the first instance he might well notice bits of lint lying about and an annoying glare on a polished floor; however, if he is calm he might notice of the same room its relatively well-kept appearance and the pleasing abundance of sunlight. Here's an example of this very thing from "Beast of the Heartland":

> *Three mornings later, as Mears waits for Leon in the gym, he listens happily to the slapping of jump ropes, the grunt and thud of someone working the heavy bag, the jabber and pop of speed bags, the meaty thump of fourteen-ounce sparring gloves. Pale winter light chutes through the high windows like a Bethlehem star to Mears' eyes. The smell is a harsh perfume of antiseptic, resin, and sweat. . . .*

But then, a little while later, after Mears learns that he is to fight a very dangerous man, here's how the same place seems to him:

> *The deal concluded, Mears feels exposed, as if a vast, luminous eye—God's, perhaps—is shining on him, revealing all his frailties. He sits up straight, holds his head very still, rubs his palms along the tops of his thighs, certain that everyone is watching. Leon's breathing is hoarse and labored, like last breaths. The light is beginning to tighten up around that sound, to congeal into*

something cold and gray, like a piece of dirty ice in which they are all embedded.

Then, a short time later:

. . . after a minute or so, he begins to relax, thinking about the money, slipping back into the peace of morning in the gym, with the starred light shining from on high and the enthusiastic shouts of the young fighters and the slap of leather making a rhythm like a river slapping against a bank and the fat man who is not his friend beginning to breathe easier now beside him.

Longish descriptive passages should do more than merely describe the landscape and the character's mood; in order to maintain the flow of the narrative and sustain the reader's interest they must be in themselves little stories, each with a beginning, a dynamic, and a sense of closure. Here are two passages—the first from "Beast"—that satisfy this condition and achieve a similar effect, that of showing a character's transition from anxiety to serenity, as well as evoking the landscape:

A tremendous billow of applause issues from the arena, and not long thereafter, Leon pops in the door and says, "Quick knockout, man. We on in five." Then it goes very fast. The shuffling, bobbing walk along the aisle through the Wichita crowd, hearing shouted curses, focusing on that vast, dim tent of white light that hangs down over the ring. Climbing through the ropes, stepping into the resin box, getting his gloves checked a final time. It's all happening too quickly. He's being torn away from important details. Strands of tactics, sustaining memories, are being burned off him. He does not feel prepared. His belly knots and he wants to puke. He needs to see where he is, exactly where, not just this stretch of blue canvas that ripples like shallow water and the warped circles of lights suspended in blackness like an oddly geometric grouping of suns seen from outer space. The heat of those lights, along with the violent, murmurous heat of the crowd, it's sapping—it should be as bright as day in the ring, like noon on a tropic beach, and not this murky twilight reeking of Vaseline and concession food and fear. He keeps working, shaking his shoulders, testing the can-

vas with gliding footwork, jabbing and hooking. Yet all the while
he's hoping the ring will collapse or Vederotta will sprain some-
thing, a power failure, anything to spare him. But when the an-
nouncer brays his weight, his record and name over the mike, he
grows calm as if by reflex and submits to fate and listens to the boos
and desultory clapping that follow.

Here's a longer and more traditionally descriptive passage from a
novella, "R&R".

The Rio Dulce was a wide blue river, heaving with a light chop.
Thick jungle hedged its banks, and yellowish reed beds grew out
from both shores. At the spot where the gravel road ended was a
concrete pier, and moored to it a barge that served as a ferry; it
was already loaded with its full complement of vehicles—two
trucks—and carried about thirty pedestrians. Mingolla boarded
and stood in the stern beside three infantrymen who were still
wearing their combat suits and helmets, holding double-barreled
rifles that were connected by flexible tubing to backpack com-
puters; through their smoked faceplates he could see green reflec-
tions from the read-outs on their visor displays. They made him
uneasy, reminding him of the two pilots, and he felt better after
they had removed their helmets and proved to have normal human
faces. Spanning a third of the way across the river was a sweep-
ing curve of white cement supported by slender columns, like a
piece fallen out of a Dali landscape: a bridge upon which con-
struction had been halted. Mingolla had noticed it from the air
just before landing and hadn't thought much about it; but now
the sight took him by storm. It seemed less an unfinished bridge
than a monument to some exalted ideal, more beautiful than any
finished bridge could be. And as he stood rapt, with the ferry's oily
smoke farting out around him, he sensed there was an analogue
of that beautiful curving shape inside him, that he, too, was a road
ending in midair. It gave him confidence to associate himself
with such loftiness and purity, and for a moment he let himself
believe that he also might have—as the upward-angled terminus
of the bridge implied—a point of completion lying far beyond the
one anticipated by the architects of his fate.

On the west bank past the town the gravel road was lined with stalls: skeletal frameworks of brushwood poles roofed with palm thatch. Children chased in and out among them, pretending to aim and fire at each other with stalks of sugar cane. But hardly any soldiers were in evidence. The crowds that moved along the road were composed mostly of Indians: young couples too shy to hold hands; old men who looked lost and poked litter with their canes; dumpy matrons who made outraged faces at the high prices; shoeless farmers who kept their backs ramrod-straight and wore grave expressions and carried their money knotted in handkerchiefs. At one of the stalls Mingolla bought a sandwich and a Coca Cola. He sat on a stool and ate contentedly, relishing the hot bread and the spicy fish cooked inside it, watching the passing parade. Gray clouds were bulking up and moving in from the south, from the Caribbean; now and then a flight of XL-16s would arrow northward toward the oil fields beyond Lake Ixtabal, where the fighting was very bad. Twilight fell. The lights of the town began to be picked out sharply against the empurpling air. Guitars were plucked, hoarse voices sang, the crowds thinned. Mingolla ordered another sandwich and Coke. He leaned back, sipped and chewed, steeping himself in the good magic of the land, the sweetness of the moment. Beside the sandwich stall, four old women were squatting by a cooking fire, preparing chicken stew and corn fritters; scraps of black ash drifted up from the flames, and as twilight deepened, it seemed these scraps were the pieces of a jigsaw puzzle that were fitting together overhead into the image of a starless night.

In the second paragraph of this section the reader is given the traditional furniture of what is considered setting: the people, the buildings, the tastes, the sky, the airplanes overhead, all details that have the bright particularity of a specific place and time. But because the reader is now in Mingolla's head, because he has come from an awful place, one furnished with sinister infantrymen and oily smoke and the uncompleted bridge, the humanity of this new place comes to the reader in the same way it does to Mingolla, as a relief, a point of release from tension, and details that might otherwise have been mere bits of travelogue are imbued with the emotionality of his passage.

In "R&R," the unfinished bridge—crossing only partway as it does from the east bank, where the war machine and the R&R town are situated, to the west where things are relatively peaceful and ordinary—takes on a metaphorical weight. Over the course of the novella it becomes part of an image system, the repetition and evolution of which serves to amplify the themes of the story and the changes taking place in the protagonist. At one point, for example, the protagonist, again riding the ferry, looks down into the water and thinks he sees reflected there "the broken curve of his life." In "Beast of the Heartland," with far less room to maneuver, I had to make do with a sketchier construct, and so, recognizing that Mears, mostly blind, would be abnormally sensitive to changes in the light, I used the light to evoke his emotions in each setting. When, for instance, he is sitting in the bar after his fight with Nazario, looking into the mirror, he sees "a black, rippling distance flocked by points of actinic light, a mysterious lake full of stars and no sign of his reflection." The hooker's sequined dress reveals itself as "the scattering of moonlight on choppy water," and the bartender "when he's visible at all, is a cryptic shadow." This confluence of black and mysterious imagery corresponds to Mears' feelings of mortality that surface moments later, his oddly contemplative and almost mystic apprehension of imminent death. Accordingly, there is the cold blue neon radiance that attends his fear; the "Bethlehem star" that lights a happy morning in the gym; "the murky twilight reeking of Vaseline and concession food and fear" that enshrouds the ring—the commonality of these associations redolent of his attitude toward his work. Toward the end of the story, once again sitting in the bar, "staring into that infinite dark mirror, feeling lost, undefined, sickly, like there's a cloud between him and the light that shines him into being, because he's not sure when he's going to fight again, maybe never, he's so busted up from Vederotta." Then, in a kind of existential panic, he goes out into the streets where:

> . . . the Christmas lights are gleaming against the black velour illusion of night like green and red galaxies, as if he's just stepped into an incredible distance hung here and there with plastic angels filled with radiance. And people, lots of people brushing past, dark and shiny as beetles, scuttling along in this holy immensity, chattering their bright gibberish, all hustling toward mysterious crossroads where they stop and freeze into silhouettes against the streams of light, and Mears, who is walking very fast because walking is dragging something out of him, some old weight of emo-

*tion, is dismayed by their stopping, it goes contrary to the flow he
wants to become part of, and he bursts through a group of shadows assembled like pilgrims by a burning river, and steps out, out
and down—he's forgotten the curb—and staggers forward into the
traffic, into squealing brakes and shouts, where he waits for a collision he envisions as swift and ultimately stunning, luscious in
its finality. . . .*

At the absolute end of the story, Mears achieves an epiphany. He
pulls his hooker girlfriend into a doorway, "a dark interval" between "two
great, diffuse masses of white light", and "the blackness of street and sky
is so uniform, it looks as if you could walk a black curve up among the
blinking red and green lights. . . ." Though no good conclusion for Mears
is stated, at least partly because of the use of light throughout the story,
because of the general progression from dimness to brightness, one cannot help but feel hopeful for him. So in this instance, setting has not only
been used to create a realistic backdrop and to inform character, it has
become a kinetic element of the narrative flow, and finally acts to bestow
unnatural significance upon what is, after all, only a man walking out
onto a street and nearly being hit by a car, something that happens many
times a day in every city of the world.

Playing around with sentence structure and narrative tone can assist
a writer in evoking a setting while at the same time establishing his protagonist's mood. Here's an example from a horror story in progress:

*He decided he would clean the kitchen. Something to do. Take
his mind off things. Jesus, these people lived like pigs. What the
hell was in that coffee cup? Compote of dead cigarettes, curdled
milk phlegm. And that shit on the stove. A green blot. Algae-fuck-
ing-green. The damn place was right out of a Poe story. Stains
dappling the countertop like the palette of a deranged artist, one
who used decomposed tissues instead of oils and acryllics. Viscous
masses, ichors, mutated jellies that might once have been eyes,
glands, vital fluids, bat brains, snail guts, puree of tomato worm,
each leaking an odious gas. The smell made him gag. He stepped
back from the sink, breathing hard, holding a steak knife whose
blade was fettered with gray scum. His heart beat wildly, errati-
cally, like something trying to hatch. Water dripped from the*

faucet. Tap. Tap. Taptaptap. Watching the drips made some-
thing heavy grow behind his skullbone. Not anger. Purpose.
Heavy metal purpose. Industrial-strength purpose. He imagined
his brain making a fist.

Obviously the materials of this paragraph go a long way toward evoking the character's agitated mood, as well as the ambience of a foul
kitchen, but the incidence of short sentences and fragments heighten the
effect. The reader has an ear for prose rhythms, even when reading
silently, and any writer would be foolish not to take advantage of this.

Sometimes a striking effect can be produced by omitting the "I saw,"
"she felt," "they heard" constructions from one's sentences, thereby per-
sonifying an inanimate object: "Their footsteps crunched in the dirt; from
the next street over, a jukebox cried out for love."

The preceding fragment is taken from a scene in which two people
who are soon to be lovers are walking together, and the effect is to add a
bit of color to their courtship. It's always good to check your sentences
to see whether or not the "I saw etc." constructions can be eliminated to
good effect.

Keep in mind that you will not be able to employ all the tricks and
knowledge at your disposal consciously to create setting while writing the
first draft of a story. Writing fiction is like taking a rubbing of your brain:
All the bulges and convolutions and fissures will show up in your work
whether you want them to or not, and it's up to you to look for the patterns that you are unconsciously developing as you work, and to select
from among them those that will be most evocative of the kind of atmosphere you want to create. And always remember that the perceptions
of your point-of-view character are the lens through which you must create your setting; if you do you not know him extremely well, you will at
best do an inconsistent job of creating the world in which he lives.

▼

This world's no blot for us,
Nor blank; it means intensely, and means good:
To find its meaning is my meat and drink.

Browning's Fra Lippo Lippi was clearly no existentialist, and although we live in an existential age, we still seek meaning—if not in the natural world, in mankind's relation to that world and what we have made or will make of it. It may well be that the peculiar appeal of science fiction is that it so often seeks to mediate between human beings and the ever more hostile environment they have created, seeks to explain the ways of the god technology to man.

Put formally, *theme* is the writer's vision of life interpreted in terms of her own personality; it is a series of perceptions which the writer believes to be accurate and significant and which she communicates in the system of values and sentiments and incidents that is the story. It is the sum of plot, character, and setting.

Isolating the theme of a story—call it intellectual concept, message, meaning, intention, moral (as in Aesop), or ontology—is a slippery business. Good stories are likely to exhibit a family of related themes, no one of which is clearly delineated. Stories in which theme is unequivocal and immediately apparent are likely to result from the subservience of art to propaganda, or at least to didacticism. Theme-hunting can be a lot of fun, and an appreciation of the thematic content of a story is important, but no one should look for ready agreement on a statement of theme unless it is very broad, and no one should attempt to find meaning where none was intended, interpolating his own personality into the story instead of carefully examining and understanding that of the writer.

It is in the development of thematic material that the writer most fully reveals himself to the perceptive reader. The writer is bound to display certain beliefs and values which can be described as *judicial* and *preferential* attitudes. A pair of judicial attitudes are *optimism* and *pessimism*, reasoned convictions that life is essentially good or evil. Another pair are *sentimentalism* and *cynicism*, emotional judgments on the same issue. The two basic preferential attitudes are *realism* and *romanticism*, the one expressing the notion that truth is found through submission to fact, the other that truth is found in escape from it. These terms are vast over-simplifications: In a given story, a writer may vary his attitudes, may equivocate, may, indeed, build his story to express his own uncertainties on the matter—itself a powerful and increasingly popular theme.

Relatively few writers begin a story with a clear and fixed concept of theme in mind (although propagandists invariably do so). More likely, a writer enters his story via some notion of plot or a burgeoning fascination with a character. This is less true of science fiction, which is preeminently a literature of ideas, and which often finds its genesis in such questions as "what would life be like if?" or "what would people do if thus-and-such should occur?" Here, with a nod of thanks to Joanna Russ, I include a caveat for the new writer: Beware of the thematic approach to writing! It can swiftly lead you into the viscous toils of allegory, which is for most writers—trying to make a living from their work—a fate worse than debt.

But whether or not the writer begins with a firm thematic intention, theme will be there buried somewhere in the first draft. At this point, she is likely to see meanings that surpass her original intentions (if she had any), and she will go back in her revision to tinker and adjust, to clarify meaning and express it more artfully. In this effort, one of the writer's principal tools is *symbolism*, the substitution of an idea or a thing for some other idea or thing less amenable to the kind of compressed expression demanded in short fiction. Good symbols are not merely decorative embellishment, are not (except at the linguistic level) stock devices with universal meanings. They are, in fact, frequently more or less ambiguous and must be interpreted solely within the little world of the story and in terms of the personality of the writer as revealed. It is there, and only there, that symbolic rhetoric can carry its greatest freight of meaning.

Freud, forgive me.

LILY RED

by Karen Joy Fowler

▼

One day Lily decided to be someone else. Someone with a past. It was an affliction of hers, wanting this. The desire was seldom triggered by any actual incident or complaint, but seemed instead to be related to the act or prospect of lateral movement. She felt it every time a train passed. She would have traded places instantly with any person on any train. She felt it often in the car. She drove onto the freeway that ran between her job and her house and she thought about driving right past her exit and stopping in some small town wherever she happened to run out of gas and the next thing she knew, that was exactly what she had done.

Except that she was stopped by the police instead. She was well beyond the city; she had been through several cities, and the sky had darkened. The landscape flattened and she fell into a drowsy rhythm in which she and the car were both passengers in a small, impellent world defined by her headlights. It was something of a shock to have to stop. She sat in her car while the police light rotated behind her and at regular intervals she watched her hands turn red on the steering wheel. She had never been stopped by the police before. In the rearview mirror she could see the policeman talking to his radio. His door was slightly open; the light was on inside his car. He got out and came to talk to her. She turned her motor off. "Lady," he said and she wondered if policemen on television always called women *lady* because that was what real policemen did, or if he had learned this watching television just as she had. "Lady, you were flying. I clocked you at eighty."

Eighty. Lily couldn't help but be slightly impressed. She had been twenty-five miles per hour over the limit without even realizing she was speeding. It suggested she could handle even faster speeds. "Eighty," she said contritely. "You know what I think I should do? I think I've been dri-

ving too long and I think I should just find a place to stay tonight. I think
that would be best. I mean, eighty. That's too fast. Don't you think?"

"I really do." The policeman removed a pen from the pocket inside
his jacket.

"I won't do it again," Lily told him. "Please don't give me a ticket."

"I could spare you the ticket," the policeman said, "and I could read
in the paper tomorrow that you smashed yourself into a retaining wall not
fifteen miles from here. I don't think I could live with myself. Give me
your license. Just take it out of the wallet, please. Mattie Drake runs a little bed and breakfast place in Two Trees. You want the next exit and bear
left. First right, first right again. Street dead-ends in Mattie's driveway.
There's a sign on the lawn. MATTIE'S. Should be all lit up this time of night.
It's a nice place and doesn't cost too much in the off season." He handed
Lily back her license and the ticket for her to sign. He took his copy. "Get
a good night's sleep," he said and in the silence she heard his boots scattering gravel from the shoulder of the road as he walked away.

She crumpled the ticket into the glove compartment and waited for
him to leave. He shut off the rotating light, turned on the headlights, and
outwaited her. He followed all the way to the next exit. So Lily had to
take it.

She parked her car at the edge of Mattie's lawn. Moths circled the
lights on the sign and on the porch. A large white owl slid through the
dusky air, transformed by the lights beneath it into something angelic. A
cricket landed on the sleeve of her linen suit. The sprinklers went on suddenly; the watery hiss erased the hum of insects, but the pathway to the
door remained dry. Lily stood on the lighted porch and rang the bell.

The woman who answered wore blue jeans and a flannel shirt. She
had the angular hips of an older woman, but her hair showed very little
gray, just a small patch right at the forehead. "Come in, darling," she said.
There was a faint southern softness in her voice. "You look tired. Do you
want a room? Have you come to see the caves? I'm Mattie."

"Yes, of course," Lily told her. "I need a room. I met some people
who were here last year. You really *have* to see these caves, they told me."

"I'll have Katherine pack you a lunch if you like," Mattie offered.
"It's beautiful hiking weather. You won't get nearly so hot as in the summer. You can go tomorrow."

Lily borrowed the phone in the living room to call David. It sat on
a small table between a glass ball with a single red rosebud frozen inside

and picture of the Virgin praying. The Virgin wore a blue mantilla and appeared to be suspended in a cloudless sky. The phone had a dial which Lily spun. She was so used to the tune their number made on the touch phone at work that she missed hearing it. She listened to the answering machine, heard her voice which sounded nothing like her voice, suggesting that she leave a message. "I'm in Two Trees at Mattie's bed and breakfast," she said. "I had this sudden impulse to see the caves. I may stay a couple of days. Will you call Harriet and tell her I won't be in tomorrow? It's real slow. There won't be a problem." She would have told David she missed him, but she ran out of time. She would have only said it out of politeness anyway. They had been married nine years. She would miss him later. She would begin to miss him when she began to miss herself. He might be missing her, too, just about then. It would be nice if all these things happened at the same time.

She took the key from Mattie, went upstairs, used the bathroom at the end of the hall, used someone else's toothbrush, rinsing it out repeatedly afterwards, unlocked her door, removed all her clothes and cried until she fell asleep.

In the morning Lily lay in bed and watched the sun stretch over the quilt and onto the skin of her arms and her hands. She looked around the room. The bed was narrow and had a headpiece made of iron. A pattern of small pink flowers papered the walls. On the bookcase next to the bed a china lady held a china umbrella with one hand and extended the other, palm up, to see if the rain had stopped. There were books. *Beauty's Secret*, one of them said on the spine. Lily opened it, but it turned out to be about horses.

A full-length mirror hung on the back of the bedroom door. Lily didn't notice until the sunlight touched its surface, doubling in brightness. She rose and stood in front of it, backlit by the sunny window, frontlit by the mirror so that she could hardly see. She leaned in closer. Last night's crying had left her eyes red and the lids swollen. She looked at herself for a long time, squinting and changing the angle. Who was she? There was absolutely no way to tell.

The smell of coffee came up the stairs and through the shut door. Lily found her clothes on the desk chair where she had left them. She put them on: stockings, a fuchsia blouse, an eggshell business suit, heels. She used the bathroom, someone else's hairbrush as well as someone else's toothbrush, and came downstairs.

"You can't go hiking dressed like that," Mattie told her and, of course, Lily couldn't. "You have nothing else? What size shoe do you wear? A six and a half? Six? Tiny little thing, aren't you? Katherine might have something that will do." She raised her voice. "Katherine? Katherine!"

Katherine came through the doorway at the bottom of the stairs, drying her hands on a dish towel. She was somewhat younger than Mattie though older than Lily, middle forties, perhaps, and heavier, a dark-skinned woman with straight black hair. On request she produced jeans for Lily, a sleeveless T-shirt, a red sweatshirt, gray socks, and sneakers. Everything was too big for Lily. Everything was wearable.

Mattie took her through the screen door and out the back porch after breakfast. Beyond the edge of Mattie's sprinklers, the lawn stopped abruptly at a hill of sand and manzanita. Mattie had stowed a lunch and a canteen in a yellow daypack. She began to help Lily into it. "You go up," Mattie said. "All the way up. And then down. You can see the trail from the other side of the fence. Watch for rattlers. You hiked much?" Lily was having trouble slipping her left arm under the second strap. It caught at the elbow, her arm pinned behind her. Mattie eased the pack off and began again.

"Oh, yes," Lily assured her. "I've hiked a lot." Mattie looked unconvinced. "I'm a rock-climber," said Lily. "That's the kind of hiking I'm used to. Crampons and ropes and mallets. I don't usually wear them on my back. I wear them on my belt. I take groups out. Librarians and school teachers and beauticians. You know."

"Well, there's just a trail here," said Mattie doubtfully. "I don't suppose you can get into trouble as long as you stay on the trail. Your shoes don't really fit well. I'm afraid you'll blister."

"I once spent three days alone in the woods without food or shelter and it snowed. I was getting a merit badge." The daypack was finally in place. "Thank you," Lily said.

"Wait here. I'm going to get some moleskin for your feet. And I'm going to send Jep along with you. Jep has a lot of common sense. And Jep knows the way. You'll be glad of the company," Mattie told her. She disappeared back into the house.

"It was in Borneo," Lily said softly, so that Mattie wouldn't hear. "You want to talk about blisters. You try walking in the snows of Borneo."

Jep turned out to be a young collie. One ear flopped over in proper collie fashion. One pointed up like a shepherd's. "I've heard some nice things about you," Lily told him. He followed Lily out to the gate and then took the lead, his tail and hindquarters moving from side to side with every step. He set an easy pace. The trail was unambiguous. The weather was cool when they started. In an hour or so, Lily removed her sweatshirt and Jep's tongue drooped from his mouth. Everyone felt good.

The sun was not yet overhead when Lily stopped for lunch. "Eleven twenty-two," she told Jep. "Judging solely by the sun." Katherine had packed apple juice and cold chicken and an orange with a seam cut into the peel and a chocolate Hostess cupcake with a cream center for dessert. Lily had not seen a cupcake like that since she had stopped taking a lunch to school. She sat with her back against a rock overhang and shared it with Jep, giving him none of the cream filling. There was a red place on her left heel and she covered it with moleskin. Jep lay on his side. Lily felt drowsy. "You want to rest a while?" she asked Jep. "I don't really care if we make the caves and you've seen them before. I could give a damn about the caves, if you want to know the truth." She yawned. Somewhere to the left a small animal scuttled in the brush. Jep hardly lifted his head. Lily made a pillow out of Katherine's red sweatshirt and went to sleep, leaning against the overhang.

When she woke, the sun was behind her. Jep was on his feet, looking at something above her head. His tail wagged slowly and he whined once. On the ground, stretching over him and extending several more feet, lay the shadow of a man, elongated legs, one arm up as though he were waving. When Lily moved away from the overhang and turned to look, he was gone.

It unsettled her. She supposed that a seasoned hiker would have known better than to sleep on the trail. She turned to go back to Mattie's and had only walked a short way, less than a city block, when she saw something she had missed coming from the other direction. A woman was painted onto the flat face of a rock which jutted up beside the trail. The perspective was somewhat flattened, and the image had been simplified, which made it extraordinarily compelling somehow. Especially for a painting on a rock. When had Lily ever seen anything painted on a rock other than "Kelly loves Eric" or "Angela puts out"? The woman's long, black hair fell straight down both sides of her face. Her dark eyes were half-closed; her skin was brown. She was looking down at her hands which she held cupped together and she was dressed all in red. Wherever the surface of the rock was the roughest, the paint had cracked, and one whole sleeve had flaked off entirely. Lily leaned down to touch the missing arm. There was a silence as if the birds and the snakes and the insects had all suddenly run out of breath. Lily straightened and the ordinary noises began again. She followed Jep back down the trail.

"I didn't get to the caves," she admitted to Mattie. "I'll go again tomorrow. But I did see something intriguing. The painting. The woman painted on the rock. I'm used to graffiti, but not this kind. Who painted her?"

"I don't know," said Mattie. "She's been here longer than I have. We get a lot of farm labor through, seasonal labor, you know. I always thought she looked Mexican. And you see paintings like that a lot in Mexico. Rock Madonnas. I read somewhere that the artists usually use their own mothers' faces for inspiration. The writer said you see these paintings by the roadside all the time and that those cultures in which men idolize their own mothers are the most sexist cultures in the world. Interesting article. She's faded a lot over the years."

"You don't often see a Madonna dressed in red," Lily said.

"No, you don't," Mattie agreed. "Blue usually, isn't it?" She helped Lily out of the pack. "Did you get blisters?" she asked. "I was worried about you."

"No," said Lily, although the spot on her heel had never stopped bothering her. "I was fine."

"You know who might be able to tell you about the painting? Allison Beale. Runs the county library, but lives here in Two Trees. She's been here forever. You could run over tonight and ask her if you like. I'll give you the address. She likes company."

So Lily got back in her car with Allison Beale's address in her pocket and a map to Allison's house. She was supposed to go there first and then pick up some dinner at a little restaurant called The Italian Kitchen, but she turned left instead of right and then left again to a bar she'd noticed on her way into Two Trees, with a neon martini glass tipping in the window. The only other customer, a man, stood with his back to her, studying the jukebox selections, but choosing nothing. Lily sat at the counter and ordered a margarita. It came without salt and the ice floated inside it uncrushed. "You're the lady staying with Mattie," the bartender informed her. "My name is Egan. Been to the caves?"

"Lily," Lily said. "I don't like caves. I can get lost in the supermarket. Wander for days without a sweater in the frozen foods. I'm afraid to think what would happen to me in a cave."

"These caves aren't deep," the bartender said, wiping the counter in front of her with the side of his hand. "Be a shame to come all the way to Two Trees and not even see the caves."

"Take a native guide," the other man suggested. He had come up behind her while she ordered. She slid around on the bar stool.

"Henry," he told her. He wore a long, black braid and a turquoise necklace. The last time Lily had seen him he had been dressed as a policeman. She'd had no sense of his hair being long like this.

"You're an Indian," Lily said.

"Can't put anything past you." He sat down on the stool next to hers. Lily guessed he was somewhere in his thirties, just about her own age. "Take off your wedding ring and I'll buy you a drink."

She slid the ring off her finger. Her hands were cold and it didn't even catch at the knuckle. She laid it on the napkin. "It's off," she said. "But that's all I'm taking off. I hope we understand each other."

The bartender brought her a second margarita. "The first one was on the house," he said. "Because you're a guest in Two Trees. The second one is on Henry. We'll worry about the third when you get to it."

Lily got to it about an hour later. She could easily have done without it. She was already quite drunk. She and Henry and the bartender were still the only people in the bar.

"It just intrigued me, you know?" she said. The bartender stood draped across the counter next to her. Henry leaned on one elbow. Lily could hear that she was slurring her words. She tried to sharpen them. "It seemed old. I thought it intrigued me enough to go talk to the librarian about it, but I was wrong about that." She laughed and started on her third drink. "It should be restored," she added. "Like the Sistine Chapel."

"I can tell you something about it," the bartender said. "I can't swear any of it's true, but I know what people say. It's a picture of a miracle." He glanced at Henry. "Happened more than a hundred years ago. It was painted by a man, a local man, I don't think anyone remembers who. And this woman appeared to him one day, by the rock. She held out her hands, cupped, just the way he drew them, like she was offering him something, but her hands were empty. And then she disappeared again."

"Well?" said Lily.

"Well, what?" Henry answered her. She turned back to him. Henry was drinking something clear from a shot glass. Egan kept it filled; Henry never asked him, but emptied the glass several times without appearing to be affected. Lily wondered if it might even be water.

"What was the miracle? What happened?"

There was a pause. Henry looked down into his drink. Egan finally spoke. "Nothing happened that I know of." He looked at Henry. Henry shrugged. "The miracle was that she appeared. The miracle was that he turned out to be the kind of person something like this happened to." Lily shook her head in dissatisfaction. "It's kind of a miracle the painting has lasted so long, don't you think?" Egan suggested. "Out there in the wind and the sand for all those years?" Lily shook her head again.

"You are a hard woman," Henry told her. He leaned closer. "And a beautiful one."

It made Lily laugh at him for being so unoriginal. "Right." She stirred her drink with her fingers. "How do Indians feel about their mothers?"

"I loved mine. Is that the right answer?"

"I'll tell you what I've always heard about Indians." Lily put her elbows on the counter between them, her chin in her hands.

"I bet I know this." Henry's voice dropped to a whisper. "I bet I know exactly what you've always heard."

"I've heard that sexual technique is passed from father to son." Lily took a drink. "And you know what I've always thought? I've always thought a lot of mistakes must be perpetuated this way. A culture that passed on sexual technique from *mother* to son would impress me."

"So there's a middle man," said Henry. "Give it a chance. It still could work." The phone rang at the end of the bar. Egan went to answer it. Henry leaned forward, staring at her intently. "You have incredible eyes," he said and she looked away from him immediately. "I can't decide what color they are."

Lily laughed again, this time at herself. She didn't want to respond to such a transparent approach, but she couldn't help it. The laugh had an hysterical edge. She got to her feet. "Take off your pants and I'll buy you a drink," she said and enjoyed the startled look on Henry's face. She held onto the counter, brushing against him by accident on her way to the back of the bar.

"End of the counter and left," the bartender told her, hanging up the phone. She gripped each stool and spun it as she went by, hand over hand, for as long as they lasted. She made it the last few steps to the bathroom on her own. The door was marked with the silhouette of a figure wearing a skirt. Lily fell through it and into the stall. On one side of her "Brian is a fox" was scratched into the wall. On the other side were the words "Chastity Chews." A picture accompanied the text, another picture of a woman, presumably chewing chastity. She had many arms like Kali and a great many teeth. A balloon rose from her mouth. "Hi," she said simply.

Lily spent some time at the mirror, fixing her hair. She blew a breath into her hand and tried to smell it, but all she could smell was the lavatory soap. She supposed this was good. "I'm going home," she announced, back in the bar. "I've enjoyed myself."

She felt around in her purse for her keys. Henry held them up and rang them together. "I can't let you drive home. You hardly made it to the bathroom."

"I can't let you take me. I don't know you well enough."

"I wasn't going to suggest that. Looks like you have to walk."

Lily reached for the keys and Henry closed his fist about them. "It's only about six blocks," he said.

"It's dark. I could be assaulted."

"Not in Two Trees."

"Anywhere. Are you kidding?" Lily smiled at him. "Give me the keys. I already have a blister."

"I could give you the keys and you could hit a tree not two blocks from here. I don't think I could live with myself. Egan will back me up on this." Henry gestured with his closed fist toward the bartender.

"Damn straight," said Egan. "There's no way you're driving home. You'll be fine walking. And, anyway, Jep's come for you." Lily could see a vague doggy shape through the screen door out of the bar.

"Hello, Jep," Lily said. The figure through the screen wagged from side to side. "All right." Lily turned back to the men at the bar. "All right," she conceded. "I'm walking. The men in this town are pitiless, but the dogs are fine. You've got to love the dogs."

She swung the screen door open. Jep backed out of the way. "Tomorrow," Egan called out behind her, "you go see those caves."

Jep walked beside her on the curbside, between her and the street. Most of the houses were closed and dark. In the front of one a woman sat on a porch swing, holding a baby and humming to it. Some heartbreak song. By the time Lily reached Mattie's she felt sober again.

Mattie was sitting in the living room. "Egan called," she said. "I made you some tea. I know it's not what you think you want, but it has some herbs in it, very effective against hangover. You won't be sorry you drank it. It's a long hike to the caves. You want to be rested."

Lily sat on the couch beside her. "Thank you. You've being very good to me, Mattie. I don't deserve it. I've been behaving very badly."

"Maybe it's just my turn to be good," said Mattie. "Maybe you just finished your turn. Did you ever get any dinner?"

"I think I may have had some pretzels." Lily looked across the room to the phone, wondering if she were going to call David. She looked at the picture of the Madonna. It was not a very interesting one. Too sweet. Too much sweetness. "I should call my husband," she told Mattie and didn't move.

"Would you like me to leave you alone?"

"No," said Lily. "It wouldn't be that sort of call. David and I, we don't have personal conversations." She realized suddenly that she had left her wedding ring back at the bar on the cocktail napkin beside her empty glass.

"Is the marriage a happy one?" Mattie asked. "Forgive me if I'm prying. It's just—well, here you are."

"I don't know," said Lily.

Mattie put her arm around Lily and Lily leaned against her. "Loving is a lot harder for some people than for others," she said. "And being loved can be hardest of all. Not for you, though. Not for a loving woman like you."

Lily sat up and reached for her tea. It smelled of chamomile. "Mattie," she said. She didn't know how to explain. Lily felt that she always appeared to be a better person than she was. It was another affliction. In many ways Mattie's analysis was true. Lily knew that her family and friends wondered how she lived with such a cold, methodical man. But there was another truth, too. Often, Lily set up little tests for David, tests of his sensitivity, tests of his commitment. She was always pleased when he failed them, because it proved the problems between them were still his fault. Not a loving thing to do. "Don't make me out to be some saint," she said.

She slept very deeply that night, dreaming on alcohol and tea, and woke up late in the morning. It was almost ten before she and Jep hit the trail. She watched for the painting on her way up this time, stopping to eat an identical lunch in a spot where she could look at it. Jep sat beside her, panting. They passed the rock overhang where she had eaten lunch the day before, finished the climb uphill and started down. The drop-off was sharp; the terrain was dusty and uninviting, and Lily, who was tired of walking uphill, found it even harder to descend. When the trail stopped at a small hollow in the side of a rock, she decided she would rest and then go back. Everyone else might be excessively concerned that she see the caves, but she couldn't bring herself to care. She dropped the day-pack on the ground and sat beside it. Jep raised his collie ear and wagged his tail. Turning, Lily was not at all surprised to see Henry coming down the hill, his hair loose and hanging to his shoulders.

"So," he said. "You found the caves without me."

"You're kidding." Lily stood up. "This little scrape in the rock? This can't be the famous Two Trees caves. I won't believe it. Tell me there are real caves just around the next bend."

"You need something more?" Henry asked. "This isn't enough? You are a hard woman."

"Oh, come on." Lily flicked her hair out of her eyes. "Are you telling me people come from all over to see this?"

"It's not the caves." Henry was staring at her. She felt her face reddening. "It's what happens in the caves." He moved closer to her. "It's what happens when a beautiful woman comes to the caves." Lily let herself look right at his eyes. Inside his pupils, a tiny Lily looked back out.

"Stay away from me," said Lily. Was she the kind of woman who would allow a strange man in a strange place to kiss her? Apparently so. Apparently she was the kind of woman who said no to nothing now. She reached out to Henry; she put one hand on the sleeve of his shirt, one hand on his neck, moved the first hand to his back. "I gave you my car and my wedding ring," she told him. "What do you want now? What will satisfy you?" She kissed him first. They dropped to their knees on the hard floor of the cave. He kissed her back.

"We could go somewhere more comfortable," said Lily.

"No," said Henry. "It has to be here."

They removed their clothes and spread them about as padding. The shadow of the rock lengthened over them. Jep whined once or twice and then went to sleep at a safe distance. Lily couldn't relax. She let Henry work at it. She touched his face and kissed his hand. "Your father did a nice job," she told him, moving as close to his side as she could, holding herself against him. "You do that wonderfully." Henry's arm lay underneath her back. He lifted her with it, turning her so that she was on top of him, facing down. He took hold of her hair and pulled her face to his own, put his mouth on her mouth. Then he let her go, staring at her, holding the bits of hair about her face in his hands. "You are so beautiful," he said and something broke inside her.

"Am I?" She was frightened because she suddenly needed to believe him, needed to believe that he might love her, whoever she was.

"Incredibly beautiful."

"Am I?" Don't say it if you don't mean it, she told him silently, too afraid to talk and almost crying. Don't make me want it if it's not there. Please. Be careful what you say.

"Incredibly beautiful." He began to move again inside her. "So beautiful." He watched her face. "So beautiful." He touched her breasts and then his eyes closed and his mouth rounded. She thought he might fly apart, his body shook so and she held him together with her hands, kissed him until he stopped and then kissed him again.

"I don't want to hurt you," Henry said.

It hurt Lily immediately, like a slap. So now she was the sort of woman men said this to. Well, she had no right to expect anything different from a man she didn't even know. She could have said it to him first if she'd thought of it. That would have been the smart thing to do. Nothing would have been stupider than needing him. What had she been thinking of? "But you will if you have to," she finished. "Right? Don't worry. I'm not making anything of this. I know what this is." She sat up and reached for Katherine's sweatshirt. She was cold and afraid to move closer to Henry. She was cold and she didn't want to be naked anymore.

"You sound angry," Henry said. "It's not that I couldn't love you. It's not that I don't already love you. Men always disappoint women. I'm not sure we can escape it."

"Don't be ridiculous," Lily told him sharply. She put her head into the red tent of the sweatshirt and pulled it through. "I should have gotten your sexual history first," she added. "I haven't done this since the rules changed."

"I haven't been with a woman in ten years," Henry said. Lily looked at his face in surprise.

"Before that it was five years," he said. "And before that three, but that was two at once. That was the sixties. Before that it was fifteen years. And twenty before that. And two. And two. And before that almost a hundred."

Lily stood up, pulling on Katherine's jeans. "I should have gotten your psychiatric history first," she said. The faster she tried to dress, the more difficulties she had. She couldn't find one of Katherine's socks. She was too angry and frightened to look among Henry's clothes. She put on Katherine's shoes without it. "Come on, Jep," she said.

"It can't mean anything," Henry told her.

"It didn't. Forget it." Lily left without the daypack. She hurried up the trail. Jep followed somewhat reluctantly. They made the crest of the hill; Lily looked behind her often to see if Henry was following. He wasn't. She went past the painting without stopping. Jep preceded her through the gate into Mattie's backyard.

Mattie and Katherine were waiting in the house. Katherine put her arms around her. "You went to the caves," Katherine said. "Didn't you? I can tell."

"Of course she did," said Mattie. She stroked Lily's hair. "Of course she did."

Lily stood stiffly inside Katherine's arms. "What the hell is going on?" she asked. She pushed away and looked at the two women. "You sent me up there, didn't you? You did! You and Egan and probably Allison Beale, too. Go to the caves, go to the caves. That's all I've heard since I got here. You dress me like some virginal sacrifice, fatten me up with Hostess cupcakes and send me to him. But why?"

"It's a miracle," said Mattie. "You were chosen. Can't you feel it?"

"I let some man pick me up in a bar. He turns out to be a nut." Lily's voice rose higher. "Where's the miracle?"

"You slept with Henry," said Mattie. "Henry chose *you*. Just like the woman in the painting chose him. That's the miracle."

Lily ran up the stairs. She stripped Katherine's clothes off and put her own on. Mattie came and stood in the doorway. Lily walked around her and out of the room.

"Listen to me, Lily," Mattie said. "You don't understand. He gave you as much as he can give anyone. That's why in the painting the woman's hands are empty. But that's *his* trap. *His* curse. Not yours. When you see that, you'll forgive him. Katherine and Allison and I all forgave him. I know you will, too. A loving woman like you." Mattie reached out, grabbing Lily's sleeve. "Stay here with us. You can't go back to your old life. You won't be able to. You've been chosen."

"Look," said Lily. She took a deep breath and wiped at her eyes with her hands. "I wasn't chosen. Quite the opposite. I was picked up and discarded. By a man in his thirties and not the same man you slept with. Maybe you slept with a god. You go ahead and tell yourself that. What difference does it make? You were still picked up and discarded." She shook loose of Mattie and edged down the stairs. She expected to be stopped, but she wasn't. At the front door, she turned. Mattie stood on the landing behind her. Mattie held out one hand. Lily shook her head. "I think you're pretty pathetic, if you want to know the truth. I'm not going to tell myself a lot of lies or listen to yours. I know who I am. I'm going. I won't be back. Don't expect me."

Her car waited at the front of the house, just where she had parked it the first night. She ran from the porch. The keys were inside. Left and left again, past the bar where the martini glass tipped darkly in the window, and onto the freeway. Lily accelerated way past eighty and no one stopped her. The foothills sped by and became cities. When she felt that she was far enough away to be safe from small town Madonnas and men who were cursed to endure centuries of casual sex with as many loving women as possible, which was damn few, in fact, if you believed the numbers they gave you, she slowed down. She arrived home in the early evening. As she was walking in the door, she noticed she was wearing her wedding ring.

David was sitting on the couch reading a book. "Here I am, David," Lily said. "I'm here. I got a speeding ticket. I never looked to see how much it was for. I lost my ring playing poker, but I mortgaged the house and won it back. I lost a lot more, though. I lost my head. I'm halfhearted now. In fact, I'm not at all the woman I was. I've got to be honest with you."

"I'm glad you're home," said David. He went back to his book.

ONCE MORE, WITH MEANING

by Karen Joy Fowler

▼

Notes on "Lily Red":

▼

I have met writers who claim to love the first draft. They attack the blank screen with white-hot fire. Their little fingers fly over the keys. We may exchange Christmas cards with these writers, but we rarely invite them to dinner.

I think of the first draft as penance or dues. I am going to have such fun in the second and the third and the tenth draft, but first I must pay the price of admission and that price is filling up the screen with an unsightly mess of words. The reason this is no fun is that I don't know what I'm doing yet. I don't know who the story is about, or why I am telling it. When I begin the story, I don't even know how or where or when it begins.

I solve these problems by writing it. I have in my head something wonderful, but vague and fragmentary. It may be an image, it may be a conversation, it may be an incident, it may be a feeling. It may be some lyrics to some rock song I have completely misheard. The one thing we can be sure it is *not* is a story. Still there is something about it, some X factor, that makes me think it could be. Not just a story, but a wonderful story. This imaginary story I haven't told yet, it shimmers in my mind like a bird in the sunlight. And then I spend the first draft removing its wings, feather by feather.

I usually force my way through the first draft on plot alone or something vaguer than plot, some shape I think the story might have. My most usual method is to choose a moment of climax or revelation and then plot backwards from it. I rarely get anywhere near the end of a first draft. By the time I've written several pages, I have a much clearer idea, and I

go back and start again on draft two. I do not save my first drafts. They
are too stupid to live. My motto: "The brain is not a pretty organ. Never
show anyone yours."

At a certain point, when some of the choices have been made, I
begin to enjoy myself. My father used to play a game with me. On a sheet
of yellow paper—yellow, mind, very important—he would draw a large,
amorphous scribble. My task was to take the scribble and turn it into a
picture. I am playing the same game still. I go through the first draft,
looking for the picture. I pick out the things I like best, the things that
seem to work and seem to work together. There will be whole paragraphs
I think are rather good, bits of dialogue that seem amusing, surprising,
or sharp.

Mainly I will be thinking about theme. I cannot reduce my own
themes to a single sentence. They are not messages, but constellations
of issues and questions. It takes me the whole story. If I could say what I
wanted to say in a sentence I would do so and save us all a lot of time.
Theme is the element I use to unify the work, the organizing principle.

When you know your themes you know which pieces belong in this
story and not some other story. So I am going through my first draft, asking, does this belong, does this, does this, and basically what I'm asking
is, why did I want to tell this story in the first place. Why does this story
matter to me? What is this story about?

The trigger for "Lily Red" was a bit of historical research left over
from my novel *Sarah Canary*. I read in a biography a paragraph about
P. T. Barnum's Wild West Show. Barnum hired a group of Indians from
Iowa to tour and perform war dances in full paint and regalia. When he
tired of these, he persuaded them to perform the Wedding Dance instead.
The Wedding Dance was a sacred ceremony. To do the dance was to actually marry: It couldn't be simulated. Barnum could not be made to understand this, or else he didn't care. He persisted, raised wages until they
agreed. They performed it twice a day for several weeks. When Do-
humme, one of the most beautiful of the squaws died, they interpreted
the death as a judgment on them all. They went home.

I was very moved by this. In using it I imagined I would be writing
a story whose themes included some of my personal favorites—the in-
tersection of cultures, imperialism, and profit. I thought I would be writing a story about the sacred and the profane, about what could not be
sold and what the price might be on something that could not be sold. I

thought I would be writing about voyeurism. I used the image of Do-humme. I painted her face on a rock.

If I have learned one thing about my own methods, it is that I never end up writing the story I thought I might be writing when I began. When I went through my first draft, what I liked best was one scene, which took place in a bar, the town of Two Trees, and Lily, my main character. I still find Lily a treat. This does not mean necessarily that I like her, although I do, or approve of her. It just means I enjoyed writing her. She is one of only a few of my characters that I think I will use again someday. And what was the story about? Something else entirely.

I recognized Lily only after I had written her. She was a figure out of American mythology—Coyote, the trickster, caught in someone else's trick. She was also the brave little tailor, a figure out of a fairy tale. She is not a powerful figure, but she is a clever one. She has a streak of amorality, a certain audacity, and she is quick on her feet. When I knew who *she* was then I began to know what the story was about.

"Lily Red" turned out to be about expectation and disappointment. It's a fairy tale about the fairy tales we tell ourselves to make it through our lives. It's about how hard they are sometimes to believe in and how hard they are not to believe in. At its most purified level, it is about the difficulty of distinguishing between what is real and what is imaginary, which, as it turns out, is the theme of all my work, THE THEME I CAN'T ESCAPE.

This theme may not be as clear to other readers as it is to me. I have talked to some readers so I make this statement with a certain authority. There are other things in the story. It contains, for example, my profound disapproval of gods who sleep with mortals. If we peruse the mythological record, we find that the immortals make for irresponsible lovers. Besides, they have never wanted to sleep with me. So forget them.

It's also about the expectations we bring to sex, the difficulties men and woman have with each other, and the role other women, our *sisters*, play in these difficulties. But these are not, as I read the story, the central themes.

I took the story in late draft to the Sycamore Hill workshop in North Carolina. There I was told, with great unanimity, that the main thing in the story which no longer worked was Barnum and the Wild West Show. The incident that triggered the whole story vanished entirely, with only a vague image on a rock and the curse left behind.

The fairy tale is a theme I care about deeply; I don't ever write stories about things that don't matter to me. Any woman can tell you how powerful and enduring the fairy tales we grew up with are. They enter our bloodstream when we read them, or else are already chemically present, waiting only to be released. We don't outgrow them. We add to them. I watch a lot of television, for research purposes only, of course, see a lot of movies, and read a lot of books. Based on this I am ready to identify some of those things I think most people want to believe.

I think we want desperately to believe in an ordered universe, with consequences and justice, even if that justice is merciless or blind.

We want to believe in our own importance. We want to believe in a universe that responds to special pleading.

We want to believe that God cares.

And even if the universe itself remains cold, then we want, most of us, to believe in the transforming power of love. We want to believe that we are sexually compatible with someone. We want to believe that in some ledger somewhere, we have already all been sorted into pairs, like the animals on Noah's ark, that someday we will find our other half.

We want to believe that love survives death, even if we then have to believe that malice does as well.

I need to believe these things as much as the next person. And just because we need to believe in these things, that need in itself doesn't automatically make them untrue. But there is no empirical basis for these things—true or untrue, they belong to the realm of magic.

Now, the world may be chock full of magical happenings, but I am never in the right place at the right time to see them. I know people who've seen UFOs, been brought to their knees by feats of mind control, remembered past lives, and received extra sensory messages. I know people who've felt the presence of the dead and I know people who've talked to Jesus personally. I know these people and in some cases I trust these people, but in my whole life I have never had one experience myself or actually seen anyone else have one experience that demanded supernatural explanation. I have seen irrationality at work in the universe and luck, too, but no magic. The miracles I have witnessed have all been the ordinary ones—birth, springtime, the red tide, the grunion run, mountains, trees.

How am I to deal with this? I could believe that the world has a magical subtext from which I am for some reason excluded. Or I could believe that these people have lied to me or, more charitably, that they were mistaken. There is simply no overestimating the gullibility of human beings and I ought to know, because I am one. But neither option appeals to me.

I try instead to maintain a position I will call belieflessness. If I tell you I don't believe in God, this is not the same as telling you I believe there is no God. Nor is this a fine distinction.

My main character Lily is at once, like me, a storyteller and a pragmatist. She is the point-of-view character, albeit in third person, and she is trying to get out of one story, when she falls into another. She imagines she's creating a new story for herself, her own story, the *real* story, but it turns out to be someone else's story entirely, even though she's the one going through it. The only story in which she is the protagonist turns out to be the story she fled in the first place.

Did we all follow that? I find all this story within story within story stuff strangely satisfying. I picture the shape of the piece turning inside out and back again, ending at the beginning point, only in a different plane, like a Möbius strip.

Lily faces each of those beliefs previously listed, all wrapped up in the character of Henry. Since Lily herself produces lies on demand, she should know better than to believe a story just because someone else tells it. And she is a hard woman to please. She slips up at one point; for one moment she believes in all of the above. I would say that the author, too, completely guiled by the male character she has created, still drunk on those imaginary margaritas a few pages earlier, slips up at exactly the same moment.

But both of us recover.

I used the trappings of fairy tales to illuminate the theme. The title is a takeoff on the story "Rose Red," and the phrase, lily white. It begins with a journey, an arrival. The prince appears in disguise—and what could be more toadish than a cop?—and directs her to the castle. The sprinklers represent the moat around the castle. She acquires an animal companion and a quest. People in fairy tales always have a task—cut through the brambles, climb the glass mountain, slay the dragon. Lily's task is to go to the caves. She has to be outfitted in magic clothing, fed with magic foods. She has to try three times, three being the number of fairy tales. She finds her prince and he's pretty damned attractive. He does a whole lot more than kiss her and he does it very nicely, too. And only after she's accomplished her task, only after she's seen it through, can she reasonably reject it.

"Lily Red" is intended as a fairy tale that dismisses all fairy tales, an anti-fairy tale. "You are nothing but a pack of cards," is the way the story ends. Almost. Except that there is some evidence of the miraculous in the ending. There is some doubt as to Lily's reliability as a witness. There is, I hope, some sympathy for Lily's determination to look at an unpleasant situation straight on, but is wanting not to believe any more commendable or persuasive than wanting to believe?

I am not a writer who provides answers or solves problems. Answers and solutions are another of those fairy tales we need to believe. And when I know the difference between fiction and nonfiction I will never write again.

In Lily's husband I tried to create a character who occupies the ledge space between sympathetic and unsympathetic. If you like her, you don't like him so much. If you don't like her, you can see his point. If you ignore the things that she herself tells you about him, and she is rather a liar, then what you are left with is his single line and his single action, which could go either way. And the last word is his, although he speaks it rather absently. He is, in fact engrossed in another story entirely. Possibly his own.

OUR NEURAL CHERNOBYL
by Bruce Sterling

▼

The late twentieth century, and the early years of our own millennium, form, in retrospect, a single era. This was the Age of the Normal Accident, in which people cheerfully accepted technological risks that today would seem quite insane.

Chernobyls were astonishingly frequent during this footloose, not to say criminally negligent, period. The nineties, with their rapid spread of powerful industrial technologies to the developing world, were a decade of frightening enormities, including the Djakarta supertanker spill, the Lahore meltdown, and the gradual but devastating mass poisonings from tainted Kenyan contraceptives.

Yet none of these prepared humankind for the astonishing global effects of biotechnology's worst disaster: the event that has come to be known as the "neural chernobyl."

We should be grateful, then, that such an authority as the Nobel prize-winning systems neurochemist Dr. Felix Hotton should have turned his able pen to the history of *Our Neural Chernobyl* (Bessemer, December 2056, $499.95). Dr. Hotton is uniquely qualified to give us this devastating reassessment of the past's wrongheaded practices. For Dr. Hotton is a shining exemplar of the new "Open-Tower Science," that social movement within the scientific community that arose in response to the New Luddism of the teens and twenties.

Such pioneering Hotton papers as "The Locus Coeruleus Efferent Network: What in Heck Is It There For?" And "My Grand Fun Tracing Neural Connections with Tetramethylbenzidine" established this new, relaxed, and triumphantly subjective school of scientific exploration.

Today's scientist is a far cry from the white-coated sociopath of the past. Scientists today are democratized, media-conscious, fully integrated into the mainstream of modern culture. Today's young people, who admire scientists with a devotion once reserved for pop stars, can scarcely imagine the situation otherwise.

But in chapter 1, "The Social Roots of Gene-Hacking," Dr. Hotton brings turn-of-the-century attitudes into startling relief. This was the golden age of applied biotech. Anxious attitudes toward "genetic tampering" changed rapidly when the terrifying AIDS pandemic was finally broken by recombinant DNA research.

It was during this period that the world first became aware that the AIDS retrovirus was a fantastic blessing in a particularly hideous disguise. This disease, which dug itself with horrible, virulent cunning into the very genetic structure of its victims, proved a medical marvel when finally broken to harness. The AIDS virus' RNA transcriptase system proved an able workhorse, successfully carrying healing segments of recombinant DNA into sufferers from myriad genetic defects. Suddenly one ailment after another fell to the miracle of RNA transcriptase techniques: sickle-cell anemia, cystic fibrosis, Tay-Sachs disease—literally hundreds of syndromes now only an unpleasant memory.

As billions poured into the biotech industry, and the instruments of research were simplified and streamlined, an unexpected dynamic emerged: the rise of "gene-hacking." As Dr. Hotton points out, the situation had a perfect parallel in the 1970s and 1980s in the subculture of computer hacking. Here again was an enormously powerful technology suddenly within the reach of the individual.

As biotech startup companies multiplied, becoming ever smaller and more advanced, a hacker subculture rose around this "hot technology" like a cloud of steam. These ingenious, anomic individuals, often led into a state of manic self-absorption by their ability to dice with genetic destiny, felt no loyalty to social interests higher than their own curiosity. As early as the 1980s, devices such as high-performance liquid chromotographs, cell-culture systems, and DNA sequences were small enough to fit into a closet or attic. If not brought from junkyards, diverted, or stolen outright, they could be reconstructed from off-the-shelf parts by any bright and determined teenager.

Dr. Hotton's second chapter explores the background of one such individual: Andrew ("Bugs") Berenbaum, now generally accepted as the perpetrator of the neural chernobyl.

Bugs Berenbaum, as Dr. Hotton convincingly shows, was not much different from a small horde of similar bright young misfits surrounding the genetic establishments of North Carolina's Research Triangle. His father was a semisuccessful free-lance programmer, his mother a heavy marijuana user whose life centered around her role as "Lady Anne of Greengables" in Raleigh's Society for Creative Anachronism.

Both parents maintained a flimsy pretense of intellectual superiority, impressing upon Andrew the belief that the family's sufferings derived from the general stupidity and limited imagination of the average citizen. And Berenbaum, who showed an early interest in such subjects as math and engineering (then considered markedly unglamorous), did suffer some persecution from peers and schoolmates. At fifteen he had already drifted into the gene-hacker subculture, accessing gossip and learning "the scene" through computer bulletin boards and all-night beer-and-pizza sessions with other would-be pros.

At twenty-one, Berenbaum was working a summer internship with the small Raleigh firm of CoCoGenCo, a producer of specialized biochemicals. CoCoGenCo, as later congressional investigations proved, was actually a front for the California "designer drug" manufacturer and smuggler Jimmy ("Screech") McCarley. McCarley's agents within CoCoGenCo ran innumerable late-night "research projects" in conditions of heavy secrecy. In reality, these "secret projects" were straight production runs of synthetic cocaine, beta-phenethylamine, and sundry tailored variants of endorphin, a natural antipain chemical ten thousand times more potent than morphine.

One of McCarley's "black hackers," possibly Berenbaum himself, conceived the sinister notion of "implanted dope factories." By attaching the drug-producing genetics directly into the human genome, it was argued, abusers could be "wet-wired" into permanent states of intoxication. The agent of fixation would be the AIDS retrovirus, whose RNA sequence was a matter of common knowledge and available on dozens of open scientific databases. The one drawback to the scheme was, of course, that the abuser would "burn out like a shitpaper moth in a klieg light," to use Dr. Hotton's memorable phrase.

Chapter 3 is rather technical. Given Dr. Hotton's light and popular style, it makes splendid reading. Dr. Hotton attempts to reconstruct Berenbaum's crude attempts to rectify the situation through gross manipulation of the AIDS RNA transcriptase. What Berenbaum sought, of course, was a way to shut off and start up the transcriptase carrier, so that the internal drug factory could be activated at will. Berenbaum's custom transcriptase was designed to react to a simple user-induced trigger— probably D, 1, 2, 5-phospholytic gluteinase, a fractionated component of "Dr. Brown's Celery Soda," as Hotton suggests. This harmless beverage was a favorite quaff of gene-hacker circles.

Finding the coca-production genomes too complex, Berenbaum (or perhaps a close associate, one Richard ["Sticky"] Ravetch) switched to a simpler payload: the just-discovered genome for mammalian dendritic growth factor. Dendrites are the treelike branches of brain cells, familiar to every modern schoolchild, which provide the mammalian brain with its staggering webbed complexity. It was theorized at the time that DG factor might be the key to vastly higher states of human intelligence. It is to be presumed that Berenbaum and Ravetch had both dosed themselves with it. As many modern victims of the neural chernobyl can testify, it does have an effect. Not precisely the one that the CoCoGenCo zealots envisioned, however.

While under the temporary maddening elation of dendritic "branch-effect," Berenbaum made his unfortunate breakthrough. He succeeded in providing his model RNA transcriptase with a trigger, but a trigger that made the transcriptase itself far more virulent than the original AIDS virus itself. The stage was set for disaster.

It is at this point that one must remember the social attitudes that bred the soul-threatening isolation of the contemporary scientific worker. Dr. Hotton is quite pitiless in his psychoanalysis of the mental mind-set of his predecessors. The supposedly "objective worldview" of the sciences is now quite properly seen as a form of mental brainwashing, deliberately stripping its victims of the full spectrum of human emotion and response. Under such conditions, Berenbaum's reckless act becomes almost pitiable; it was a convulsive overcompensation for years of emotional starvation. Without consulting his superiors, who might have shown more discretion, Berenbaum began offering free samples of his new wetwares to anyone willing to shoot them up.

There was a sudden brief plague of eccentric genius in Raleigh, before the now-well-known symptoms of "dendritic crash" took over, and plunged the experimenters into vision-riddled, poetic insanity. Berenbaum himself committed suicide well before the full effects were known. And the full effects, of course, were to go far beyond even this lamentable human tragedy.

Chapter 4 becomes an enthralling detective story as the evidence slowly mounts.

Even today the term "Raleigh collie" has a special ring for dog fanciers, many of whom have forgotten its original derivation. These likable, companionable, and disquietingly intelligent pets were soon transported all over the nation by eager buyers and breeders. Once it had made the jump from human host to canine, Berenbaum's transcriptase derivative, like the AIDS virus itself, was passed on through the canine maternal womb. It was also transmitted through canine sexual intercourse and, via saliva, through biting and licking.

No dendritically enriched "Raleigh collie" would think of biting a human being. On the contrary, these loyal and well-behaved pets have even been known to right spilled garbage cans and replace their trash. Neural chernobyl infections remain rare in humans. But they spread through North America's canine population like wildfire, as Dr. Hotton shows in a series of cleverly designed maps and charts.

Chapter 5 offers us the benefit of hindsight. We are now accustomed to the idea of many different modes of "intelligence." There are, for instance, the various types of computer Artificial Intelligence, which bear no real relation to human "thinking." This was not unexpected — but the diverse forms of animal intelligence can still astonish in their variety.

The variance between *Canis familiaris* and his wild cousin, the coyote, remains unexplained. Dr. Hotton makes a good effort, basing his explication on the coyote neural mapping of his colleague, Dr. Reyna Sanchez of Los Alamos National Laboratory. It does seem likely that the coyote's more fully reticulated basal commissure plays a role. At any rate, it is now clear that a startling advanced form of social organization has taken root among the nation's feral coyote population, with the use of elaborate coded barks, "scent-dumps," and specialized roles in hunting and food storage. Many of the nation's ranchers have now taken to the "protection system," in which coyote packs are "bought off" with slaughtered, barbecued livestock and sacks of dog treats. Persistent reports in Montana, Idaho, and Saskatchewan insist that coyotes have been spotted wearing cast-off clothing during the worst cold of winter.

It is possible that the common household cat was infected even earlier than the dog. Yet the effects of heightened cat intelligence are subtle and difficult to specify. Notoriously reluctant lab subjects, cats in their infected states are even sulkier about running mazes, solving trick boxes, and so on, preferring to wait out their interlocutors with inscrutable feline patience.

It has been suggested that some domestic cats show a heightened interest in television programs. Dr. Hotton casts a skeptical light on this, pointing out (rightly, as this reviewer thinks) that cats spend most of their waking hours sitting and staring into space. Staring at the flickering of a television is not much more remarkable than the hearthside cat's fondness for the flickering fire. It certainly does not imply "understanding" of a program's content. There are, however, many cases where cats have learned to paw-push the buttons of remote-control units. Those who keep cats as mousers have claimed that some cats now torture birds and rodents for longer periods, with greater ingenuity, and in some cases with improvised tools.

There remains, however, the previously unsuspected connection between advanced dendritic branching and manual dexterity, which Dr. Hotton tackles in his sixth chapter. This concept has caused a revolution in paleoanthropology. We are now forced into the uncomfortable realization that *Pithecanthropus robustus*, formerly dismissed as a large-jawed, vegetable-chewing ape, was probably far more intelligent than *Homo sapiens*. CAT scans of the recently discovered Tanzanian fossil skeleton, nicknamed "Leonardo," reveal a *Pithecanthropus* skull ridge obviously rich with dendritic branching. It has been suggested that the pithecanthropoids suffered from a heightened "life of the mind" similar to the life-threatening, absentminded genius of terminal neural chernobyl sufferers. This yields the uncomfortable theory that nature, through evolution, has imposed a "primate stupidity barrier" that allows humans, unlike *Pithecanthropus*, to get on successfully with the dumb animal business of living and reproducing.

But the synergetic effects of dendritic branching and manual dexterity are clear in a certain nonprimate species. I refer, of course, to the well-known "chernobyl jump" of *Procyon lotor*, the American raccoon. The astonishing advances of the raccoon, and its Chinese cousin the panda, occupy the entirety of chapter 8.

Here Dr. Hotton takes the so-called "modern view," from which I must dissociate myself. I, for one, find it intolerable that large sections of the American wilderness should be made into "no-go areas" by the vandalistic activities of our so-called "striped-tailed cousins." Admittedly, excesses may have been committed in early attempts to exterminate the verminous, booming population of these masked bandits. But the damage to agriculture has been severe, and the history of kamikaze attacks by self-infected rabid raccoons is a terrifying one.

Dr. Hotton holds that we must now "share the planet with a fellow civilized species." He bolsters his argument with hearsay evidence of "raccoon culture" that to me seems rather flimsy. The woven strips of bark known as "raccoon wampum" are impressive examples of animal dexterity, but to my mind it remains to be proven that they are actually "money." And their so-called "pictographs" seem little more than random daubings. The fact remains that the raccoon population continues to rise exponentially, with raccoon bitches whelping massive litters every spring. Dr. Hotton, in a footnote, suggests that we can relieve crowding pressure by increasing the human presence in space. This seems a farfetched and unsatisfactory scheme.

The last chapter is speculative in tone. The prospect of intelligent rats is grossly repugnant; so far, thank God, the tough immune system of the rat, inured to bacteria and filth, has rejected retroviral invasion. Indeed, the feral cat population seems to be driving these vermin toward extinction. Nor have opossums succumbed; indeed, marsupials of all kinds seem immune, making Australia a haven of a now-lost natural world. Whales and dolphins are endangered species; they seem unlikely to make a comeback even with the (as-yet-unknown) cetacean effects of chernobyling. And monkeys, which might pose a very considerable threat, are restricted to the few remaining patches of tropical forest and, like humans, seem resistant to the disease.

Our neural chernobyl has bred a folklore all its own. Modern urban folklore speaks of "ascended masters," a group of chernobyl victims able to survive the virus. Supposedly, they "pass for human," forming a hidden counterculture among the normals, or "sheep." This is a throwback to the dark tradition of Luddism, and the popular fears once projected onto the dangerous and reckless "priesthood of science" are now transferred to these fairy tales of supermen. This psychological transference becomes clear when one hears that these "ascended masters" specialize in advanced scientific research of a kind now frowned upon. The notion that some fraction of the population has achieved physical immortality, and hidden it from the rest of us, is utterly absurd.

Dr. Hotton, quite rightly, treats this paranoid myth with the contempt it deserves.

   Despite my occasional reservations, this is a splendid book, likely to
be the definitive work on this central phenomenon of modern times. Dr.
Hotton may well hope to add another Pulitzer to his list of honors. At
ninety-five, this grand old man of modern science has produced yet another stellar work in his rapidly increasing oeuvre. His many readers, like
myself, can only marvel at his vigor and clamor for more.

for Greg Bear

ABOUT "OUR NEURAL CHERNOBYL"

by Bruce Sterling

▼

Although I am a science fiction critic by choice and conviction, I find it a little difficult to discuss my own work as a fiction writer. This book's worthy editor, however, has asked me to talk about the "theme" of "Our Neural Chernobyl." His assignment has proved impossible for me to avoid, but at least it seems pretty straightforward. "Our Neural Chernobyl" is nothing *but* theme.

The theme of this so-called "story" is, of course, chernobyls—our cheerful acceptance of technological risks that seem quite insane. What is it about technology and science—or rather, the politicized rhetoric of contemporary technology and science—that allows us to menace our entire planet with dangerous, brittle technologies, and yet accept this action as something wise and plausible and somehow good for us? How is it that people get fast-talked into accepting nutty schemes such as strip-mining, freon, supertankers, traffic jams, nuclear power, and genetic recombination? It can't merely be the money to be made from these efforts, because there are a million easier ways to make money. A few days of arbitrage in the contemporary currency markets, for instance, would yield enough paper profit to buy out every nuclear reactor in the former Soviet Union and then some. No, this is done for cultural reasons. It's done because of the culturally unquestionable sublimity of the technological imperative.

Science fiction is an aspect of this phenomenon. Only a culture crazily enamored of any kind of knowledge and furiously hungry for any kind of power could create a literature like science fiction. Science fiction is the true native literature of a chernobylized society. The core values expressed by science fiction transcend traditional economics, business sense, democratic politics, literary standards, and other such primitive fripperies. Throughout the twentieth century, science fiction was enormously popular in both communist and capitalist countries. In fact the SF cult (as I have repeatedly discovered with pleasure) has roots in almost every country on earth. The only places where science fiction doesn't flower nowadays are dismal locales like Iran, Cambodia, and Burma, where a future-shocked populace of one-party Luddites cowers in terror before a rest-of-the-world that seems to them to have gone entirely berserk.

You may notice in reading "Our Neural Chernobyl" that it is not a story. It is, in point of fact, an imaginary book review. There is no hero. There are practically no characters. There is no plot. There is no dramatic tension. There is certainly nothing in the way of eternal verities or humanistic values. What there is, is a third-hand bare narrative of the weird results of a hideous action committed by a deranged techno-criminal who is the native son of a pair of classic science fiction fans: a turbo-dork hard-SF computer programmer and a ditzy cape-wearing medievalist fantasy chick. This cruel lampoon of the contemporary genre readership might have proven unbearable for my chosen audience, if not for the prophylactic presence of our anonymous narrator-reviewer, a pompous fathead who has mastered the archly mandarin review-style typical of highbrow science magazines. Thanks to this cunningly obscurantist deployment of pseudo-objective scientific rhetoric, "Our Neural Chernobyl" was quite popular with hardcore SF fans and was even a Hugo Award finalist back in 1988.

The unorthodox form of this story accomplishes its function effectively. Imagine this nonexistent "story" recast as an actual no-kidding commercial sci-fi story with plot and characters and everything. We'll make Andrew "Bugs" Berenbaum the protagonist. He's a petty criminal high as a kite on experimental dope who works to manufacture narcotics for a sordid drug-smuggling ring. Our plot: Berenbaum commits a horrible gene-splicing disaster that contaminates the entire world, so he goes insane and commits suicide. Even *Interzone* (Q: How many British science fiction writers does it take to change a lightbulb? A: None, they prefer to sit around in the gloom)—anyway, as I was saying, even the noble *Interzone*, Britain's greatest modern gift to our genre, would consider that story to be too dark and morbid. But Berenbaum is not the hero. And there is no story here at all. So his terrible plight and horrible activities are actually *funny*.

One key sentence in this story is the following: "Chapter 4 becomes an enthralling detective story as the evidence slowly mounts." Note that you are not actually *reading* an enthralling detective story. You are merely being baldly *told* that some chapter of some imaginary book—a book which is not even a work of fiction—appears to some reviewer to be "an enthralling detective story." Nevertheless the pace of the narrative picks up quite perkily at this point, and for quite a while "Our Neural Chernobyl" actually *functions* as if it were an enthralling detective story, even though it's nothing of the kind. It's a little genre miscegenation there, as the cognitive estrangement native to SF discourse disguises itself as the cerebral puzzle-kick that one gets from suspense fiction. This story-less story actually *achieves real suspense* in the midst of its endless demented wisecracking about raccoon wampum and TV-watching cats. I wish I knew exactly how I achieved that effect. I promise you that I didn't do it on purpose.

But that's just a narrative riff. Another and far less graceful line is crucial to the theme. It's this one: "We are now forced into the uncomfortable realization that *Pithecanthropus robustus*, formerly dismissed as a large-jawed, vegetable-chewing ape, was probably far more intelligent than *Homo sapiens*." This line and the foofaraw which follows forms a core thematic statement for "Our Neural Chernobyl," which is itself a single-minded exercise in forcing us into uncomfortable realizations about our own very modern and very human stupidity. Notice that this paragraph has rather little to do with the MacGuffin of the story, i.e. an intelligence-amplifying virus running wild. Instead this apparent diversion is a systematic deployment of Darwinian thematics.

It was Darwin's discovery of the origin of man as a species that shattered Christian culture in the nineteenth century and led to an intense sense of ontological disenfranchisement. In our twentieth century, this deep Western culture-crisis was conflated with the more modern mythos of technological progress into Big Science's crypto-Christian Rocket Transcendentalism, a major pillar in the contemporary temple of mystical scientism, the cultural headquarters from which our culture's chernobyls emerge. If you don't believe this unorthodox social analysis of mine, well, just take it on faith for a minute. And let me assure you that, in our society, the entire issue of proto-hominids really bugs people for a galaxy of reasons which they are basically unable to confront, due to puissant mechanisms of large-scale social psychological denial. Okay? Still with me? This explains why one writes science fiction stories instead of essays on political science.

So anyhow, when "Our Neural Chernobyl" then declares that we have dug up extinct ape-man Missing Links who were *much smarter than humans*, this creates all kinds of fruitful cognitive-dissonant mischief that the story would be unable to provoke without this apparent digression. The core social value of human intelligence, already under severe attack from other aspects of the story, is dealt a sudden and stunning low blow. Thematically speaking this throw-away paragraph is pressing on a deep cultural bruise. It works even better *because of its apparent offhandedness*.

I could have written a very different science fiction story full of ponderous metaphoric intent, about how some team of walking-shorts-clad Richard Leakey yuppie paleo people dig up bones of a superintelligent extinct hominid in Kenya, followed by much consternation from Catholic theologians and so forth. But I'm a writer of the Pat Cadigan school—I believe in cutting people in half before they even realize they're hurt. If you're going to kill a sacred cow, eat it with a big smile and some ketchup.

The ending is the weakest part of this "story" because, not being a story, it can't really have an ending. Instead, it has to have a topper, a kind of punchline rim shot so the reader can finish the reading experience with some vague sense of catharsis. There's no real catharsis to be found in rim shots. More's the pity. If there were, all my stories would probably look like this. Instead, I just make a point of getting away with them when I suspect that I can.

This story is dedicated to Greg Bear, the author of *Blood Music*, a very fine science fiction novel of the 1980s. *Blood Music* is about intelligence run amuck on the microbe-level thanks to the goofing around of some sociopathic hacker geek. Attentive readers may notice a certain thematic connection here. Greg Bear is the world's most reluctant cyberpunk, but he probably deserves this (to my ears) noble term ten times more than many other people far more eager to have it. The story owed a lot to Bear's inspiration, and even some to his literary technique.

It also owed a great debt to Stanislaw Lem, author of *A Perfect Vacuum*, which is an entire book consisting of science-fictional reviews of non-existent books. I'm quite the Lem devotee, in my modest, non-Polish fashion. I once wrote an admiring critical piece about Stanislaw Lem called "The Spearhead of Cognition," a term of his that I have found very useful while considering the Thing That Is SF. In his critical writing (to be found in the fine book *Macroworlds*) Stanislaw Lem demonstrates that science fiction is not and should not be a conventional literature. To Lem's piercing and prescient eye, science fiction would be better off abandoning narrative and character entirely, rather than debasing the enormous majesty of SF's natural thematics with outworn narrative kitsch borrowed from pulp thrillers, bastardized fairy tales, and outworn preindustrial myths. The guy has got a point.

Stanislaw Lem ranks with Olaf Stapledon as a monumental refutation of the notion that science fiction writers are storytellers. We are not the Shakespeares or the Molières of this world, or even its quirky and minor-league Lucians or Cyrano de Bergeracs. If we science fiction writers were honest, we would recognize ourselves as brothers- and sisters-in-arms of Andrew "Bugs" Berenbaum, though we happen to use word processors instead of outlaw DNA sequencers. I think our world and our genre would both be better places if we boldly admitted this sort of thing to ourselves. It's a question of how much honesty one can bear, I suppose. Personally, I've found that one can bear almost unlimited amounts of honesty as long as it's funny.

▼

". . . and in the final, shattering explosion, we all died."

The neophyte writer who ended his story with this language has posed his reader a rather obvious logical question, one that exists less obviously in all works of fiction: Who's telling the story? The author, of course, creates the story, but in the complex transaction between author and reader, between manufacturer and consumer, it is reasonable to ask: Who's minding the store?

The "who" in these questions may be one or several entities variously referred to as *narrator, persona, mask, center of consciousness, auctorial presence,* or *implied author.* Whatever this "who," whatever term used to describe it, it is not to be confused with the living creator, the person who pays taxes and raises a family and hassles with editors and finds herself, some day, the subject of doctoral dissertations on her life and times.

For the moment, call the "who" *narrator,* recognize that it can be either inside or outside the story, and term its relationship to the story *point of view.*

Internal point of view is written in the first person as though by a participant in the action or at least a witness to it. Here the "I" of the story may be a principal character, a minor character, or a group of characters *(composite point of view).* Stories written from the point of view of the principal character are the most limiting; only one mind is revealed, and the revelation is perforce subjective. A minor character who tells a story can be a little more detached, can speculate about the actions of the principal character and provide a running gloss on those actions that would be implausible if attributed to the principal character. Still less limiting is the *composite point of view* such as that employed in the Japanese film *Roshomon* or Wilkie Collins' *The Moonstone* or Browning's *The Ring and the Book.* It is typical of the epistolary story and frequently used in tales of crime and mystery, perhaps in the form of court transcripts or tape recordings.

The *external point of view*, written in the third person, gives the author far more scope, particularly in characterization. If she employs an omniscient point of view, her knowledge of the events in the story and of the minds of her characters is all-inclusive. She may move where she will, see what she wishes, understand all, even predict the future within the little world of the story. She is, in that little world, God. But gods tend to be remote, and an author may wish to sacrifice some power to gain greater immediacy or deeper reader identification with a principal character. To do so, she arbitrarily limits her omniscience.

The *limited point of view* confines the author's knowlege to one character; knowledge of other characters comes only through their interaction with the focal character; events unknown to him remain unknown to the reader. Strether in James' *The Ambassadors* is such a focal character.

Even more constrictive is the *detached point of view*, in which the author reports, without comment or analysis, what might be seen or heard by a detached observer. The narrator is a camera and tape recorder and a series of olfactory and tactile sensors, free to move into implausible places, but otherwise incapable of reporting more than the sensors indicate. This is Hemingway in "The Killers," the technique of the pseudo-documentary, or Lawrence Sanders' *The Anderson Tapes*.

A final and dreadfully complex aspect of point of view: However we define "narrator," there is likely to be yet another personality involved in the creative transaction. This *auctorial presence* may correspond precisely with the narrator (either within or outside the story), in which case it is lost in him and will not trouble us. In other cases, the auctorial presence seems to haunt the narrator, injecting in subtle ways the personality of the artist. When it is perceptible, the auctorial presence occupies a mediating position between author, characters, and reader.

The distance between this presence and the other parties to the writer-reader-story transaction varies along scales of moral, philosophical, or even physical values. The gullible Gulliver is far away from the perceptive Dean Swift, but close to the reader, his closeness fostered by his ingenuous first-person narrative. The Houyhnhnms are close, at least philosophically, to the Dean, enormously far away from him physically and geographically, and totally divorced from the Yahoos, the race to which we readers are forced to admit we belong. And somewhere within the circle of Dean and Gulliver and Yahoo and Houyhnhnm and reader is the auctorial presence, mediating, making us aware of closeness and distance, of our identification with Yahoo and longing for Houyhnhnm, so that at the end we feel the pathos of Gulliver's departure and then laugh wryly at ourselves for being affected by this passage with its final gem of a periodic sentence (see "Style"):

> *. . . I took a second leave of my Master: But as I was going to prostrate myself to kiss his Hoof, he did me the honor to raise it gently to my Mouth. I am not ignorant how much I have been censured for mentioning this last Particular. Detractors are pleased to think it improbable, that so illustrious a Person should descend to give so great a Mark of Distinction to a Creature so inferior as I.*

FEEDBACK

by Joe Haldeman

▼

This game was easier before I was famous, or infamous, and before the damned process was so efficient. When I could still pretend it was my own art, or at least about my art. Nowadays, once you're doped up and squeezed into the skinsuit, it's hard to tell whose eye is measuring the model. Whose hand is holding the brush.

It was more satisfying back then, twenty years ago, even though it was physically painful, with actual electrodes and blood samples to effect the transfer. Now I just take the buffer drug and let them roll the skinsuit over me after I fall asleep. When I wake up I'm in the customer's body. The collaborator's.

It works best when I can interview the collaborator beforehand and find out whether he or she has any artistic training or talent. Some of the most interesting work I produce in collaboration comes from the totally inexperienced, their unfamiliarity with the tools and techniques resulting in happy accidents, spontaneity. It's best to know about that ahead of time, so I can use the meditative period before the drug kicks in, to prepare myself for a tighter or looser approach. But I can work cold if I have to; if the millionaire can't spare the time for an interview before the session.

I'll work in any painting or drawing medium the customer wants, within reason, but through most of my career people naturally chose my own specialty, transparent water color. Since I became famous, though, with the Manhattan Monster thing, people want to trowel on thick acrylics in primary colors. Boring. But they take the painting home and hang it up and ask their friends, isn't that just as scary as shit? Because of the stylistic association, usually, rather than the subject matter. Most people's nightmares stay safely hidden when they pick up a brush. Good thing, too. After the Monster a lot of right-thinking citizens wanted to make my profession illegal, claiming it could bring out "the beast" hidden in Everyman. The fact that it had never happened before didn't make a dent in their righteousness. The Supreme Court did.

All an art facilitator does is loan his or her mechanical skills and esthetic sensibilities to the customer. If the customer is a nut case, the collaboration may be truly disturbing—and perhaps revealing. A lot of us find employment in mental institutions. Some of us find residence in them. Occupational hazard.

At least I make enough per assignment now, thanks to notoriety from the Monster case, that I can take off half the year, to travel and paint for myself. This year I was leaving the first of February, start off the vacation sailing in the Caribbean. One week to go, I could already feel the sun, taste the rum. I'd sublet the apartment and studio and already had all my clothes and gear packed into two small bags. Watercolors don't take up much space and you don't need a lot of clothes where I was headed.

I was tempted to pre-empt my itinerary and go on to the islands early. It would have cost extra and confused my friends, who know me to be methodical and punctual. But I should have done it. God, I should have done it.

We had one of those fast hard snows that make Manhattan beautiful for a while. I walked to and from lunch the long way, through Central Park, willing to trade the slight extra danger for the beauty. Besides, my walking stick supposedly holds enough electricity to stun a horse.

The man waiting for me in the lobby didn't look like trouble, though you never know. Short, balding, old-fashioned John Lennon-style spectacles.

He introduced himself while I was fumbling with overcoat and boots. Juan Carlos Segura, investment counselor.

"Have you ever painted before?" I asked him. "Drawn or sculpted or anything?"

"No. My talents lie elsewhere." I think I was supposed to be able to tell how wealthy he was by upper-class lodge signals—the cut of his conservative blue pin-stripe, the heavy gold mechanical watch—but my own talents lie elsewhere. So I asked him directly. "You understand how expensive my services are."

"Exactly. One hundred thousand dollars a day."

"And you know you must accept the work as produced. No money-back guarantee."

"I understand."

"We're in business, then." I buzzed my assistant Allison to start tea while we waited for the ancient elevator.

People who aren't impressed by my studio, with its original Picasso, Monet, Dali, and Turner, are often fascinated by Allison. She is beautiful but very large, six foot three but perfectly proportioned, as if some magic device had enlarged her by twenty percent. Mr. Segura didn't blink at her; didn't notice the paintings on the walls. He accepted his tea and thanked her politely.

I blew on my tea and studied him over the cup. He looked serious, studious, calm. So had the Manhattan Monster.

The direct approach sometimes costs me a commission. "There's half a page of facilitators in the phone book," I said. "Every single one of them charges less than I do."

He nodded, studying me back.

"Some people want me just because I *am* the most expensive. Some few want me because they know my work, my own work, and it's very good. Most want a painting by the man who released the Monster from Claude Avery."

"Is it important for you to know?"

"The more I know about you, the better picture you'll get."

He nodded and paused. "Then accept this. Maybe fifty percent of my motivation is because you are the most costly. That is sometimes an index of value. Of your artistic abilities, or anybody else's, I am totally ignorant."

"So fifty percent is the Monster?"

"Not exactly. In the first place, I don't care to pay that much for something that other people have. Two of my acquaintances own paintings they did with you in that disturbing mode.

"Looking at their paintings, it occurred to me that something more subtle was possible. You. Your own anger at being used in this way."

"I've expressed that in my own paintings."

"I am sure that you have. What I want, I suppose, is to express my own anger at my customers, through yours."

That was a new wrinkle. "You're angry at your customers?"

"Not all of them. Most. People give me large amounts of money to invest for them. Once each quarter, I extract a percentage of the profit." He set down the cup and put his hands on his knees. "But most of them want some input. It is their money, after all."

"And you would prefer to follow a single strategy," I said. "The more capital you had behind your investment pattern, the less actual risk— since I assume that you don't have to pay *back* a percentage, if an investment fails."

"For an artist, you know a lot about money."

I shrugged. "I'm a *rich* artist."

"People are emotionally connected to their money, and they want to do things with it, other than make more money. My largest client last year was a bug about space exploitation."

"Oh, no."

"And when the lunar colony collapsed, so did his fortune. I got the blame."

"But you didn't advise him to—"

"No. I tried to talk him out of it, and did manage to convince him to diversify slightly, into related energy and defense issues. Of course, they were depressed too, or nosedived along with the space stocks. Naturally it was my fault for not choosing the *right* collateral investments. He had to sell two of his cars and his ivory collection."

"Poor thing."

"He is only the most obvious, the most amusing. Most of my clients are at least mildly resentful if I don't make them a fortune every quarter. Even though I explain that it's my business to protect their money first; increase it second. A conservative strategy takes real work. Anybody can gamble."

"Interesting. And you see a connection with my work?"

"I saw it when I read the profile in *Forbes* a couple of years ago."

"And you waited for my price to come down?"

"I waited until I could afford the luxury. Your price actually has come down nine percent, because of inflation, since the article. You'll be raising it soon."

"Good timing. I like round numbers, but I'm going up to one-twenty when I return from vacation in August." I picked up a stylus and touch-pad and began drawing close parallel lines. It helps me think. "The connection, the analogy, is good. I know that many of my clients must be dissatisfied with the abstract smearing that cost them six figures. But they get exactly what they paid for. I explain it to them beforehand, and if they choose not to hear me, that's their problem."

"You said as much in the article. But I don't want abstract smearings. I want your customary medium, when you work seriously. Old-fashioned hyperrealism."

"You want me to do a Boston School watercolor?"

"Exactly. I know the subject, the setting—"

"That's three week's work, minimum. More than two million dollars."

"I can afford it."

"Can you afford to leave your own work for three weeks?" I was drawing very fast lines. This would really screw up my vacation schedule. But it would be half a year's income in three weeks.

"I'm not only going to leave for three weeks . . . I'm going exactly where you are. The Cayman Islands. George Town."

I just looked at him.

"They say the beach is wonderful."

I never asked him how he'd found out about my vacation plans. Through my credit card company, I supposed. That he would take the trouble before our initial interview was revealing. He was a man who left nothing to chance.

He wanted a photo-realist painting of a nude woman sitting in a conference room, alone, studying papers. Horn-rimmed glasses. The conference room elegant, old-fashioned.

The room would be no problem, given money, since George Town has as many banks and insurance buildings as bikinis. The model was another matter. Most of the models in George Town would be black, which would complicate the text of the painting, or would be gorgeous beach bums, with tan lines and silicone breasts. I told him I thought we wanted an ordinary woman, trim but severe-looking; someone whose posture would radiate dignity without clothing. (I showed him *Maja Desnuda* and some Delacroix, and a few of Wyeth's Helgas that had that quality.) She also would have to be a damned good model, to do three weeks of sitting in the same position. I suggested we hire someone in New York and fly her down with us. He agreed.

Allison had been watching through the ceiling bug, part of her job. She came in and poured herself a cup of tea. "Nut case," she said.

"Interesting nut case, though. Rich."

"If you ever took on a charity nut case, I wasn't watching." She stirred a spoonful of marmalade into her tea, Russian style. She only does that to watch me cringe. "So I should get tickets to the Caymans for me and M & M?"

"Yeah, Friday."

"First class?"

"What's it worth to you?"

"I don't know. You want a cup of tea in your lap?"

"First class."

Finding the right model was difficult. I knew two or three women who would fill the bill in terms of physical appearance and sitting ability, but they were friends. That would interfere with the client's wishes, since he obviously wanted a cold, clinical approach. I spent an afternoon going through agency files, and another afternoon interviewing people, until I found the right one. Rhonda Speck, thirty, slender enough to show ribs. I disliked her on sight and liked her even less when she took her clothes off, for the way she looked at me—her expression a prim gash of disapproval. Even if I were heterosexual I wouldn't be ogling her unprofessionally. That edge of resentment might help the painting, I thought. I didn't know half of it.

I told Rhonda the job involved a free trip to the Cayman Islands and she showed as much enthusiasm as if I had said Long Island. She did brighten a little when I described the setting. She was working on her law degree, and could study while she sat. That also helped to distance me from her, since I am not a great admirer of that profession. I dealt with a lot of lawyers during the years of litigation following the Manhattan Monster, and I liked perhaps one out of five. (One that I liked was a prosecutor, the only one who had the grace not to bring up my sexual orientation, which was irrelevant. I knew that Claude Avery was gay, and I knew he was troubled by it—a facilitator does almost literally get under his client's skin—but there was no way I could tell that he was going to work out his problems by dismembering, or at least de-membering, male prostitutes.)

I called my banker in George Town and described the office I needed. She knew of a small law firm that was closing for a February vacation, and would inquire.

It had been a few years since I'd painted nudes, and had done only two photo-realist ones. I didn't want to work with Rhonda any more than I had to, or pay her more than I had to, so I had a friend with a similar figure come over and sit. For two days I did sketches and photographs, experimenting with postures and lightings. I took them to Segura and we agreed on the pose, the woman looking up coldly from her papers, as if interrupted, strong light from the desk lamp putting half of her face in shadow. Making the desk lamp the only source of light also isolated the figure from the details of the office, which would be rendered in photo-realist detail, but darkly, making for a sinister background.

Then I spent three days doing a careful portrait of the model, head and upper body, solving some technical problems about rendering the glossy hair and the small breasts. I wanted them to look hard, unfeminine, yet realistic.

I took the portrait up to Segura's office and he approved. His only reservations were about himself. "You're sure I'll be able to produce something with this kind of control? I literally can't draw a face that looks like a face."

"No problem. Your hands will be stiff, from using undeveloped muscles, but while you're in the skinsuit your movements will be precisely the same as mine.

"Have I told you about the time I hired a facilitator myself?" He said no. "I was curious about how it felt on the other end. I hired a guitarist-composer, and we spent two days writing a short fugue in the style of Bach. We started with the four letters of my last name—which coincidentally form an A-minor-seventh chord—and made up a marvelously complicated little piece that was unequivocably *mine*. Even though I can't play it."

"You could play it in the skinsuit, though."

"Beautifully. I have a tape of it, the facilitator sitting beside me playing a silent solid-body guitar while I roam around the frets with brilliant sensitivity." I laughed. "At the end of each day my hands were so weak I couldn't pick up a fork, let alone a brush. My fingers were stiff for a week."

"Your experience will be less extreme. Using a brush doesn't involve the unnatural stretching that playing a guitar does."

Not completely convinced, Segura was willing to part with an extra hundred grand for a one-day demonstration. A predictable course, given hindsight, knowing him to be a man boxed in by distrust and driven, or at least directed, by what I would call paranoia.

He suggested a self-portrait. I told him it would have to be done from photographs, since the skinsuit distorts your face almost as much as a bank robber's pantyhose disguise. That interested him. He was going to spend three weeks in the skinsuit; why not have a record of what it was like? I pretended that nobody had come up with the idea before and said sure, sounds interesting.

In fact, I'd done it twice, but both times the collaborators produced thick impasto abstractions that didn't resemble anything. Segura would be different.

By law, a doctor has to be present when you begin the facilitation. After it gets under way, any kind of nurse or medic is adequate for standing guard. A few collaborators have blood pressure spikes or panic attacks. The nurse can terminate the process instantly if the biosensors show something happening. He pushes a button that releases a trank into my bloodstream, which breaks the connection. It also puts me into a Valium haze the rest of the day. A good reason to have people pay in advance.

There's a doctor in my building who's always willing to pop up and earn a hundred dollars for five minutes' work. I always use the same nurse, too, a careful and alert man with the unlikely name Marion Marion. He calls himself M & M, since he's brown and round.

I soaked and taped down four half-sheets of heavy D'Arches cold-press, allowing for three disasters, and prepared my standard portrait palette. I set up the session to begin at 9:30 sharp. M & M came over early, as usual, to have tea and joke around with Allison and me. He's a natural comic and I think also a natural psychologist. Whatever, he puts me at ease before facing what is usually a rather trying experience.

(I should point out here that it's not always bad. If the collaborator has talent and training and a pleasant disposition, it can be as refreshing as dancing with a skilled partner. The facilitator has the satisfaction of doing mechanically effortless work without the anxiety that's always there to some extent, working alone: Is this *really* any good? Am I going to make a mistake that consigns it to the rubbish bin?)

The others showed up on time and we got down to business. An anteroom off my studio has two parallel examining tables. Segura and I stripped and lay down and were injected with six hours' worth of buffer. I was asleep for most of it, but know what happens: M & M glued the induction electrodes to the proper places on our shaven heads. The doctor looked at them, signed a piece of paper, and left. Then M & M, with

Allison's assistance, rolled the loose skinsuits over us, sealed them, and pumped the air out.

Segura and I woke up simultaneously when M & M turned on the microcurrent that initiated the process. It's like being puppet and puppeteer simultaneously. I saw through Segura's eyes. His body sat me up and slid me to the floor, and walked me into the studio. He perched me on a stool in front of the nearly horizontal easel and the mirror. Then I took over.

If you were watching us work, you would see two men sitting side by side, engaged in what looks like a painstakingly overpracticed mime routine. If one of us scratches his ear, the other one does. But from the inside it is more complicated: we exchange control second by second. This is why not every good artist can be a good facilitator. You have to have an instinct for when to assert your own judgment, your own skills, and let the client be in control otherwise. It is literally a thousand decisions per hour, for six hours. It's exhausting. I earn my fee.

My initial idea for the portrait was, in compositional terms, similar to what our nude would be—a realistic face in harsh light glowing in front of an indistinct background. There wouldn't be time to paint in background details, of course.

I made a light, precise drawing of the head and shoulders, taking most of an hour. Not quite centered on the paper. Then I took a chisel brush and carefully painted in the outlines of the drawing with frisket, a compound like rubber cement. You can paint over it and, when the paint dries, rub it off with an eraser or your fingertip, exposing the white paper and the drawing underneath.

When the frisket was dry I mopped the whole painting with clear water and then made an inky wash out of burnt umber and French ultramarine. I worked the wash over the whole painting and, while it was still damp, floated in diffuse shapes of umber and ultramarine that would hint at shadowy background. Then I buzzed Allison in to dry it while I/we walked around, loosening up. She came in with a hair dryer and worked over the wet paper carefully, uniformly, while I didn't watch. Sometimes a dramatic background wash just doesn't work when it dries—looks obvious or cheesy or dull—and there is never any way to fix it. (Maybe you could soak the paper overnight, removing most of the pigment. Better to just start over, though.)

I walked Segura across to the bay window and depolarized it, and looked out over the city. The snow that remained on the shaded part of rooftops was gray or black. Traffic crawled in the thin bright light. Pedestrians hurried through the wind and slush.

Segura's body wanted a cigarette and I allowed him to walk me over to his clothes and light one up. The narcotic rush was disorienting. I had to lean us against a wall to keep from staggering. It was not unpleasant, though, once I surrendered control to him. No need for me to dominate motor responses until we had brush in hand.

Allison said the wash was ready and looked good. It did, vague gloomy shapes suggesting a prison or asylum cell. I rolled up a kneaded eraser and carefully rubbed away the frisket. The light pencil drawing floated over the darkness like a disembodied thought.

I had to apply frisket again, this time in a halo around the drawing, and there was a minor setback: I'd neglected to put the frisket brush into solvent, and the bristles had dried into a solid useless block. I surprised myself by throwing it across the room. That was Segura acting.

I found another square brush and carefully worked a thin frisket mask around the head and shoulders, to keep the dark background from bleeding in, but had to stop several times and lift up the brush because my hand was trembling with Segura's suppressed anger at the mistake. Relax, it was a cheap brush. You must be hell on wheels to work for.

First a very dilute yellow wash, New Gamboge, over the whole face. I picked up the hair dryer and used it for six or seven minutes, making sure the wash was bone dry, meanwhile planning the next couple of stages.

This technique, "glazing," consists of building up a picture with layer upon layer of dilute paint. It takes patience and precision and judgment—sometimes you want the previous layer to be completely dry, and sometimes you want it damp, to diffuse the lines between the two colors. If it's too damp, you risk muddying the colors, which can be irreversable and fatal. But that's one thing that attracts me to the technique, the challenge of gambling everything on the timing of one stroke of the brush.

Segura obviously felt otherwise. Odd, for a man who essentially gambles for a living, albeit with other people's money. He wanted each layer safely dry before proceeding with the next, once he understood what I was doing.

Well, that's a technique, but it's not *my* technique, which is what he was paying for. It would also turn this portrait, distorted as it was, into a clown's mask.

I could have picked up a pencil and written out that argument for him to see through our eyes, but it's a mistake for the facilitator to blatantly take over that way. It *is* the customer's painting, after all. If he wants to screw it up, let him.

That kind of disassociation was easy with the usual thick acrylic messes, but I was reluctant to screw up a watercolor, especially at that level of subtlety. The prospect of spending three weeks producing a profoundly flawed work was not appealing either.

So I pushed back a little, establishing my authority, so to speak. I didn't want this to become a contest of wills. I just wanted control over the hair dryer, actually, not over Juan Carlos Segura.

There was a slight battle, lasting only seconds. It's hard to describe the sensation to someone who hasn't used a facilitator. It's something like being annoyed at yourself for not being able to make up your mind, rather intensified—"being of two minds," literally.

Of course I won the contest, having about ten thousand times more experience at it than Segura. I set down the hair dryer and the next layer, defining the hollows of the face visible through the skinsuit, went on with appropriately soft edges. I checked the mirror and automatically noted the places I would come back to later with the paper dry, to make actual lines, defining the bottom of the goggle ridges, the top of the lip, the forward part of the ear mass.

The portrait was finished in two hours, but the background still needed something. Pursuing a vague memory from a week before, I flipped through a book of Matthew Brady photographs, visions of the Civil War's hell. Our face in the skinsuit resembled those of some corpses, open-mouthed, staring. I found the background I wanted, a ruined tumble of brick wall, and took the book back to the easel. I worked an intimation of the wall into the background, drybrushing umber and ultramarine with speckles and threads of clotted blood color, alizarin muted with raw umber. Then I dropped the brushes in water and looked away, buzzing M & M. I didn't want to see the painting again until I saw it with my own eyes.

Coming out of the facilitation state takes longer than going in, especially if you don't go the full six hours. The remaining buffer has to be neutralized with a series of timed shots. Otherwise, Segura and I would hardly have been able to walk, expecting the collaboration of another brain that was no longer there.

I was up and around a few minutes before Segura. Allison had set out some cheese and fruit and an ice bucket with a bottle of white burgundy. I was hungry, as always, but only nibbled a bit, waiting for lunch.

Segura attacked the food like a starved animal. "What do you think?" he said between bites. "Is it any good?"

"Always hard to tell while you're working. Let's take a look." I buzzed Allison and she brought the painting in. She'd done a good job, as usual, the painting set off in a double mat of brick red and forest green, inside a black metal frame.

"It does look good," he said, as if surprised.

I nodded and sipped wine, studying it. The painting was technically good, but it would probably hang in a gallery for years, gathering nervous compliments, before anybody bought it. It was profoundly ugly, a portrait of brutality. The skinsuit seemed to be straining to contain a mask of rage. Something truly sick burned behind the eyes.

He propped it up on the couch and walked back and forth, admiring it from various angles. For a moment I hoped he would say "This will do fine; forget about the nude." I could use the two million but didn't look forward to three weeks of his intimate company.

"It captures something," he said, grinning. "I could use it to intimidate clients."

"The style suits you?"

"Yes. Yes, indeed." He looked at me with a sort of squint. "I vaguely remember fighting over some aspect of it."

"Technical matter. I prevailed, of course—that's what you pay me for."

He nodded slowly. "Well. I'll see you in George Town, then." He offered his hand, dry and hot.

"Friday morning. I'll be at the Hilton." Allison put the painting in a leather portfolio and ushered him out.

She came back in with a color Xerox of it. "Sick puppy."

I examined the picture, nodding. "There's some talent here, though. A lot of artists are sick puppies."

"Present company excluded. Lunch?"

"No, I'm meeting Harry."

"Harry? You'll be with him all winter."

"Yeah, but we didn't plan on three weeks' business first. I'm taking him to Seasons as a peace offering. One last French meal before we descend to goat curry and fish stew."

"Well, have fun. I'm still on rabbit food until we get down there." She was coming on Thursday. Harry and I were leaving that night, for a few days of sunshine and rest before I had to deal with Segura.

I poured another glass of wine and carried it over to the window. The icy wind was audible through the double-pane glass. The people on the sidewalk hurried hunched over against the gale. Tomorrow I'd be lying on snow-white sand, swimming in blood-warm water. I drank the wine and shivered.

In the eighteenth century, George III was sailing in the Gulf of Mexico when a sudden storm, probably a hurricane, smashed his ship to pieces. Fishermen from one of the Caymans braved the storm to go out and pick up survivors. Saved from what he'd thought would be certain death, King George expressed his gratitude by declaring that no resident of the island would ever have to pay taxes to the British crown, for the rest of eternity.

So where other Caribbean islands have craft shops and laid-back bars, George Town has high-rise banks and insurance buildings. A lot of expatriate Brits and Americans live and work there, doing business by satellite bounce.

I have a bank account in George Town myself, and may retire there some day. For this time of my life, it's too peaceful, except for the odd hurricane. I need Manhattan's garish excitement, the constant input, the dangerous "edge."

But it's good to get away. Harry and I are both pretty good sailors. We rented a thirty-two-foot racing sloop; the original plan had been to hang around George Town for a week, getting the feel of the boat while skindiving in the wreck-strewn harbor, with an afternoon or so given over to banking business. Then lay a course for Jamaica and points east.

The Segura commission set that back almost a month. Harry was good enough to come down anyhow. He's on a year's sabbatical from teaching duties, finishing a book about Athebaskan dialects, and he can work anyplace that has AA batteries and Razorpoints.

So we had two days of thawing out on the beach, swimming, imbibing rum drinks full of vegetation, appreciating the beautiful men and women—and, one must admit, being appreciated in return. Money can't buy everything, but can stave off flab and wrinkles, perhaps until you're old enough for them not to matter.

The beach is an ideal place for quick figure sketches, so I loosened up for the commission by filling a notebook with pictures of women as they walked by or played in the sand and water. Drawing forces you to see, so for the first time I was aware that the beauty of the native black women was fundamentally different from that of the tourists, white or black. It was mainly a matter of posture and expression, dignified and detached. The tourist women were always to some extent posing, even at their most casual. Which I think was the nature of the place, rather than some characteristic female vanity. I normally pay much closer attention to men, and believe me, we corner the market on that small vice.

My staff came down on Thursday. M & M tore off into town, to find out whether either of his girlfriends had learned about the other. Allison joined Harry and me on the beach.

Impressive as she is in office clothes, Allison is spectacular out of them. She has never tanned; her skin is like ivory. Thousands of hours in the gym have given her the sharply defined musculature of a classical statue. She wore a black leather string bikini that revealed everything not absolutely necessary for reproduction or lactation, but I don't think most straight men would characterize her as "sexy." She was too formidable. That was all right with Allison, since she almost never was physically attracted to any man shorter or less well built than she. That dismissed all but a tenth of one percent of the male race. She had yet to find an Einstein, or even a Schwarzenegger, among the qualifiers. They usually turned out to be gentle but self-absorbed, predictably, and sometimes more interested in me than her. The couple of times that happened, she was more understanding than Harry.

The two of them got along well, and we had a pleasant day. We rented a small skiff in the afternoon and went reef fishing. Allison and I watched while Harry caught enough for dinner. We'd brought masks and snorkels but a big gray hammerhead showed up, and we decided that drinking beer was healthier than swimming.

The chef at the Hilton did a good job with Harry's fish, snapper almondine. We resisted the urge to have one last night on the town. I went over after dinner and made sure everything was ready in the office we'd rented, because I knew that otherwise I'd wake up in the middle of the night worrying about some detail.

The message light was on when I got back to the hotel; both Rhonda Speck and Segura had arrived. It wasn't quite ten, but Harry and I agreed it was too late to return their calls, and retired.

▼

I set up the pose and lighting before we went under, explaining to Rhonda exactly what we were after. Segura was silent, watching. I took longer than necessary, messing with the blinds and the rheostats I'd put on the two light sources. I wanted Segura to get used to Rhonda's nudity. He was obviously straight as a plank, and we didn't want the painting to reveal any sexual curiosity or desire. Rhonda was only slightly more sexy than a mackerel, but you could never tell.

For the same reason, I didn't want to start the actual painting the first day. First we'd do a series of charcoal roughs. I explained to Segura about negative spaces and how important it was to establish balance between the light and dark areas. That was something I'd already worked out, of course. I just wanted him to stare at Rhonda long enough to become bored with the idea.

It didn't quite work out that way.

We didn't need a doctor's certification in George Town, so the setting up took a little less time. Artist and client lockstepped into the office where Rhonda waited, studying the pages of notes stacked neatly on her desk.

There were two piano stools with identical newsprint pads and boxes of charcoal sticks. The idea was to sketch her from eight or ten slightly different angles, Segura moving around her in a small arc while I worked just behind him, looking over his shoulder. Theoretically, I could be anywhere, even in another room, since I was seeing her through his eyes. But it seems to work better this way, especially with a model.

The sketches had a lot of energy—so much energy that Segura actually tore through the paper a few times, blocking out the darkness around the seated figure. I actually got excited myself, and not just by feedback from Segura. The "negative-space" exercise is just that, an art-school formalism, but Segura didn't know that, and the result came close to being actual art.

I showed him that after we came out of the buffer. The sketches were good strong abstractions. You could turn them upside-down or sideways, retaining symmetry while obliterating text, and they still worked well.

I had a nascent artist on my hands. Segura had real native talent. The combination could have produced a painting of some value, one that I wouldn't have been able to do by myself. If things had worked out.

Harry and I took the boat out after lunch—or rather, Harry took the boat out with me as ballast, baking inertly under a heavy coat of total sunblock. (Allison and I are almost equally pale, and that's not all we have in common; I'm also nearly as well-muscled. We met at the weight machines in a Broadway gym.) He sang songs in Athabaskan, probably about blizzards and clubbing seals. I watched billowing clouds form abstract patterns in the impossible cobalt sky. The soothing sounds of the boat lulled me to sleep—the keel slipping through warm water, the lines creaking, the ruffle of the sails.

Harry woke me to help bring her back in. He'd tacked out quite a few miles, the highrises and cruise ships below the horizon, and had expected a quick run back on a following wind. Of course the wind shifted seaward, and we had to fight it back to the island, dark clouds gathering. One person can handle the thirty-two-foot sloop, but it's a lot easier with two, especially tacking into a strong wind. There was a cool mist of rain that became intermittantly heavy. A couple of miles from shore we started to see lightning, so we struck sail and revved up the little motor and drove straight in, prudence conquering seamanship.

We dried off at the marina bar and drank hot chocolate laced with rum, watching a squall line roll across land and water, feeling lucky to be inside.

Sometimes I have difficulty talking with Harry. Circumstances of birth and upbringing left me "cultured" but not particularly well educated; Harry is quite the opposite. How can a person earn four degrees and still be unable to learn how to hold a wineglass? But he can talk knowledgably about anything from astrophysics to Zoroastrianism. He doesn't draw or paint, but he knows art history and criticism, so we usually wind up talking about my work rather than his, cultural linguistics and anthropology—though in a weak moment I did agree to go up to the Arctic with him one summer. Paint mud landscapes while he chats with the natives, compiling examples for a cassette that will go with his book.

Anyhow, I had earlier described to him the morning's surprising successes. He'd given it some thought.

"I don't want to see them yet," he said. "They'll be more interesting in the context established by the final painting."

"You just don't want to say anything that might rain on my parade." He shrugged and laughed. "We know each other too well, Harry. You know you'd have to be honest, and you're afraid honesty might not be the best policy now."

"Further deponent sayeth not." He smiled and turned his attention back to the storm. "Wet and wild. Photography tomorrow?"

"Yeah. And then drawing drawing drawing."

"The part you like best."

"Oh yes." Actually, I halfway do like it, the way an athlete can enjoy warming up, in expectation of the actual event.

I could have done the photography and drawing without Segura, but I wanted him involved, so that he would have a lot of time and concentration invested before we started painting. It affects your attitude toward both subject and working surface.

The next morning I set up the cameras before we went into the skinsuits. The main one was a fairly complex and delicate piece of equipment, an antique eight by ten view camera that took hairline-accurate black and white negatives. I could have accomplished the same thing with a modern large-format camera, but I liked the smooth working of the gears, the smell of the oak and leather, the sense of contact with an earlier, less hurried, age. The paradox of combining the technology of that age with ours.

The other camera was a medium-format Polaroid. Buffered and suited, I led Segura through the arcane art and science of tweaking lights, model, f-stop, and exposure to produce a subtle spectrum of prints: a sequence of ninety-eight slightly different, and profoundly different, pictures of one woman. We studied the pictures and her and finally decided on the right combination. I set up the antique eight by ten and reproduced the lighting. We focused it with his somewhat younger eyes and took three slightly different exposures.

Then we took the film into the darkroom that M & M had improvised in the firm's executive washroom. We developed each sheet in Rodinal, fixed and washed them, and hung them weighted up to dry.

We left the darkroom and spent a few minutes smoking, studying

Rhonda as she studied her law. I told her she was free for three days; show up Thursday morning. She nodded curtly and left, resentful.

Her annoyance was understandable. She'd been sitting there naked for all that time we were playing in the darkroom. I should have dismissed her when we finished shooting.

We lit up another cigarette and I realized that it wasn't me who had kept her waiting. It was Segura. I'd started to tell her to go and then he manufactured a little crisis that led straight to the darkroom. From then on I hadn't thought of the woman except as a reversed ghost appearing in the developer tray.

Under the circumstances, it wasn't a bad thing to have her hostile toward us, if we could capture the hostility on paper. But it goes against my grain to mistreat an employee, even a temporary one.

We examined each of the negatives with lightbox and loupe, then took the best one back into the darkroom for printing. Plain contact prints on finest-grain paper. The third one was perfect: rich and stark, almost scary in its knife-edge sharpness. You could see one bleached hair standing out from her left nipple.

That was enough work for the day; in fact, we'd gone slightly over the six-hour limit, and both of us were starting to get headaches and cramps. Another half-hour and it would be double vision and tremors. More than that—though I'd never experienced it—you wind up mentally confused, the two minds still linked electrically but no longer cooperating. Some poor guinea pigs took it as far as convulsions or catatonia, back when the buffer drug was first being developed.

M & M eased us out of it and helped us down to a taxi. It was only five blocks to the hotel, but neither of us was feeling particularly athletic. (For some reason the buffer hangover hits people like me, in very good shape, particularly hard. Segura was somewhat flabby and overweight, but he had less trouble getting out of the car.)

Harry wasn't in the room, which suited me fine. I pulled the blackout blinds and collapsed, desperately hungry but too tired to do anything about it but dream of food.

▼

Allison had set up the paper, one large sheet of hand-made hotpressed 400-pound rag, soaking it overnight and then taping it down with plenty of time to dry completely. That sheet of paper, the one Segura would be drawing on, cost more than some gallery paintings. The sheet I'd be working on was just paper, with a similar tooth. My drawing would be a random scribble, though it would look fine while I was working on it.

We had set up two drawing tables with their boards at identical angles, mine a little higher since I have a larger frame. An opaque projector mounted above Segura shot a duplicate of yesterday's photo onto the expensive paper. Our job for the next three days was to execute a meticulously accurate but ghost-light tracing of the picture, which would be gently erased after the painting was done.

Some so-called photorealists bypass this step with a combination of photography and xerography—make a high-contrast print and then impress a light Xerox of it onto watercolor paper. That makes their job a high-salaried kind of paint-by-numbers. Doing the actual under-drawing puts you well "into" the painting before the first brush is wet.

We sat down and went to work, starting with the uniformly bound law books on the shelves behind Rhonda. It was an unchallenging, repetitive subject to occupy us while we got used to doing this kind of labor together.

For a few minutes we worked on a scrap piece of the same kind of paper that was in front of me, until I was absolutely confident of his eye and hand. Then we started on the real thing.

After five grueling hours we had completed about a third of the background, an area half the size of a newspaper page. I was well pleased with that progress; working by myself I would have done little more.

Segura was not so happy. In the taxi, he cradled his right hand and stared at it, the wrist quivering, the thumb frankly twitching. "How can I possibly keep this up?" he said. "I won't even be able to pick up a pencil tomorrow."

I held out my own hand and wrist, steady, muscular. "But *I* will. That's all that counts."

"It could permanently damage my hand."

"Never happened." Of course, I'd never worked with anyone for three weeks. "Go to that masseur, the man whose card I gave you. He'll make your hand good as new. Do you still have the card?"

"Oh, yeah." He shifted uncomfortably. "I don't mean to be personal, or offensive . . . but is this man gay? I would have trouble with that."

"I wouldn't know. We don't have little badges or a secret hand-shake." He didn't laugh, but he looked less grim. "My relationship with him is professional; I wouldn't know whether he was gay or not." Actu-ally, since our professional relationship included orgasm, if he wasn't gay, he was quite a method actor. But I assumed he would divine Segura's orientation as quickly as I had. A masseur, so to speak, ought to have a feel for his clients.

The next day went a lot better; like myself, Segura was heartened by the sight of the previous day's careful work outline. We worked faster and with equal care, finishing all of the drawing except for the woman and the things on the desk in front of her.

It was on the third day that I had the first inkling of trouble. Work-ing on the image of Rhonda, Segura wanted to bear down too hard. That could be disastrous; if the pencil point actually broke the fibers of paper along a line, it could never be completely erased. You can't have "out-lines" in this kind of painting; just sharply defined masses perfectly join-ing other sharply defined masses. A pencil line might as well be an inkblot.

If I had correctly interpreted the energy behind that pencil point, I might have stopped the project right then. Give Segura his money back, put the model, Allison, and M & M back on the plane to New York and set sail for Jamaica. I say "might." I'm as curious about human nature as the next person, maybe more curious because of the peculiar insights fa-cilitating gives me. If I had known Segura then as well as I came to know him, I might have gone ahead with it anyhow. Just to see the painting.

At the time, though, I put it down to simple muscular fatigue. Se-gura was not in good physical shape. His normal work day comprised six hours in conference and six hours talking on the phone or dictating cor-respondence. He took a perverse pride in not even being able to keyboard. He never lifted anything heavier than a cigarette.

People who think art isn't physically demanding ought to try to sit in one position for six hours, brush or pencil in hand, staring at some-thing or someone and trying to transfer its essence to a piece of paper or canvas. Even an athletic person leaves that arena with aches and twinges. A couch potato like Segura can't even walk away without help.

He never complained, though, other than expressing concern that his fatigue might interfere with the project. I reassured him almost every day. In fact, I had once completed a successful piece with a hemiplegic so frail he couldn't sign his name the same way twice. We taught ourselves how to hold the brush in our teeth.

It was a breathtaking moment when we turned off the overhead projector for the last time. The finished drawing floated on the paper, an exquisite ghost of what the painting would become. Through Segura's eyes I stared at it hungrily for fifteen or twenty minutes, mapping out strategies of frisket and mask, in my mind's eye seeing the paper glow through layer after careful layer of glaze. It would be perfect.

Rhonda wasn't in a great mood, coming back to sit after three days on her own, but even she seemed to share our excitement when she saw the underdrawing. It made the project real.

The first step was to paint a careful frisket over her figure, as well as the chair, lamp, and table with its clutter. That took an hour, since the figure was more than a foot high on the paper. I also masked out reflections on a vase and the glass front of a bookcase.

I realized it would be good to start the curtains with a thin wash of Payne's Gray, which is not a color I normally keep on my palette, so I gave Rhonda a five-minute break while I rummaged for it. She put on a robe and walked over to the painting and gasped. We heard her across the room.

I looked over and saw what had distressed her. The beautifully detailed picture of her body had been blotted out with gray frisket, and it did look weird. She was a non-being, a featureless negative space hovering in the middle of an almost photographic depiction of a room. All three of us laughed at her reaction. I started to explain, but she knew about frisketing; it had just taken her by surprise.

Even the best facilitators have moments of confusion, when their client's emotional reaction to a situation is totally at odds with their own. This was one of those times: My reaction to Rhonda's startled response was a kind of ironic empathy, but Segura's reaction was malicious glee.

I could see that he disliked Rhonda at a very deep level. What I didn't see (although Allison had known from the first day) was that it wasn't just Rhonda. It was women in general.

I've always liked women, even though I've known since thirteen or fourteen that I would never desire them. It's pernicious to generalize, but

I think that my friendships with women have usually been deeper and more honest than they would have been if I were straight. A straight man can simply like a woman and desire her friendship, but there's always a molecule or two of testosterone buzzing between them, if they are both of an age and social situation where sex might be a possibility, however remote. I have to handle that complication with some men whom I know or suspect are gay, even when I feel no particular attraction toward them.

The drawing had gone approximately from upper left to lower right, then back to the middle for the figure, but the painting would have to proceed in a less straightforward way. You work all over the painting at once: a layer of rose madder on the spines of one set of books, and on the shady side of the vase, and on two of the flowers. You need a complete mental picture of the finished painting so you can predict the sequence of glazes, sometimes covering up areas with frisket or, when there were straight lines, with drafting tape. The paper was dry, though, so it was usually just a matter of careful brush work. Pathologically careful: You can't erase paint.

Of course Rhonda had to sit even though for the first week her image would be hidden behind frisket. Her skin tones affected the colors of everything else. Her emotional presence affected the background. And Segura's feeling toward her "colored" the painting literally.

The work went very smoothly. It was a good thing Segura had suggested the trial painting; we'd been able to talk over the necessity for occasional boldness and spontaneity, to keep the painting from becoming an exercise in careful draftsmanship. Especially with this dark, sinister background, we often had to work glazes wet-into-wet. Making details soft and diffuse at the periphery of a painting can render it more realistic rather than less. Our own eyes see the world with precision only in a surprisingly small area around the thing that has our attention. The rest is blur, more or less ignored. (The part of the mind that is not ignoring the background is the animal part that waits for a sudden movement or noise; a painting can derive tension from that.)

Segura and I worked so well together that it was going to cost me money; the painting would be complete in closer to two weeks than three. When I mentioned this he said not to worry; if the painting was good he'd pay the second million regardless of the amount of time (he'd paid a million down before we left New York), and he was sure the painting would be good.

Of course there was arithmetic involved there, as well as art. *Fortune* had listed his before-tax income last year as $98,000,000. He probably wanted to get back to his quarter-million-a-day telephone.

So the total time from photography to finished background was only eleven days, and I was sure we could do the figure and face in a day. We still had a couple of hours' buffer left when we removed the frisket, but I decided to stop at that point. See whether we could finish her completely in one session. We studied her for an hour or so, sketching.

The sketches were accurate, but in a way they were almost caricatures, angular, hostile. As art, they were not bad, though like Segura's initial self-portrait, they were fundamentally, intentionally, ugly. I could feel Manet's careful brush and sardonic eye here: How can a well-shaped breast or the lush curve of a hip be both beautiful and ugly? Cover the dark, dagger-staring face of *Olympia* and drink in the lovely body. Then uncover the face.

That quality would be submerged in the final painting. It would be a beautiful picture, dramatic but exquisitely balanced. The hatred of women there but concealed, like an underpainting.

It was a great physical relief to be nearing the end. I'd never facilitated for more than five days in a row, and the skinsuit was becoming physically repulsive to me. I was earning my long vacation.

That night I drank too much, Harry and I finishing more than a litter of rum, watching two bad movies on television while a serious storm rattled the windows.

The morning was brilliant but I was not. M & M injected me with a cocktail of vitamins and speed that burned away the hangover. I knew I'd come back down hard by nightfall, but the painting would be done long before then.

Segura was jittery, snappish, as we prepared for the last day. Maybe M & M gave him a little something along with the buffer, to calm him down. Maybe it wasn't a good idea.

Rhonda was weird that morning, too, with good reason. She was finally the focus of our attention and she played her part well. Her concentration on us was ferocious, her contempt palpable.

I dabbed frisket on a few highlights—collarbone, breast, eye, and that glossy raven hair—and then put in a pale flesh-colored wash over everything, cadmium yellow light with a speck of rose. While it dried, we smoked a cigarette and stared at her. Rhonda had made it clear that she didn't like smoke, and we normally went into another room or at least stood by an open window. Not today, though.

I had a little difficulty controlling Segura: He was mesmerized by her face and kept wanting to go back to it. But it doesn't work that way; the glazes go on in a particular order, one color at various places on the body all at once. If you finished the face and then worked your way down, the skin tones wouldn't quite match. And there was actual loathing behind his obsession with her face, the force that compels you to keep looking back at a hideous photograph.

He also had the amateurish desire to speed up; find out what the picture was going to look like. In retrospect, I wonder whether there might have been something sinister about that, as well.

It was obvious that the face and figure would take longer than I had planned, maybe half again as long, with so much attention going into hauling on the reins. His impatience would cost us an extra day in the skinsuits, which made me angry, and further slowed us down.

Here I have to admit to a lack of empathy, which for a facilitator is tantamount to a truck driver admitting falling asleep at the wheel. My own revulsion at having to spend another day confined in plastic masked what Segura was feeling about his own confinement. I was not alert. I had lost some of my professional control. I didn't see where his disgust was leading him; leading us.

This is hindsight again: One of the talents that Segura translated into millions of dollars was an ability to hide his emotions, to make people misread him. This was not something that was usually under his conscious control; he did it automatically, the way a pathological liar will lie even when there's nothing at stake. The misogyny that seemed to flood his attitude toward the painting—and Rhonda—was only a small fraction of what he must have actually felt, emotions amplified by the buffer drug and empath circuitry. Some woman must have hurt him profoundly, repeatedly, when he was a child. Maybe that's just amateur psychology. I don't think so. If it were an antipathy that developed after puberty, as I had encountered in other clients, it would have felt quite different; there would have been a sexual component. His hate was more primitive, inchoate.

Most people reveal themselves during facilitation, but a few tighten up. I knew Segura was that kind, which was a relief; they're easier to work with. Doubly a relief with Segura, since from the beginning I had a feeling I didn't want to know him all that well.

I might have prevented it by quitting early. But I wanted to do all the light passages and then start the next day with a fresh palette, loaded with dark. Perhaps I also wanted to punish Segura, or push him.

The actions were simple, if the motivations were not. We had gone twenty minutes past the six-hour mark, and had perhaps another half-hour to go. I had an annoying headache, not bad enough to make me quit. I assumed Segura felt the same.

Every now and then we approached Rhonda to adjust her pose. Only a mannequin could retain exactly the same posture all day. Her chin had fallen slightly. Segura got up and walked toward her.

I don't remember feeling his hand slip out and pick up the large wash brush, one we hadn't used since the first day. Its handle is a stick of hardwood almost an inch in diameter, ending in a sharp bevel. I never thought of it as a weapon.

He touched her chin with his left forefinger and she tilted her head up, closing her eyes. Then with all his strength he drove the sharp stick into her chest.

The blast of rage hit me without warning. I fell backwards off the stool and struck my head. It didn't knock me out, but I was stunned, disoriented. I heard Rhonda's scream, which became a horrible series of liquid coughs, and heard paper and desk accessories scattering as (we later reconstructed) she lurched forward and Segura pushed her face down onto the desk. Then there were three meaty sounds as he punched her repeatedly in the back with the brush handle.

About this time M & M and Allison came rushing through the door. I don't know what Allison did, other than not scream. M & M pulled Segura off Rhonda's body, powerful forearm scissored across his throat, cutting off his wind.

I couldn't breathe either, of course. I started flopping around, gagging, and M & M yelled for Allison to unhook me. She turned me over and ripped off the top part of the skinsuit and jerked the electrodes free.

Then I could breathe, but little else. I heard the quiet struggle between M & M and Segura, the one-sided execution.

Allison carried me into the prep room and completed the procedure that M & M normally did, stripping off the skinsuit and giving me the shot. In about ten minutes I was able to dress myself and go back into the office.

M & M had laid out Rhonda's body on a painter's dropsheet, face-down in a shockingly large pool of blood. He had cleaned the blood off the desk and was waxing it. The lemon varnish smell didn't mask the smell of freshly butchered meat.

Segura lay where he had been dropped, his limbs at odd angles, his face bluish behind the skinsuit mask.

Allison sat on the couch, motionless, prim, impossibly pale. "What now?" she said softly. M & M looked up and raised his eyebrows.

I thought. "One thing we have to agree on before we leave this room," I said, "is whether we go to the police or . . . take care of it ourselves."

"The publicity would be terrible," Allison said.

"They also might hang us," M & M said, "if they do that here."

"Let's not find out," I said, and outlined my plan to them.

It took a certain amount of money—a good thing I had the million in advance—and there was the added complication of having to work around Harry. But we did it: We staged a tragic accident, transferring both of their bodies to a small boat whose inboard motor leaked gasoline. They were less than a mile from shore when thousands saw the huge blossom of flame light up the night, and before rescuers could reach the hulk, the fire had consumed it nearly to the waterline. Burned almost beyond recognition, the "artist" and his model lay in a final embrace.

I finished the face of the picture myself. A look of pleasant surprise, mischievousness. The posture that was to have communicated hardness was transformed into that of a woman galvanized by surprise, perhaps expectation.

We gave it to Segura's family, along with the story we'd given to the press: Crusty financier falls in love with young law student/model. It was an unlikely story to anyone who knew Segura well, but the people who knew him well were busy scrambling after his fortune. His sister put the picture up for auction in two weeks, and since its notoriety hadn't faded, it brought her $2.2 million.

There's nothing like a good love story that ends in tragedy.

Harry didn't buy it, since he knew too much about Segura and Rhonda—and human nature, for that matter. We did sail to Jamaica, and that trip was a story in itself: a day becalmed followed by a day where ten-

foot waves marched at right angles to twenty-foot swells. A pod of whales
that inexplicably followed us for days. Crystalline nights where the Milky
Way seemed as bright as the full moon.

But it was a voyage full of silences. Harry wanted me to tell him what
had really happened. If I had been the only one involved, I would have
told him everything, but I had to protect M & M. So we drifted together
for a month and then, as they say, we drifted apart.

Back in New York, I looked at my overall situation and decided I
could afford to quit. I gave Allison and M & M generous severance pay,
and what I got for the studio paid for even nicer places in Maine and Key
West.

I sold the facilitating equipment and have since devoted myself to
pure watercolors and photography. People understood. This latest tragedy
on top of the grotesque experience with the Monster.

But I downplayed that angle. I wanted to do my own work. I was tired
of collaboration, and especially tired of the skinsuit.

You never know whose hand is picking up the brush.

POINT OF VIEW

by Joe Haldeman

▼

Every story is *somebody's* story. "Point of view" determines who is telling the story, and what his or her relationship is to the story, and how it's going to be told.

Or you can say that every story involves three "people": I, you, and him or her. "I" am the author; "you" are the audience; "he or she" is who-ever the story is about. (All of these pronouns can be plural, of course.) "I want to tell you a story about him" is the implicit or explicit beginning of nearly every story. (In fact, the oldest recorded story in our culture starts out "I sing to you the anger of Achilles!")

Most storytellers, since ancient times, have instinctively understood the necessity of a point of view, but the theory of point-of-view as a re-strictive device in fiction goes back less than a hundred years, to Henry James (1907). James said that every story requires a "central intelligence," through whose limitations the information that makes up the story's plot is filtered.

E.M. Forster sums up the device well, in writing about Percy Lub-bock's *The Craft of Fiction*, saying that a writer "can either describe the characters from outside, as an impartial or partial onlooker; or he can as-sume omniscience and describe them from within; or he can place him-self in the position of one of them and affect to be in the dark as to the motives of the rest; or there are certain intermediate attitudes."

That statement covers ninety percent of the device's usefulness, and when I'm teaching writing, I'm always tempted to leave it at that. But there are other ways of looking at the problem, some more general and some more complicated. Some are of particular interest to science fiction.

Most serious readers eventually come across the book *Points of View*. It's an anthology of excellent short stories arranged according to eleven named points of view, which the editors Moffet and McElheny say are parts of a diffuse continuum, ordering the stories "so as to call attention to who the narrator is, when and where he is telling the story, who he is telling it to, what relation to the events he stands in, and what kind of knowledge he claims." Their saying it's a continuum, of course, makes it difficult to criticize their list in terms of completeness or redundancy, but it's useful nevertheless:

> interior monologue
> dramatic monologue
> letter narration
> diary narration
> subjective narration
> detached autobiography
> memoir, or observer narration
> anonymous narration — single character POV
>   ˝   ˝   — dual character POV
>   ˝   ˝   — multiple character POV
>   ˝   ˝   — no character POV

Rust Hills, in *Writing in General and the Short Story in Particular* (Bantam, 1977) pooh-poohs the Moffett/McElheny system, offering a simpler four-part division:

> **Omniscient**: author knows everything
> **First Person**: author is in the story
> **Scenic**: the author is almost not there, sort of like a camera's eye
> **Central Intelligence**: author inhabits the mind of one character

This system does cover almost everything, but you could argue that it doesn't make sufficiently fine distinctions. I like to go completely overboard, and look at the problem diagrammatically:

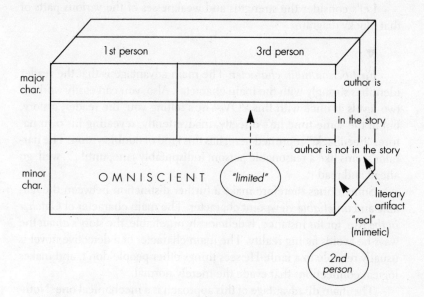

I think that covers more POVs than any writer would care to use in one lifetime. The reason to make a three-dimensional diagram is to recognize that almost all of these structures can be presented either as if they were actually happening or as if they had been recalled and written down. For instance, the most famous first person/minor character POV in English literature is good old Doctor Watson. He often starts out a story by reminding the reader that this is a written memoir, as in "The Adventure of the Speckled Band":

> *On glancing over my notes of the seventy-odd cases in which I have during the last eight years studied the methods of my friend Sherlock Holmes . . .*

This adds veracity to the account, at the expense of immediacy and a certain amount of suspense, since you do know that the narrator survived to write about it. It's a handy device for a story that requires technical explanation, as many of the Holmes stories do, because the author can avoid the artificial situation of characters standing around explaining things to each other.

Let's consider the strengths and weaknesses of the various parts of that blocky diagram:

First person/main character: The main advantage is that the reader identifies strongly with the main character. Also, you can easily work on two levels at once with this POV—he's telling you, the reader, a story, but at the same time he's directly, inadvertently, revealing his own nature. "Feedback," reprinted here, has this kind of double vision. The narrator seems like a reasonable person, indisputably sane, until . . . well, go ahead and read it.

Some critics therefore make a further distinction between the *reliable* and *unreliable* viewpoint character. The main character of *Catcher in the Rye*, for for instance, is deliciously unreliable; the story's *about* the ways he avoids facing reality. The main character of a detective novel is usually reliable to a fault: He sees things other people don't, and makes logical connections that evade the merely normal.

The main disadvantage of this approach is a mechanical one: Nothing that happens offstage can be directly reported. Everything has to be filtered through the main character's perceptions.

Many critics feel that this is the hardest form to bring off effectively, though it's probably the easiest, most natural, to write in. It could be that critics are thrown off because most first novels, and so many bad novels, are written this way.

First Person/minor character: The minor character is sometimes called the *observer.* Using this POV gives you more "distance." You do lose some reader involvement, but you gain in that the observer can quite naturally sit back and comment on what's going on. He can also directly describe the main character, and evaluate what he's doing, which would be arch and artificial in the previous POV.

Henry James, in discussing POV, admits to a weakness for this approach:

> *I have already betrayed, as an accepted habit, and even to extravagance commented on, my preference for dealing with my subject matter, for "seeing my story," through the opportunity and the*

sensibility of someone more or less detached, some not strictly in-volved, though thoroughly interested and intelligent, witness or reporter, some person who contributes to the case mainly a cer-tain amount of criticism and interpretation of it.

A common problem is that the observer can take over the story. William Price Fox, writing the novel *Ruby Red*, about a country singer, got fascinated by the voice of the observer, an old storytelling bootlegger, and after about a hundred pages found the story drifting away from Ruby. He threw the hundred pages away and started over—something I don't think I could do!

Sometimes it could be that you're telling the wrong story—maybe this minor character ought to be stage front. If it's handled properly, though, delicately, you can tell two stories simultaneously; the observer's and the main character's.

Third Person/Main Character: This is probably the most popular POV in modern fiction, certainly in genre fiction. It remains close to the main character but allows the author to say things outside of the main frame of the story. He can legitimately comment on the character and, often by flashback, elucidate his actions.

The main problem with this POV is controlling it, not allowing it to broaden into "Omniscient Author." The writer can only make direct observations about the main character, *who can't read anybody else's mind* (unless he's a telepath, okay).

This POV is sort of a compromise between the elbow room you get with the omniscient author and the reader-identification you get with first person/main character. It maintains suspense because you can legiti-mately withhold information the main character is seeking.

Third person/minor character: This isn't done too often. In a way, you have as much "distance" disadvantage as the omniscient author, but no real insight advantage to compensate for it. It can be useful, though, for telling two stories at once—the minor character in the action-story being the major one in a parallel story of character development. In Hemingway's famous story "Indian Camp," young Nick Adams fills this

role, passively watching his father during the dramas of childbirth and
suicide.

Omniscient Author: This is the loosest way to write, and some people find it the easiest. It has the disadvantage of being the most distant. Also, you have to maintain suspense without being silly about it—not letting the reader know the main character's a robot until the last line.

It's often used in genre fiction because it's a natural mode for transmitting information:

> *Bat Durston walked through the door. He had a Mark II West-*
> *inghouse laser on his hip. That's the kind that operates through*
> *the mutual destruction of matter and anti-matter.*
>
> *"Howdy, Bat," said Fred Deadhead, leaning against the bar.*
> *He gestured at the weapon. "Thought you used a Mark I."*
>
> *"Use' ta." The Mark I Westinghouse laser was powered by*
> *translation of the weak interaction force in metastable isotopes of*
> *transuranian elements. "Gah damn plutonium burned mah hip."*

Some writers are more subtle than that.

Finally, *second person* is a rarely seen mutant where, at least in terms of formal grammar, the reader becomes the main character, with an invisible narrator describing what he or she does, in present tense:

> *You walk into this bar and there's a lady, a* real *lady, sitting at*
> *the bar in a nice red dress. You've been in here a hundred times*
> *and never seen a woman.*
>
> *She looks right at you. "You took your time."*
>
> *"Yeah." You ease onto the seat next to her. "I'm usually here*
> *at six." You take one of her cigarettes and tap it on the bar. "So*
> *who are you?"*
>
> *"Your worst nightmare, John." She takes the unlit cigarette*
> *from between your fingers and puts the end against her palm. It*
> *lights.*

Alternate or *multiple viewpoints:* This is where you mix and match among the various alternatives described above. You might tell the story from the viewpoint of two or more people, or you might alternate, say, a first-person main character with a detached "omiscient author" who steps in occasionally to explain things.

This is a technique more appropriate to a novel than a short story. Ask yourself what it is in the story that requires more than one POV. It could be that you're just bored with your main character, in which case you should probably chuck the story and start another one. Maybe you think, at least unconsciously, that the story isn't impressive enough, told simply. That's usually a mistake, too.

It can work, though. The first time I was ever aware of point of view was a multiple viewpoint—in grade school, about forty years ago. I'd picked up a 3-D comic, with the old red and blue glasses, that was the story of a simple Western shoot-out. A cowboy came in through the swinging doors of a saloon and got into an argument with a guy at the bar. They finally went out on the street and slapped leather, bang, end of story. But no, then the story started over, written and drawn from the POV of the guy at the bar. Then again, from the shootist POV. I think there was another, too, perhaps the bartender.

A gimmick, but a good one. In a short story, without the glasses, I'm pretty sure it would be too thin a gimmick.

Don't be afraid to experiment, though. Once you have the story down on paper, or phosphor, you can go back and easily change the viewpoint. Look at them side by side. There's no perfect way to tell any given story, but there usually is a best viewpoint, reflecting exactly what the author wants to reveal and conceal. Find it.

"Feedback" is odd in that it is *about* point of view, in two different senses, neither of them abstract. One is the graphic artist's deliberate limitation and distortion of what he or she sees—which part of the scene in front of you should wind up on the canvas; what do you leave out, tone down, exaggerate? And then there's the science-fictional riff: Suppose some future cyberpunk tinkering allowed you to take over another person's point of view, literally—and suppose that person's view of the world was a little crazy.

BUDDHA NOSTRIL BIRD
by John Kessel

▼

After we killed the guard, Glaucon and I ran down the corridor away from the Well. Glaucon had been seriously aged in the fight. He limped and cursed, a piece of dying meat and he knew it. I brushed my hand along the wall looking for a door.

"We'll make it," I said.

"Sure," he said. He held his arm against his side.

We ran past a series of ontological windows: a forest fire, a sun in space, a factory refashioning children into flowers. I worried that the corridor might be a loop. For all I knew, the sole purpose of such corridors was to confuse and recapture escapees. Or maybe the corridors were just for fun. The Relativists delight in such absurdities.

More windows: a snowstorm, a cloudy seascape, a corridor exactly like the one we were in, in which two men wearing yellow robes—prison kosodes like ours—searched for a way out. Glaucon stopped. The hand of his double reached out to meet his. The face of mine stared at me angrily; a strong face, an intelligent one. "It's just a mirror," I said.

"Mirror?"

"A mirror," a voice said. Protagoras appeared ahead of us in the corridor. "Like sex, it reproduces human beings."

An old joke, and typical of Protagoras to quote it without attribution.

Glaucon raised his clock. In the face of Protagoras' infinite mutability it was less than useless: There was no way Glaucon would even get a shot off. My spirit sank as I watched the change come over him. Protagoras dripped fellowship. Glaucon liked him. Nobody but a maniac could dislike Protagoras.

It took all my will to block the endorphin assault, but Glaucon was never as strong as I. A lot of talk about brotherhood had passed between us, but if I'd had my freedom I would have crisped him on the spot. Instead I hid myself from Protagoras' blue eyes, as cold as chips of aquamarine in a mosaic.

"Where are you going?" Protagoras said.

"We were going—" Glaucon started.

"—nowhere," I said.

"A hard place to get to," said Protagoras.

Glaucon's head bobbed like a dog's.

"I know a short way," Protagoras said. "Come along with me."

"Sure," said Glaucon.

I struggled to maintain control. If you had asked him, Protagoras would have denied controlling anyone: 'The Superior Man rules by humility." Another sophistry.

We turned back down the corridor. If I stayed with them until we got to the center, there would be no way I could escape. Desperation forced me to test the reality of one of the windows. As we passed the ocean scene, I pushed Glaucon into Protagoras and threw my shoulder against the glass. The window shattered; I was falling. My kosode flapped like the melting wings of Icarus as sky and sea whirled around me, and I hit the water. My breath exploded from me. I flailed and tumbled. At last I found the surface. I sputtered and gasped, my right arm in agony; my ribs ached. I kicked off my slippers and leaned onto my back. The waves rolled me up and down. The sky was low and dark. At the top of each swell I could see to the storm-clouded horizon, flat as a psychotic's affect—but in the other direction was a beach.

I swam. The bad shoulder and the kosode made it hard, but at that moment I would not have traded places with Glaucon for all the enlightenment of the ancients.

When they sent me to the penal colony they told me, "Prisons ought to be places where people are lodged only temporarily, as guests are. They must not become dwelling places."

Their idea of temporary is not mine. Temporary doesn't mean long enough for your skin to crack like the dry lakebed outside your window, for the memory of your lover's touch to recede until it's only a torment in your dreams, as distant as the mountains that surround the penal colony. These distinctions are lost on Relativists, as are all distinctions. Which, I suppose, is why I was sent there.

They keep you alone, mostly. I don't mind the isolation—it gave me time to understand exactly how many ways I had been betrayed. I spent hours thinking of Areté, etching her ideal features in my mind. I remembered how they'd ripped me away from her. I wondered if she still lived, and if I would ever see her again. Eventually, when memory had faded, I conquered the passage of time itself: I reconstructed her image from incorruptible ideas and planned the revenge I would take once I was free again, so that the past and the future became more real to me than the endless, featureless present. Such is the power of idea over reality. To the guards I must have looked properly meditative. Inside I burned.

Each day at dawn we would be awakened by the rapping of sticks on our iron bedsteads. In the first hour we drew water from the Well of Changes. In the second we were encouraged to drink (I refused). In the third we washed floors with the water. From the fourth through the seventh we performed every other function that was necessary to maintain the prison. In the eighth we were tortured. At the ninth we were fed. At night, exhausted, we slept.

The torture chamber is made of ribbed concrete. It is a cold room, without windows. In its center is a chair, and beside the chair a small table, and on the table the hood. The hood is black and appears to be made of ordinary fabric, but it is not. The first time I held it, despite the evidence of my eyes I thought it had slipped through my fingers. The hood is not a material object: You cannot feel it, and it has no texture, and although it absorbs all light it is neither warm nor cold.

Your inquisitor invites you to sit in the chair and slip the hood over your head. You do so. He speaks to you. The room disappears. Your body melts away, and you are made into something else. You are an animal. You are one of the ancients. You are a stone, a drop of rain in a storm, a planet. You are in another time and place. This may sound intriguing, and the first twenty times it is. But it never ends. The sessions are indiscriminate. They are deliberately pointless. They continue to the verge of insanity.

I recall one of these sessions, in which I lived in an ancient city and worked a hopeless routine in a store called the "World of Values." The values we sold were merchandise. I married, had children, grew old, lost my health and spirit. I worked forty years. Some days were happy, others

sad; most were neither. The last thing I remembered was lying in a hospital bed, unable to see, dying, and hearing my wife talk with my son
about what they should have for dinner. When I came out from under
the hood, Protagoras yanked me from the chair and told me this poem:

> *Out from the nostrils of the Great Buddha*
> *Flew a pair of nesting swallows.*

I could still hear my phantom wife's cracking voice. I was in no mood
for riddles. "Tell me what it means."

"Drink from the Well and I'll tell you."

I turned my back on him.

It was always like that. Protagoras had made a career out of
tormenting me. I had known him for too many years. He put faith in nothing, was totally without honor, yet he had power. His intellect was available for any use. He wasted years on banalities. He would argue any side
of a case, not because he sought advantage, but because he did not care
about right or wrong. He was intolerably lucky. Irresponsible as a child.
Inconstant as the wind. His opaque blue gaze could be as witless as a scientist's.

And he had been my first teacher. He had introduced me to Areté,
offered me useless advice throughout our stormy relationship, given ambiguous testimony at my trial, and upon the verdict abandoned the university in order to come to the prison and become my inquisitor. The
thought that I had once idolized him tormented me more than any session under the hood.

After my plunge through the window into the sea, I fought my way
through the surf to the beach. For an unknown time I lay gasping on the
wet sand. When I opened my eyes I saw a flock of gulls had waddled up
to me. An arm's length away the lead gull, a great bull whose ragged feath-
ers stood out from his neck in a ruff, watched me with beady black eyes.
Others of various sizes and markings stood in a wedge behind him. I
raised my head; the gulls retreated a few steps, still holding formation. I
understood immediately that they were ranked according to their stations
in the flock. Thus does nature shadow forth fundamental truth: the rule
of the strong over the weak, the relation of one to the many in hierarchical
order.

Off to the side stood a single scrawny gull, quicker than the rest, but separate, aloof. I supposed him to be a gullish philosopher. I saluted him, my brother.

A sandpiper scuttled along the edge of the surf. Dipping a handful of seawater, I washed sand and pieces of shell from my cheek. Up the slope, saw grass and sea oats held the dunes against the tides. The scene was familiar. With wonder and some disquiet I understood that the window had dumped me into the Great Water quite near the Imperial City.

I stumbled up the sand to the crest of the dunes. In the east, beneath piled thunderheads, lightning flashed over the dark water. To the west, against the sunset's glare, the sand and scrub turned into fields. I started inland. Night fell swiftly. From behind me came clouds, strong winds, then rain. I trudged on, singing into the downpour. The thunder sang back. Water streamed down the creases of my face, the wet kosode weighed on my chest and shoulders, the rough grass cut my feet. In the profound darkness I could continue only by memorizing the landscape revealed by flashes of lightning. Exhilarated, I hurried toward my lover. I shouted at the raindrops, any one of which might be one of my fellow prisoners under the hood. "I'm free!" I told them. I forded the swollen River of Indifference. I stumbled through Iron Tree Forest. Throughout the night I put one foot before the other, and some hours before dawn, in a melancholy drizzle, passed through the Heron's Gate into the city.

In the Processor's Quarter I found a doorway whose overhang kept out the worst of the rain. Above hung the illuminated sign of the Rat. In the corner of this doorway, under this sign, I slept.

I was awakened by the arrival of the owner of the communications shop in whose doorway I had slept.

"I am looking for the old fox," I said. "Do you know where I can find him?"

"Who are you?"

"You may call me the little fox."

He pushed open the door. "Well, Mr. Fox, I can put you in touch with him instantly. Just step into one of our booths."

He must have known I had no money. "I don't want to communicate. I want to see him."

"Communication is much better," the shop owner said. He took a towel, a copper basin, and an ornamental blade from the cupboard beneath his terminal. "No chance of physical violence. No distress other than psychological. Completely accurate reproduction. Sensory enhancement: olfactory, visual, auditory." He opened a cage set into the wall and seized a docile black rat by the scruff of the neck. "Recordability. Access to a network of supporting information services. For slight additional charge we offer intelligence augmentation and instant semiotic analysis. We make the short man tall. Physical presence has nothing to compare."

"I want to speak with him in private."

Not looking at me, he took the rat to the stone block. "We are bonded."

"I don't question your integrity."

"You have religious prejudices against communication? You are a Traveler?"

He would not rest until he forced me to admit I was penniless. I refrained from noting that, if he was such a devout communicator, he could easily have stayed home. Yet he had walked to his shop in person. Swallowing my rage, I said, "I have no money."

He sliced the rat's neck open. The animal made no sound.

After he had drained the blood and put the carcass into the display case, he washed his hands and turned to me. He seemed quite pleased with himself. He took a small object from a drawer. "He is to be found at the university. Here is a map of the maze." He slipped it into my hand.

For this act of gratuitous charity, I vowed that one day I would have revenge. I left.

The streets were crowded. Dusty gold light filtered down between the ranks of ancient buildings. Too short to use the moving ways, I walked. Orange-robed messengers threaded their way through the crowd. Sweating drivers in loincloths pulled pedicabs; I imagined the perfumed lottery winners who reclined behind the opaqued glass of their passenger compartments. In the Medical Quarter, street-side surgeons hawked their services in front of racks of breasts and penises of prodigious size. As before, the names of the streets changed hourly to mark the progress of the sun across the sky. All streets but one, and I held my breath when I came to it: the Way of Enlightenment, which ran between the reform temple and the Imperial Palace. As before, metamorphs entertained the faithful on the stage outside the temple. One of them changed shape as

I watched, from a dog-faced man wearing the leather skirt of an athlete to a tattooed CEO in powered suit. "Come drink from the Well of Changes!" he called ecstatically to passersby. "Be reformed!"

The Well he spoke of is both literal and symbolic. The prison Well was its brother; the preachers of the temple claim that all the Wells are one Well. Its water has the power to transform both body and mind. A scientist could tell you how it is done: viruses, brain chemistry, hypnosis, some insane combination of the three. But that is all a scientist could tell you. Unlike a scientist, I could tell you why its use is morally wrong. I could explain that some truths are eternal and ought to be held inviolate, and why a culture that accepts change indiscriminately is rotten at its heart. I could demonstrate, with inescapable logic, that reason is better than emotion. That spirit is greater than flesh. That Relativism is the road to hell.

Instead of relief at being home, I felt distress. The street's muddle upset me, but it was not simply that: The city was exactly as I had left it. The wet morning that dawned on me in the doorway might have been the morning after I was sent away. My absence had made no discernible difference. The tyranny of the Relativists that I and my friends had struggled against had not culminated in the universal misery we had predicted. Though everything changed minute to minute, it remained the same. The one thing that ought to remain constant, Truth, was to them as chimerical as the gene-changers of the temple.

They might have done better, had they had teachers to tell them good from bad.

Looking down the boulevard, in the distance, at the heart of the city, I could see the walls of the palace. By midday I had reached it. Vendors of spiced cakes pushed their carts among the petitioners gathered beneath the great red lacquered doors. One, whose cakes each contained a free password, did a superior business. That the passwords were patent frauds was evident by the fact that the gatekeeper ignored those petitioners who tried using them. But that did not hurt sales. Most of the petitioners were halflings, and a dim-witted rabbit could best them in a deal.

I wept for my people, their ignorance and illogic. I discovered that I was clutching the map in my fist so tightly that the point of it had pierced my skin. I turned from the palace and walked away, and did not feel any relief until I saw the towers of the university rising above Scholars' Park. I remembered my first sight of them, a young boy down from the hills, the smell of cattle still about me, come to study under the great Protagoras. The meticulously kept park, the calm proportions of the buildings, spoke to the soul of that innocent boy: Here you'll be safe from blood and passion. Here you can lose yourself in the world of the mind.

The years had worn the polish off that dream, but I can't say that, seeing it now, once more a fugitive from a dangerous world, I did not feel some of the same joy. I thought of my mother, a loutish farmer who would whip me for reading; of my gentle father, brutalized by her, trying to keep the flame of truth alive in his boy.

On the quadrangle I approached a young woman wearing the topknot and scarlet robe of a humanist. Her head bounced to some inner rhythm, and as I imagined she was pursuing some notion of the Ideal, my heart went out to her. I was about to ask her what she studied when I saw the pin in her temple. She was listening to transtemporal music: her mind eaten by puerile improvisations played on signals picked up from the death agonies of the cosmos. Generations of researchers had devoted their lives to uncovering these secrets, only to have their efforts used by "artists" to erode people's connections with reality. I spat on the walk at her feet; she passed by, oblivious.

At the entrance to the humanities maze I turned on the map and followed it into the gloom. Fifteen minutes later it guided me into the Department of Philosophy. It was the last place I expected to find the fox—the nest of our enemies, the place we had plotted against tirelessly. The secretary greeted me pleasantly.

"I'm looking for a man named Socrates," I said. "Some call him 'the old fox.' "

"Universe of Discourse 3," she said.

I walked down the hall, wishing I had Glaucon's clock. The door to the hall stood open. In the center of the cavelike room, in a massive support chair, sat Socrates. At last I had found a significant change: He was grossly obese. The ferretlike features I remembered were folded in fat. Only the acute eyes remained. I was profoundly shaken. As I approached, his eyes followed me.

"Socrates."

"Blume."

"What happened to you?"

Socrates lifted his dimpled hand, as if to wave away a triviality. "I won."

"You used to revile this place."

"I reviled its usurpers. Now I run it."

"You run it?"

"I'm the dean."

I should have known Socrates had turned against our cause, and perhaps at some level I had. If he had remained true, he would have ended up in a cell next to mine. "You used to be a great teacher," I said.

"Right. Let me tell what happens when a man starts claiming he's a great teacher. First he starts wearing a brocade robe. Then he puts lifts in his sandals. The next thing you know the department's got a nasty paternity suit on its hands."

His senile chuckle was like the bubbling of water in an opium pipe.

"How did you get to be dean?"

"I performed a service for the Emperor."

"You sold out!"

"Blume the dagger," he said. Some of the old anger shaded his voice. "So sharp. So rigid. You always were a prig."

"And you used to have principles."

"Ah, principles," he said. "I'll tell you what happened to my principles. You heard about Philomena the Bandit?"

"No. I've been somewhat out of touch."

Socrates ignored the jab. "It was after you left. Philomena invaded the system, established her camp on the moon, and made her living raiding the empire. The city was at her mercy. I saw my opportunity. I announced that I would reform her. My students outfitted a small ship, and Areté and I launched for the moon."

"Areté!"

"We landed in a lush valley near the camp. Areté negotiated an audience for me. I went, alone. I described to Philomena the advantages of politic behavior. The nature of truth. The costs of living in the world of shadows and the glory of moving into the world of light. How, if she should turn to Good, her story would be told for generations. Her fame would spread throughout the world and her honor outlast her lifetime by a thousand years.

"Philomena listened. When I was finished she drew a knife and asked me, 'How long is a thousand years?'

"Her men stood all around, waiting for me to slip. I started to speak, but before I could she pulled me close and pushed the blade against my throat.

" 'A thousand years,' Philomena said, 'is shorter than the exposure of a neutrino passing through a world. How long is life?'

"I was petrified. She smiled. 'Life,' she said, 'is shorter than this blade.'

"I begged for mercy. She threw me out. I ran to the ship, in fear for my life. Areté asked what happened: I said nothing. We set sail for home.

"We landed amid great tumult. I first thought it was riot but soon found it celebration. During our voyage back Philomena had left the moon. People assumed I had convinced her. The Emperor spoke. Our enemies in philosophy were shortened, and the regents stretched me into dean.

"Since then," Socrates said, "I have had trouble with principles."

"You're a coward," I said.

Despite the mask of suet, I could read the ruefulness in Socrates's eyes. "You don't know me," he said.

"What happened to Areté?"

"I have not seen her since."

"Where is she?"

"She's not here." He shifted his bulk, watching the screen that encircled the room. "Turn yourself in, Blume. If they catch you, it will only go harder."

"Where is she?"

"Even if you could get to her, she won't want to see you."

I seized his arm, twisted. "Where is Areté!"

Socrates inhaled sharply. "In the palace," he said.

"She's a prisoner?"

"She's the Empress."

That night I took a place among the halflings outside the palace gate. Men and women regrown from seed after their deaths, imprinted with stored files of their original personalities, all of them had lost resolution, for no identity file could encapsulate human complexity. Some could not speak, others displayed features too stiff to pass for human, and still others had no personalities at all. Their only chance for wholeness was to petition the Empress to perform a transfinite extrapolation from their core data. To be miraculously transformed.

An athlete beside me showed me his endorsements. An actress showed me her notices. A banker showed me his lapels. They asked me my profession. "I am a philosopher," I said.

They laughed. "Prove it," the actress said.

"In the well-ordered state," I told her, "there will be no place for you." To the athlete I said, "Yours is a good and noble profession." I turned to the banker. "Your work is more problematical," I said. "Unlike the actress, you fulfill a necessary function, but unlike the athlete, by accumulating wealth you are likely to gain more power than is justified by your small wisdom."

This speech was beyond them: The actress grumbled and went away. I left the two men and walked along below the battlements. Two bartizans framed the great doors, and archers strolled along the ramparts or leaned through the embrasures to spit on the petitioners. For this reason the halflings camped as far back from the walls as they might without blocking the street. The archers, as any educated man knew, were there for show: The gates were guarded only by a single gatekeeper, a monk who could open the door if bested in a battle of wits, but without whose acquiescence the door could not be budged.

He sat on his stool beside the gate, staring quietly ahead. Those who tried to talk to him could not tell whether they'd get a cuff on the ear or a friendly conversation. His flat, peasant's face was so devoid of intellect that it was some time before I recognized him as Protagoras.

His disguised presence could be one of his whims. Or it could be he was being punished for letting me escape; it could be that he waited for me. I felt an urge to run. But I would not duplicate Socrates' cowardice. If Protagoras recognized me he did not show it, and I resolved to get in or get caught. I was not some half-wit, and I knew him. I approached. "I wish to see the Empress," I said.

"You must wait."

"I've been waiting for years."

"That doesn't matter."

"I have no more time."

He studied me. His manner changed. "What will you pay?"

"I'll pay you a story that will make you laugh until your head aches."

He smiled. I saw that he recognized me; my stomach lurched. "I know many such stories," he said.

"Not like mine."

"Yes. I can see you are a great breeder of headaches."

Desperation drove me forward. "Listen, then: Once there was a warlord who discovered that someone had stolen his most precious possession, a jewel of power. He ordered his servants to scour the fortress for strangers. In the bailey they found a beggar heading for the gate. The lord's men seized him and carried him to the well. 'The warlord's great jewel is lost,' they said to him. They thrust the beggar's head beneath the water. He struggled. They pulled him up and asked, 'Where is the jewel?'

" 'I don't know,' he said.

"They thrust him down again, longer this time. When they pulled him up he sputtered like an old engine. 'Where is the jewel?' they demanded. 'I don't know!' he replied.

"Furious at his insolence, fearful for their lives if they should rouse their lord's displeasure, the men pushed the beggar so far into the well that a bystander thought, 'He will surely drown.' The beggar kicked so hard it took three strong men to hold him. When at last they pulled him up he coughed and gasped, face purple, struggling to speak. They pounded him on the back. Finally he drew breath enough for words.

" 'I think you should get another diver,' the beggar said. 'I can't see it anywhere down there.' "

Protagoras smiled. "That's not funny."

"What?"

"Maybe for us, but not for the beggar. Or the bystander. Or the servants. The warlord probably had them shortened."

"Don't play games. What do you really think?"

"I think of poor Glaucon. He misses you."

Then I saw that Protagoras only meant to torment me, as he had so many times before. He would answer my desperate need with feeble jokes until I wept or went mad. A fury more powerful than the sun itself swept over me, and I lost control. I fell on him, kicking, biting. The petitioners looked on in amazement. Shouts echoed from the ramparts. I didn't care. I'd forgotten everything but my rage; all I knew was that at last I had him in my hands. I scratched at his eyes, I beat his head against the pavements. Protagoras struggled to speak. I pulled him up and slammed his head against the doors. The tension went out of his muscles. Cross-legged, as if preparing to meditate, he slid to the ground. Blood glistened in the torchlight on the lacquered doors. "Now that's funny," he whispered, and died.

The weight of his body against the door pushed it ajar. It had been open all along.

No one came to arrest me. Across the inner ward, at the edge of an ornamental garden, a person stood in the darkness beneath a plane tree. Most of the lights of the palace were unlit, but radiance from the clerestory above heightened the shadows. Hesitantly I drew closer, too unsteady after my sudden fit of violence to hide. In my confusion I could think to do no more than approach the figure in the garden, who stood patiently as if in long expectation of me. From ten paces away I saw it was a woman dressed as a clown. From five I saw it was Areté.

Her laughter, like shattering crystal, startled me. "How serious you look!"

My head was full of questions. She pressed her fingers against my lips, silencing them. I embraced her. Red circles were painted on her cheeks, and she wore a crepe beard, but her skin was still smooth, her eyes bright, her perfume the same. She was not a day older.

The memory of dead Protagoras' slack mouth marred my triumph. She ducked out of my arms, laughing again. "You can't have me unless you catch me!"

"Areté!"

She darted through the trees. I ran after her. My heart was not in it, and I lost her until she paused beneath a tree, hands on knees, panting. "Come on! I'm not so hard to catch."

The weight was lifted from my heart. I dodged after her. Beneath the trees, through the hedge maze, among the night-blooming jasmine and bougainvillea, the silver moon tipping the edges of the leaves, I chased her. At last she let herself be caught; we fell together into a damp bed of ivy. I rested my head on her breast. The embroidery of her costume was rough against my cheek.

She took my head in her hands and made me look her in the face. Her teeth were pearly white, breath sweet as the scented blossoms around us.

We kissed, through the ridiculous beard (I could smell the spirit gum she'd used to affix it), and the goal they had sought to instill in me at the penal colony was attained: My years of imprisonment vanished into the immediate moment as if they had never existed.

▼

That kiss was the limit of our contact. I expected to spend the night with her; instead, she had a slave take me to a guesthouse for visiting dignitaries, where I was quartered with three minor landholders from the mountains. They were already asleep. After my day of confusion, rage, desire, and fear, I lay there weary but hard awake, troubled by the sound of my own breathing. My thoughts were jumbled white noise. I had killed him. I had found her. Two of the fantasies of my imprisonment fulfilled in a single hour. Yet no peace. The murder of Protagoras would not long go unnoticed. I assumed Areté already knew but did not care. But if she was truly the Empress, why had he not been killed years before? Why had I rotted in prison under him?

I had no map for this maze and eventually fell asleep.

In the morning the slave, Pismire, brought me a wig of human hair, a green kimono, a yellow silk sash, and solid leather sandals: the clothes of a prosperous nonentity. My roommates appeared to be barely lettered country bumpkins, little better than my parents, come to court seeking a judgment against a neighbor or a place for a younger child or protection from some bandit. One of them wore the colors of an inferior upland collegium; the others no colors at all.

I suspected at least one of them was Areté's spy; they might have thought me one as well. We looked enough alike to be brothers.

We ate in a dining room attended by machines. I spent the day studying the public rooms of the palace, hoping to get some information. At the tolling of sixth hour Pismire found me in the vivarium. He handed me a message under the Imperial seal, and left. I turned it on.

"You are invited to an important meeting," the message said.

"With whom?" I asked. "For what purpose?"

The message ignored me. "The meeting begins promptly at ninth hour. Prepare yourself." There followed directions to the place.

When I arrived, the appointed room was empty. A long oak table, walls lined with racks of document spindles. At the far end, French doors gave onto a balcony overlooking an ancient city of glass and metal buildings. I could hear the faint sounds of traffic below.

A side door opened and a woman in the blue suit of the Lawyer entered, followed by a clerk. The woman's glossy black hair was stranded with gray, but her face was smooth. She wore no makeup. She stood at the end of the table, back to the French doors, and set down a leather box. The clerk sat at her right hand. I realized that this forbidding figure was Areté. She had become as mutable as Protagoras.

"Be seated," she said. "We are here to take your deposition."

"Deposition?"

"Your statement on the matter at hand."

"What matter?"

"Your escape from the penal colony. Your murder of the gatekeeper, the honored philosopher Protagoras."

The injustice of this burned through my dismay. "Not murder. Self-defense. Or better still, euthanasia."

"Don't quibble with us. We are deprived of his presence."

"Grow a duplicate. Bring him back to life."

For reply she merely stared at me across the table. The air tasted stale, and I felt a bead of sweat run down my breast beneath my robe. "Is this some game?"

"You may well wish it a game."

"Areté!"

"I am not Areté. I am a Lawyer." She leaned toward me. "Why were you sent to prison?"

"You were with me! You know."

"We are taking your version of events for the record."

"You know as well as I that I was imprisoned for seeking the Truth."

"Which truth?"

There was only one. "The one that people don't want to hear," I said.

"You had access to a truth people did not acknowledge?"

"They are blinded by custom and self-interest."

"You were not?"

"I had, through years of self-abnegation and study, risen above them. I had broken free of the chains of prejudice, climbed out of the cave of shadows that society lives in, and looked at the sun direct."

The clerk smirked as I made this speech. It was the first expression he'd shown.

"And you were blinded by it," Areté said.

"I saw the truth. But when I came back they said I was blind. They would not listen, so they put me away."

"The trial record says that you assisted in the corruption of youth."

"I was a teacher."

"The record says you refused to listen to your opponents."

"I refuse to listen to ignorance and illogic. I refuse to submit to fools, liars, and those who let passion overcome reason."

"You have never been fooled?"

"I was, but not now."

"You never lie?"

"If I do, I still know the difference between a lie and the truth."

"You never act out of passion?"

"Only when supported by reason."

"You never suspect your own motives?"

"I know my motives."

"How?"

"I examine myself. Honestly, critically. I apply reason."

"Spare me your colossal arrogance, your revolting self-pity. Eyewitnesses say you killed the gatekeeper in a fit of rage."

"I had reason. Do you presume to understand my motives better than I? Do you understand your own?"

"No. But that's because I am dishonest. And totally arbitrary." She opened the box and took out a clock. Without hesitation she pointed it at the clerk. His smugness punctured, he stumbled back, overturning his chair. She pressed the trigger. The weapon must have been set for maximum entropy: Before my eyes the clerk aged ten, twenty, fifty years. He died and rotted. In less than a minute he was a heap of bones and gruel on the floor.

"You've been in prison so long you've invented a harmless version of me," Areté said. "I am capable of anything." She laid the clock on the table, turned and opened the doors to let in a fresh night breeze. Then she climbed onto the table and crawled toward me. I sat frozen. "I am the Destroyer," she said, loosening her tie as she approached. Her eyes were fixed on mine. When she reached me she pushed me over backward, falling atop me. "I am the force that drives the blood through your dying body, the nightmare that wakes you sweating in the middle of the night. I am the fiery caldron within whose heat you are reduced to a vapor, extended from the visible into the invisible, dissipated on the winds of time, of fading memory, of inevitable human loss. In the face of me, you are incapable of articulate speech. About me you understand nothing."

She wound the tie around my neck, drew it tight. "Remember that," she said, strangling me.

I passed out on the floor of the interview room and awoke the next morning in a bed in a private chamber. Pismire was drawing the curtains on a view of an ocean beach: Half-asleep, I watched the tiny figure of a man materialize in a spray of glass, in midair, and fall precipitously into the sea.

Pismire brought me a breakfast of fruit and spiced coffee. Touching the bruises on my neck, I watched the man resurface in the sea and swim ashore. He collapsed on the sand. A flock of gulls came to stand by his head. If I broke through this window, I could warn him. I could say: Socrates is fat. Watch out for the gatekeeper. Areté is alive, but she is changed.

But what could I tell him for certain? Had Areté turned Relativist, like Socrates? Was she free, or being made to play a part? Did she intend to prosecute me for the murder of Protagoras? But if so, why not simply return me to the penal colony?

I did not break through the window, and the man eventually moved up the beach toward the city.

That day servants followed me everywhere. Minor lords asked my opinions. Evidently I was a taller man than I had been the day before. I drew Pismire aside and asked him what rumors were current. He was a stocky fellow with a topknot of coarse black hair and shaved temples, silent, but when I pressed him he opened up readily enough. He said he knew for a fact that Protagoras had set himself up to be killed. He said the Emperor was dead and the Empress was the focus of a perpetual struggle. That many men had sought to make Areté theirs, but none had so far succeeded. That disaster would surely follow any man's success.

"Does she always change semblance from day to day?"

He said he had never noticed any changes.

In midafternoon, at precisely the same time I had yesterday received the summons to the deposition, a footman with the face of a frog handed me an invitation to dine with the Empress that evening.

Three female expediters prepared a scented bath for me; a fourth laid out a kimono of blue crepe embroidered with gold fishing nets. The mirror they held before me showed a man with wary eyes. At the tolling of ninth hour I was escorted to the banquet hall. The room was filled with notables in every finery. A large, low table stretched across the tesselated floor, surrounded by cushions. Before each place was an enamel bowl, and in the center of the table was a large three-legged brass caldron. Areté, looking no more than twenty, stood talking to an extremely handsome man near the head of the table.

"I thank you for your courtesy," I told her.

The man watched me impassively. "No more than is your due," Areté replied. She wore a bright costume of synthetics with pleated shoulders and elbows. She looked like a toy. Her face was painted into a hard mask.

She introduced me to the man, whose name was Meno. I drew her away from him. "You frightened me last night," I said. "I thought you had forgotten me."

Only her soft brown eyes showed she wasn't a pleasure surrogate. "What makes you think I remember?"

"You could not forget and still be the one I love."

"That's probably true. I'm not sure I'm worth such devotion."

Meno watched us from a few paces away. I turned my back to him and leaned closer to her. "I can't believe you mean that," I said quickly. "I think you say such things because you have been imprisoned by liars and self-aggrandizers. But I am here for you now. I am an objective voice. Just give me a sign, and I will set you free."

Before she could answer, a bell sounded and the people took their places. Areté guided me to a place beside her. She sat, and we all followed suit.

The slaves stood ready to serve, waiting for Areté's command. She looked around the table. "We are met here to eat together," she said. "To dine on ambrosia, because there has been strife in the city, and ambition, and treachery. But now it is going to stop."

Meno now looked openly angry. Others were worried.

"You are the favored ones," said Areté. She turned to me. "And our friend here, the little fox, is the most favored of all. Destiny's author — our new and most trusted adviser."

Several people started to protest. I seized the opportunity given by their shock. "Am I indeed your adviser?"

"You may test it by deeds."

"You and you—" I beckoned to the guards. "Clear these people from the room."

The guests were in turmoil. Meno tried to speak to Areté, but I stepped between them. The guards came forward and forced the men and women to leave. After they were gone, I had the guards and slaves leave as well. The doors closed and the hall was silent. I turned. Areté had watched it all calmly, sitting cross-legged at the head of the table.

"Now, Areté, you must listen to me. Your commands have been twisted throughout this city. You and I have an instinctive sympathy. You must let me determine who sees you. I will interpret your words. The world is not ready to understand without an interpreter; they need to be educated."

"And you are the teacher."

"I am suited to it by temperament and training."

She smiled meekly.

I told Areté that I was hungry. She rose and prepared a bowl of soup from the caldron. I sat at the head of the table. She came and set the bowl before me, then kneeled and touched her forehead to the floor.

"Feed me," I said.

She took the bowl and a napkin. She blew on the ambrosia to cool it, lips pursed. Like a serving girl, she held the bowl to my lips. Areté fed me all of it, like mother to child, lover to lover. It tasted better than anything I had ever eaten. It warmed my belly and inflamed my desire. When the bowl was empty I pushed it away, knocking it from her hand. It clattered on the marble floor. I would be put off no longer. I took her right there, amid the cushions.

She was indeed the hardest of toys.

▼

It had taken me three days from my entrance to the palace to become Areté's lover and voice. The Emperor over the Empress. On the first day of my reign I had the shopkeeper who had insulted me whipped the length of the Way of Enlightenment. On the second I ordered that only those certified in philosophy be qualified to vote. On the third I banished the poets.

Each evening Areté fed me ambrosia from a bowl. Each night we shared the Imperial bed. Each morning I awoke calmer, in more possession of myself. I moved more slowly. The hours of the day were drained of their urgency. Areté stopped changing. Her face settled with a quiet clarity into my mind, a clarity unlike the burning image I had treasured up during my years in the prison.

On the morning of the third day I awoke fresh and happy. Areté was not there. Pismire entered the room bearing a basin, a towel, a razor, a mirror. He washed and shaved me, then held the mirror before me. For the first time I saw the lines about my eyes and mouth were fading, and realized that I was being reformed.

I looked at Pismire. I saw him clearly: eyes cold as aquamarines.

"It's time for you to come home, Blume," he said.

No anger, no protest, arose in me. No remorse. No frustration. "I've been betrayed," I said. "Some virus, some drug, some notion you've put in my head."

Protagoras smiled. "The ambrosia. Brewed with water from the Well."

Now I am back in the prison. Escape is out of the question. Every step outward would be a step backward. It's all relative.

Instead I draw water from the Well of Changes. I drink. Protagoras says whatever changes will happen to me will be a reflection of my own psyche. That my new form is not determined by the water, but by me. How do I control it, I ask. You don't, he replies.

Glaucon has become a feral dog.

Protagoras and I go for long walks across the dry lake. He seldom speaks. I am not angry. Still, I fear a relapse. I am close to being nourished, but as yet I am not sure I am capable of it. I don't understand, as I never understood, where the penal colony is. I don't understand, as I never understood, how I can live without Areté.

Protagoras sympathizes. "Can't live with her, can't live without her," he says. "She's more than just a woman, Blume. You can experience her, but you can't own her."

Right. When I complain about such gnomic replies, Protagoras only puts me under the hood again. I think he knows some secret he wants me to guess, yet he gives no hints. I don't think that's fair.

After our most recent session, I told Protagoras my latest theory of the significance of the poem about the swallows. The poem, I told him, was an emblem of the ultimate and absolute truth of the universe. All things are determined by the ideas behind them, I said. There are three orders of existence, the Material (represented by the physical statue of the Buddha), the Spiritual (represented by its form), and the highest, which transcends both the Physical and the Spiritual, the Ideal (represented by the flight of the birds). Humbly I begged Protagoras to tell me whether my analysis was true.

Protagoras said, "You are indeed an intellectual. But in order for me to reveal the answer to a question of such profound spiritual significance, you must first bow down before the sacred Well."

At last I was to be enlightened. Eyes brimming with tears of hope, I turned to the Well and, with the utmost sincerity, bowed.

Then Protagoras kicked me in the ass.

UNCLE HENRY, UNCLE ZORP, AND CRAZY COUSIN BINGO

by John Kessel

▼

One of the tricks a science fiction writer can use to conjure up a world that's alien and values that aren't ours is to select the right viewpoint character. By choosing the proper character, and placing the camera close to or even inside him, one can introduce an altered world while burdening the reader with a minimum of explanations.

One way to see this is to imagine two characters introduced to the world of the future, Uncle Henry and Uncle Zorp. Uncle Henry is just like us, familiar with the world today but not particularly up on the possibility of change. When presented with the virtual reality hardware or the space invasion or the legal marriage between adults and children, he is nonplussed, offended, confused. At the very least, he notices.

Uncle Zorp is a native of the altered world. He's not surprised by the virtual reality hardware; in fact he knows where you can get a deal on an interactive date with Cleopatra. His first marriage, to a forty-year-old veteran of the war against the Sirians, occurred when he was eight. The advantage of telling the story from Uncle Zorp's perspective is that the future is natural to him, and therefore does not demand as much explanation.

One way to tell SF readers from non-SF readers is by their reaction to this game. SF readers enjoy the kick they get from being forced into a perspective from which things they consider natural are unnatural, and vice versa. Many non-SF readers, not lacking in intellect or sophistication, will reject or be confused by the same material. I have a writer friend who reacts to SF elements in workshop stories with "I don't read science fiction, so I can't criticize this." This same writer wouldn't hesitate to offer a blunt critique of a mainstream story. I think this is a case of his assumptions about what's appropriate in a story being invalidated by the science fiction premise. Once one detail of reality as we know it has been violated, such readers can't figure out why everything can't be violated. Break the bonds of realism and they are in the wasteland.

If the character's automatic acceptance of the VR gear automatically means you don't expect consistency of personality or motivation from him, you're going to get lost. You'll feel you can't trust or identify with Uncle Zorp's perceptions. He's unnatural, uncouth, unpredictable.

In "Buddha Nostril Bird," my narrator Blume is an avatar of Uncle Zorp, completely familiar with his odd world. When he refers to a "clock" that can be set for "maximum entropy," that is used later in the story to reduce a bystander to gruel on the floor, his only shock is at the arbitrariness of the assault; he accepts the weapon without question. When he says he is too "short" to use the public transportation system, and later, upon being taken into the palace, awakes to find himself a "taller" man than he was the night before, I expect the reader to grasp that his physical stature has not changed, but that the people in my future world use the language of height to describe changes of status.

I take pleasure in imagining this strange world, trying to make it as consistent as possible, and constructing it from these linguistic pieces. The science fiction reader takes pleasure from decoding it.

The reader can be made to see Uncle Zorp's perspective in the third person viewpoint, where the author remains technically exterior to the character and holds the power to comment on the action directly, as well as the first person (as in "Buddha Nostril Bird"), where the author is hidden behind the mask of a character who speaks to us directly. This is a matter of managing what John Gardner called the psychic distance—the distance the reader perceives between himself and the character.

There is, however, some difference between first and third persons. The third person narrator, because it puts us at least nominally outside the character, necessarily invokes more distance, no matter how close, than the first person narrator, where we are necessarily inside. In third, even if all the opinions are those of the protagonist, there is an implied observer other than the character.

The third person voice thus enables a cooler, more ironic look at the action and character, and for me, paradoxically, this results in more sympathy. When I really want to present an attitude I don't agree with, I lean toward first person. I want to be inside the head of the person whose opinions I find questionable.

Which leads me to the main point of this essay. One of the gratifications writers can take in their fictions is revenge. You can get back at someone you disapprove of by making him the hero of the story, then tormenting him in a world that reveals how wrong he is.

Think of this character as Crazy Cousin Bingo. Unlike Uncle Henry, Bingo may be perfectly at home in his world, but you can't trust his view of it. He's your annoying or amusing or tragic cousin who's so fatally deluded about many things: He thinks that combing his hair over his bald spot makes him look handsome, that women can't do math, that he didn't get the job at McDonald's because of scheming by the Trilateral Commission. He's the dreaded unreliable narrator, familiar to mainstream readers, not so common in science fiction (though since the late fifties we find versions of him in stories from Damon Knight's "The Country of the Kind" to Connie Willis' "A Letter From the Clearys").

What's unreliable about Cousin Bingo isn't that he lies about the facts, but that his opinions are not trustworthy. The events of the story aren't untrue—even an unreliable narrator is reliable about many, perhaps most things—but his judgments about them are. Often he isn't so much unreliable as he is *unsympathetic*. As far as the physical events go (and that's not very far—one of the insights of unreliability is how few "facts" are independent of interpretation), Blume, the narrator of "Buddha Nostril Bird," tells us what happens accurately, more or less. But we can't take his word for what these events mean. And we most definitely cannot trust his judgments of the other characters, their motives, their morality.

Why not? How would I know this if I weren't the author?

Well, for one thing, his reactions are out of proportion to their causes. For example, when Glaucon, with whom he has planned an escape, falls under the sway of Protagoras and is recaptured, Blume thinks, "Glaucon was never as strong as I. A lot of talk about brotherhood had passed between us, but if I'd had my freedom I would have crisped him on the spot." A rather harsh judgment on a man who has been his friend and co-escapee. In isolation such a reaction is not enough to mark Blume— he may be speaking out of his frustration and rage at being himself recaptured, out of his struggle to keep himself from becoming Protagoras' slave. But as the story progresses, my intention is for the accumulation of such harsh judgments by Blume ultimately to reflect against him, so that in the end sentences like "Nobody but a maniac could dislike Protagoras," come to be true in a way that Blume does not intend, more revealing of my attitude toward Blume than Blume realizes.

When he vows revenge against the shopkeeper for his "gratuitous act of charity," is this a sign of a cultural difference of this future world as revealed to the reader through an "Uncle Zorp" narrator, or evidence of Blume's own lack of charity? In some ways I want it to be both. Blume is a cross between Uncle Zorp and Crazy Cousin Bingo, a man at home in the future and one whose opinions you cannot trust.

There are two dangers of the unreliable narrator. The first is that the irony-challenged reader may assume that I agree with Blume. Many SF readers, perfectly able to pick up the slightest implication about the future world from a chance comment the narrator makes about dilating doors or drugstore strippers, have difficulty realizing when the narrator's opinions are not to be taken as the author's. To avoid this I marshal the attitudes and behaviors Blume exhibits and play them counter to his judgments of his own righteousness, in the hope that the accumulation will make it evident to the reader that I could not possibly intend this arrogant pedant to be the hero. Blume seeks revenge obsessively. He consistently portrays himself as superior to others. He judges immediately and without doubt. He never questions his own motives. He believes in the rule of the strong over the weak.

The second danger of the unreliable narrator is that in pursuit of one's ideological end one can cease writing fiction and produce propaganda instead. The writer can go overboard and end up evoking sympathy for a character he doesn't intend to be sympathetic, or annoyance at himself for being so unfair.

The way to avoid this is to allow the narrator his humanity. In "Buddha Nostril Bird" I tried hard not to deny Blume's sincere love for Areté, his joy at being free of the prison, his dismay and confusion at the torment he suffers under the hood. He has reason to feel anger. There is not one of us who has not acted as Blume does, shown the same arrogance, surety of judgment, conviction that we have been wronged and desire for revenge. His pain is real. His dismay is real. His confusion is real. When I have him say "The meticulously kept park, the calm proportions of the buildings, spoke to the soul of the innocent boy: Here you'll be safe from blood and passion. Here you can lose yourself in the world of the mind," I want you to see both Blume's neurotic fear of human emotion, and his vulnerability. This balance of sympathy is crucial to the success of a story using an unsympathetic narrator.

Let me say a bit more about the implied author, who hints at his judgments of Blume from behind Blume's voice. In all stories, whether we are in first or third person, an author's viewpoint is implied somewhere within, behind, and between the statements on the page. Not only must readers be able to figure out the judgments and values of the author, in the end they must accept them, or they will reject the story.

Imagine the viewpoints of the author, the story's characters and the reader at the beginning of the story as points on a triangle:

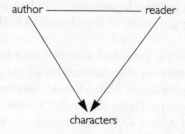

By the end of the story, the diagram should look something like this:

In the successful story, the distance between the author's and the reader's points on this triangle must approach zero by the end of the story; they must come to view the characters from the same perspective in the end. A reader may decide the protagonist is disgusting and still like the story, if the author intends for the reader to feel disgust. The problem comes when we feel a character the author wants us to *like* is disgusting or the character the story wants us to *dislike* arouses our sympathy; in such a case the *story* arouses our disgust. Most of us have had the experience of reading a book where the author wants us to see the hero as brave and principled, yet we see him as inflexible and cruel, or where the author sees the character as sensitive and we regard her as full of self-pity.

This is of course to a degree out of the author's control. Not only will some readers be unwilling or unable to see things the way the writer does; historically, some characters that were seen as heroic seem less so to the modern reader. No matter how close the author thinks he's closed the gap between himself and the reader, social change occurring after the story's publication can pry it apart. So, for instance, in *Heart of Darkness* Joseph Conrad has his narrator Marlow describe the African fireman on a steamboat as "an improved specimen . . . to look at him was as edifying as seeing a dog in a parody of breeches and a feather hat walking on its hind legs."

At the time this was published in 1899 it must have seemed merely an ironic commentary on the inadvisability of trying to civilize black Africans; but today we recoil from Marlow's easy racism in a way that undercuts his judgment. To the degree that Conrad wants us to accept Marlow's vision of Africa, such passages call into question his entire story.

Compare a similar passage in Herman Melville's "Benito Cereno," written forty-five years earlier. The viewpoint character Captain Delano sees an African slave on a ship, sleeping "like a doe, in the shade of a woodland rock. Sprawling at her lapped breasts was her wide-awake fawn, stark naked . . ." Once again the African is seen as an animal. But in this story later events call into question all of Delano's perceptions, and in the end we see that every judgment he has made about the slaves on the *San Dominick* has been completely off the mark. Melville *intends* for us, in the end, to reject Delano's assessments; the whole point of the story is to show how much more than dumb animals the slaves are, and how blind Delano's racial stereotyping has made him. So although Melville's character and Conrad's express similar racist opinions, the authors' handling of these opinions, as shown by their treatment of the characters expressing them, causes us to come away with different estimations of the authors: Conrad is guilty of a racism that Melville is criticizing. Note that it's not the opinions the viewpoint character expresses that determine our attitude toward the author, but the author's *attitude toward* the character, as expressed in the way the author presents the character, the context in which the character's opinions appear.

So although I would not be surprised if attitudes in Blume's story that I take for granted look perverse or old-fashioned thirty or forty years from now, I try the best I can to manage the story's tone to bring the reader into agreement with me. Tone can match, emphasize, or contradict the meaning of the words. Speaking is not always a matter of what is said. In the end, we authors want the reader's opinion to coincide, not necessarily with our character's, but with our own.

Or do we? Another way of thinking about this is that creating an unsympathetic narrator helps a writer discover exactly how he does feel about the acceptability of certain attitudes. The degree to which you can push the viewpoint character's defects and still feel like you are being fair is an estimation of what you feel the truth of the world to be. Your actual beliefs are to be found in the way you treat your character. If I can offer any defense of my mistreatment of poor Blume in "Buddha Nostril Bird," it is that this story is a comedy, and Blume receives enlightenment as well as a kick in the pants in the end.

I recently heard Karen Joy Fowler quote the poet Robert Hass as saying that the thing the writer habitually argues for is the lesson he feels he most needs to teach himself. The themes writers write about most obsessively are the things we have personal trouble with. What this suggests to me is that the arrogance I show you in Blume is a trait I must fight in myself, and in the end Blume is *me*, John Kessel the human being, as cleverly portrayed by "John Kessel" the author, speaking as a ventriloquist through Blume the character, in a fabricated world of the distant future. It may be that the reason I resort to first person when writing a character I disagree with is that I see in these people undesirable traits I am prone to myself. Therefore I admonish myself by writing as if I were the narrator.

▼

Style is the dress of thought; a modest dress,
Neat, but not gaudy, will true critics please.

This is Sam Wesley, the Vicar of Epworth, two of whose eighteen children brought neatness—nothing gaudy—to Protestantism and to Savannah, Georgia. Like religious reformers, good writers have a style uniquely their own, a way of going about artistic creation that is as individual as genetic coding. The dress of thought: Style is the choice of words, their arrangement in sentences, and their exploitation as sources of sensuous imagery.

Words delivered to the reader are ink marks on paper, symbols of great abstraction, largely meaningless in themselves, a *medium* through which meaning is triggered in the mind. In themselves, words, even if not vocalized, carry sound, can be musical, can carry such intellectual freight as music is capable of, but that is all. The writer is aware of the musical quality of words and phrases and he takes whatever advantage of it he can. His real concentration, however, is on the capacity of the words he chooses to tap the reader's store of remembered sense-images, intellectual associations, and emotions.

Words can deliver *denotative* and *connotative* meanings. The good journalist or technical writer seeks the former, meanings as given in the dictionary, as little confused by additional, equivocal meanings as possible. The fiction writer—like the advertising copy writer or political propagandist—depends heavily on connotation, choosing words which can trigger in the reader's mind all sorts of additional meanings—emotional, intellectual, or sensuous. "Sensuous" and "sensual," for example, carry much the same denotative meaning; they connote very different things.

When a writer combines words in a sentence, she pays attention to the shape and structure of the sentence. She manipulates the natural *rhythm* of a series of words and exploits its ability to reinforce their meaning. She avoids awkward concatenations of eye-obstructing poly-syllables and the fractionally distracting action of unconscious jingles, and she tries to suit the pace of her phrasing to the action she is describing. She is more likely to construct a *loose* or *cumulative* sentence, one whose meaning is complete well before it ends, in passages of little physical movement, when the loose sentence's capacity for subtle rhythmic effects can be employed for all its musical worth, and additional meanings can be strung like beads on a string in a succession of clauses. She uses the *periodic* sentence to suspend full meaning, however many interruptions she permits, however complex the sentence may be, to the end. Either sentence may employ the device of *balance*—equal rhetorical elements on either side of a conjunction whose meanings are complementary—or *antithesis*—balanced elements whose meanings contrast. Loose sentences are the meandering streams of language; periodic are the breaking waves; balanced convey the antiphonal rhythm of the diurnal tides.

The preceding sentence attempts to make certain fairly abstract notions concrete through a series of sense-images. There are a great many such rhetorical devices, and if you have a fondness for Greek you may wish to take a look at *litotes, hyperbole, apostrophe, synecdoche*, and the like. Two such devices—metaphor and simile—are worth distinguishing. *Metaphor* is an implied comparison between two unlike things (usually one is abstract, the other concrete and sensuous in its appeal): "Life is just a bowl of cherries. . . ." *Simile* is explicit comparison: "O, my Luve's like a red, red rose. . . ." Language—and particularly slang—is full of one-word metaphors: "Hey dude! Dig that chick in the shades. . . ." which are more properly described as *kennings*. Good writers coin them or steal them from street corners with delight.

Most of style is conscious, although not self-conscious. But experienced writers have usually so internalized the rhetorical elements of style they have adopted as theirs, that they exercise full conscious control primarily in revision, the process by which competent writing becomes beautiful. And here I offer four rules handed down to me by my English-professor father along with a ten-dollar bill, a bottle of pretty good whiskey, and a used bible. Wilson *pere's* Four Rules of Good Writing (which I all too often violate) are:

1. Never use a big word if a little one will do.
2. Never use two words if one will do.
3. Avoid the passive voice like the plague.
4. And let the verbs carry the load.

PRETTY BOY CROSSOVER

by Pat Cadigan

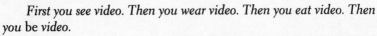

First you see video. Then you wear video. Then you eat video. Then you be video.

— The Gospel According to Visual Mark

Watch or Be Watched.

— Pretty Boy Credo

"Who made you?"

"You mean recently?"

Mohawk on the door smiles and takes his picture. "You in. But only you, okay? Don't try to get no friends in, hear that?"

"I hear. And I ain't no fool, fool. I got no friends."

Mohawk leers, leaning forward. "Pretty Boy like you, no friends?"

"Not in this world." He pushes past the Mohawk, ignoring the kissy-kissy sounds. He would like to crack the bridge of the Mohawk's nose and shove bone splinters into his brain but he is lately making more effort to control his temper and besides, he's not sure if any of that bone splinters in the brain stuff is really true. He's a Pretty Boy, all of sixteen years old, and tonight could be his last chance.

The club is Noise. Can't sneak into the bathroom for quiet, the Noise is piped in there, too. Want to get away from Noise? Why? No reason. But this Pretty Boy has learned to think between the beats. Like walking between the raindrops to stay dry, but he can do it. This Pretty Boy thinks things all the time—*all* the time. Subversive (and, he thinks so much that he knows that word *subversive*, sixteen, Pretty, or not). He thinks things like *how many Einsteins have died of hunger and thirst under a hot African sun* and *why can't you remember being born* and *why is music common to every culture* and especially *how much was there going on that he didn't know about and how could he find out about it.*

And this is all the time, one thing after another running in his head, you can see by his eyes. It's for def not much like a Pretty Boy but it's one reason why they want him. That he *is* a Pretty Boy is another and one reason why they're halfway home getting him.

He knows all about them. Everybody knows about them and everybody wants them to pause, look twice, and cough up a card that says, Yes, we see possibilities, please come to the following address during regular business hours on the next regular business day for regular further review. Everyone wants it but this Pretty Boy, who once got five cards in a night and tore them all up. But here he is, still a Pretty Boy. He thinks enough to know this is a failing in himself, that he likes being Pretty and chased and that is how they could end up getting him after all and that's b-b-b-bad. When he thinks about it, he thinks it with the stutter. B-b-b-bad. B-b-b-bad for him because he doesn't God help him want it, no, no, n-n-n-no. Which may make him the strangest Pretty Boy still live tonight and every night.

Still live and standing in the club where only the Prettiest Pretty Boys can get in any more. Pretty Girls are too easy, they've got to be better than Pretty and besides, Pretty Boys like to be Pretty all alone, no help thank you so much. This Pretty Boy doesn't mind Pretty Girls or any other kind of girls. Lately, though, he has begun to wonder how much longer it will be for him. Two years? Possibly a little longer? By three it will be for def over and the Mohawk on the door will as soon spit in his face as leer in it.

If they don't get to him.

And if they *do* get to him, then it's never over and he can be wherever he chooses to be and wherever that is will be the center of the universe. They promise it, unlimited access in your free hours and endless hot season, endless youth. Pretty Boy Heaven, and to get there, they say, you don't even really have to die.

He looks up to the dj's roost, far above the bobbing, boogieing crowd on the dance floor. They still call them djs even though they aren't discs any more, they're chips and there's more than just sound on a lot of them. The great hyper-program, he's been told, the ultimate of ultimates, a short walk from there to the fourth dimension. He suspects this stuff comes from low-steppers shilling for them, hoping they'll get auditioned if they do a good enough shuck job. Nobody knows what it's really like except the ones who are there and you can't trust them, he figures. Because maybe they *aren't*, any more. Not really.

The dj sees his Pretty upturned face, recognizes him even though it's been awhile since he's come back here. Part of it was wanting to stay away from them and part of it was that the thug on the door might not let him in. And then, of course, he *had* to come, to see if he could get in, to see if anyone still wanted him. What was the point of Pretty if there was nobody to care and watch and pursue? Even now, he is almost sure he can feel the room rearranging itself around his presence in it and the dj confirms this is true by holding up a chip and pointing it to the left.

They are squatting on the make-believe stairs by the screen, reminding him of pigeons plotting to take over the world. He doesn't look too long, doesn't want to give them the idea he'd like to talk. But as he turns away, one, the younger man, starts to get up. The older man and the woman pull him back.

He pretends a big interest in the figures lining the nearest wall. Some are Pretty, some are female, some are undecided, some are very bizarre, or wealthy, or just charity cases. They all notice him and adjust themselves for his perusal.

Then one end of the room lights up with color and new noise. Bodies dance and stumble back from the screen where images are forming to rough music.

It's Bobby, he realizes.

A moment later, there's Bobby's face on the screen, sixteen feet high, even Prettier than he'd been when he was loose among the mortals. The sight of Bobby's Pretty-Pretty face fills him with anger and dismay and a feeling of loss so great he would strike anyone who spoke Bobby's name without his permission.

Bobby's lovely slate-grey eyes scan the room. They've told him senses are heightened after you make the change and go over but he's not so sure how that's supposed to work. Bobby looks kind of blind up there on the screen. A few people wave at Bobby—the dorks they let in so the rest can have someone to be hip in front of—but Bobby's eyes move slowly back and forth, back and forth, and then stop, looking right at him.

"Ah . . ." Bobby whispers it, long and drawn out. "Aaaaaahhhh."

He lifts his chin belligerently and stares back at Bobby.

"You don't have to die anymore," Bobby says silkily. Music bounces under his words. "It's beautiful in here. The dreams can be as real as you want them to be. And if you want to be, you can be with me."

He knows the commercial is not aimed only at him but it doesn't matter. This is *Bobby*. Bobby's voice seems to be pouring over him, caressing him, and it feels too much like a taunt. The night before Bobby went over, he tried to talk him out of it, knowing it wouldn't work. If they'd actually refused him, Bobby would have killed himself, like Franco had.

But now Bobby would live forever and ever, if you believed what they said. The music comes up louder but Bobby's eyes are still on him. He sees Bobby mouth his name.

"Can you really see me, Bobby?" he says. His voice doesn't make it over the music but if Bobby's senses are so heightened, maybe he hears it anyway. If he does, he doesn't choose to answer. The music is a bumped up remix of a song Bobby used to party-till-he-puked to. The giant Bobby-face fades away to be replaced with a whole Bobby, somewhat larger than life, dancing better than the old Bobby ever could, whirling along changing scenes of streets, rooftops, and beaches. The locales are nothing special but Bobby never did have all that much imagination, never wanted to go to Mars or even to the South Pole, always just to the hottest club. Always he liked being the exotic in plain surroundings and he still likes it. He always loved to get the looks. To be watched, worshipped, pursued. Yeah. He can see this is Bobby-heaven. The whole world will be giving him the looks now.

The background on the screen goes from street to the inside of a club; *this* club, only larger, better, with an even hipper crowd, and Bobby shaking it with them. Half the real crowd is forgetting to dance now because they're watching Bobby, hoping he's put some of them into his video. Yeah, that's the dream, get yourself remixed in the extended dance version.

His own attention drifts to the fake stairs that don't lead anywhere. They're still perched on them, the only people who are watching *him* instead of Bobby. The woman, looking overaged in a purple plastic sac-suit, is fingering a card.

He looks up at Bobby again. Bobby is dancing in place and looking back at him, or so it seems. Bobby's lips move soundlessly but so precisely he can read the words: *This can be you. Never get old, never get tired, it's never last call, nothing happens unless you want it to and it could be you. You. You.* Bobby's hands point to him on the beat. *You. You. You.*

Bobby. Can you really see me?

Bobby suddenly breaks into laughter and turns away, shaking it some more.

He sees the Mohawk from the door pushing his way through the

crowd, the real crowd, and he gets anxious. The Mohawk goes straight
for the stairs, where they make room for him, rubbing the bristly red strip
of hair running down the center of his head as though they were greeting a favored pet. The Mohawk looks as satisfied as a professional glut-
ton after a foodrace victory. He wonders what they promised the Mohawk
for letting him in. Maybe some kind of limited contract. Maybe even a
try-out.

Now they are all watching him together. Defiantly, he touches a tall
girl dancing nearby and joins her rhythm. She smiles down at him, moving between him and them purely by chance but it endears her to him
anyway. She is wearing a flap of translucent rag over secondskins, like an
old-time showgirl. Over six feet tall, not beautiful with that nose, not even
pretty, but they let her in so she could be tall. She probably doesn't know
that; she probably doesn't know anything that goes on and never really
will. For that reason, he can forgive her the hard-tech orange hair.

A Rude Boy brushes against him in the course of a dervish turn, asking acknowledgement by ignoring him. Rude Boys haven't changed in
more decades than anyone's kept track of, as though it were the same little group of leathered and chained troopers buggering their way down
the years. The Rude Boy isn't dancing with anyone. Rude Boys never do.
But this one could be handy, in case of an emergency.

The girl is dancing hard, smiling at him. He smiles back, moving
slightly to her right, watching Bobby possibly watching him. He still
can't tell if Bobby really sees anything. The scene behind Bobby is still
a double of the club, getting hipper and hipper if that's possible. The
music keeps snapping back to its first peak passage. Then Bobby gestures
like God and he sees *himself.* He is dancing next to Bobby, Prettier than
he ever could be, just the way they promise. Bobby doesn't look at the
phantom but at him where he really is, lips moving again. *If you want to
be, you can be with me. And so can she.*

His tall partner appears next to the phantom of himself. She is also
much improved, though still not Pretty, or even pretty. The real girl turns
and sees herself and there's no mistaking the delight in her face. Queen
of the Hop for a minute or two. Then Bobby sends her image away so
that it's just the two of them, two Pretty Boys dancing the night away,
private party, stranger go find your own good time. How it used to be
sometimes in real life, between just the two of them. He remembers
hard.

"B-b-b-bobby!" he yells, the old stutter reappearing. Bobby's image seems to give a jump, as though he finally heard. He forgets everything, the girl, the Rude Boy, the Mohawk, them on the stairs, and plunges through the crowd toward the screen. People fall away from him as though they were re-enacting the Red Sea. He dives for the screen, for Bobby, not caring how it must look to anyone. What would they know about it, any of them. He can't remember in his whole sixteen years ever hearing one person say, *I love my friend.* Not Bobby, not even himself.

He fetches up against the screen like a slap and hangs there, face pressed to the glass. He can't see it now but on the screen Bobby would seem to be looking down at him. Bobby never stops dancing.

The Mohawk comes and peels him off. The others swarm up and take him away. The tall girl watches all this with the expression of a woman who lives upstairs from Cinderella and wears the same shoe size. She stares longingly at the screen. Bobby waves bye-bye and turns away.

"Of course, the process isn't reversible," says the older man. The steely hair has a careful blue tint; he has sense enough to stay out of hip clothes.

They have laid him out on a lounger with a tray of refreshments right by him. Probably slap his hand if he reaches for any, he thinks.

"Once you've distilled something to pure information, it just can't be reconstituted in a less efficient form," the woman explains, smiling. There's no warmth to her. *A less efficient form.* If that's what she really thinks, he knows he should be plenty scared of these people. Did she say things like that to Bobby? And did it make him even *more* eager?

"There may be no more exalted a form of existence than to live as sentient information," she goes on. "Though a lot more research must be done before we can offer conversion on a larger scale."

"Yeah?" he says. "Do they know that, Bobby and the rest?"

"Oh, there's nothing to worry about," says the younger man. He looks as though he's still getting over the pain of having outgrown his boogie shoes. "The system's quite perfected. What Grethe means is we want to research more applications for this new form of existence."

"Why not go over yourselves and do that, if it's so *exalted.*"

"There are certain things that need to be done on this side," the woman says bitchily. "Just because—"

"Grethe." The older man shakes his head. She pats her slicked-back hair as though to soothe herself and moves away.

"We have other plans for Bobby when he gets tired of being featured in clubs," the older man says. "Even now, we're educating him, adding more data to his basic information configuration—"

"That would mean he ain't really *Bobby* any more, then, huh?"

The man laughs. "Of course he's Bobby. Do you change into someone else every time you learn something new?"

"Can you prove I *don't?*"

The man eyes him warily. "Look. You *saw* him. Was that Bobby?"

"I saw a video of Bobby dancing on a giant screen."

"That *is* Bobby and it will remain Bobby no matter what, whether he's poured into a video screen in a dot pattern or transmitted the length of the universe."

"That what you got in mind for him? Send a message to nowhere and the message is him?"

"We could. But we're not going to. We're introducing him to the concept of higher dimensions. The way he is now, he could possibly break out of the three-dimensional level of existence, pioneer a whole new plane of reality."

"Yeah? And how do you think you're gonna get Bobby to do *that?*"

"We convince him it's entertaining."

He laughs. "That's a good one. Yeah. Entertainment. You get to a higher level of existence and you'll open a club there that only the hippest can get into. It figures."

The older man's face gets hard. "That's what all you Pretty Boys are crazy for, isn't it? Entertainment?"

He looks around. The room must have been a dressing room or something back in the days when bands had been live. Somewhere overhead he can hear the faint noise of the club but he can't tell if Bobby's still on. "You call this entertainment?"

"I'm tired of this little prick," the woman chimes in. "He's thrown away opportunities other people would kill for—"

He makes a rude noise. "Yeah, we'd all kill to be someone's data chip. You think I really believe Bobby's real just because I can see him on a *screen?*"

The older man turns to the younger one. "Phone up and have them pipe Bobby down here." Then he swings the lounger around so it faces a nice modern screen implanted in a shored-up cement-block wall.

"Bobby will join us shortly. Then he can tell you whether he's real or not himself. How will that be for you?"

He stares hard at the screen, ignoring the man, waiting for Bobby's image to appear. As though they really bothered to communicate regularly with Bobby this way. Feed in that kind of data and memory and Bobby'll believe it. He shifts uncomfortably, suddenly wondering how far he could get if he moved fast enough.

"My *boy*," says Bobby's sweet voice from the speaker on either side of the screen and he forces himself to keep looking as Bobby fades in, presenting himself on the same kind of lounger and looking mildly exerted, as though he's just come off the dance floor for real. "Saw you shakin' it upstairs awhile ago. You haven't been here for such a long time. What's the story?"

He opens his mouth but there's no sound. Bobby looks at him with boundless patience and indulgence. So Pretty, hair the perfect shade now and not a bit dry from the dyes and lighteners, skin flawless and shining like a healthy angel. Overnight angel, just like the old song.

"My *boy*," says Bobby. "Are you struck, like, shy or *dead?*"

He closes his mouth, takes one breath. "I don't like it, Bobby. I don't like it this way."

"Of course not, lover. You're the Watcher, not the Watchee, that's why. Get yourself picked up for a season or two and your disposition will *change.*"

"You really like it, Bobby, being a blip on a chip?"

"Blip on a chip, your ass. I'm a universe now. I'm, like, *everything*. And, hey, dig—I'm on every channel." Bobby laughed. "I'm happy I'm sad!"

"S-A-D," comes in the older man. "Self-Aware Data."

"Ooo-eee," he says. "Too clever for me. Can I get out of here now?"

"What's your hurry?" Bobby pouts. "Just because I went over you don't love me any more?"

"You always were screwed up about that, Bobby. Do you know the difference between being loved and being watched?"

"Sophisticated boy," Bobby says. "So wise, so learned. So fully packed. On this side, there *is* no difference. Maybe there never was. If you love me, you watch me. If you don't look, you don't care and if you don't care I don't matter. If I don't matter, I don't exist. Right?"

He shakes his head.

"No, my boy, I *am* right," Bobby laughs. "You believe I'm right, because if you *didn't*, you wouldn't come shaking your Pretty Boy ass in a place like *this*, now, would you? You *like* to be watched, get seen. You see me, I see you. Life goes on."

He looks up at the older man, needing relief from Bobby's pure Prettiness. "How does he see me?"

"Sensors in the equipment. Technical stuff, nothing you care about."

He sighs. He should be upstairs or across town, shaking it with everyone else, living Pretty for as long as he could. Maybe in another few months, this way would begin to look good to him. By then they might be off Pretty Boys and looking for some other type and there he'd be, out in the cold-cold, sliding down the other side of his peak and no one would *want* him. Shut out of something going on that he might want to know about after all. Can he face it? He glances at the younger man. All grown up and no place to glow. Yeah, but can *he* face it?

He doesn't know. Used to be there wasn't much of a choice and now that there is, it only seems to make it worse. Bobby's image looks like it's studying him for some kind of sign, Pretty eyes bright, hopeful.

The older man leans down and speaks low into his ear. "We need to get you before you're twenty-five, before the brain stops growing. A mind taken from a still-growing brain will blossom and adapt. Some of Bobby's predecessors have made marvelous adaptation to their new medium. Pure video: There's a staff that does nothing all day but watch and interpret their symbols for breakthroughs in thought. And we'll be taking Pretty Boys for as long as they're publicly sought-after. It's the most efficient way to find the best performers, go for the ones everyone wants to see or be. The top of the trend is closest to heaven. And even if you never make a breakthrough, you'll still be entertainment. Not such a bad way to live for a Pretty Boy. Never have to age, to be sick, to lose touch. You spent most of your life young, why learn how to be old? Why learn how to live without all the things you have now—"

He puts his hands over his ears. The older man is still talking and Bobby is saying something and the younger man and the woman come over to try to do something about him. Refreshments are falling off the tray. He struggles out of the lounger and makes for the door.

"Hey, my *boy*," Bobby calls after him. "Gimme a minute here, gimme what the problem is."

He doesn't answer. What can you tell someone made of pure information anyway?

There's a new guy on the front door, bigger and meaner than His Mohawkness but he's only there to keep people out, not to keep anyone *in*. You want to jump ship, go to, you poor un-hip asshole. Even if you are a Pretty Boy. He reads it in the guy's face as he passes from noise into the three A.M. quiet of the street.

They let him go. He doesn't fool himself about that part. They *let* him out of the room because they know all about him. They know he lives like Bobby lived, they know he loves what Bobby loved—the clubs, the admiration, the lust of strangers for his personal magic. He can't say he doesn't love that, because he *does*. He isn't even sure if he loves it more than he ever loved Bobby, or if he loves it more than being alive. Than being live.

And here it is, three A.M., clubbing prime time, and he is moving toward home. Maybe he *is* a poor un-hip asshole after all, no matter what he loves. Too stupid even to stay in the club, let alone grab a ride to heaven. Still he keeps moving, unbothered by the chill but feeling it. Bobby doesn't have to go home in the cold anymore, he thinks. Bobby doesn't even have to get through the hours between club-times if he doesn't want to. All times are now prime time for Bobby. Even if he gets unplugged, he'll never know the difference. Poof, it's a day later, poof, it's a year later, poof, you're out for good. Painlessly.

Maybe Bobby has the right idea, he thinks, moving along the empty sidewalk. If he goes over tomorrow, who will notice? Like when he left the dance floor—people will come and fill up the space. Ultimately, it wouldn't make any difference to anyone.

He smiles suddenly. Except *them*. As long as they don't have him, he makes a difference. As long as he has flesh to shake and flaunt and feel with, he makes a pretty goddamn big difference to *them*. Even after they don't want him any more, he will still be the one they didn't get. He rubs his hands together against the chill, feeling the skin rubbing skin, really *feeling* it for the first time in a long time, and he thinks about sixteen million things all at once, maybe one thing for

every brain cell he's using, or maybe one thing for every brain cell yet to
come.

He keeps moving, holding to the big thought, making a difference,
and all the little things they won't be making a program out of. He's light-
headed with joy—he doesn't know what's going to happen.

Neither do they.

THE S WORD
by Pat Cadigan

▼

The Catcher in the Rye is one of the most oft-cited examples of it. Cordwainer Smith's remains positively unique and unduplicated. Harlan Ellison is both famous and notorious for it. The British New Wave SF of the late 1960s is rife with its more experimental forms. Mainstream writer Jay McInerny successfully applied it in a way that normally gets a beginning writer flayed alive in the workshop. All the unreadable prose I've ever come across has been unreadable because of it.

You can't use it to fool anybody if you have no real story. But if you don't have a good one, or an appropriate one, even the most fascinating plot is rendered as blah as, say, a television set tuned to a dead channel — a phrase which, I'd say, puts the lie to the accusation that most cyberpunk (for lack of a better and equally well-known word) science fiction is the triumph of style over substance.

There, I finally said it. The dreaded S word: style.

Many SF readers — and a good number of writers — tend to clench up at the mention of the dreaded S word. For them, it would seem to suggest preposterous metaphors, overwrought similes, and strange tricks with typography that make reading an exercise in visual gymnastics.

And yet, if you surveyed their favorite stories and novels, I'd bet that all of them have a distinctive style. You can call it voice, or texture, or atmosphere, and it is all of those things. But it's also the entryway to the world of the story, and the conveyance that propels you through it; it's why you won't forget the last thing you see/hear/feel on your way out of that world.

Style, like time, is one of those ubiquitous intangibles that affects everything whether you want it to or not; you ignore it at your peril. Unlike time, however, style must be subordinate to the needs of your material. Form follows function and, in the most successful cases, makes it more than the sum of its parts.

What would *The Catcher in the Rye* be lacking the direct and colloquial voice of Holden Caulfield? Holden makes the novel the classic that it is—style working as characterization.

The style of John Brunner's visionary and monumental *Stand On Zanzibar*, on the other hand, is an example of style as setting. At various points throughout the book, Brunner gives us a series of quick cuts to inform us of the status and position of the main characters and many minor ones as well. This also reinforces our perception of Brunner's future world, a high-tech hyperactive reality watching itself on its own various media. Even more striking, though, is how it portrays channel-surfing a good dozen years before such a thing became routine. But while Brunner's style keeps the story both vivid and fast-paced, it does so by not being personal and familiar. It is as unblinking, impersonal, and merciless as the steady, cold gaze of a surveillance camera.

My own short story, "Pretty Boy Crossover," is told in the same type of slangy language the characters speak, but at the remove of third person. I wanted the reader to see, feel, and hear the textures of the Boy's world but at the same time, I wanted it to remain a strange and uncomfortable place, a distortion of the familiar. I also wanted a sense of immediacy, happening now and now and now, before your very eyes, so I tried present tense rather than past tense. The story rolled itself out, which told me I had made the right choice.

Actually, I'm making it sound like choosing a style for "Pretty Boy Crossover" was far more considered than it actually was. Ideas come to writers in various ways, often at the strangest times, and frequently the style of the story will suggest itself as the idea unfolds in the mind.

But suppose that for some reason, this doesn't happen. Say you have an idea, a situation, even a whole plot, but every time you start to make a beginning, the damned thing just won't come to life for you. At a time like this, I recommend breaking a rule or two, or twenty. No one will know what you write in private, so it doesn't matter if it's a mess. Try anything, try everything; try the kinds of voices writing instructors always warn against using. The only way to hear your voice is to use it, and the only way to discover the telling of a story is to go ahead and start telling it. If you get it wrong, you'll know to start over.

▼

Some writers seem to be capable of a broad range of styles over an equally broad range of stories, while others appear to have hit on the style most useful to them and so decided to stick with it. Wondering which is better is a bit like wondering which kind of fingerprints are better, whorls or lines—or perhaps which kind of story itself is better. I submit that while this last may be a subjective judgment, there is a best kind of style. And once again, that is the style that serves the story best.

Ultimately, of course, it is up to the writer to decide what sort of voice suits the story in question. If the style calls attention to itself; if, in the course of the story, the writer has been so self-indulgent that readers can sense the auctorial self-gratification that the late John Gardner called the "Look-Ma-how-good-I'm-writing" syndrome; if we feel that the writer told us everything but showed us nothing, the style has defeated the story and defeated the whole point of writing something in the first place.

On the other hand, if the story displays its plot and creates what I think of as the inner-eye theater, if the words draw the reader into the story, propel the reader through the story, yet seem to disappear for the duration of the story, you can be certain that the style did its job.

While style is an important consideration to the writer, it should be the last thing that the reader would think to comment on. When readers comment on your wonderful plots, your strong characterization, and your realistic action and outcome without mentioning your style, then your style has served its purpose, and your story is successful.

Everything else is gravy.

FAIR GAME

by Howard Waldrop

▼

"AN OLD MAN IS A NASTY THING."

He heard church bells ringing anxiously on the wind.

He felt the cool air on his skin.

He saw the valley spread out below him like a giant shell.

It was a valley he had known, thirty-five or forty years ago, when he had been there for the skiing. It was a small valley in Bavaria, with its small town. He had never seen it in this season, having been here only in winter. This was spring. Patches of snow still lay in the shade, but everything was greening, the air was a robin-egg blue above the hovering mountains.

He was on the road into town, moving toward the sound of the bells. He lifted his eyes up a little past the village (the glare hurt them, but in the last few years so had all bright lights). Through a slight haze he saw a huge barn, far off on the road leading out the other side of the town.

He looked quickly back down at his feet. He did not like looking at the barn.

He noticed his boots, his favorites, the ones he had hunted in until two years ago when his body had turned on him after all the years he had punished it, when he couldn't hunt anymore. When he could no longer crouch down for the geese in the blinds, he had taken to walking up pheasant and chukar. But then even that ability had left him, like everything else he ever had.

Walking toward the town was tiring. His pants were that tattered old pair from the first hunt in Africa, the one the book came out of. He had kept those pants in the bottom of an old trunk filled with zebra hides.

He put his hands to his broad chest and felt a flannel shirt and his fishing vest. It was the one he'd been wearing in that picture with the two trout and the big smile, taken the first time he'd come to Idaho.

He felt his face as he walked. His beard was still scraggly on his chin. He reached up and felt the big lump on his forehead, the one he'd gotten when he'd butted his way through a jammed cabin door, out of a burning airplane, his second plane crash in two days seven years before.

His hat was the big-billed marlin cap from the days of Cuba and Bimini and Key West, back when everything was good: the writing, the hunting and fishing, the wives, the booze.

He remembered that morning in Idaho when he was in his bathrobe, just back from the hospital, and both the house and the shotgun had been still and cool.

Now he was walking down the hill toward the ruckus in town, dressed in odds and ends of his old clothing. It was a fine spring morning in the mountains half a world away.

Many houses stood with doors open, all the people now at the town square. Still, the pealing of the bells echoed off the surrounding peaks.

From way off to the left he could hear the small flat bells of cattle being driven toward him, and the shouts of the people who herded them.

A woman came from a house and ran past him without a glance, toward the milling people and voices ahead.

A child looked down at him from one of the high third-story windows, the ones you sometimes had to climb out of in the winter if you wanted to go outside at all.

He was winded from the half-mile walk into town.

The crowd stood looking toward the church doors, perhaps three hundred people in all, men, women, a few of the children.

The bells stopped ringing, slowed their swings, stopped in the high steeple. The doors opened up, and the priest and bürgermeister came out onto the broad steps.

The crowd waited.

"There he is," said the priest.

Heads turned, the crowd parted, and they opened a path for him to the steps. He walked up to the priest and the mayor.

"Ernst," said the bürgermeister. "We're so glad you came."

"I'm a little confused," he heard himself say.

"The Wild Man?" said the priest. "He's come down into the villages again. He killed two more last night and carried off a ram three men couldn't lift. Didn't you get our cablegram?"

"I don't think so," he said.

"We sent for you to come hunt him for us. Some townspeople remembered you from the Weimar days, how you hunted and skied here. You're the only man for the job. This Wild Man is more dangerous than any before has ever been."

Ernst looked around at the crowd. "I used to hunt in the old days, and ski. I can't do either anymore. It's all gone, all run out on me."

It hurt him to say those things aloud, words he had said over and over to himself for the last two years, but which he had told only two people in the world before.

The faces in the crowd were tense, waiting for him or the official to say something, anything.

"Ernst!" pleaded the bürgermeister, "you are the only man who can do it. He has already killed Brunig, the great wolf hunter from Axburg. We are devastated."

Ernst shook his head slowly. It was no use. He could not pretend to himself or these people. He would be less than useless. They would put a faith in him when he knew better than to put any hopes in himself.

"Besides," said the young priest, "someone has come to help you do this great thing."

Somebody moved in the crowd, stepped forward. It was a withered old black man, dressed in a loincloth and khaki shirt. On its sleeve was a shoulder patch of the Rangers of the Ngorongoro Crater Park, and from the left pocket hung the string of a tobacco pouch.

"Bwana," he said, with a gap-toothed smile.

Ernst had not seen him in thirty years. It was Mgoro, his gunbearer from that first time in Africa.

"Mgoro," he said, taking the old man's hands and wrists, shaking them.

He turned to the officials.

"If he's come all this way, I guess we'll have to hunt this Wild Man together," said Ernst. He smiled uneasily.

The people cheered, the priest said a prayer of thanksgiving, and the mayor took him and Mgoro inside his house.

▼

Later they took them to a home on the south side of town. The house looked as if a howitzer shell had hit one corner of it. Ernst saw that it wasn't exploded. The thin wall of an outbuilding had been pulled off, and a window clawed out from what had been a child's bedroom.

"The undertaker," said the mayor, "is sewing the arms and legs back on. His mother heard him scream and came down to see what was wrong. They found her half a kilometer from here. When the Wild Man got through with her, he tossed her down and picked up the sheep.

"We tried to follow his trail earlier this morning. He must live in the caves on the other side of the mountain. We lost his trail in the rocks."

Ernst studied the tracks in the dirt of the outbuilding, light going in, sunken and heavy-laden coming out with the woman. They were huge, oddly shaped, missing one of the toes on the left foot. But they were still the prints of a giant barefoot man.

"I'll hunt him," said Ernst, "if you'll put some men up by that barn on the edge of town. I don't want him running near there." He looked down, eyes not meeting those of the bürgermeister.

"We can put some men up there with shotguns," said the priest. "I doubt he'll go close with the smell of many men there. If you want us to."

"Yes. Yes, I do want that."

"Let's go to your guns, then," said the mayor.

▼

"We have a few small bore rifles and shotguns for the men of the village," said the priest, "but these are the heaviest. We saved them for you."

Ernst took his glasses out of his pocket, noticing they were the new bifocals he'd gotten for reading after those plane crashes in '54. He looked the weapons over.

One was a Weatherby .575 bolt action, three-shot magazine with a tooled stock and an 8X scope. He worked the bolt; smooth, but still a bolt action.

"Scope comes off, eh, bwana?" asked Mgoro.

"Yes. And check the shells close."

The second was an eight-gauge shotgun, its shells the size of small sticks of dynamite. Ernst looked in the boxes, pulled out a handful each of rifled slugs and 00 shot. He put the slugs in the left bottom pocket of his fishing vest, the shotshells in the right.

The third was an ancient wheel-lock boar gun. Its inlaid silver and gilt work had once been as bright and intricate as the rigging on a clipper ship, but was now faded and worn. Part of the wood foregrip that had run the length of the barrel was missing. Its muzzle was the size of the exhaust pipe on a GMC truck.

"We shall have to check this thing very well," said Ernst.

"That gun was old when Kilimanjaro was a termite mound," said Mgoro.

Ernst smiled. "Perhaps," he said. "I'd also like a pistol each for Mgoro and me," he said to the mayor. "Anything, even .22's.

"And now, while Mgoro goes over these guns, I'd like to read. Do you have books? I used to have to bring my own when I came for the skiing."

"At the parish house," said the priest. "Many books, on many things."

"Good."

He sat at the desk where the priest wrote his sermons, and he read in the books again about the Wild Men.

Always, when he had been young and just writing, they had thought he was a simple writer, communicating his experience with short declarative sentences for the simple ideas he had.

Maybe that was so, but he had always read a lot, and knew more than he let on. The Indian-talk thing had first been a pose, then a defense, and at the last, a curse.

He had known of the Wild Men for a long time. There used to be spring festivals in Germany and France, and in the Pyrenees, in which men dressed in hairy costumes and covered themselves with leaves and carried huge clubs in a shuffling dance.

In Brueghel's painting, *The Battle Between Carnival and Lent*, one of his low-perspective canvases full of the contradictions of carnival, you can see a Wild Man play going on in the upper left corner, the Wild Man player looking like a walking cabbage with a full head of shaggy hair.

The Wild Men—feral men, abandoned children who grew up in solitary savagery, or men who went mad—became hirsute. Lichens and moss grew on their bodies. They were the outlaws who haunted the dreams of the Middle Ages. All that was inside the village or the manor house was Godmade and good, everything outside was a snare of the devil.

More than the wolf or the bear, the serf feared the Wild Man, the unchained human without conscience who came to take what he wanted, when he wanted.

Ernst was reading Bernheimer's book again, and another on Wild Man symbolism in the art of the Middle Ages and the Renaissance. All they had agreed upon was that there had been Wild Men and that they had been used in decorative arts and were the basis of spring festivals. All this Ernst remembered from his earlier reading.

He took off his glasses and rubbed the bridge of his nose, felt again the bump above his eye.

What was the Wild Man? he asked himself. This thing of the woods and crags—it's nothing but man unfettered, unrestrained by law and civilization. Primitive, savage man. Rousseau was wrong—let man go and he turns not into the Noble Savage but into pure chaos, the chaos of Vico, of the totem fathers. Even Freud was wrong about that—the totem fathers, if they were Wild Men, would never compete with their offspring. They would eat them at birth, like Kronos.

What about this Wild Man, then? Where did he stay during the day? On what did he live when not raiding the towns? How do you find him, hunt him?

Ernst went back to the books. He found no answers there.

Mgoro said, "We are ready."

It was dusk. The sun had fallen behind the mountains. What warmth the day had had evaporated almost instantly. Ernst had taken a short nap. He had wakened feeling older and more tired than he had for years, worse than he had felt after the shock therapy in the hospital, where you woke not knowing where you were or who you were.

The other men had gone to places around the village, posted in the outlying structures, within sight and sound of each other, with clear fields of vision and fire toward the looming mountains.

Four others, with him and Mgoro, set out in the direction the Wild Man had taken that morning. They showed Ernst the rocky ground where the misshapen footprints ended.

"He'll be up and moving already," said Ernst. "Are the dogs ready?"

"They're coming now," said the bürgermeister. Back down the trail they heard men moving toward them. "Are we to try to drive him out with them?"

"No," said Ernst. "That's what he'll be expecting. I only want him to think about them. The most likely place he'll be is the caves?"

"Yes, on the other side of the mountain. It's very rocky there."

"Take the dogs over that way, then. Make as much noise as you can, and keep them at it all night, if need be. If they come across his spoor, so much the better. It would be good if they could be made to bark."

Three hounds and a Rottweiler bounded up, straining at their leashes, whimpering with excitement. The man holding them doffed his cap to the bürgermeister.

"Ernst would like to know if you can make the dogs howl all night, Rudolf."

The man put a small whistle to his mouth and blew a soundless note. The four dogs began to bark and whine as if a stag had stepped on them.

Ernst laughed for the first time in many months.

"That will do nicely," he said. "If they don't find anything, blow on that every quarter hour. Good luck."

The dogs, Rudolf, the bürgermeister, and the others started up the long trail that would take them around the mountain. Night was closing in.

"Where do you think he is?" asked Mgoro.

"Back down a quarter mile," said Ernst, "is where we should wait. He'll either pass us coming down, or back on the way up if they spot him in the village."

"I think so too," said Mgoro. "Though this is a man, not lion or leopard."

"I have to keep telling myself that," said Ernst.

"Moon come up pretty soon," said Mgoro. "Damn mountains too high, or already be moonlight."

"It's the full moon that does it maybe," said Ernst. "Drives them to come into the towns."

"You think he crazy man? From last war?"

"The bürgermeister said this is the first Wild Man attack since before the war, from before that paperhanging sonofabitch took over."

Mgoro wrapped a blanket around himself, the shotgun, the wheel-lock. Ernst carried the Weatherby across his arm. It was already getting heavy.

The outline of the mountains turned silvery with the light from the rising, still unseen moon.

Then from up the side of the mountain, the dogs began to bark.

Nothing happened after they reached the ravine where they would wait. The dogs barked, farther and farther away, their cries carried on the still, cool air of the valley.

Lights were on in the town below. Ernst was too far away to see the men standing guard in the village itself, or what was happening in the church where most of the women and children waited.

Mgoro sat in his blanket. Ernst leaned against a rock, peering into the dark upper reaches of the ravine. The moonlight had frosted everything silver and gold, with deep shadows. He would have preferred an early, westering moon lighting this side of the mountain. This one was too bright and you had to look into it. Anything could be hiding in the shadowed places. It would be better later, when the moon was overhead, or west.

The dogs barked again, still farther away. Maybe this moon was best. If they ran anything up on that side, the men over there could see it, too.

"Bwana," said Mgoro, sniffing the air. "Snow coming."

Ernst breathed deeply, sniffed. He was seized with coughing, quieted himself, choked, coughed again. His eyes stung, tears streamed down his face. He rubbed them away.

"Damn," he said. "Can't smell it yet. How long?"

"Don't know this land. One, mebbe two hours away."

Just what we need, a spring blizzard, Ernst thought.

An hour passed. Still they had bright moonlight. They heard the sound of the dogs far off. Nothing had come down the ravine. There had been no alarm from the town.

Ernst's back was knotted. His weak legs had gone to sleep several times. He'd had to massage them back to stinging life.

Mgoro sat in his blanket, the gun barrels made him look like a teepee in the moonlight. Ernst had seen him sit motionless for hours this way at waterholes, waiting for eland, wildebeest, lions. He was the best gun-bearer Ernst had ever seen.

Something about Mgoro was gnawing at the back of Ernst's mind.

Ernst looked around, back down at the village. There were fewer lights now (the guards had been turning off a few at a time). He looked at the church, and he looked farther across the valley at the huge barn, a blot on the night.

He looked away, back up the ravine.

He thought something was wrong, then realized it was the light.

He looked up. High streaked cirrus raced across the moon. As he watched, it changed to altocumulus and the moon dimmed more. A dark, thicker bank slid in under that, blotting the stars to the north.

In ten minutes the sky was solidly overcast and huge, wet flakes of snow began to fall.

Two hours into the storm, Mgoro sat up, his head turned sideways. Snow already covered the lower part of his blanket, merging with the wet line of melted snow against the upper part of his body.

His finger pointed left of the ravine.

Ernst could barely make out Mgoro, much less anything further away.

But they heard it snuffling in the wet air as it went by down the rugged gully.

They waited. Ernst had eased the safety off the .575. But the sound grew fainter, continued on toward the village.

For an instant, Ernst smelled something in the air—sweat, dirt, mold, wet leaves, oil?—then it was gone. The thing must have missed their scent altogether.

The snow swirled down for another ten minutes, then stopped as abruptly as it had begun.

Another five minutes and the moon was out, bright and to the west, shining down on a transformed world of glass and powder.

The thing had come by close.

When they turned to look down the ravine they could see the shad-owed holes of the footprints leading in a line down toward the town. The end of the tracks was still more than a kilometer from the village. They strained their eyes, then Ernst took out a pair of night binoculars, passed them to Mgoro. He scanned the terrain past where the footprints disappeared near a road.

He shook his head, handed them back.

Ernst put them to his eyes. It was too bright to make out anything through the glasses—the snow threw back too much glare, made the shadows too dark.

"If he decides not to go in, he'll come back this way," said Ernst.

"If we shoot to warn them, he go anywhere," said Mgoro.

"If nothing happens in the next hour, we follow his tracks," said Ernst.

The moon was dropping to the right of the village. Ernst checked his watch. Fifty minutes had passed.

If they stayed, they had the high ground, command of the terrain. They would be able to see him coming.

If they tracked him, and the Wild Man got above them, he could wait for them anywhere.

Do I treat this like stalking a lion, or following an airborne ranger? Ernst asked himself. He moved in place, getting the circulation back in his leg, the one with the busted kneecap and the shrapnel from three wars back.

He didn't want the Wild Man to get too far ahead of them. It could have circled the town and gone up the other side of the valley, sensing something wrong, or not wanting to leave tracks in the snow. Or it could be holed up just ahead, watching and waiting.

The dogs barked again. Now they sounded nearer, and they were holding the tone. They must have crossed the Wild Man's path somewhere and were trailing him now.

Ernst felt his pulse rise, like you do when beagles begin to circle, indicating the rabbit somewhere ahead of you is coming your way, or when a setter goes on point, all tense, and you ready yourself for the explosion of quail.

Shouts from the village cut across his reverie. Shots followed, and banging on pots and pans. The bells began to toll rapidly.

Mgoro stood against a rock so as to give no silhouette to anything down the ravine. Lights went on in town, flashlight beams swung up and around. They converged toward this side of town. Lights crossed the field and came toward the ravine, with sporadic small arms fire. The sounds from the town grew louder, like an angry hornet's nest.

Mgoro pointed.

Far down, where the footprints had ended, there was a movement. It was only a blur against the snow, a dull change in the moonlit background, but it was enough.

Mgoro dropped the blanket from his shoulders, held the shotgun and wheel-lock, one in each hand, two feet to the side and one foot back of Ernst.

The movement came again, much closer than it should have been for so close a space of time, then again, closer still.

First it was a shape, then a man-shape.

It stopped for a few seconds, then came on in a half-loping ape shamble.

Behind and below, flashlight beams reached the far end of the ravine and were starting up, slowly, voices still too indistinct with the distance.

Now the shape moved from one side of the gully to the other, running. Now it was two hundred meters away in the moonlight. Now a hundred. Eighty.

It was too big for a man.

The baying of the dogs, up the mountain behind Ernst, got louder.

The man-shape stopped.

Ernst brought the Weatherby up, held his breath, squeezed.

The explosion was loud, louder than he remembered, but he worked the bolt as the recoil brought the muzzle up. He brought the sights back down, centered them on the gully before the shell casing hit the ground.

There had been a scream with the shot. Whatever had screamed was gone. The ravine was empty.

He and Mgoro ran down the gully.

It had jumped three meters between one set of prints and the next, and there was a spray of blood four meters back. A high hit, then. Maybe, thought Ernst, as they ran up out of the ravine to the left, maybe we'll find him dead twenty meters from here.

But the stride stayed long, the drops in the snow far apart.

Ernst's lungs were numb. He could hardly breathe in enough air to keep going. His legs threatened to fold, and he realized what he was— an old, half-crippled man trying to run down something that was twice his size, wounded and mad.

Mgoro was just behind him. His lungs labored, too, but still he held both guns where he could hand them to Ernst in seconds.

The flashlights and lanterns from the town headed across the front of the village, between the town and the Wild Man. Behind Ernst and Mgoro, the dogs neared in the ravine.

Ernst and Mgoro slowed. The footprints were closer together now, and there was a great clot of blood that seemed to have been coughed up. Internal bleeding maybe, thought Ernst, maybe a better shot than I thought I could ever make again.

The moon was on the edge of the far mountain. They would lose the light for a while, but it should be nearing dawn.

The tracks led in an arc toward the roadway south of the village. Lights from the men in town and those halfway up the hill led that way.

They heard the dogs behind them, whining with urgency when they came to the place of the hit. Now they left the ravine and came straight behind the two men.

"Off the tracks. Off!" puffed Ernst. He grabbed Mgoro, pulled him five paces down the mountainside.

In a moment the dogs flashed by, baying, running full speed. As they passed, the last of the direct moonlight left the valley. The dogs ran on into darkness.

"Come," said Mgoro, through gritted teeth. "We have him."

They heard the dogs catch up to the Wild Man. One bark ended in a squeal, another just ended. Two dogs continued on, and the sound of the pursuit moved down the valley.

Ernst ran on, his feet and chest like someone else's.

He realized that the Wild Man was heading toward the barn. When Ernst was thirteen, up in Michigan one summer, he got lost. It was the last time in his life he was ever lost.

He had been fishing, and had a creel full of trout. But he had crossed three marshy beaver ponds that morning, skirted some dense woods getting to the fishing. On the way back he had taken a wrong turn. It was that easy to get lost.

He had wandered for two hours trying to find his way back to his own incoming tracks.

Just at dusk, he came to a clearing and saw in front of him a huge barn, half-gone in ruin. He wondered at it. There was no house with it. It was in the middle of the Michigan woods. There were no animals around, and looked as if there never had been.

He walked closer.

Someone stepped from around one corner, someone dressed in a long grey cloak, wearing a death's head mask.

Ernst stopped, stunned.

The thing reached down inside its cloak and exposed a long, diseased penis to him.

"Hey, you, Bright Boy," it said. "Suck on this."

Ernst dropped his rod, his creel, and ran in a blind panic until he came out on the road less than half a mile from the cabin his family had rented.

One dog still barked. They had found the other three on the way. Two dead, torn up and broken. The third had run until it had given out. It lay panting in a set of tracks, pointing the way with its body like an arrow.

Now the sky to the east was lighter. Ernst began to make things out—the valley floor, the lights of the men as they ran, the great barn up ahead beside the road.

Something ran through a break in the woods, the sound of the dog just behind it.

Ernst stopped, threw the .575 to his shoulder, fired. A vip of snow flew up just over the thing's shoulder, and it was gone into the woods again. The dog flashed through the opening.

Ernst loaded more shells in.

The great barn was a kilometer ahead when they found the last dog pulled apart like warm red taffy.

Ernst slid to a stop. The prints crossed a ditch, went up the other side, blood everywhere now.

Ernst jumped into the ditch just as he realized the prints were doubled, had been trodden over by something retracing its steps.

He tried to stop himself from going just as Mgoro, on the bank behind him, saw the prints and yelled.

Ernst's arms windmilled, he let go of the rifle, fell heavily, caught a rock with his fingers, slipped, his bad knee crashing into the bottom of the ditch.

Dull pain shot through him. He pulled himself to his other knee.

The Wild Man charged.

It had doubled back, jumped off into a stand of small trees fifty feet up the ditch. Now it had them.

The Weatherby was half-hidden in the ditch snow. Did he have time to get it? Was the action ready? Was the safety off? Was there snow in the barrel and would it explode like an axed watermelon in his hands when he fired?

Not on my knees, Ernst thought, and stood up.

"Gun!" he said, just as Mgoro slammed the shotgun butt down into his right shoulder from the bank above.

Ernst let the weight of the barrels bring the eight-gauge into line. He was already cocking both hammers as his left arm slid up the foregrip.

The Wild Man was teeth and beard and green-grey hair in front of him as the barrels came level with its chest.

Ernst pulled both triggers.

All the moments come down to this. All the writing and all the books and the fishing and the hunting and the bullfights. All the years of banging yourself around and being beaten half the time.

The barrels leaped up with recoil.

All the years of living by your code. Good is what makes you feel good. A man has to do what a man has to do.

A huge red spot appeared on the Wild Man's shoulder as the slug hit and the right hand, which had been reaching for Ernst, came loose and flew through the air behind the buckshot.

Ernst let the shotgun fall.

"Gun!" he said.

And then you get old and hurt and scared, and the writing doesn't work anymore, and the sex is gone and booze doesn't help, and you can't hunt or fish, all you have is fame and money and there's nothing to buy.

Mgoro put the butt of the wheel-lock against his shoulder.

The Wild Man's left hand was coming around like a claw, reaching for Ernst's eyes, his face, reaching for the brain inside his head.

Ernst pulled the trigger-lever, the wheel spun in a ratcheting blur, the powder took with a *floopth* and there was an ear-shattering roar.

Then they take you to a place and try to make you better with electricity and drugs and it doesn't make you better, it makes you worse and you can't do anything anymore, and nobody understands but you, that you don't want anything anymore.

Ernst lies under a shaggy wet weight that reeks of sweat and mushrooms. He is still deaf from the explosion. The wheel-lock is wedged sideways against his chest, the wheel gouging into his arm. He pushes and pulls, twisting his way out from under, slipping on the bloody rocks.

Mgoro is helping him, pulling his shoulders.

"It is finished," he says.

Ernst stands, looking down at the still-twitching carcass. Blood runs from jagged holes you can see the bottom of the ditch through. It is eight feet tall, covered with lichen and weeds, matted hair, and dirt.

Now it is dead; this thing that was man gone mad, man without law, like all men would be if they had nothing to hold them back.

And one day they let you out of the place because you've acted nice, and you go home with your wife, and you sing to her and she goes to sleep and next morning at dawn you go downstairs in your bathrobe and you go to your gun cabinet and you take out your favorite, the side-by-side double barrel your actor friend gave you before he died and you put it on the floor and you lean forward until the barrels are a cool infinity mark on your forehead . . .

Ernst stands and looks at the big barn only a kilometer away, and he looks at Mgoro, who, he knows now, has been dead more than thirty years, and Mgoro smiles at him.

Ernst looks at the barn and knows he will begin walking toward it in just a moment, he and Mgoro, but still there is one more thing he has to do.

He reaches down, pulling, and slowly turns the Wild Man over, face up.

The hair is matted, ragged holes torn in the neck and chest and stomach, the right arm missing from the elbow down.

The beard is tangled, thick and bloody. Above the beard is the face, twisted.

And Ernst knows that it is his face on the Wild Man, the face of the thing he has been hunting all his life.

He stands then, and takes Mgoro's arm, and they start up the road toward the barn.

The light begins to fade, though it is crisp morning dawn. Ernst knows they will make the barn before the light gives out completely.

And above everything, over the noise of the church bells back in town, above the yelling, jubilant voices of the running people, there is a long, slow, far-off sound, like the boom of surf crashing onto a shore.

Or maybe it is just the sound of both triggers being pulled at once.

ICEBERG, GOLDBERG, IT'S ALL
THE SAME TO ME. . . .
by Howard Waldrop

▼

Being a literary chameleon ain't easy.

By literary chameleon, I don't mean someone who can imitate the style or phrasing or outward trappings of a certain writer or writers.

I mean (and this is the ideal) that they can alter their points of view, types of characters, levels of diction and phrasing to tell, in the best possible way, the exact story that needs to be told.

The SF and fantasy field has had, historically, about three: Henry Kuttner, the early Robert Silverberg, and Theodore Sturgeon.

The first two are special cases; their chameleonhood was an adjunct of their special status as Demon Writers who turned out, at their heights, a "mere" million words or so a year.

Kuttner was so busy he was more famous as his pen names than his own; the standard thought was that Henry Kuttner was a competent writer, but that Lewis Padgett and Lawrence O'Donnell were wows. (Sometimes Padgett was Kuttner and his wife C.L. Moore, sometimes not.) It got so bad that when Jack Vance came along, everybody thought *he* was another Kuttner pseudonym.

The early Robert Silverberg, by his own admission, could turn out anything, at any length, in any style, to anybody who paid anything. Both Kuttner and Silverberg made a lot of money, and a lot of that was at a penny a word.

Kuttner literally dropped dead after doing it for twenty years. Silverberg closed down (in someone's words) the literary sausage factory but continued on as a literary chameleon (at the "reduced" rate of less than half a million words a year) in truth, in the stories and novels that made him the absolute best writer in the field from the mid 1960s to the late '70s.

Theodore Sturgeon was the true chameleon from the beginning. He instinctively chose the right *everything*—point of view, incident, episode, even the exact right words, to tell a story.

(Go right now and pick up some of his collections, if they're still in print. Read, say, "It" and then "Killdozer!" and "The [Widget], the [Wadget] and Boff" and ask yourself, why were there three people named Theodore Sturgeon all writing at the same time?)

I've been accused of being like Theodore Sturgeon.

No, not because I'm some kind of corn-fed genius like he could sometimes be, but because: 1) both of us take a real long time sometimes to write a story, and 2) neither of us ever made a lot of money in this business.

If you're just the garden variety lit. cham. (as opposed to lit. cham. and demon writer), you won't. Be warned.

This field, SF, fantasy, spec fic, *realismo magico norteamericano*, whatever they're calling it this week, for all its insistence on its cutting edge, its ground-breaking, its meaningfulness; this field positively thrives on sameness.

Nowhere is this more apparent than in the matter of style.

What readers want more than anything (even another rewrite of Tolkein) is the same style from their favorite writers telling them their favorite type of stories, whether it's appropriate or not.

Some writers' styles work only with stories that need to be told by sleazy con men in the first person. *That* doesn't work for stories that need to be told by Martians in the second person plural, or by an omniscient narrator in the third person future conditional. Like as not, you read a story crying out for Martian narrative from the hive-nest, and there'll be Throwout Jones telling it to you. . . .

If *one* style could cover all this, and pull the old literary plow, we would only *have* one style. Since we don't, it doesn't. *Tertio et Q.E.D.*

Let's get a few things out of the way first before we get to the nougat of this concoction, which is style. This story, "Fair Game," was written on the (up till then) worst night of my life in the large closet I used for an office at the time. I'd been thinking about the story, and reading up on it for a long time (long time = 10 years). It was only when I'd recently done research on the Wild Men of the Woods (one has a minor role in my "What Makes Hieronymus Run?") that I had the thing I knew would make the story work. That, and the events of that godawful night, made me go in, turn on the light, and write this between eleven P.M. and seven the next morning. (One answer to "How long did it take you to write 'Fair Game'?" is "Eight Hours," the other is "Ten years, eight hours, and however long it takes a brain to fry itself out.") There was a rewrite the next afternoon, but this is pretty much the way it came out. The story was written for, and appeared in Pamela Sargent and Ian Watson's *Afterlives*, an anthology of after-death stories. Sometime in the publishing process, long after the book was scheduled, a minor editor at the publisher wanted changes in the story, feeling "I hadn't been fair to the protagonist" (whom they'd evidently known). Pam and Ian were ready to pull the book if it came to that. I said, "Wait." I sent the book editor a list of the thirty-five books, a recording, and two videotapes I'd used lately in the research of the story, and said "Call me back after you read these; we'll talk." The story was printed exactly as Watson and Sargent had accepted it (they're the heroes of this anecdote, not me), and I had a nice apology from the editor-in-chief at the publisher for the whole incident.

▼

Which brings us, slowly, to Hemingway the man and writer.

The fascinating (and cautionary) lesson for any writer is not exemplified by the career (it was the most public literary career anyone had ever had up to that time) or the craft (we'll talk about that later, but I might as well say it here: He changed the way the short story was written, for good or bad, for fifty years).

It is the dying fall, the one perceived only in retrospect—how could somebody so good go so bad so quick? And was the suicide, so to speak, the last squeal of the talent on the way out of the room?

(Several books that have come out since the story was written, like Tom Dardis' *The Thirsty Muse*, tell us that the drinking, if nothing else, had gotten so heavy it would have killed a water buffalo; and that the accumulation of old war and accident wounds and illnesses, especially the two airplane crashes in two days in Africa in 1954, did more harm than anyone, even the writer, knew or would admit.)

Part of the public career as a literary he-man is that you can grimace as you limp, but you can't talk about it except as a joke.

But what's the literary equivalent of a grimace when you can't write anymore, either?

When you have bought your *own* load of hooey, you know exactly what it's worth.

Now, let's talk about style.

When I knew, intellectually at least, that I was going to write this story, one of the few things I promised myself, is that I would not do what everybody else did.

What everybody else did, when they wrote a story about Hemingway (there are *very* many) was try to write it *like* Hemingway.

This is a Bozo No-No.

That's what the Bad Hemingway contest is, and that's also why people find out even the Bad Hemingway Contest is not easy. ("Now we must go into the tall grass to finish the wounded *simba* which is the typewriter." "The novel came up and made two long jumps, heavy against the rod, and pulled toward the tangled snags of the literary quarterlies. . . ."

(There is a big difference between writing "a Hemingway story" and "a story about Hemingway." Since "Fair Game" I've written both "a story about Thomas Wolfe" and "a Damon Runyon story.")

The things that make up "the Hemingway style" are:

1. Fairly simple declarative sentences held together with conjunctions.

2. Use of words that are concrete, which also carry some extra freight.

3. Totally commonplace (but because of context) unexpected metaphors.

4. And most important, a controlled range of emotions expressed by the narrator (or the narration). People screw up, get drunk, punch each other out, break hearts, blow up bridges, shoot and kill and get shot and killed in horrible ways in his stories and novels, but *the narration never does*.

5. Repetition. What you really find, as someone said, is not repetition so much as *insistence*. There was a reason for this at first—to show a character looking at something, then thinking about it again like a mantra, then showing a second character saying or doing the same thing, with an entirely different emphasis.

Unless you know exactly what you're doing, insistence becomes mere repetition. (Like all his other innovations, and the public persona, they became albatrosses at the end—he'd acted and written that way for so long he couldn't do it any other way—A *Moveable Feast*, a sort of fictionalized nonfiction memoir of the Paris years, was as far as he ever got away from himself—whereas *The Old Man and the Sea* and *Islands in the Stream* weren't far enough after the (critical) *merde*-pile that was *Across the River and into the Trees*. That was the one where they accused the once-fresh style of evolving into "baby talk.")

▼

So how do you write a story, doing all this stuff, not in the Hemingway style but with the same concerns and some of the same elements?

My "usual" style, the one I use when I'm not particularly doing anything else, is, as Steve Utley once said, "pretty short and punchy" anyway, so I had to ease off *that* a little. One problem of being a lit. cham. is that there are times when writing like yourself is all wrong, like this one. (In the years since "Fair Game" I've intentionally chosen stories to write where I had to lengthen sentences, changed my syntax and levels of diction, and write much longer stories and novellas, in efforts to make myself find the right way to tell something. If you do your job right, as I said, the reader will not be able to imagine *any* other way the story could have been written. The worst thing a writer can do—besides telling a very bad story well and adding to the clutter—is to tell a great story all wrong, ruining it for the reader, themselves, and any other writer with the same concerns—like the old baseball story of the guy who played first base so badly nobody could ever play the position again.)

Starting with some of the same equipment, fairly short sentences, a few concrete adjectives, we go to how the thing would look to the character. As Brad Denton (another literary chameleon) says, what you should be doing in a story about Hemingway is trying to figure out how things *look* to Hemingway, since you can't talk about style separate from character and point of view. He's right. (In "Night of the Cooters" I tried to imagine what a Martian invasion would have looked like to Slim Pickens in 1890s Texas if he'd have been a sheriff there instead of an American character actor playing those kinds of roles in movies in the 1960s and '70s.)

Let's start with the barn.

The image, and what it meant, is from a conversation Hemingway had with Gary Cooper (friends for thirty years) when Cooper first knew he had the cancer that would kill him. He was talking about everything in an elegaic mood, when Hemingway, more banged up physically and mentally than anyone knew, said "Race you to the barn."

(Coop won, by the way, which probably hastened the depression and shock treatments that finally put Hemingway over. As I mention, it was the shotgun Gary Cooper had had custom-made for Hemingway that the writer used that morning in Ketchum, Idaho.)

The barn was important to Hemingway, then. But subservient to the hunt. So when I begin to mention the barn, I wanted Ernst uncomfortable for some reason he doesn't understand. First he tries not to think about it; then he wants men put around it so the Wild Man of the Woods can't lead him there. (Having to hunt the Wild Man of the Woods *in* the barn would have made this another whole cheap story that you would not have seen.) Each mention — insistence — of the barn, until I just stop and tell you what happened up in Michigan, and I made that part up, gives another take on it, sometimes to Ernst, sometimes to the villagers. The test is: Does the reader know the barn's important without knowing the Cooper-Hemingway anecdote?

Same way with the guns. A shiny new Weatherby that would stop a train, a huge old goose gun, an antique wheel-lock. As he uses them, he goes further back in time, and it's the wheel-lock, a weapon that was around when there were *still* Wild Men of the Woods around, that gets the job done. If you didn't notice this, I've done my job. If you did notice this, I've done my job.

Icebergs:

Hemingway said a lot of stuff. Some of it came out of a horse's patoot; a lot of it's way politically incorrect (which should never stop a writer from saying it if it's the *truth*) but he said a couple of things that still hold.

One of them's usually referred to as the Iceberg Theory of Literature. He said something a writer knows, and knows completely, the reader will know too, without it ever being mentioned.

Like an iceberg, seven-eighths of what's going on in a story is under the surface.

Since I do not Come Right Out and Say in the first paragraph, "This is a story about Ernest Hemingway and what happened between the time he pulled the triggers and the time the top of his head hit the dish cabinet," the reader has to come to this realization from the words I do use. Hopefully, I let you know without having to tell you.

(I crash the *Titanic* of exposition into the iceberg of my narrative exactly twice: Once when I tell you what happened up at the barn, then again about Mgoro, and both of these are close to the end. I *had* to do those two things because—well, imagine the story *without* me telling you those two facts—so you would know what Ernst had been hunting all his life just before I show you. Otherwise you would have accused me of pulling a cheap psychoanalytical rabbit out of my Freudian butt at the last minute.)

One of the things this involves is withholding information, another Bozo No-No, which is called smoke-and-mirrors and handwaving in the writing biz. You are depending on the juggernaut of your narrative to carry the reader past such niggling questions as what's a Ngorongoro Crater Forest Ranger doing in Austria, why Ernst's wearing clothing from thirty years of personal history, why Mgoro and the barn unsettle him so? I tell students in writing workshops *never* to do this.

Then they read this story and say "But *you* did it!" and I say "I did it because I knew *exactly*, what I was doing and why, and when you know that you can do that," and they say, "Well, how will I know *when* I can do that?" and I will scream back "You'll know it when you *can* do it!"

Talking about style in this story, and Hemingway's stories can't be talked about apart from the story itself—if the story had needed another style, I would have tried to find it. That I needed to write with some of Hemingway's arsenal (or bag o' tricks, if you prefer) *dulce et decorum est*, in my opinion. But that I refused to write it *like* Hemingway is proper, too. (It's a little like trying to describe any kind of fishing without using the word *water*.)

▼

So being a literary chameleon isn't all it's cracked up to be. For one thing, it's hard work, and nobody notices but other writers, anyway. (As Leadbelly used to say, you can't *stand* around and pick a thousand pounds of cotton a day.) If you do it right, the old iceberg fairly zips along. It's only when somebody anchors to it, and starts chipping away and doing core samples that you find out how the snowfall was in 1612 A.D., what kind of trees there were in Spitzbergen, when the first radioactive fallout started showing up, whether or not there's a frozen seal carcass near the summit, that you begin to see how long it took to make the goddamn thing.

If I did my job right, you enjoyed the view of the thing going abaft the port rail, blue and pink in the Atlantic sunset, with its barns and wheel-locks, Wild Men and forest rangers, while under the waves was a big old lump of stuff.

And, unlike that first publisher's editor, you might think a large part of that undersea mass was me being pretty nice to that frightened, burnt-out old fart after all.

A WORKSHOP LEXICON

by Bruce Sterling

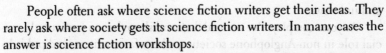

People often ask where science fiction writers get their ideas. They rarely ask where society gets its science fiction writers. In many cases the answer is science fiction workshops.

Workshops come in many varieties—regional and national, amateur and professional, formal and frazzled. In science fiction's best-known workshop, Clarion, would-be writers are wrenched from home and hearth and pitilessly blitzed for six weeks by professional SF writers, who serve as creative writing gurus. Thanks to the seminal efforts of Robin Wilson, would-be SF writers can receive actual academic credit for this experience.

But the workshopping experience does not require any shepherding by experts. Like a bad rock band, an SF writer's workshop can be set up in any vacant garage by any group of spotty enthusiasts with nothing better to occupy their time. No one has a copyright on talent, desire, or enthusiasm.

The general course of action in the modern SF workshop (known as the "Milford system") goes as follows. Attendees bring short manuscripts, with enough copies for everyone present. No one can attend or comment who does not bring a story. The contributors read and annotate all the stories. When that's done, everyone forms a circle, a story is picked at random, and the person to the writer's right begins the critique. (Large groups may require deliberate scheduling.)

Following the circle in order, with a minimum of cross-talk or interruptions, each person emits his/her considered opinions of the story's merits and/or demerits. The author is strictly required, by rigid law and custom, to make no outcries, no matter how he or she may squirm. When the circle is done and the last reader has vented his or her opinion, the silently suffering author is allowed an extended reply, which, it is hoped, will not exceed half an hour or so, and will avoid gratuitously personal ripostes. This harrowing process continues, with possible breaks for food, until all the stories are done, whereupon everyone tires to repair ruptured relationships in an orgy of drink and gossip.

No doubt a very interesting book could be written about science fiction in which the writing itself played no part. This phantom history could detail the social demimonde of workshops and their associated cliques: Milford, the Futurians, Milwaukee Fictioneers, Turkey City, New Wave, Hydra Club, Jules Verne's Eleven Without Women, and year after year after year of Clarion—a thousand SF groups around the world, known and unknown.

Anyone can play. I've noticed that workshops have a particularly crucial role in non-Anglophone societies, where fans, writers, and publishers are often closely united in the same handful of zealots. This kind of fellow-feeling may be the true heart's blood of the genre.

We now come to the core of this piece, the SF Workshop Lexicon. This lexicon was compiled by Mr. Lewis Shiner and myself from the work of many writers and critics over many years of genre history, and it contains buzzwords, notions, and critical terms of direct use to SF workshops.

The first version, known as the "Turkey City Lexicon" after the Austin, Texas writers' workshop that was a cradle of cyberpunk, appeared in 1988. In proper ideologically-correct cyberpunk fashion, the Turkey City Lexicon was distributed uncopyrighted and free of charge: a decommodified, photocopied chunk of free literary software. Lewis Shiner still thinks that this was the best deployment of an effort of this sort, and thinks I should stop fooling around with this fait accompli. After all, the original Lexicon remains uncopyrighted, and it has been floating around in fanzines, prozines and computer networks for seven years now. I respect Lew's opinion, and in fact I kind of agree with him. But I'm an ideologue, congenitally unable to leave well enough alone.

In September 1990 I rewrote the Lexicon as an installment in my critical column for the British magazine *Interzone*. When Robin Wilson asked me to refurbish the Lexicon yet again for *Paragons*, I couldn't resist the temptation. I'm always open to improvements and amendments for the Lexicon. It seems to me that if a document of this sort fails to grow it will surely become a literary monument, and, well, heaven forbid. For what it's worth, I plan to re-release this latest edition to the Internet at the first opportunity. You can e-mail me about it: I'm bruces@well.com.

And if you want to photocopy this document for handy use in your own workshop — well, this book is copyrighted. Which means this essay is similarly copyrighted. That means that if you dare to reproduce these pages, your photocopier will swell up and explode. If you don't believe this assertion, try it for yourself. Just keep in mind that I can't be held responsible.*

Some Lexicon terms are attributed to their originators, when I could find them; others are not, and I apologize for my ignorance.

Science fiction boasts many specialized critical terms. You can find a passel of these in Gary K. Wolfe's *Critical Terms for Science Fiction and Fantasy: A Glossary and Guide to Scholarship* (Greenwood Press, 1986). But you won't find them in here. This lexicon is not a guide to scholarship. The Workshop Lexicon is a guide (of sorts) for down-and-dirty hairy-knuckled sci-fi writers, the kind of ambitious subliterate guttersnipes who actually write and sell professional genre material. It's rough, rollicking, rule-of-thumb stuff suitable for shouting aloud while pounding the table.

THE LEXICON

▼ PART ONE: WORDS AND SENTENCES

"Said-book" ism. An artificial verb used to avoid the word "said." "Said" is one of the few invisible words in the English language and is almost impossible to overuse. It is much less distracting than "he retorted," "she inquired," "he ejaculated," and other oddities. The term "said-book" comes from certain pamphlets, containing hundreds of purple-prose synonyms for the word "said," which were sold by aspiring authors from tiny ads in American magazines of the pre-World War II era.

Tom Swifty. An unseemly compulsion to follow the word "said" with a colorful adverb, as in " 'We'd better hurry,' Tom said swiftly." This was a standard mannerism of the old Tom Swift adventure dime-novels. Good dialogue can stand on its own without a clutter of adverbial props.

---

*Editor's Note: The editor agrees with Lewis Shiner; Science fiction writers, readers, editors, and critics are herewith granted explicit permission to copy and distribute Sterling's "A Workshop Lexicon" by any means they wish. Neither the editor nor the publisher, however, may be held responsible for exploding copy machines.

Brenda Statr dialogue. Long sections of talk with no physical background or description of the characters. Such dialogue, detached from the story's setting, tends to echo hollowly, as if suspended in midair. Named for the American comic strip in which dialogue balloons were often seen emerging from the Manhattan skyline.

Burly Detective syndrome. This useful term is taken from SF's cousin-genre, the detective-pulp. The hack writers of the Mike Shayne series showed an odd reluctance to use Shayne's proper name, preferring such euphemisms as "the burly detective" or "the red-headed sleuth." This syndrome arises from a wrong-headed conviction that the same word should not be used twice in close succession. This is only true of particularly strong and visible words, such as "vertiginous." Better to reuse a simple tag or phrase than to contrive cumbersome methods of avoiding it.

Pushbutton words. Words used to evoke a cheap emotional response without engaging the intellect or the critical faculties. Commonly found in story titles, they include such bits of bogus lyricism as "star," "dance," "dream," "song," "tears," and "poet," clichés calculated to render the SF audience misty-eyed and tender-hearted.

Brand name fever. The overuse of commercial brand names to create a false sense of gritty verisimilitude. It is useless to stock the future with Hondas, Sonys, and Brauns without accompanying visual and physical detail.

"Call a Rabbit a Smeerp." A cheap technique for false exoticism, in which common elements of the real world are renamed for a fantastic milieu without any real alteration in their basic nature or behavior. "Smeerps" are especially common in fantasy worlds, where people often ride exotic steeds that look and act just like horses. (Attr. James Blish)

Roget's Disease. The ludicrous overuse of farfetched adjectives, piled into a festering, fungal, tenebrous, troglodytic, ichorous, leprous, synonymic heap. (Attr. John W. Campbell)

Gingerbread. Useless ornament in prose, such as fancy sesquipedalian Latinate words where short clear English ones will do. Novice authors sometimes use "gingerbread" in the hope of disguising faults and conveying an air of refinement. (Attr. Damon Knight)

Not Simultaneous. The misuse of the present participle is a common structural sentence-fault for beginning writers. "Putting his key in the door, he leapt up the stairs and got his revolver out of the bureau." Alas, our hero couldn't do this even if his arms were forty feet long. This fault shades into "Ing Disease," the tendency to pepper sentences with words ending in "-ing," a grammatical construction which tends to confuse the proper sequence of events. (Attr. Damon Knight)

▼ PART TWO: PARAGRAPHS AND PROSE STRUCTURE

Bathos. A sudden, alarming change in the level of diction. "There will be bloody riots and savage insurrections leading to a violent popular uprising unless the regime starts being lots nicer about stuff."

Countersinking. A form of expositional redundancy in which the action clearly implied in dialogue is made explicit. " 'Let's get out of here!' he shouted, urging her to leave."

Show Don't Tell. A cardinal principle of effective writing. The reader should be allowed to react naturally to the evidence presented in the story, not instructed in how to react by the author. Specific incidents and carefully observed details will render auctorial lectures unnecessary. For instance, instead of telling the reader "She had a bad childhood, an unhappy childhood," a specified incident—involving, say, a locked closet and two jars of honey—should be shown.

Rigid adherence to show-don't-tell can become absurd. Minor matters are sometimes best gotten out of the way in a swift, straightforward fashion.

Laughtrack. Characters grandstand and tug the reader's sleeve in an effort to force a specific emotional reaction. They laugh wildly at their own jokes, cry loudly at their own pain, and rob the reader of any real chance of attaining genuine emotion.

Squid in the Mouth. The failure of an author to realize that his/her own weird assumptions and personal in-jokes are simply not shared by the world at large. Instead of applauding the wit or insight of the author's remarks, the world at large will stare in vague shock and alarm at such a writer, as if he or she had a live squid in the mouth.

Since SF writers as a breed are generally quite loony, and in fact make this a stock in trade, "squid in the mouth" doubles as a term of grudging praise, describing the essential, irreducible, divinely unpredictable lunacy of the true SF writer. (Attr. James P. Blaylock)

Squid on the Mantelpiece. Chekhov said that if there are dueling pistols over the mantelpiece in the first act, they should be fired in the third. In other words, a plot element should be deployed in a timely fashion and with proper dramatic emphasis. However, in SF plotting the MacGuffins are often so overwhelming that they cause conventional plot structures to collapse. It's hard to properly dramatize, say, the domestic effects of Dad's bank overdraft when a giant writhing kraken is levelling the city. This mismatch between the conventional dramatic properties and SF's extreme, grotesque, or visionary thematics is known as the "squid on the mantelpiece."

Handwaving. An attempt to distract the reader with dazzling prose or other verbal fireworks, so as to divert attention from a severe logical flaw. (Attr. Stewart Brand)

You Can't Fire Me, I Quit. An attempt to diffuse the reader's incredulity with a pre-emptive strike — as if by anticipating the reader's objections, the author had somehow answered them. "I would never have believed it, if I hadn't seen it myself!" "It was one of those amazing coincidences that can only take place in real life!" "It's a one-in-a-million chance, but it's so crazy it just might work!" Surprisingly common, especially in SF. (Attr. John Kessel)

Fuzz. An element of motivation the author was too lazy to supply. The word "somehow" is a useful tip-off to fuzzy areas of a story. "Somehow she had forgotten to bring her gun."

Dischism. The unwitting intrusion of the author's physical surroundings, or the author's own mental state, into the text of the story. Authors who smoke or drink while writing often drown or choke their characters with an endless supply of booze and cigs. In subtler forms of the Dischism, the characters complain of their confusion and indecision — when this is actually the author's condition at the moment of writing, not theirs within the story. "Dischism" is named after the critic who diagnosed this syndrome. (Attr. Thomas M. Disch)

Signal from Fred. A comic form of the Dischism in which the author's subconscious, alarmed by the poor quality of the work, makes unwitting critical comments: "This doesn't make sense." "This is really boring." "This sounds like a bad movie." (Attr. Damon Knight)

False Interiorization. A cheap labor-saving technique in which the author, too lazy to describe the surroundings, afflicts the viewpoint-character with a blindfold, an attack of space-sickness, the urge to play marathon whist games in the smoking room, etc.

False Humanity. An ailment endemic to genre writing, in which soap-opera elements of purported human interest are stuffed into the story willy-nilly, whether or not they advance the plot or contribute to the point of the story. The actions of such characters convey an itchy sense of irrelevance, for the author has invented their problems out of whole cloth, so as to have something to emote about.

Wiring Diagram Fiction. A genre ailment related to "False Humanity," "Wiring Diagram Fiction" involves "characters" who show no convincing emotional reactions at all, since they are overwhelmed by the author's fascination with gadgetry or didactic lectures.

White Room Syndrome. A clear and common sign of the failure of the author's imagination, most often seen at the beginning of a story, before the setting, background, or characters have gelled. "She awoke in a white room." The "white room" is a featureless set for which details have yet to be invented—a failure of invention by the author. The character "wakes" in order to begin a fresh train of thought—again, just like the author. This "white room" opening is generally followed by much earnest pondering of circumstances and useless exposition; all of which can be cut, painlessly.

It remains to be seen whether the "white room" cliché will fade from use now that most authors confront glowing screens rather than blank white paper.

▼ **PART THREE: COMMON WORKSHOP STORY TYPES**

The Jar of Tang. A story contrived so that the author can spring a silly surprise about its setting, For instance, the story takes place in a desert of coarse orange sand surrounded by an impenetrable vitrine barrier; surprise! our heroes are microbes in a jar of Tang powdered orange drink. (Attr. Stephen P. Brown)

When done with serious intent rather than as a passing conceit, this type of story can be dignified by the term "Concealed Environment." (Attr. Christopher Priest)

The "Poor Me" Story. Autobiographical piece in which the male viewpoint character complains that he is ugly and can't get laid. (Attr. Kate Wilhelm)

The Grubby Apartment Story. Similar to the "poor me" story, this autobiographical effort features a miserably quasi-bohemian writer, living in urban angst in a grubby apartment. The story commonly stars the author's friends in thin disguises—friends who may also be the author's workshop companions, to their considerable alarm.

The Shaggy God Story. A piece which mechanically adopts a Biblical or other mythological tale and provides flat science-fictional "explanations" for the theological events. (Attr. Michael Moorcock)

Adam and Eve Story. Nauseatingly common subset of the Shaggy God Story in which a terrible apocalypse, spaceship crash, etc., leaves two survivors, man and woman, who turn out to be Adam and Eve, parents of the human race!

Deus ex Machina or "God in the Box." Story featuring a miraculous solution to the story's conflict, which comes out of nowhere and renders the plot struggles irrelevant. H. G. Wells warned against SF's love for the deus ex machina when he coined the famous dictum that "If anything is possible, then nothing is interesting." Science fiction, which specializes in making the impossible seem plausible, is always deeply intrigued by godlike powers in the handy pocket size. Artificial Intelligence, virtual realities, and nanotechnology are three contemporary SF MacGuffins that are cheap portable sources of limitless miracle.

Just-Like Fallacy. SF story which thinly adapts the trappings of a standard pulp adventure setting. The spaceship is "just like" an Atlantic steamer, down to the Scottish engineer in the hold. A colony planet is "just like" Arizona except for two moons in the sky. Space westerns and futuristic hard-boiled detective stories have been especially common versions.

Re-Inventing the Wheel. A novice author goes to enormous lengths to create a science-fictional situation already tiresomely familiar to the experienced reader. Reinventing the Wheel was traditionally typical of mainstream writers venturing into SF. It is now often seen in writers who lack experience in genre history because they were attracted to written SF via SF movies, SF television series, SF role-playing games, SF comics, or SF computer gaming.

The Cozy Catastrophe. Story in which horrific ever is are overwhelming the entirety of human civilization, but the action concentrates on a small group of tidy, middle-class, white Anglo-Saxon protagonists. The essence of the cozy catastrophe is that the hero should have a pretty good time (a girl, free suites at the Savoy, automobiles for the taking) while everyone else is dying off. (Attr. Brian Aldiss)

The Motherhood Statement. SF story which posits some profoundly unsettling threat to the human condition, explores the implications briefly, then hastily retreats to affirm the conventional social and humanistic pieties, i.e. apple pie and motherhood. Greg Egan once stated that the secret of truly effective SF was to deliberately "burn the motherhood statement." (Attr. Greg Egan)

The Kitchen-Sink Story. A story overwhelmed by the inclusion of any and every new idea that occurs to the author in the process of writing it. (Attr. Damon Knight)

The Whistling Dog. A story related in such an elaborate, arcane, or convoluted manner that it impresses by its sheer narrative ingenuity, but which, as a story, is basically not worth the candle. Like the whistling dog, it's astonishing that the thing can whistle—but it doesn't actually whistle very well. (Attr. Harlan Ellison)

The Rembrandt Comic Book. A story in which incredible craftsmanship has been lavished on a theme or idea which is basically trivial or subliterary, and which simply cannot bear the weight of such deadly-serious artistic portent.

The Slipstream Story. Non-SF story which is so ontologically distorted or related in such a bizarrely non-realist fashion that it cannot pass muster as commercial mainstream fiction and therefore seeks shelter in the SF or fantasy genre. Postmodern critique and technique are particularly fruitful in creating slipstream stories.

The Steam-Grommet Factory. Didactic SF story which consists entirely of a guided tour of a large and elaborate gimmick. A common technique of SF utopias and dystopias. (Attr. Gardner Dozois)

▼ PART FOUR: PLOTS

Idiot Plot. A plot which functions only because all the characters involved are idiots. They behave in a way that suits the author's convenience, rather than through any rational motivation of their own. (Attr. James Blish)

Second-Order Idiot Plot. A plot involving an entire invented SF society which functions only because every single person in it is necessarily an idiot. (Attr. Damon Knight)

And Plot. Picaresque plot in which this happens, and then that happens, and then something else happens, and it all adds up to nothing in particular.

Kudzu Plot. Plot which weaves and curls and writhes in weedy organic profusion, smothering everything in its path.

Card Tricks in the Dark. Elaborately contrived plot which arrives at (a) the punchline of a private joke no reader will get, or (b) the display of some bit of learned trivia relevant only to the author. This stunt may be intensely ingenious, and very gratifying to the author, but it serves no visible fictional purpose. (Attr. Tim Powers)

Plot Coupons. The basic building blocks of the quest-type fantasy plot. The hero collects sufficient plot coupons (magic sword, magic ring, magic cat) to send off to the author for the ending. The author decrees that the hero will pursue his quest until sufficient pages are filled to complete a trilogy. (Attr. Dave Langford)

Bogus Alternatives. A list of plot-paths that a character could have taken, but didn't. In this nervous mannerism, the author stops the action dead to work out complicated plot problems at the reader's expense. "If

I'd gone along with the cops they would have found the gun in my purse. And anyway, I didn't want to spend the night in jail. I suppose I could have just run away instead of stealing their squad car, but then . . ." Best dispensed with entirely.

▼ **PART FIVE: BACKGROUND**

Info-dump. Large chunk of indigestible expository matter intended to explain the background situation. Info-dumps can be covert, as in fake newspaper or "Encyclopedia Galactica" articles, or overt, in which all action stops as the author assumes center stage and lectures. Info-dumps are also known as "expository lumps." The use of brief, deft, inoffensive info-dumps is known as "kuttnering," after Henry Kuttner. When information is worked unobtrusively into the story's basic structure, this is known as "heinleining."

Stapledon. Name assigned to the auctorial voice which takes center stage to deliver a massive and magisterial info-dump. Actually a common noun, as in "I like the way your stapledon describes the process of downloading brains into computer memory, but when you try to heinlein it later, I can't tell what the hell is happening."

Frontloading. Piling too much exposition into the beginning of the story, so that it becomes so dense and dry that it is almost impossible to read. (Attr. Connie Willis)

Nowhere Nowhen Story. Putting too little exposition into the story's beginning, so that the story, while physically readable, seems to take place in a vacuum and fails to engage any readerly interest. (Attr. L. Sprague de Camp)

"As You Know, Bob." A pernicious form of info-dump through dialogue, in which characters tell each other things they already know, for the sake of getting the reader up to speed. This very common technique is also known as "Rod and Don dialogue" (attr. Damon Knight) or "maid and butler dialogue" (attr. Algis Budrys).

I've Suffered For My Art (And Now It's Your Turn). A form of info-dump in which the author inflicts upon the reader hard-won, but irrelevant bits of data acquired while researching the story. As Algis Budrys once pointed out, homework exists to make the difficult look easy.

Used Furniture. The use of a cliched genre background right out of Central Casting. We can, for instance, use the Star Trek universe, only we'll file the serial numbers off it and call it the Imperium instead of the Federation.

Eyeball Kicks. Vivid, telling details that create a kaleidoscopic effect of swarming visual imagery against a baroquely elaborate SF background. One ideal of cyberpunk SF was to create a "crammed prose" full of "eyeball kicks." (Attr. Rudy Rucker)

Ontological riff. Passage in an SF story which suggests that our deepest and most basic convictions about the nature of reality, space-time, or consciousness have been violated, technologically transformed, or at least rendered thoroughly dubious. The works of H. P. Lovecraft, Barrington Bayley, and Philip K. Dick abound in "ontological riffs."

▼ PART SIX: CHARACTER AND VIEWPOINT

Viewpoint glitch. The author loses track of point of view, switches point of view for no good reason, or relates something that the viewpoint character could not possibly know.

Submyth. Classic character-types in SF which aspire to the condition of archetype but don't quite make it, such as the mad scientist, the crazed supercomputer, the emotionless super-rational alien, the vindictive mutant child, etc. (Attr. Ursula K. Le Guin)

Funny-hat characterization. A character distinguished by a single identifying tag, such as odd headgear, a limp, a lisp, a parrot on his shoulder, etc.

Mrs. Brown. The small, downtrodden, eminently common, everyday little person who nevertheless encapsulates something vital and important about the human condition. "Mrs. Brown" is a rare personage in the SF genre, being generally overshadowed by swaggering submyth types made of the finest gold-plated cardboard. In a famous essay, "Science Fiction and Mrs. Brown," Ursula K. Le Guin decried Mrs. Brown's absence from the SF field. (Attr: Virginia Woolf)

▼ **PART SEVEN: MISCELLANEOUS**

AM/FM. Engineer's term distinguishing the inevitable clunky real-world faultiness of "Actual Machines" from the power-fantasy techno-dreams of "Fucking Magic."

Intellectual sexiness. The intoxicating glamor of a novel scientific idea, as distinguished from any actual intellectual merit that it may some-day prove to possess.

Consensus Reality. Useful term for the purported world in which the majority of modern sane people generally agree that they live—as op-posed to the worlds of, say, Forteans, semioticians or quantum physicists.

The Ol' Baloney Factory. "Science Fiction" as a publishing and pro-motional entity in the world of commerce.

Greg Bear was born in San Diego, California, in 1951 and now lives in a suburb of Seattle. He holds an AB from San Diego State University. He was awarded a Nebula, Hugo, and Prix Apollo for his novelette "Blood Music" (1983). He won a Nebula Award for his novella "Hardfought," and Hugo and Nebula Awards for the short story "Tangents" (1986). His novel *Moving Mars* won the 1994 Nebula Award for best novel. Bear served as President of The Science Fiction and Fantasy Writers of America, 1988–89. He has taught at the Clarion Writers Workshop-West and once worked as a lecturer at the San Diego Aerospace Museum.

Pat Cadigan was born in Schenectady, New York, and now lives in Overland Park, Kansas. A former student at James Gunn's University of Kansas Writers Workshop, she sold her first story in 1980. In the late '70s she was co-editor of *Shayol*, a semi-professional magazine which was honored with a World Fantasy Award in 1981. Her second novel, *Synners*, won the Arthur C. Clarke Award (1991), as did her third, *Fools*. She has taught at Clarion-West.

Karen Joy Fowler was born in Bloomington, Indiana, in 1950 and now lives in Davis, California, where she took a Masters Degree in Political Science. She won the John W. Campbell Memorial Award for Best New Writer in 1987 and the Commonwealth Club Medal for *Sarah Canary* in 1991. She has been a National Endowment for the Arts grant recipient, serves as Writer-in-Residence at Cleveland State University, and is a frequent lecturer at both the Clarion-East and Clarion-West Workshops.

Joe Haldeman was born in Oklahoma City, in 1943. He holds a baccalaureate in Physics and Astronomy from the University of Maryland and the MFA in creative writing from the University of Iowa. He was dangerously employed (he received a Purple Heart) as an Army combat en-

gineer in Vietnam in 1968. His novel *The Forever War*, one of the defining books of the seventies, won both Nebula and Hugo Awards in 1976.
He won another Hugo Award in 1977 for "Tricentennial" and both Hugo
and Nebula Awards again in 1991 for his novella, "The Hemingway
Hoax." His story, "Graves," won the 1993 World Fantasy and Nebula
Awards for short story. Haldeman lives half the year in Gainesville,
Florida and half in Boston, where he is Adjunct Professor of Writing at
the Massachusetts Institute of Technology. He has been a frequent lecturer at Clarion-East, has taught at Clarion-West, and was President of
the Science Fiction and Fantasy Writers of America, 1992–94.

James Patrick Kelly was born in Mineola, New York, in 1951 and now
lives in Portsmouth, New Hampshire. He is a graduate of Notre Dame
University and an alumnus of Clarion-East. He has established a rep-
utation as a master of the short story form, as a writers' writer, and he
returned to East Lansing fifteen years after his student tenure to begin
regular service as a lecturer. He has also lectured at the Writers Forum
of the State University of New York at Brockport and at the University of
New Hampshire, and has held writing residencies at more than forty primary and secondary schools under the auspices of the New Hampshire
State Council of the Arts.

John Kessel was born in Buffalo, New York, in 1950 and received his doctorate at the University of Kansas in 1981. He now lives in Raleigh, North
Carolina, where he is Professor of American Literature and Creative
Writing at North Carolina State University. His novella "Another Or-
phan" won the Nebula Award in 1983, and his short story "Buffalo" won
the Locus Award and the Theodore Sturgeon Award in 1991. In 1994
his play, *Faustfeathers*, won North Carolina's Paul Green Playwriting
Prize. He has been a frequent lecturer at Clarion-East.

Nancy Kress was born in Buffalo, New York and now lives in Brockport.
She holds an MA degree from the State University of New York at Brockport, where she has served as an adjunct instructor. Her story "Beggars
in Spain" won both Hugo and Nebula Awards in 1992; another story,
"Out of All Them Bright Stars" won a Nebula Award in 1986. She has
taught fourth grade, high school, and college-level English, and at writing workshops from Alaska to New York. She has lectured at both
Clarion-East and Clarion-West.

Pat Murphy was born in 1955, holds the BA from the University of California, Santa Cruz, and now lives in San Francisco, where she is Director of Publications at the Exploratorium, working with publishers and museum staff to create science books. "Rachel in Love" (which appears in this volume) won the Nebula Award for short story in 1988, as did her second novel *The Falling Woman*. She is one of a double handful of writers to be nominated for Nebula Awards in all four fiction categories (novel, novelette, novella, and short story). In 1991 her *Points of Departure* won the Philip K. Dick Award for the best original paperback, and she won the World Fantasy Award that same year for her novella "Bones." *Nadya: The Wolf Chronicles* is forthcoming from Tor Books. She is a Clarion-East alumna and has taught at Stanford and at UC Santa Cruz, and has become both a Clarion-East and a Clarion-West lecturer.

Kim Stanley Robinson was born in Waukegan, Illinois, in 1952. He won the World Fantasy Award in 1984 for his story "Black Air," the Nebula Award in 1987 for his novella "The Blind Geometer," and the John W. Campbell Award in 1992 for his novel *Pacific Edge*. In 1993 his novel *Red Mars* won the British Science Fiction Award and in 1994 the Nebula Award. *Green Mars* won both Locus and Hugo Awards that same year. He holds a doctorate from the University of California, San Diego, and has served as visiting lecturer at that institution and at the University of California, Davis. He is a Clarion-East alumnus who has returned as a lecturer, and he participated in the National Science Foundation's Antarctic Artists and Writers Program in 1995.

Lucius Shepard was born in Lynchburg, Virginia, in 1947 and now lives in Seattle. He was 1985's John W. Campbell Award winner for Best New Writer. In 1987 he won the Nebula Award for his novella "R & R", and his short story collection, *The Jaguar Hunter*, won a World Fantasy Award in 1988. *The Ends of the Earth* won him another World Fantasy Award in 1992 for best story collection. "Barnacle Bill the Spacer," a novella, won the Hugo in 1993. He is a Clarion-East alumnus who has returned as a lecturer. He has also taught at Clarion-West and has been considerably surprised to be invited to lecture at the United States Military Academy at West Point.

Bruce Sterling was born in Brownsville, Texas, in 1954. He attended the University of Texas, and now lives in Austin. One of the progenitors of the greatly influential cyberpunk movement, his approach to science fiction expands the genre. His critical and analytical bent is revealed both in his superb fiction and in such non-fiction as his remarkable study of First Amendment issues, *The Hacker Crackdown: Law and Disorder on the Electronic Frontier,* and in his sprightly essay on workshoppery appended to this volume.

Howard Waldrop was born in Houston, Mississippi, in 1946 and attended the University of Texas-Arlington. He now lives near Seattle. His short story "The Ugly Chickens" won both the World Fantasy Award and the Nebula Award in 1981. He has taught at Cleveland State University and at both Clarion-West and Clarion-East.

Robin Wilson was born in Columbus, Ohio, in 1928 and now lives in Carmel-by-the-Sea, California. He holds a doctorate from the University of Illinois. After twelve years as a naval officer and CIA operative in Europe, he took up English professoring, founded and sporadically taught at the Clarion Writers Workshop, and in 1980 fell from grace into a college presidency in California. He is the author of quantities of academic journalism, a couple dozen science fiction short stories and novelettes, and two novels.